WHERE
COURAGE
CALLS

Books by Janette Oke

Return to Harmony • *Another Homecoming*
Tomorrow's Dream • *Dana's Valley***

ACTS OF FAITH*
The Centurion's Wife • *The Hidden Flame* • *The Damascus Way*

CANADIAN WEST
When Calls the Heart • *When Comes the Spring*
When Breaks the Dawn • *When Hope Springs New*
Beyond the Gathering Storm
When Tomorrow Comes

LOVE COMES SOFTLY
Love Comes Softly • *Love's Enduring Promise*
Love's Long Journey • *Love's Abiding Joy*
Love's Unending Legacy • *Love's Unfolding Dream*
Love Takes Wing • *Love Finds a Home*

A PRAIRIE LEGACY
The Tender Years • *A Searching Heart*
A Quiet Strength • *Like Gold Refined*

SEASONS OF THE HEART
Once Upon a Summer • *The Winds of Autumn*
Winter Is Not Forever • *Spring's Gentle Promise*

SONG OF ACADIA*
The Meeting Place • *The Sacred Shore* • *The Birthright*
The Distant Beacon • *The Beloved Land*

WOMEN OF THE WEST
The Calling of Emily Evans • *Julia's Last Hope*
Roses for Mama • *A Woman Named Damaris*
They Called Her Mrs. Doc • *The Measure of a Heart*
A Bride for Donnigan • *Heart of the Wilderness*
Too Long a Stranger • *The Bluebird and the Sparrow*
A Gown of Spanish Lace • *Drums of Change*

Also look for *Janette Oke: A Heart for the Prairie* by Laurel Oke Logan

*with Davis Bunn
**with Laurel Oke Logan

WHERE COURAGE CALLS

A *When Calls the Heart* NOVEL

JANETTE OKE
LAUREL OKE LOGAN

BETHANYHOUSE
a division of Baker Publishing Group
Minneapolis, Minnesota

© 2014 by Janette Oke and Laurel Oke Logan

Published by Bethany House Publishers
11400 Hampshire Avenue South
Bloomington, Minnesota 55438
www.bethanyhouse.com

Bethany House Publishers is a division of
Baker Publishing Group, Grand Rapids, Michigan

Printed in the United States of America

Library of Congress Cataloging-in-Publication Data
Oke, Janette.
    Where courage calls : a When Calls the Heart novel / Janette Oke and
Laurel Oke Logan.
        pages cm
    Summary: "In the early 20th century, new schoolteacher Beth Thatcher
is assigned a post in a remote mining community in Western Canada. There
her courage—and her heart—will be tested in unexpected ways"—Provided
by publisher.
    ISBN 978-0-7642-1232-1 (cloth : alk. paper)
    ISBN 978-0-7642-1231-4 (pbk.)
    ISBN 978-0-7642-1233-8 (large-print pbk.)
    1. Women pioneers—Fiction. 2. Canada, Western—Fiction. I. Logan,
Laurel Oke. II. Title.
PR9199.3.O38W54 2014
813′.54—dc23   2013039789

Scripture quotations are from the King James Version of the Bible.

Cover design by Dan Thornberg, Design Source Creative Services

14 15 16 17 18 19 20   7 6 5 4 3 2 1

Dedicated with deepest affection
to some very special people.

Ashley Carolyn & Steve
Nathanael Edward
Jessica Brianne & Steve
Kathryn Louise & Jeff
Courtney Elizabeth
Jacquelyn Leigh & Daniel
Alexander Nicolas
Kristalyn Lorene
Emily Marie
Vladimir David
Connor Edward
Anastasia Kimberly
Brian Carl
Wesley Frederick
Curtis Craig
And in loving memory of our little Amanda Janette.

And yes, thanks to the blessings of our heavenly Father,
they are all ours.

CHAPTER

1

THE ENTIRE FIRST FLOOR of the large stone house had become a hive of swarming bodies. With glasses of pink lemonade in hand and dressed to the nines in long gowns, beaded shifts, and formal tuxedos, the guests bumbled out from the formal drawing room onto the wide veranda in clusters of three or four, buzzing with fresh gossip as they went. As Beth pushed through the crowd it seemed that everyone who was anyone in Toronto society had arrived in high energy, boisterous greetings, arms reaching for polite hugs, and hands presenting unnecessary going away gifts. Father's more-than-ample home was quickly becoming stifling, though every window was thrown wide. But there was not a whisper of a breeze to lift the overpowering scent of Mother's lavish floral bouquets on this late-summer night.

For one with a gentle spirit and acute sensitivity, it was overwhelming. Beth felt she would smother if she were not allowed some space—some quiet, some fresh air—if only for a few minutes, until she was able to calm her heartbeat and ease the pulsing in her temples. If only she could slip away.

Then opportunity presented itself. Mr. Woodworth, a leading light in Canada's railroad industry, captured the crowd's attention. One hand on the grand piano as though to introduce an upcoming performance, the other waving in dramatic flourish, he began to spin one of his legendary tales. And with the crowd's eyes fastened on him, Beth was able to duck into the hallway unnoticed and find a place to catch her breath before she must face them all again.

Mother, in her enthusiasm, must have invited everyone they knew from the past and the present. But Mother had always taken advantage of any excuse for a party, and she was known among her peers as excelling in the art of the hostess. *At least she hasn't insisted on chaperoning party games on the veranda tonight.* Beth's habit of counting small blessings couldn't help but bring a smile to her lips. She was glad that even in her current agitation, she was able to see some humor. As her father reminded her on occasion, "A sense of humor is a requisite to surviving in our demanding world."

Beth took the final steps through a narrow door into her little haven of safety and solitude between the servants' stairway and the door into the yard. Leaning close to a small open window, she noted the scent of fresh-mown grass and the peaceful chirping of crickets under the porch steps, and gazed up at the moon climbing its way over the trees. This was exactly what she needed. If her absence could go undetected for a short while, she would survive.

"She means well," Father murmured behind her shoulder.

Before turning to face him, Beth's response was a disheartened sigh. "Yes, I suppose she does."

Beth was not surprised that her father had noticed her slip out from the crowd of well-wishers. He knew Mother's social events often stretched Beth beyond her personal sense of ease. The number of guests, the elegant attire, the fussy refreshments, and the endless and overly loud conversations seemed to Beth to be shallow, superficial.

"It's just that I'd told her I wanted a *family* dinner on my last night at home."

"Yes, I know, my dear."

In the sweet, close silence, Beth leaned her head against her father's shoulder and attempted to sort through her thoughts aloud. "I'm not afraid of going away. I'll just miss you all so much." She thought of her sister's baby, asleep upstairs. "And JW—how much will he have grown by the time I see him again?"

She could hear the smile in her father's voice when he said, "Babies do grow up, Beth. It's usually considered a marvelous thing."

She raised her gaze to his. "Not when you're the auntie who isn't around to see it." The pouty tone in her voice did not make Beth proud, but since only Father could hear, she gave in to the emotions of the moment. Her throat began to tighten and tears welled in her eyes.

Footsteps in the short hall brought Beth upright and quickly wiping her eyes. Father stepped aside in order to allow Emma to pass, but the young domestic paused at the bottom of the stairs, the basket she was carrying balanced on her hip.

"They're looking for you, Miss Beth," Emma cautioned under her breath.

"Thank you, Emma." Beth drew herself up and did a quick check of her appearance, smoothing the lace collar of her dress, adjusting the wide silk band around her hips, and pinching her cheeks just a little for some color. She noticed Father smiling down at her and reached up to straighten his black bow tie.

His grin widened. "Do I pass inspection?"

9

"Always." Beth pulled her shoulders back, gave him an appreciative smile, and forced herself back toward the laughter and voices in the crowded drawing room. The moment she appeared in the doorway she knew she had been spotted.

"There she is! The woman of the hour! Our daring adventurer . . ." And on and on the voices filled the air around her.

"Come here, Beth dear. Miss Thompson would like to hear about the town in which you plan to teach."

"Yes, darling. Tell us all about your new school."

Beth could not prevent her deep sigh. She hoped no one noticed. The truth was, she knew so little—well, practically nothing—about the new town or new school. That very fact caused much of the unsettled feeling in the pit of her stomach. The interrogation by those who crowded close, begging for details, pushed her distress even higher. In spite of it all, Beth knew she must respond in some way to the avalanche of questions she had grown painfully tired of hearing. Perhaps it wasn't the repetitious answers that she had come to dread. More likely it was the familiar comments and quips that were sure to follow, particularly from the younger crowd with whom Beth had shared her growing-up years.

"But, Beth, you *do know* they haven't any servant girls in the western wilds, don't you?"

"Can you even cook for yourself?"

"Or boil water for tea?" More titters.

"And who will do your laundry?" This was always followed by a ripple of laughter. But she attempted to join in with the gaiety, hoping to deflect further jibes.

Edward Montclair, poised and impeccably garbed in full evening attire, pushed a wayward mop of dark hair from his eyes and grinned. "Better get yourself a pair of those Levi work pants, Elizabeth—you know you can't wear your fancy dresses among those mountain miners."

Beth tried to hold on to her smile. Edward had been inserting himself into her conversations for all the years they had grown up together. She wished his whole family would just move away so she would never see him again, even if it damaged Father's business dealings with Mr. Montclair. And then a new thought emerged. *She* was leaving *Edward* behind! The revelation brought a genuine smile, but the conversation had continued on around her.

"I heard they don't even bother to learn English! How can you possibly be expected to teach their children?"

Another young man, conveying a self-proclaimed knowledge of any subject at hand, sagely added, "That's true. Most of the men who work in the mining towns are *foreigners*. You know, just here to make money off our land for their families back home. Sometimes they leave a wife behind and take another here in Canada."

Gasps followed his pronouncement.

Not everyone in the group was as quick to pass judgment, but it seemed to Beth that those who were the most disparaging had the most to say. Mercifully, Father extended a teacup to her, and Beth accepted it gratefully.

Truth be told, Beth had little interest in either the tea or Mother's fancy sandwiches and pastries, but it did give her an excuse to gradually pull away from the circle around her and, with nods and smiles, work her way toward the laden tables. She purposefully gave the spread her full attention as she carefully chose from the fruit and vegetable trays, taking also two small crackers with her favorite cheese and a rosemary-cucumber garnish.

She had not been nibbling at her selections long when, as if on cue, her sister Julie stepped to the center of the room, waved an arm high, and called for everyone's attention. "Dear friends, a moment of your time, please." The conversations around them quickly faded. Julie turned dramatically, the pale green beaded fringe on her skirt whirling around her as she called out, "I know all of you are enjoying the refreshments that Mother has provided this evening." She waited just long enough to allow a respectful patter of applause. Then another graceful turn and a sweeping arm in Beth's direction. "And I hope you've all had a chance to converse with our guest of honor—dear Bethie—who shall be leaving us tomorrow on a train for the West."

Beth tried not to squirm, and instead smiled around the room. It was already getting late, with no end in sight for the festivities. Her train was scheduled to leave at ten o'clock the next morning, and she still had some final things to pack.

Julie continued, "I've been asked to explain that my sister has a great need for a good night's rest before embarking on such a journey. Reverend Collins has graciously offered to bless her travels with prayer, and then Beth will be retiring for the night." There was a collective murmur, then scattered nods of understanding. "But," Julie added, "you're all welcome to stay as long as you wish. There's so much more to eat. We need your help with that." This was met with laughter and nods, particularly from the row of young men toward whom Julie bestowed one of her coquettish smiles.

Reverend Collins stepped forward. Feet shuffled and all heads bowed.

Beth heard little of his prayer. She was occupied with one of her own. *Thank you, thank you, God* was all she could think of, and then added, *And bless Father for managing it,* overwhelmed by her unexpected emancipation earlier than expected, which she was certain he had engineered.

Even with her sister's announcement, it took almost half an hour for Beth to extract herself gracefully from all the well-wishers. When she finally slipped up the stairs, the list of last-minute things to do was spinning round and round in her mind. She pulled off the uncomfortable shoes—"to go with your lovely frock," her mother had insisted—and relished the feel of thick carpet under her tired feet. But as she hurried down the long hall, she could not resist a last visit into the nursery and a peek at JW.

As she tiptoed in, to her surprise she discovered the sweet-tempered baby was not asleep. He was lying quietly in the same crib that she and sisters Margret and Julie had used as babies. "Just for the times he will visit," Mother explained as she created a new nursery for this grandson. And, of course, for all of the brothers, sisters, and cousins she hoped would eventually follow.

In the moonlight Beth watched the baby's face light up in a smile of pleasure at seeing a beloved auntie appear above him. "Hi, darling." Casting a guilty glance over her shoulder, she scooped him up and moved to the rocking chair, ignoring the tears that started to slide down her cheeks. "And how is the nicest baby in the whole world tonight?" she crooned with a catch in her voice, settling back to rock with him for a while.

The sounds of guests were still drifting up from below when at last she pulled the door closed on the nursery and moved on to her own room, leaving the sleeping baby tucked among the soft blankets of his crib. Her mind was quiet enough now to sort through the remaining few items to fold and place in her suitcase. She tucked her Bible in last and checked to see that the suitcase would still shut.

How will I ever be able to carry it? she wondered, marveling that it could be so heavy when there were two additional trunks already packed and strapped to the back of Father's Rolls-Royce. She got ready for bed, took down her hair, and brushed it out. So many of the young ladies she knew were cutting their hair short in the modern style, but she and Julie had not been allowed to do so. Mother was distrustful of the current fashion trends. Even their dresses were always a few inches longer than most of their friends. That was fine with Beth, but Julie found it nearly impossible to bear. So much so that Beth suspected when she returned she would find her younger sister had won the battle, bobbing her hair and shortening her skirts. The thought brought a small grin. How often had Julie been stifled with Mother's answer, "But Beth doesn't have any trouble with our rules."

And Julie would always retort, "Oh, yes she does! She just doesn't say so!"

As if knowing that Beth's thoughts had wandered in her direction, a quiet knock was followed by Julie's whisper at the door. "Bethie, you awake?"

"Come in, darling."

Julie entered, already in nightgown and robe. "Can I sleep in here—one last time?"

"Yes, but it's not the last time, silly. This trip won't last forever. You know the position they offered is only for one year."

Julie drew off her robe and threw herself into the thick feather bed and under the blankets. "I hope you're right," she mused. "But what if you meet some fine young man—a shopkeeper, perhaps?" She sat up, eyes wide. "Surely there are businessmen even in the West. And then you'll marry and settle down. You'll never come back if that happens."

"The trains travel in both directions, dear. It's not so isolated as it used to be. Please, don't be so dramatic."

"Hmph," Julie answered, throwing herself back onto the pillow.

"I'm surprised at you, Julie." There was a wink in Beth's voice, and she turned to look over her shoulder at her sister. "You haven't once suggested what I thought you would."

Julie's head popped up above the covers. "What's that?"

Beth laid aside her hairbrush and rose to switch off the electric light.

"What do you mean?" Julie coaxed as Beth slid into the bed.

"Well . . . I would have thought—because you're such a daring adventurer yourself—that you already would have asked Father to be allowed to—"

"Come visit you!" Julie scrambled upright again and clasped her hands together in delight.

"He might say yes."

"Not Mother. She would never allow it."

Beth moved closer, fluffing her pillow beneath her head and snuggling down into the warmth. "She might. After all, I would already be there—and she knows I'm able to restrain most of your foolish notions."

"Hmph" was Julie's answer once again, but she joined in with Beth's chuckle and cozied down among the blankets. "You might be right. And anyway, it's worth a try."

As the grandfather clock in the hall called out periodic warnings of how quickly the night was slipping away, Beth and Julie whispered on in the darkness, forging plans and making promises.

※

Beth slid out of bed so as not to awaken Julie, then scrambled for her list, written in careful hand and laid beside her brush the night before. She skimmed it quickly, bathed, dressed, and pinned up her long tresses with Emma's assistance, then hastened downstairs for breakfast. Margret and John had spent the night at the family home but would not be driving with the rest of them to the train station. So Beth held on to baby JW, her elder sister's little John William, until the last possible moment before releasing him into his father's arms and hugging Margret good-bye.

"Be careful, Beth." Then Margret forced a rather strained smile, cupped Beth's face in her hands so she could look deeply into her eyes, and corrected herself softly. "No, I already *know* you will be careful. So, little sister, I'll tell you to be *brave* instead."

Beth's tears spilled out, and she circled her sister's shoulders in a long embrace. "I love you, Margret," she whispered. "Take good care of baby JW for me," she added with a wobbly smile.

Father was propelling them all out the door before Beth felt she truly was ready. She waved back toward her home and the little group watching from the open doorway, then ducked into the sleek automobile. Julie slipped in beside her, followed by her mother, and then her father settled into the jump seat. He nodded toward their driver, and the car rolled forward. Beth strained around for a last look out the back window.

This would not be the first time she had traveled on the train. Grandmama and Grandpapa lived in a neighboring city, so she had been on several short family excursions for visits with them. And sometimes there were concerts or operas or lectures in nearby towns that Father felt merited a train ride.

But for the most part Beth had done little in the way of travel—and never unchaperoned. Even at a time when long summer vacations in the United States or even Europe were commonplace for many of those in their social circle, her family had remained at home. Now Beth wished she were more familiar with the larger world—beyond the bits and pieces of knowledge she had gained from books.

But Father, whose business it was to travel—who had spent a great deal of Beth's childhood away at sea building a notable import company—had taken care of everything. Nothing was left for Beth to manage but the cumbersome suitcase and the heartrending good-byes. With Mother's careful planning, there was even time to sit in the station café to share a cup of tea before the first whistle announced Beth's approaching departure.

On the platform, Father was the first to draw Beth aside and pull her close. He said, his voice low, "I won't say much. I won't be able." He cleared his throat. "But I do want to give you this." Drawing something from his overcoat pocket, Father produced a small brass piece.

Beth gasped. "Oh, I can't, Father," she said, her hand over her mouth.

"Please," he insisted. "I want you to have it. I know you've always loved it." That was true. Father's compass had been special to Beth since she was a little girl, enamored by anything that had to do with her father's work at sea—but this object more than any other was her delight. And it had been a symbol to them both of his love and guidance to his daughter.

Then her father added huskily, "So you will always be able to find your way home."

Beth couldn't breathe.

He cleared his throat again. "I wrote a Bible verse on a slip of paper inside. Don't forget its words, Beth. They are absolutely true, and especially for you as you begin this . . ." But he couldn't finish.

She threw her arms around his neck and struggled not to weep. When she felt a hand touch her back, Beth turned toward her mother and another painful good-bye.

"It's so hard to let you go, darling," her mother said, obviously doing her best to keep her voice steady. "Do try to get your rest, dear. And remember to take your Scott's Emulsion daily. I worry so about your constitution being strong enough for this endeavor. And I shall be praying each day—you know that."

How fully Beth knew that to be true. "I love you, Mother," she told her, embracing her tightly.

"Yes, dear. I love you too." Beth leaned back and saw rare tears forming in her mother's eyes.

"Don't forget, my darling, I shall want to know all about everything, and I will watch rather impatiently for each of your letters," her mother added.

"Yes, Mother."

"I'm sorry, Priscilla, but it's time," Father prompted solemnly. "We need to let Beth get on her way."

Mother's expression betrayed a pitiful sorrow. "It's just for a year, I know. Yet that seems ever so long just now." She dabbed at her eyes with a lace hankie, kissing Beth's cheek one last time.

Then Julie pushed forward and flung her arms around Beth. "I'll miss you! I'll miss you so much!"

Emotions were threatening to overwhelm Beth now. She buried her face against Julie's shoulder.

After a moment Father interrupted. "Come, Beth. The train is just about to pull out."

Then everything happened at once. A porter took Beth's case, and she turned to follow as directed. She climbed the steps into the train's vestibule and, stopping to wave just once more to her beloved family, she turned the corner and entered the confining hallway. The porter had already disappeared around a bend not far ahead, and Beth hurried to catch up.

The man ushered her to a private sleeping compartment, and motioning toward each of its amenities, he explained their use. However, Beth was not in a state to understand a word of what he was saying, staring around her blankly. She finally moved to the window and drew back the thick velvet curtain, only to find she was looking out on the wrong side of the train to catch one more glimpse of her family, finding instead the looming windows of another motionless train.

Dutifully, Beth turned back to the porter and pulled out the coins Father had given her for a tip. The man doffed his funny little hat and pulled the door closed behind him.

She had never felt so alone.

CHAPTER

2

ETH PASSED THE LONG DAY watching the countryside slide past her window, reading half-heartedly, and
eventually venturing out to find her way around the train.
Covered vestibules between cars helped to make these walks
feel more secure. But she was far too conscious of the train's
speed to fully trust her balance, especially as she stepped over
the demarcation separating one car from the next—and when
a curve sent the cars to jostling and swaying.

The many stops at towns large and small along the way
would have provided some diversion, but Beth dared not dis-
embark even for a short walk for fear of not being safely on
board again before the iron beast, spitting steam in a most
forceful manner, glided away.

The dining car was an elegant restaurant on wheels, though
she wondered what she could possibly eat without further
upsetting her fluttering stomach. The constant clatter of the
wheels on the tracks, along with the motion from side to side,
left her feeling slightly queasy much of the time. Surveying
the menu, Beth quickly ruled out trying to spoon soup to her

mouth without a disaster on her clothing or the tablecloth. Instead, she chose some tea along with a pastry roll and tore off little bites as she half listened to the amiable chatter of two women at a table directly behind her. Their cheerful voices served only to increase her loneliness. If only she were sharing the table with her own family.

Forlorn, Beth allowed her gaze to take in the rest of the passengers. *What type of fellow travelers would journey so far?* Clearly this car would cater only to the wealthy heading west. Others who were less affluent would eat sack lunches while sitting in the humbler seats of their passenger cars. Beth frowned at the familiar guilt of being surrounded by luxury when she knew others were not given such privileges.

To her left was a table where one lone, suited gentleman dined. Beth noted his rumpled jacket and dusty shoes, a clear contrast to the refined air of the man himself. Beth suspected that he might have been having a difficult time traveling too— that he was out of his familiar element. It made her wonder if others around could perceive as clearly that she felt entirely out of place and alone.

At the table in front of her was a young woman with two children. One little boy was sitting quietly, though he appeared rather sullen. The second was a bundle of energy, driving his mother to distraction. Just as she would reprimand him for one action, he would think of something equally mischievous to take up. In just the few moments that Beth observed their table, he had knocked over the crystal salt shaker, dipped his linen napkin into his water glass, and kicked at the wall repeatedly, leaving several scuff marks on the paneled wood. *Edward was just like that when he was the same age,* mused Beth, then found herself blushing for such a judgmental attitude.

Earlier in the summer she had heard a rumor that Edward

Montclair's father had given him an ultimatum in hopes of encouraging him to take life more seriously and to assume some responsibility for his own livelihood—join the Mounted Police or sign on to one of the many ships owned by his father's company—and not in a position of importance either, but as a regular lowly sailor. Beth was not surprised to hear that Edward had chosen the force, though she had rolled her eyes and gossiped to Julie, "I'm amazed they were willing to take him." She blushed now, remembering the less-than-gracious words, and silently wished him well wherever he might find himself employed.

Her thoughts returned to the young mother and her tired face. *She does have her hands full.* For a moment Beth considered asking if she could be of assistance in any way, but quickly convinced herself that her offer would be more embarrassing than helpful.

The couple seated across from the little family listened to the ruckus with rather stern faces. Beth could tell by their stiff postures and grim expressions that they did not approve of such a display. They were older and probably had already raised their own children. Periodically the husband would clear his throat and his wife would answer with an ever so slight shake of her head to express her shared perturbation. But they neither spoke to one another nor made eye contact. Instead the rhythm of fork to mouth never ceased, almost keeping time with the swaying of the train.

The sound of laughter came again from the ladies dining together, and then their voices from behind Beth carried forward. "My mother would never have allowed me to behave so atrociously," one whispered.

"I wouldn't have stayed in my seat long if I had tried. My daddy would have marched me right outside for a 'chat'—if you know what I mean."

Beth hoped their exchange had not been overheard by the young mother.

"Your father?" came the retort. "I don't believe it. Charlie always said you were your daddy's favorite—the apple of his eye. To hear him talk, I can't imagine that your daddy ever spoke to you harshly. Believe me, your brother says he got more than his share of your daddy's wrath."

"Don't be fooled. Charlie remembers things the way he wants to remember them. I suppose we all do." The woman laughed. "And then we spend the rest of our lives basing the way we think about our families on what we *thought* happened—instead of what really did."

What a provocative thought. Beth turned it round and round in her mind, musing silently as she stirred at her tea. *Could it be true of my childhood too? And if so, how would I ever realize the error in order to correct it?* All at once memories of home came rushing back to Beth so quickly she could almost forget everything around her. The faces she had left behind at the train station were safely fastened in place in her memory. Father, one arm pulling Mother close against him, the other waving slowly as she boarded. And Julie's tears flowing unchecked over her cheeks.

Then more memories followed. Father in the parlor behind his newspaper, Julie in the sunroom sketching some new image, even Margret during their frequent visits—up in the nursery rocking JW to sleep while husband John leaned over her shoulder to smile at his son. And of course Mother moving deftly through the house, presiding competently over all. Beth pictured the attic where she and Julie had found such lovely isolation as schoolgirls, whispering and planning the great adventures they were certain to share. Even the long-ago nursery, with favorite toys and special books lining its tidy shelves.

A slow tear escaped Beth's clouded eyes. She hurried to dab it away with the corner of her napkin. But nostalgia had already taken hold, and she found herself reveling in the images. Her earliest memory came easily to mind, washing over her with a warm sense of safety and pleasure.

She recalled with vivid clarity the feeling of cuddling on Father's lap when he retreated in the evening with a book to his overstuffed chair, Beth having come fresh from a bath ready to say good-night, hoping that Mother would not rush her too quickly off to bed. Father would pull one side of his silk lounging jacket around Beth's small shoulders and she would tuck her bare feet deep inside the folds on the other, pressing her tiny ear against his broad chest and listening to his deep voice reverberate as he shared aloud with her from whatever he had been reading.

Pausing a moment to contemplate, Beth was certain she could have been no more than three at the time. *That old chair*, she thought, smiling to herself. *How Mother despised it.* There were relatively few times when Father had put his foot down, particularly in regard to home furnishings in their fine Victorian residence. Mother had filled it with beautiful objects small hands were not allowed to touch. But because of Father's insistence, the chair remained. And in Beth's mind it belonged to the two of them only. Whenever he was home from his travels, it was their little haven in Mother's perfectly ordered world where even the nursery was arranged just so, and Polly the nurse was instructed to keep toys picked up as soon as Beth or big sister Margret had laid them aside.

With fondness Beth recalled too the precious brass compass, perched on the table beside Father's chair. Sometimes he would allow her to hold it—smooth and cold, heavy and mysterious, its tiny needle spinning and bobbing at will.

When she had been a bit older, Father had told her the story of how the simple yet vital little instrument had brought his ship's crew safely home during a frightening and dangerous storm at sea. Father had demonstrated that the pointer always turned toward magnetic north—no matter which way the box was held. "The compass needle tells the truth, Beth, even in a storm. And then one must adjust the rest of one's circumstances in accordance—even though sometimes it feels amiss. It reminds me that the Bible is like that too. It tells us the truth, and then we must adjust our thinking, our actions, to match." The deep significance of the compass made Beth even more determined to keep careful watch over such a family treasure on this year-long adventure.

A riot of noise drew Beth's attention. The mother was gathering her boys to leave the dining car and having much difficulty now in coaxing the troublesome one from his chair. With terse commands interspersed with hushed begging from his mother, a slow smile crept across the boy's face when at last he slid slowly from the seat. It was readily apparent that he enjoyed the attention his behavior was drawing. He tossed his napkin to the floor and eyed his frazzled mother as if daring her to make a scene.

Suddenly the youngster became aware of the maître d' towering over him. The smirking eyes grew wide at such an imposing form. But the man smiled kindly to the mother, then placed a hand firmly on the boy's shoulder and reached far down to the floor beside him to lift the discarded napkin, calmly placing it on the table, where it belonged. Stiffly, the lad fell in line behind his mother while the maître d' called after them cheerfully, "Have a good evening, madam. We'll see you in the morning for breakfast." It was an unexpected kindness. The beleaguered mother managed a feeble thank-you in return.

Beth pushed back her plate, deciding to abandon the re-
mains of her meager supper. By the time she returned to her
sleeper, the porter had prepared her bed, and she anticipated
settling into it and passing the time with a good night's sleep.
But the rumble of the wheels and the rocking motion made it
almost impossible for her to remain asleep. She rose several
times for a drink of water or just to stretch restless limbs, returning to her bed only to struggle further for a comfortable
position that might elicit sleep.

All at once Beth's eyes opened wide in fright, a flash of
flickering light filled the cabin, and then—only darkness. For
several hazy moments she struggled to grasp where she was.
There was only a suffocating fear pressing down on her until,
at last, her mind cleared enough to recall and understand. It
had been a nightmare. In reality she was still on the train and
headed west.

She threw aside the blankets and rose to a seated position,
wiping the perspiration from her forehead with the sleeve of
her nightgown. Outside in the passageway, Beth could hear
footsteps and then became aware of the heavy drone of rain
on the roof.

It was a familiar enough dream—one that had haunted
her since childhood. Perhaps she should not be surprised at
its reappearance at a time when she was so unsettled and
anxious—and when her thoughts had been reveling in childhood memories.

It began as always with a vision of the snow-white bassinet.
Slowly the tiny childish version of herself would make her
way across the room to peer inside at baby William, her precious infant brother. But as her gaze lifted over the side ex-
pectantly, she found the bed empty, and the horror of those
tragic days descended anew. Immediately in the nightmare, a

bout of uncontrollable coughing overcame Beth, leaving her desperately laboring to breathe, crying out silently for her absent father, hearing nearby the sound of Mother weeping. And in that state she would awake, gasping even now to draw a satisfying breath.

Whooping cough—it had stolen away Mother's baby, her little Sweet William. And it had forever altered Beth's world, leaving her own small body frail and sickly, and causing Mother to hover and brood and stifle. From that moment on Beth had suffered under the limitations that the illness had effected. Now she tried to shake away the terrible emotion of it all—to remember where she was and why. How troubling that as she took this momentous step toward independence and accomplishment, the nightmare had returned with its suffocating fears. Beth found it even more difficult to sleep again.

When morning finally arrived the rain had stopped, but daylight revealed another dismal, cloudy day. There were few choices for an engaging pastime. Beth set herself to read until even she—an ardent reader—had lost interest. She wandered a little and sat frequently in the dining car. But she could not escape the gloomy shadow that hung over her nor the agitated, turbulent thoughts about where she was going . . . about the enormous unknown ahead.

By her third day on the train, Beth felt thoroughly miserable and desperately bored. The clouds had burst open again, and strong winds drove sheets of rain against her window, blocking out any scenery there might have been to help the passage of time.

Then came Winnipeg, and it was in the worst of the weather that Beth faced a train change. She looked at the water streaming down the outside of her window and drew an umbrella from the crammed suitcase. It was foolish, she knew, to expect much protection from such a small, frilly contraption designed for fashion more than function.

She gathered her belongings and found herself swept along with the crowd of passengers, down the narrow steps and across the train platform. Even the covered loading area, meant to keep passengers out of the elements, was not able to protect them from the rain driven crossways by the winds.

Other travelers, their heads ducked beneath umbrellas, hats, and newspapers, were heading toward a second train. Beth fell in step and arrived at the end of the huddled line, awaiting a turn to climb aboard the next long row of cars. There too was the mother with her two boys, grasping at their hands and dragging them along behind a porter who carried their luggage.

Even with her umbrella clutched tightly above her, Beth could feel the rain coursing down the back of her neck and soaking through her traveling suit all the way to her skin. The wind pulled wildly in one direction and then the other, almost whipping the ineffective umbrella from her hands. It was no use. There was nothing she could do but let the torrent soak in and endure the shivering. She folded the useless accessory and tucked it under one arm. Beth's past experience with these late-summer rains often had included the threat of another round of illness.

If Mother were here, what on earth would she say? "Elizabeth, you'll be sick. For pity's sake, ask for assistance at the train station. There are people whose job it is to carry your bags and see that you arrive safely. A girl like you should take full advantage of their services. There is no earthly reason to suffer difficulties. And"—she could almost hear aloud her mother's repeated warning—"if you expect to endure life in the West, you shall need much assistance."

The very memory of such belittling words caused Beth

to hoist the suitcase higher and step in closer to the others ready to board. Her eyes strained through the mist to read the numbers painted on the side of the train.

She stared in shock—*205? That is not right.* She put her suit-case down and hurriedly reached into her jacket sleeve for the ticket Father had purchased. *It says 308.* Panic gripped her as she cast a look around. There were other waiting trains at the station.

"Please, sir," she called to a porter standing nearby. "Excuse me, please! I think I must find number 308."

The man took quick steps toward her and reached for her ticket. "Well, miss, that one leaves from the far end of the station."

Beth choked out a thank-you and grasped the handle of the suitcase. Just then she heard the man shout, "Darby! Help this young lady with her bag; see that she gets to the right train." A young porter was by her side in an instant with a much larger umbrella. He took the ticket, lifted her suitcase effortlessly, and tipped his elbow out for her to grasp. Beth breathed a sigh of gratitude and clutched his offered arm as he held the umbrella over her. *Perhaps Mother is right. It's easier to allow others to assist.* Yet it was disheartening to admit she was already failing at the capability she had hoped to demonstrate during her adventure west.

"We'll have to step it up, miss. Your train's about ready to leave."

They hastened toward a second waiting train—the farthest away. It was a struggle for Beth to keep up with the porter's long stride as he fairly pulled her along through the crowds. Her fitted tweed skirt allowed for only tiny, quick steps. The hurried clicking of Beth's heels was swallowed up in all the confusion, noise, and rain.

The man delivered her to the steps leading onto the proper

train, and Beth reached for the next offered hand that easily drew her small frame up into the vestibule. She made a vain attempt to shake off the rain and pushed a stray strand of hair from her eyes, sure that the new hat purchased specifically for this trip must be ruined beyond repair. She could feel the left side of the velvet brim, now soaked through, resting on her ear. She knew she must look an absolute fright, but Mother had taught her to always be dignified, even in difficult circumstances. So she drew in a deep breath, lifted her chin, and moved into the passageway. A third porter was standing ready to carry her suitcase and see that she found the right sleeping compartment.

"Oh," she exclaimed, "I didn't tip the other porter—"

"Not to worry, miss, we're just doing our jobs," the current attendant assured her, but she wished she had been more aware and had thought to express her gratitude properly.

At last she was able to close a door between herself and the rest of the world. She collapsed against it for a moment, not certain how to proceed. Just then the train lurched forward and only her hand grabbing for support from the nearby door handle kept her on her feet.

Beth knew she had come perilously close to being left on the station platform. She squeezed her eyes shut. "Thank you, God," she whispered. "I have no idea what I would have done had I missed this train!"

In short order she had locked the passageway door, pulled the curtains closed, slipped out of her wet garments, dried herself as best she could with a small linen hand towel she found hanging at the washstand, wrestled her suitcase open, and donned dry clothing. Even then Beth could not stop shivering. She dug through the case once again and found a sweater to add to her outfit. The pieces did not work together, but there was no one near enough to criticize.

Next she had to determine what to do with the sopping clothing she had removed. But there seemed to be no ready answer. The washbowl was far too small to contain it all, and there was no other receptacle of any kind. So, holding each piece well away to avoid soaking wet patches into her dry clothes, she folded them neatly, tucking personal garments discreetly in the middle of the pile, and laid the bundle on newspaper pages that she'd spread over one corner of the floor. She had tried to imagine what her mother would do, but had concluded that Mother would never be found in such an out-of-control situation. Beth could only hope the train had some type of laundry service.

Reminded of her mother, Beth rummaged again in the suitcase to bring out the familiar bottle of Scott's Emulsion. Had Mother been present, she would certainly have insisted Beth take a draught now of the dreadful fluid. Mother had long ago concluded that Beth's bout with whooping cough had rendered her lungs unable to properly supply oxygen to her body and that this was causing her many ailments—even her small stature. It wasn't as if any doctor had pronounced such a conclusive diagnosis, but no one doubted Mother's veracity. And armed with that verdict she had set out to find the right medicines and tonics and elixirs to bring Beth to a state of perfect health. Beth could remember the dreaded spoon being held to her mouth each night, carrying some new smelly, ill-tasting concoction. It made this current adventure all the more unexpected that Beth, then, would be the one of the three sisters to brave a journey alone so far from home. But even here she surrendered to Mother's prescribed treatment.

Tucking the bottle away, she dropped to the seat and looked

31

around for something to pass the time and help her relax. Reading came first to mind. But she had already finished the books she had packed in her suitcase. With a glance toward the corner, she bemoaned the fact that she had rendered the courtesy newspaper useless. All her other books except her Bible had been packed in the trunks that had been checked—

The trunks! Would they have been sent to the wrong train? Beth's mind whirled in panic. She took a deep breath to calm herself and sort through what she knew. Father had placed her trunks together on a cart at the platform in Toronto, and they had been wheeled away by a porter. Father had told her they were "checked through." So they should have been transferred to the proper train, probably before she herself had managed to arrive there. She blew out a long breath of relief.

She considered spending some time reading her Bible. But she was sure she lacked the proper frame of mind right then, so she settled herself onto the padded velvet seat and tucked her feet up beside her. Drawing the window curtain back, she cast a glance outside, finding only the river of rain still streaming down the glass panes.

No diversion there, she concluded. She felt rather tired after her chase across the station, so she leaned back against the seat and let her mind wander. She much preferred to be alone with her thoughts just now and focused her mind back toward her childhood memories—hoping to overshadow the recent nightmare with happier recollections.

It was a simple matter of remembering Julie. It seemed to Beth that no one could deny the charms of the new baby sister who'd arrived about a year after William's death. The chubby cherub burst into the world smiling and laughing. Every chance Beth was given she asked to hold the new baby in her bundle of blankets, though sometimes she was only allowed to sit very close to Mother and offer one finger to the plump curling fist of her tiny sister as she nursed.

However, Mother often let Beth stand beside the crib and sing lullabies until Julie drifted off to sleep. Beth recalled with fondness how she had also been permitted to place a toy or dolly next to Julie, where she could look at it and smile. But Mother would chide Beth whenever she discovered all the toys lined up inside the walls of the crib like soldiers keeping watch over their sleeping baby. The thought brought a tightness to Beth's throat even now. She remembered how closely they had all guarded Julie.

In time Julie began to walk and talk. From that moment on there seemed for Beth to be no memory in which the two of them were not together. They played together in the nursery and almost always shared nicely. When Julie demanded a toy that Beth had already claimed, it was not so very difficult to give it up for the sake of her young sibling, particularly because doing so always made Mother smile approvingly.

Even while they were very young, Beth, Julie, and big sister Margret enjoyed most the pleasure of being read to. Together with Mother, or with Father whenever he was present, they shared tales of all the talking animals in Rudyard Kipling's *Just So Stories* and imagined the chaotic world of *Alice in Wonderland* by Lewis Carroll. They read too from a book of Bible stories illustrated for children, growing familiar with the lives of Father Abraham, and brave Daniel, and kind Jesus. And after just a few sessions spent with Father, Beth had quickly learned to decipher the letters of the alphabet and was soon reading on her own.

A change in the train's speed brought Beth back to her present surroundings. Familiar now with the train's motion, Beth could sense the gradual slowing of the chugging engine while the effort of the brakes rippled from car to car in jerking fashion. Even though she would have loved to get out on firm ground for a short walk, she determined to ignore another stop.

She closed her eyes instead to shut out the present and drew upon a favorite event from childhood. With a deep, longing breath, Beth summoned the feelings once more.

She had been seven and Julie was three. They had been allowed to accompany their parents for the first time to the expansive home of the Montclairs, who were hosting a concert. Holding hands and sitting close together, the sisters were still and solemn with full-moon eyes at the display of bright brass instruments so near at hand trumpeting out their songs above the quivering of the strings. The loud boom of drums and sudden clash of cymbals always made the sisters tremble just a little. But in spite of the moments of startling crescendo, Beth was so enthralled by the music she could hardly breathe. She could almost hear it echoing now despite the thrum of the train's engine.

The very next day young Auntie Elizabeth had arrived at their home with a gift for Beth—a child-size violin she herself had used for lessons years before. The little girl's rapture at the concert had not gone unnoticed, and soon Beth was struggling with every ounce of determination in her soul to coax out the same sounds that had come from the strings that night, lifting her eyes to watch her instructor as he bobbed his chin in rhythm with her labored efforts. Over time, his face seemed to grimace less and less while Beth played. She became quite proficient at an early age. So with her dual loves of music and books, it was as if for Beth that reading brought the whole world closer while music filled it with color and joy.

She thought of her concert violin—the full-size version

that Father had given her when she turned thirteen—and the discussion with him about bringing it along. It was packed away safely now in one of the trunks. Beth was glad to know that it was close, but couldn't help but be concerned that it might be damaged on the trip. She chose to trust that Father had wrapped it well.

Thinking back with fondness, Beth stirred on the confining train seat as she remembered again how very fascinating it was that she would now be following in Auntie's footsteps, traveling to the West to teach. And even though Beth had later come to discover that her namesake Elizabeth was not truly an aunt—being the daughter of Father's eldest brother Ephraim and thus an older cousin whom Mother insisted be addressed respectfully—Beth and her sisters chose to continue the term of endearment. She had rarely seen Aunt Elizabeth, who had moved west not long after the concert and rarely returned to visit, but Beth nurtured a delightful sense of pleasure at their similarities, particularly as she was offered the position out west.

Beth contemplated again the remark she had overheard in the dining car. Perhaps childhood memories were actually fickle things, she thought now. That what one comes to understand about a particular person or event sometimes beguiles the mind, fashioning simple, unadorned truth into something slightly askew from reality. She wondered how many small alterations she had woven into her own memories over the years.

Beth gave a long sigh and leaned forward for another look out the window. Still raining . . . From the hallway she heard the porter's voice calling the dinner hour and prepared to make her way to the dining car. Maybe she would work up the nerve to invite someone to join her.

She reached eagerly for her Bible and carried it along with her to the table. A beloved psalm assured her once again that her heavenly Father was with her even when her dearest earthly father could not be. She prayed for her family and settled in for more hours of travel, spending time between the dining car and her cabin.

Another emotionally exhausting afternoon dragged on, and she was not close yet to her destination. The tight compartment in which she had already spent dreary hours offered small comfort. After supper Beth stood in the center of it and shook her head wearily. Too early to dress for bed and too late to spend any more time in aimless strolls, she chose to surrender the day and struggled to pull her high-heeled shoes from her aching feet.

Just then there came a firm knock on the door.

CHAPTER

3

𝓡ATHER MYSTIFIED, Beth stood to answer the knock. As she reached for the door handle, she remembered the obvious. It would be the porter, there to pull out the bed and prepare her compartment for the night.

"Yes, one moment," she called, turning the latch.

But instead of the porter's black coat, the doorway was filled with a bright red jacket. She stepped back and quickly realized it was that of an officer of the Royal Canadian Mounted Police.

"How nice to see you again, Elizabeth." The familiar voice came just as Beth's eyes lifted to see a face she knew all too well. The wavy brown hair hung over dark green eyes eagerly fastened on hers.

"Edward?"

He bowed slightly. "Yes, ma'am, it is I."

"But what—what are you doing here?" She was so astounded—and mortified—she could hardly speak.

Edward cleared his throat. "May I?" He gestured into the compartment.

She would have rather denied his request, but her mother's

training forbade it. Beth heard her voice answer, "Yes, of course."

She drew back as Edward stepped across the threshold, leaving the door wide behind him. His manners weren't always what Beth would have desired, but in this case he was acting appropriately. "Your father requested that I accompany you during your travels—see you safely through to Coal Valley," he explained.

His explanation only left Beth more bewildered. "My father? He asked you to accompany me? Whatever for?"

"I also have been posted in the West," he hurried to explain, "and was traveling at this time. As a favor to your family, I agreed to see to your needs and safety."

Beth's thoughts rushed back over the day—the thorough soaking while she struggled with her own suitcase and nearly missed her connection. "But—" she labored to find expression for her dismay—"then where have you been?" Immediately she wished she could take back the question. That was not the point. She did not *want* nor *need* his help.

Sounding aloof and defensive, Edward replied, "I boarded this train at the last stop. My company already had other travel arrangements. But at the suggestion of your father, I received special permission to travel with you instead. I have gone to considerable trouble to be of assistance, I assure you."

Beth refused to soften her tone. "And I assure you, Mr. Montclair, that it was entirely unnecessary. I have been managing just fine." Beth knew her words sounded weak and pathetic and, worst of all, were far from the truth. Just at that moment she remembered the soggy pile of discarded clothing still stacked in the far corner of the cabin. She shifted slightly to shield the sorry mess from Edward.

Her conscience brought to mind the two helpful porters.

What would she have done without them? But *this?*—this was too much. How could her father—

"Nevertheless," Edward was saying, "I intend to keep my word to your father." He cleared his throat again. "I shall return in the morning at eight o'clock to escort you to breakfast. Is that acceptable to you?"

"I need a *police escort* for breakfast?" she shot back, further incensed at his callous presumption.

He didn't budge. "So should I come at eight?" Then Beth could see his eyes actually crinkle ever so slightly at the corners. "Of course," he said, "I would be more than happy to come at six—or at five. As you wish, Elizabeth."

Beth knew the impudent expression well enough to know he would be very pleased to awaken her far earlier than she was ready to rise. She had been bested—and by *him*, of all people. She could feel her face burning with anger. "Fine. Fine. But not before eight. Or I shall call the porter and . . ." She let the threat hang. What could she do? How could she complain to a porter about the conduct of a *police officer?* One who had been sent by her father? Edward had won.

Bowing once more, he retreated and closed the door behind him. Beth stood in the center of the room, trembling. Aloud she muttered, "Only the devil at the door would be worse than Edward Montclair!" Immediately she rebuked herself for such a dreadful pronouncement. But the truth was, she wanted to hide from him—to lock herself away or . . . or jump from the train. And even as she knew she was being childish and nonsensical, she could only pace out her frustrations during the short steps between door and window. *This is absolutely unacceptable—that he has found a way to intrude on my plans even here. I thought . . . I thought I was well rid of him!*

Edward had been a nuisance back as long as Beth could

remember. And because his family was intrinsically connected with Father's shipping business, there had been far more obligations requiring her to cross paths with him than she would have preferred.

The Montclairs had their roots in old England, and Beth had often heard that nobility was included in Mrs. Montclair's family line, though specifics were left conspicuous by their absence. Edward frequently found a way to work his "stately lineage" into conversation. But his obvious pride was the least of Beth's issues against him.

She had concluded even as a little girl that he was a trouble-maker and a good-for-nothing. Just because the Montclairs had considerable wealth and resources, she didn't believe it gave Edward the social advantages that he seemed to so boldly claim. And wield about.

Edward's father must have similar impressions about his son, she concluded a bit smugly. *No doubt this is the reason Edward is now with the Royal Canadian Mounted Police, with the hope that discipline and order will knock some sense of a worthwhile, productive gentleman into him!*

Rather more vigorously than necessary, Beth pulled the pins from her hair, shaking it loose and brushing it out, all the while casting further criticisms of her unwanted chaperone at her reflection in the mirror. "He thinks he's superior to everyone else!" she muttered.

She couldn't help remembering her first encounter with Edward Montclair, sitting in church with his parents. Beth had watched him from across the aisle trying to provoke an answering smile from Margret, who had *not* responded to his attempts at flirting. After service the sisters had turned their backs on him when he approached, giggling together about how foolish he was to try to elicit a smile from an older girl.

"He should know better," they'd agreed with the great assurance of the young.

Beth banged the brush down on the washstand and shook herself in an effort to regain some composure. But she went back to her list of accusations. He'd also chased her—just her—with a dead lizard he found behind the church. Her Sunday school classmates had insisted that he was sweet on her, of all things. Her trembling fingers fumbled with the buttons of her shirtwaist as she prepared for bed.

Oh, how Beth had spurned him back in those days. She had abandoned conversations with others if Edward joined the group. Had refused to even acknowledge him when he called out her name. And on one occasion at a church social when she was quite young, she had dared stamp her foot at her mother's instructions to sit next to the infuriating youngster. Inexplicably, Mother had acquiesced, and a triumphant Beth was allowed to scoot into a chair safely away from her tormenter.

Beth paused as she hung the shirtwaist in the tiny closet and studied the memory further. For the first time, it struck her as odd that Mother had given in. She certainly could not recall other times when a flash of willfulness had caused Mother to concede. *Had Mother known? Could she possibly have understood a young girl's feelings about the matter?* Yet Edward was here, thrust back into Beth's life at a most inopportune time.

Surely this can't be Mother's doing, can it? Beth had sometimes suspected that her mother and Mrs. Montclair secretly played matchmaker between Edward and her—hoping to tie their families together even further through matrimony. *And no doubt Mother is intrigued by the "nobility" of the family,* Beth acknowledged ruefully. It certainly didn't matter to her.

But Edward had said Father was the instigator of these

unfortunate circumstances. *Perhaps blaming Mother is unfair.* Beth determined to push the conflicted feelings out of her mind for the time being. She pulled her nightgown over her head and . . . *Oh my!* It was far too early to retire for the night. The sun was still rather high in the sky, and the porter had not yet arrived. And here she stood, mindlessly ready for bed. In utter frustration, Beth reached for her clothing and hurried to replace her attire before a second knock at the door.

"I'll tell you one thing," she mumbled to no one, "if he calls me Elizabeth the Great just once more, I shall not speak to him again—even if it means I don't speak to him for the entire remainder of the trip!"

When the porter arrived to make up Beth's bed, she was seated comfortably in her cabin, the picture of serenity. She was even able to pose a question about laundry service in a dignified manner and was pleased that the porter seemed perfectly able to be of assistance. To her relief, the evidence of her rain mishap was whisked away. And for the second time in one evening, Beth prepared herself for bed.

Before putting out her light, she drew a long breath and picked up her Bible from the suitcase. She tucked her feet down under the covers, plumped both pillows behind her back, and opened to where she had been reading last—the book of Ephesians. Words about anger, about ministering grace to others, being kind and tenderhearted, seemed to leap off the page. She couldn't help but compare her own childish behavior toward Edward to God's desire for her and how she should treat others.

"I'm sorry, Father God," she finally sighed. "I should not have behaved that way." And then she quickly followed with, "Please help me to be respectful tomorrow. Even if I don't desire his company, I don't want to dishonor You."

Just at that moment Beth remembered her father's words as they parted. She was shocked that she could have so quickly forgotten about the verse he had written on paper and tucked inside the compass. Tossing aside the covers and scrambling to retrieve the brass instrument from where she had wrapped it carefully and packed it away, she flipped up the lid and a little slip of paper tumbled out.

Written in Father's careful cursive was, "I can do all things through Christ which strengtheneth me. Philippians 4:13."

Beth drew in a long, slow breath. Thoughts and emotions tumbled around inside her as she pondered the words and her father's intentions. She wondered what might have been different if she'd had that Scripture in mind during her meeting with Edward. She wondered what her father would say if he had seen her during the appalling episode. Her cheeks flushed. Even though she knew Father would be gracious and forgiving, she felt ashamed for not better representing his family . . . better representing the Lord.

Kneeling beside her open suitcase on the shuddering floor of the passenger train, Beth whispered aloud, "I'm already failing, God—I've embarrassed myself and treated another person badly." Then another verse came to her mind and she added with a trembling little smile, "But You promised that Your mercies are new every morning. Thank You for that. I need those mercies tonight. And tomorrow."

Beth returned the compass to its place, slid the suitcase back under the bed, and settled in again for the night. She had positioned the little slip of paper on the windowsill nearby and repeated it over and over until she had drifted off to sleep.

CHAPTER

4

TRUE TO HIS WORD, Edward Montclair arrived in full uniform with Stetson in hand to escort Beth to breakfast—two minutes early. He was visibly surprised by her smile when she met him at the door, but he made no comment. Beth continued to smile as Edward stepped back and motioned for her to precede him down the narrow aisle.

"Isn't it a lovely day today?" she offered, as if making conversation with a recent acquaintance. "I'm so glad it isn't raining anymore. I'd like to see some of the countryside."

"Yes," he agreed cautiously. "Though I've been told it's mostly open prairie we'll be crossing."

"Fine. That will be a nice contrast from city sights back home."

He shrugged. "There will be fewer stops—so we should make better time."

Beth smiled once more. "Fine," she repeated with a nod as they entered the dining car.

Edward held Beth's chair for her and ordered a pot of tea. She put in her breakfast order, then settled back and turned toward the window. She tried not to notice how his red jacket drew attention from all around the room.

"I can't even believe that it's already Sunday," she said. "It's certainly a bright day. The sky is so clear . . . as blue as—as blue as—" She paused and then said, "Well, I guess as blue as JW's eyes." Beth smiled to herself as she drew up the vision of her nephew's welcome the night before she left. Edward remained silent, so Beth chatted on. "Milo Phelps traveled to Saskatchewan last summer, and he said the skies over the prairie are unrivaled anywhere."

There was a moment of quiet and then Edward remarked, "It's the very same sky, you know."

"Excuse me?"

"It's precisely the same sky that covers everything."

"Hmm. Well then, maybe it's just that one can see so much more of it here."

Edward shook his head. "Well, maybe it's just that there's nothing else to see." Beth was certain by his tone that he was mocking her for her attempts at congeniality. She let the comment pass.

The maître d' set a plate before her containing a freshly baked scone, three small dollops of jellies spread like leaves around a little rose-shaped pat of butter, and a dainty china egg holder with a hard-boiled egg still steaming from the already opened top. *As beautiful and refined as any restaurant in Toronto.* Beth thanked the man and reached for her knife.

But Edward noted slyly over his own heaping plate, "That's not much of a meal, Elizabeth. What would your mother say?"

Before a terse retort could pass her lips, Beth forced herself to remain even-tempered. "Traveling is somewhat upsetting to my stomach. I think my mother would understand."

Looking puzzled that he was unable to bait her, Edward

responded awkwardly, "I'm sorry you don't feel well," and turned his attention to his own meal. For some time there was silence between them, and Beth was relieved to enjoy her breakfast and the scenery in peace.

Then Edward broke into her thoughts. "I was very surprised that your family allowed you to travel alone—and so far from home. I would have thought your mother would forbid it."

Again Beth struggled to respond calmly. "She was in support of my becoming a teacher. Though, of course, she would have preferred that I found a position nearby."

His eyes held a hint of something she couldn't identify. "I would expect that she would have preferred you to marry and settle down—as Margret did."

"Perhaps." Beth was finding it a little easier to continue to answer calmly but honestly. "Teaching is what I *chose* to pursue." She thought about Mother's first attempts to advise her away from college and teaching, but preferred to remember the pride in Mother's eyes on graduation day. "It's true that Mother would not have selected this path for me. But neither did she forbid it. And I do believe she's supportive now."

"That's ridiculous."

"Pardon me? I don't—"

"I said it's *ridiculous*." Edward leaned forward, elbows on the table, and lowered his voice. "I would have thought at least your father could control you."

Beth couldn't help but press herself into her seat. "This is not about being controlled, Edward. It's about—"

"It's about you acting like a stubborn, headstrong woman— like so many others in our generation," he shot back, "those females who feel it necessary to try to act like men, all in an effort to avoid leading boring lives at home."

Beth forced herself to return his steely expression. "Is that what you think I'm doing?"

"Yes. You, and Sigrid Freeman . . . and Ruth Shields. You have your fancy debutante parties and lead everyone to believe you're prepared to marry—and then you go off to college instead, thinking you can get jobs and take care of yourselves. Well, it won't work, Elizabeth. You'll see. You'll spend a month or two—maybe even a year—in some godforsaken wasteland, and then you'll come running back home, ready to be rescued."

Beth watched her hands slowly smooth the napkin across her lap as she edited her thoughts. "But Sigrid is in Ottawa playing with the philharmonic. And Ruth is a nurse."

"For now," he nodded grimly, leaning back again, his voice still muted but full of tension. "For now—but I'll give them less than a year and they'll both be engaged. Because that's the way the world works. When women get enough of pretending they can earn a living, they fall back on men to take care of them. We don't have the luxury of playing at an occupation for a while and then having someone else support us as soon as we're tired of it all. Men work hard their whole lives."

Beth waited in hard-won silence while each angry, quarrelsome response paraded through her mind. She considered commenting on the fact that he would inherit much of what he needed to support himself, that men benefit as much by marriage as women, that married women are not women of leisure but hardworking helpmates to their husbands, or that choosing a career did not even *imply* she was not interested in becoming a wife also. Instead, she dismissed each of these as argumentative and renewed her determination not to allow him to ruffle her feathers with declarations she doubted even he actually believed. What puzzled her most, however, was that he of all people would become so agitated by her life decisions. Such things had nothing to do with him. *Perhaps after leaving this train I indeed will never see him again*, she reminded herself.

She paused a moment longer and took a slow sip of tea, replaced the cup gently on its saucer, and lifted her napkin to the corners of her mouth. "I'm sorry you feel this way, Edward. I can see you don't understand my decision, but it is one I have reached under the counsel and protection of my parents. I'm afraid it does not require your approval." As calmly as she could, Beth excused herself and walked away. Her pace did not slow until she had returned to her cabin and lowered herself onto the seat. Only then did she notice she was trembling.

"I don't know if my response was proper, God. I hope I wasn't wrong in what I said to him. I truly do not understand how it would have been possible at that moment to say anything that would have been edifying to him." But Beth was rather satisfied that she had not spoken the words she really wanted to say. She felt it was a small victory, a great improvement from their previous interchange.

There was nothing she could do further to change Edward's opinion on the matter. He had again proven himself to be just as she had always seen him—a bully of a boy who had turned into a brute of a man. She wondered for a moment if he were the only one of their circle of friends to interpret her actions as he did, yet doubted that anyone else could be so narrow-minded and belligerent as Edward.

He had called her a "stubborn, headstrong woman." Even now, as she replayed the words spoken so pointedly against her, Beth could feel their sting. *After all*, she told herself, *this teaching position is perhaps the first truly assertive step I have ever taken. The problem is not that I have been stubborn—the problem is that my own hopes and wishes have been suffocated far too long by what has been expected of me.* Yes, Beth was more than aware that Mother would have chosen marriage and conformity to the norm—particularly when considering Beth's physical limitations.

She turned her back to recline against the end of the settee, kicking off her shoes and drawing her knees up to her chin. Still brooding over the conversation, more of her responses to Edward flooded into her mind. *It's true Mother would not have chosen this path for me. But neither did she forbid it. And I do think she's supportive now.* That is what she had told him, but she knew it was a pale reflection of the full truth. Mother had actually been quite set against Beth's even leaving for college, must less the "wild west."

Truth be told, Mother eventually *had* been very proud, standing in the college reception hall after Beth had graduated. But Mother also had hustled her home again as quickly as her bags could be packed and hasty good-byes said. It was clear that in her maternal way of viewing things, an unmarried daughter was to be kept close by and safe from the world—especially this daughter with a "weak constitution."

Beth felt old feelings rising up and turned once again to prayer. "Father God, I'm so tired of being told what I can't do. And maybe that does mean I'm being stubborn and headstrong. I don't want to seem rebellious—I just want to be what I feel You made me to be. And I believe You called me to this job and this place. If my attitudes are wrong, please help me understand so I can change them. But please, please, Father, give me the strength I need to do whatever it is that You're asking me to do. That's what I want. To please You—*not* to *displease* my mother."

Beth thought about the letter she must soon begin. It was

difficult to contemplate how to convey "all about everything" that Mother had requested. What she wanted most was to show that her decisions had been right and that she would be fine on her own. *Is there anything wrong with that?* she wondered.

CHAPTER

5

WITH ONLY BREAKFAST ACCOMPLISHED and no other
activity—not even a Sunday service—to fill her hours
until dinner would be served at noon, Beth's day returned to
boredom. She stared out at the enormous stretch of prairie
and imagined her family on a pleasant ride to church, seating
themselves together on the same pew they all had shared since
the sisters were little girls, joining in with the singing—which
Beth had always loved—and listening to the message . . . *without me*, she couldn't help but add as she finished the memory.

Somehow she managed to make it to noon and hurried to
arrive early at the dining car and hopefully miss her appointed
escort. She had eaten and returned to her compartment without crossing Edward's path. But when evening finally rolled
around, she was required to once more accept his company
for supper. They were seated with two gentlemen traveling
west on business, and a grateful Beth allowed the three to
carry most of the conversation, nodding politely and smiling
at what she hoped were appropriate moments.

In awkward silence Edward escorted her back to her cabin,

where she managed to thank him for his attentions. But before she could excuse herself and close the door, he reached out a hand to gently grasp her elbow. "I'm sorry, Elizabeth. I should not have spoken to you as I did this morning. I didn't intend— I wasn't trying to . . ." He struggled for words and finished with a faltering "I *am* sorry."

Lifting her face to search his, Beth was surprised at the sincerity she saw there. It was so unexpected she also was at a loss for words. "I see. It's fine. I accept your apology—I do."

"So we're still . . . friends?" He wore an expression she could not remember ever seeing on his face before.

"Friends?" she answered. "We're still—that is to say, nothing has changed as far as I am concerned." Beth was surprised he would make such a claim. She had never considered him anything more than a son of her parents' friends. *And a rather obnoxious one at that*, she couldn't help but silently add.

His relief at her forgiveness was obvious. "We arrive in Lethbridge tomorrow. Please wait here until I've made arrangements for our luggage. I'd at least like to be helpful there, as I've been a poor traveling companion so far."

She smiled but did not disagree with his assessment. "Yes, of course."

"Then I'll see you for breakfast," he pressed again, rather anxiously.

Confused by this sudden change in him, Beth dropped her gaze. "Yes, I'll be ready again at eight."

He released her arm, stepped back just a little, and nodded his acknowledgment.

⌘

After breakfast the next morning, Beth hurried to gather up the last of her belongings and tuck them into the suitcase she already had mostly filled. The porter had returned her laundered clothing when he prepared the bed last night. Taking up the slip of paper with Father's verse, she folded it until it was tiny enough to tuck inside her locket. She was just able to close its latch. She patted the necklace in place, grateful once more for the treasured truth it held.

The train pulled into Lethbridge with whistles, squealing of steel on steel, and lots of steam. Edward's knock came soon afterward. Though she greeted him amiably enough, he remained somewhat remote. He nodded briefly and reached to lift her suitcase. She fell in line behind him with her handbag safely at her side. Despite his unexplained demeanor, she was pleased that Edward was there to assist her. She quickly followed, free from worries about finding her way and making her own arrangements.

She took the last, long step down to solid ground, grateful for Edward's helping hand. She was tired and depleted by her travels thus far. Beth hoped some of that might be soothed away by a hot bath in the hotel.

Edward had arranged for a porter, and her two large trunks were already loaded on a wheeled cart, as well as what she assumed to be Edward's duffel. They added her suitcase to the stack, and Edward pushed a tip into the man's ready hand.

"See that these are delivered to the Alpine View Inn immediately."

"Yes, sir." Something about the man's tone and shifting eyes caught Beth's attention, and she frowned and turned to ask Edward about him.

But Edward already had placed his hand behind her back and was guiding her toward the train station. "We'll go first to the hotel. That should give us time to wash up and change before lunch. Then I hope we can take a taxi out of the city just a little way. I'm told there is an excellent view of the mountains from a ridge nearby, and I would also like to see the famed Lethbridge railroad bridge. I read that it's the longest in Canada—or anywhere." He sounded as if he had some claim to it all—at the very least, he seemed proud to be able to share his knowledge. "I shall be required to report to my post after lunch, but when I return we should still have much of the afternoon to spend together."

A wave of his extended arm and a taxicab slid into place before them. Edward reached for the door and Beth slid across the seat. They set off for the hotel, Beth watching out the window beside her. She couldn't help but be impressed by the up-to-date city—paved roads, modern buildings, and a lovely central garden. Eventually turning away from the city center, the taxi bumped along on dirt roads, swerving to avoid other vehicles and periodically a rider on horseback. Now Beth could see what seemed to her to be the true West.

The Alpine View Inn did not actually look out toward the mountains—at least not that Beth could tell. But it was large and tidy and looked like a suitable place to lodge. In short order she was shown to her room and told which door in the long hallway led to a shared washroom. There would be no leisurely soak in a tub, but at least she could freshen up a bit. The thought of a basin of water that did not slosh from side to side brought an amused smile to her lips. Beth could now appreciate what luxury was to be found in simply a room on terra firma—another blessing.

She disliked the idea of remaining in the clothing she had donned that morning, but the porter had not yet arrived with her suitcase and trunks. What she was wearing would simply have to suffice. At least her clothes had been fresh and clean when she had begun the day, though wrinkled from the suitcase.

Having accomplished the immediate task, Beth stretched out on the bed to wait for her bags. Mentally she calculated what the hotel would cost and added to that what she had already spent while on the train. She idly wondered if there were things she should buy while she was still near modern stores.

At last there came a loud knock at the door. "Elizabeth, it's Edward," she heard. She rose and crossed the room, but before she could open it, she heard again, "Elizabeth, are you there?" Something in Edward's tone hinted at panic.

She quickly opened the door and stepped aside as Edward strode into the room.

"He's gone."

"Who—?"

"The man who took our bags, your trunks. He's stolen everything!"

Beth couldn't move or speak.

Edward raked his fingers through his hair, making it stand on end. "I don't understand it! He looked just like all the others. But it turns out he doesn't work for the station. He is just a—just a common thief!"

Now Beth was frantic too. "Where did he go? Can you find him?"

Edward threw his hands up in the air. "If I could find him, don't you think I would have already done so?"

"There's no reason to be short with me," Beth said evenly. But she couldn't help but add, "I didn't select him."

"Oh, so it's my fault, I suppose?"

Beth swallowed her reply, her mind a jumble of questions. How could they find him? What could be done? Who could help? Edward obviously was beside himself, uncertain how to proceed. Beth's next question escaped before she realized its full import. "Did you contact the police?"

Edward seemed frozen in place. He did not turn to look at her nor did he utter a sound. She watched him straighten, draw back his shoulders, and pull down the bottom edges of his red jacket. He strode toward the door and grasped the handle. "I shall go to the post and report the theft." And he was gone.

Beth stared at the closed door and her hand went to her mouth. *What will it be like for the newly arrived RCMP to be forced to admit he has been duped?* She shook her head. *Poor Edward! He will be utterly humiliated.* She actually felt sorry for him, she truly did. But the picture in her mind of him walking into his new headquarters, hat in hand, to report a theft that had been perpetrated against him while dressed in full uniform was almost amusing.

It was not until she began to do a mental inventory of the contents of her luggage that Beth ceased to see any humor in her situation. All her clothes were gone. But more than that, her books and teaching materials. *Oh no—my violin!* Tears spilled over as she remembered that her most cherished possession of all—Father's compass—had been taken as well. Sobs now shook her body, and her legs gave way. She crumpled into a heap beside the bed, her hands clutching at the spread, and wept until she had no more tears.

CHAPTER

6

THERE HAD NEVER BEEN A TIME when Beth had found Edward to be so humbled. It had been necessary for her to return with him to the RCMP post to make a full report of her missing belongings, and Beth had succeeded in doing so rather stoically despite her headache. Edward sat dejectedly on a bench not far away, his head hung in shame as she quietly enumerated each item now lost. She was thankful she actually had made a list for reference as she packed, fearful she might miss something, and tucked it in her handbag.

Julie had teased, *"Bethie the organizer. Bethie the meticulous."* But Beth had responded that she could always think better with a pen in her hand. Julie had laughed and said, *"I do hope you never run out of paper or ink."*

But right now Beth had to think about all the things besides paper and ink she had run out of. With her head aching and her mind swirling with emotions, she never would have been able to remember half of what had been in those two trunks without that list.

Edward waited silently, penitently, his eyes fixed on his

boots, and now feigning composure as Beth's recital went on and on. She heaved a great sigh of relief when she finished and was excused. She thought she heard Edward sigh as well.

He rose and went over to the officer in charge, withdrew a paper from his coat pocket, and requested a telephone call to Elizabeth's father. A clerk took his note and made arrangements with the operator. Beth noticed how Edward's shoulders drooped as he delivered his subdued confession to her father, then turned solemnly and presented the receiver to Beth.

She knew she would not be able to control her emotions, but she reached for the telephone. Just the sound of Father's voice would have been enough to elicit tears, present situation aside.

"I'm so sorry, Beth. I know this is tremendously difficult for you," the beloved voice said.

Beth turned her back on the men around her, tucked the phone closer, and whispered in a trembling voice, "I miss you, Father."

"I'm here, my darling. We all love you, and we understand how terrible this is for you. Truly, we are so sorry. But everything can be replaced. In no time at all this will be only an unpleasant memory. You're safe, and that's what truly matters."

Her face crumpled as more tears wet her cheeks. "But we can't replace the compass, Father. Nor the violin."

His voice held calm and comfort. "Now, Beth dear, you know those are mere things. And all our worldly possessions are temporary at best. We can't allow ourselves to make idols of anything. Even the compass—it's not the item that's important, it's how it reminds us of our memories and our feelings for one another. And those can never be stolen." He paused. "Beth?"

Even though her throat had tightened further, she forced a dutiful whisper, "Yes, Father."

"I realize it's a terrible shame. My heart aches for you just now. I know you're upset, and that this will be a hardship—but this is life, my darling. These things will happen. You must choose to persist." He was quiet for another moment. "Or else give up and come back home."

Her brow furrowed, and she pressed a cool hand to her forehead, hoping to lessen the throbbing in her temples. "I can't give up, Father."

"No, of course not. I know you're going to choose to persevere through this—and more. Beth, darling, without question there will be more for you to endure. Not a comforting thought right now, but each one of these tests of character and fortitude will prepare you for the next one."

She could feel her emotions loosening their hold, her mind beginning to clear. His words were honest, loving, and best of all, true. In fact, he also could have reminded her that she had been warned—that he himself had cautioned her to expect that her new undertaking would be fraught with hardships. And she had boldly and naïvely asserted that she was ready for whatever they turned out to be. Here at the very first test of her wings, she had been reduced to a blubbering mess.

She gathered herself together. "I can endure this, Father. I know I can."

"Yes, darling, you can. Do you remember the verse? That's where you can find the strength, the wisdom to do what needs to be done."

Her lip quivered, remembering the precious paper still safely tucked away in her locket. Her hand reached up to finger it once more. "Yes, Father—I mean, I did forget, but I do remember now."

"Good. Keep it in mind, dear. You are never alone—and you always have God's strength to draw upon. Not just on the days when you feel like you've reached your limit. We must each seek God first every day—in all things. When things are going well as well as dreadful."

"Yes. Yes, I believe that."

"I know we shouldn't speak for very long. . . ." A pause, and then he coaxed softly, "Don't be too hard on Edward, Beth. I've seen unfortunate things like this happen time and time again to men far more worldly-wise than he. It could have happened to anyone. You'll forgive Edward, won't you?"

She could not refuse him. "Yes, Father." They talked only a short time more before saying their good-byes, Beth near tears once again. But her heart felt less heavy, her feelings more settled.

⌘

Beth and Edward spoke little as they ate their supper, and he was gone soon afterward. She returned to her room and through the long evening hours made another list of what she would need for the immediate future. She washed out her underthings, hoping they would be dry for wearing in the morning. She opened the second-floor window to capture some breezes, and hung the wet garments from the curtain rod. The morning would bring an opportunity to replace some of her possessions, she consoled herself. Father had assured her that Mother would take on the task of replacing and shipping the bulk of what she would need, but he had suggested that Beth gather what was available in Lethbridge for the time being.

She remembered how she and Mother had worked together to assemble all those items in the first place, so Mother would well know what was lost. Beth shuddered to think how the event would be interpreted at home. *Is this the evidence Mother needs to declare the whole venture a fiasco? Will there soon be a letter—or even a telegram—with instructions for me to return home?*

Though Edward's knock at the door came early the next morning, Beth was dressed and ready to begin a new day. But his first words stopped her short. "I've arranged for our travel on to Coal Valley. A car is waiting below."

"Oh, I can't leave just yet. There are some things I will need to purchase."

"I'm sorry, Elizabeth. We have time for just a quick breakfast, but then the car will be leaving. It's some distance—"

"Then I shall have to make other arrangements," she calmly said, standing her ground. "I have shopping that must be done today."

Edward seemed equally determined. "I spent much of the evening finding this car and driver. You must believe me, there will be nothing else available for several more days. Your father instructed me to see that you arrive at Coal Valley today, and that is precisely what I plan to do."

"But what about the things I need? I have nothing else but what I am wearing!"

His expression softened a little. "I'm very sorry, Elizabeth. But I *cannot* fail him again." Then he added, somewhat feebly, "Surely there will be stores in your new town."

Beth shook her head in despair, but she would not go against what Father had instructed. She grasped at the locket and whispered a little prayer that God would provide for her.

The road from Lethbridge across the prairies was long but rather pleasant. Beth watched in awe as the mountains rose before her, looming larger on the western horizon with each hill they crested. She could see train tracks nearby—at times out of sight but always appearing again. Beth wondered why she had not been able to continue beyond Lethbridge by train. But she dared not raise the question in the current circumstances. Infrequently the road passed through a small town, and signs along the way pointed toward others not far from the road. Yet Beth was amazed by the vast stretches of land broken only by the occasional farm.

Once they reached the foothills of the mountain range, their way became more rugged and winding, weaving between wooded hills into a wide valley and finally angling upward, then down again between the mountains. The only other vehicles they encountered were large logging trucks with heavy loads, passing far too close to Beth's window for comfort.

At last a small sign indicated Coal Valley to the right, and their vehicle turned off the main road. Soon swallowed by thick forests, this road wove its haphazard way through the valley and aimlessly ascended countless hills, only to wander back down again toward the river.

She had a sudden realization of how lost and disoriented she was. If she were required to find her way out again on her own, only the winding road would save her. Then she thought of her father's compass, and it reopened the recent ache in her heart.

Edward leaned forward toward the driver, his face betraying his own concerns. "How often does your company send cars in and out of this place?" he queried.

"Oh," the man said, scratching at his whiskers, "sometimes once a week—sometimes not that often. Depends."

"On the weather? Or is it somewhat seasonal?"

The craggy face puckered in thought. "Oh, we don't come

out here in winter," he said. "Ain't hardly nobody sends a car out then. Sometimes the coal company'll push a truck through—but then, sometimes even the coal trains can't make it."

"Are there passenger trains available as well?" Beth dared ask.

"Naw, not out this way. Just a spur to carry out the coal, bring in supplies. The men from the company sometimes ride in the caboose—but they don't take no passengers ever."

Beth felt her heart drop. She wasn't even there yet, and she already felt isolated and confined. *So I'll never get out except by car . . . and who knows when one will come.* Clutching at any handhold just to keep from bumping against Edward on the back seat, she stared ahead and tried not to picture what such a trip would be like on the slippery, slushy roads of winter. Much less in deep snow . . .

Finally, the trees thinned out a little to reveal a small cluster of buildings clinging to a hillside.

"This here's it," the driver announced and drew up to a stop in a swirl of dust.

Edward and the driver emerged from their side of the dusty vehicle. Edward hurried around and pulled Beth's door open. She reached for her handbag and stepped out. For a moment she stood awkwardly, stretching her tired limbs as she assessed Coal Valley.

Main Street, if it could be labeled such, was a rutted dirt road, scarcely wide enough for two cars to pass. By the looks of things, though, Beth doubted there had ever been a need. To the left were two large buildings crowding unceremoniously against a rough boardwalk. One structure was broad and square, the other low and long, boasting large dirt-encrusted front windows and the appearance of some type of store.

Opposite was a two-story building skulking behind over-grown bushes, though a well-beaten path led to its front door. Stairs outside headed upward to what must be second-floor living quarters. Next, a vacant lot that may have once been someone's garden, and beside that a large weathered house tucked behind a rickety picket fence. With no building's surface having been painted for many years, if ever, it could have simply been a forgotten ghost town but for the thick odor of woodsmoke and the steady chugging of machinery not far away.

From every direction, the forest crowded close, as if to swallow the town whole. Just past the storefront the road curled downward along the face of the hill. Along this straight stretch of road was a series of small homes, duplicate in structure . . . and shabbiness.

Beth roused herself and noticed Edward also surveying the surroundings. He looked genuinely concerned. The driver waited motionless nearby. *Was he expecting something from them?* Beth glanced toward Edward again, assuming he would make a move to pay the driver. When he did not, she began to rummage in her handbag for the travel money Father had provided.

She felt a hand on her arm, and Edward was bending to whisper—not too quietly, "He insisted on payment in advance—including his gratuity." A slow grin played over the driver's face. He could have been paid twice!

One wave of the driver's hand directed them toward the only structure, with its well-traveled path, showing any evidence of inhabitants. Over the door was a sign simply announcing "Tavern."

Beth drew in a breath. "Can—are they able to do that? Serve liquor here?"

"No, Elizabeth, they cannot. There are prohibition laws in effect." Edward indicated she should wait, and he stepped toward the building, drawing himself up to his full height before entering. Beth waited outside for some time, clutching her handbag tightly. Edward finally reappeared and motioned her forward.

"I've been told it's an old sign," he said, but his solemn expression conveyed he was still wary.

Beth followed him into the building. The entrance hall inside was dimly lit and stuffy, with stale tobacco smoke. She could hear low voices from somewhere, and Edward turned a corner toward the sound. To Beth's surprise, a small circle of women gathered next to the long bar.

"Oh, yer here at last! We been waitin' so long!" a voice called out, and the group hurried toward them, all exclaiming at once. "They told us you'd arrive today, so we all come ta meet ya," the first woman explained over the commotion.

Beth tried to smile at each in turn, overwhelmed by the hubbub. Edward remained between the door and a heavy wooden coat rack. A large pool table filled the farthest corner of the room, with other round tables in between. Beth felt her knees going weak and grasped the back of a nearby chair, trying to conceal her turbulent thoughts.

Quickly a middle-aged woman with an Irish accent took charge. "Now, ladies, we don't want to be scaring her off soon as she gets here, do we? Make way. Give a body room to breathe. Katie, fetch the coffee. Abbie dear, the cups. Let's have a bit o' order now."

She motioned Beth toward one of the tables while others hurried to set out various baked goods, obviously contributed by each woman of the welcoming committee. Without pausing for usual civilities, the Irish woman seated herself next to

Beth and began explaining the situation while another put a cup of coffee in front of her. "We've had ourselves some terrible days, Miss Thatcher." At Beth's nod, she continued, "It's been powerful hard keeping body and soul together since the trouble at the mine. But we be hoping and praying having a teacher be a step toward something better."

Beth answered weakly, "Thank you."

"Tell her 'bout the company, Frances. Tell her what they done."

The Irish woman waved away the suggestion. "There's what she needs to know and there's what shouldn't be her burden, not today." With confident eyes and soft features, she turned back to face Beth, continuing in her thick brogue, "What you *need* to know, miss, is that we mothers decided to bring you here. And though that comes dear, the school that we had afore wasn't fit for our young, and that's the truth of it, plain as day."

Beth was working hard to clearly comprehend what had *not* been said. "I see. The mining company provided a teacher?"

"No, dear, not a teacher. Just a man to make a poor show of it. He were no more a teacher than I be a queen. And what with all his yelling and cursing, we all up and stopped sending our kids."

"I'm so sorry."

"But now that yer here, and we can see yer a woman o' breeding, we can start over, miss."

"I shall do my best, I assure you." Beth thought about the loss of her teaching materials and decided against mentioning her own troubles. She cleared her throat. "Perhaps if I could see the school, I could—"

A titter of laughter swept the room, and the woman next to Frances announced, "Yer sittin' in it, miss."

66

"Excuse me?"

"This is our school. It's all we got that ain't mine-company owned."

Beth cast a glance toward Edward, whose face looked pale. She hoped her own expression betrayed less alarm. "This tavern . . . is to be our schoolroom?"

A voice sounding defensive called from across the room, "It ain't no tavern no more! We already told the brass standin' over there. It's a respectable pool hall now. We don't serve nothin' more than coffee and food." She added, "An' you can only use it in the day. I need it back by supper. An' ya gotta have all the school stuff put aside in the back by then too. Them company men don't want no books in their way when they're playin' pool."

Frances clarified, "You see, Helen's man runs the pool hall. But they're willin' to let us meet here for lessons." She gestured around enthusiastically. "It's plenty big. Room for all. And we already got a chalkboard painted on the back o' that board. James and Gabe, they'll hang it up for you every day. It'll be all ready tomorrow—if you are." All eyes fixed on Beth's face.

Purposefully, Beth placed her cup back on its saucer and met Frances's gaze, the words of Father's verse playing over in her mind. She swallowed nervously. "I'm not certain I can be ready by tomorrow." She offered a feeble smile around the room and hurried on, "But I shall be pleased to begin lessons on the day after that. At any rate, I shall do the best I can."

There was a collective sigh of relief and then a flurry of voices and activity. It sounded like the women had not been certain that the new teacher would be willing to remain when she saw what they could offer. Beth's heart was already warming toward them, seeing their delight that those fears had been allayed. Only Edward stood aloof before their happy exclamations.

When the coffee and sweets were gone and the ladies were dispersing, Edward drew Beth aside. His voice was strained as he said, "The driver is ready to leave, Elizabeth. And you should come too. This is unacceptable. Your father would not approve of this situation."

She raised her eyes and searched his face. "I think he would, Edward. I truly think he would. It's just—well, it's that I hope I am up for the challenge. I wish I had been better prepared."

He shook his head and stooped closer to whisper, "It's too much to ask of anyone, Elizabeth. No one could properly teach under such conditions."

Beth's mind was already whirling with preparations to be made. She turned for another glance around the room. Edward grasped her elbow and pulled her nearer. His voice softened to plead, "No, Elizabeth. Let them send someone else. Let them send a man—"

"They already sent a man, Edward." Beth drew in a deep breath. "It's my turn now."

He released her and turned to leave, frustration evident in his whole demeanor. Beth hurried after him, bursting into the bright sunshine. She squinted against the sudden light and trailed Edward to the car. Instantly she realized what a fearful thing it would be to watch the car take him out of sight.

"You're not angry, are you?" she said to his back. He paused and turned, and she approached cautiously. "Edward, are you angry with me?"

"No, Elizabeth. I have no reason to be angry." But his tone was severe.

"Then why . . . ?"

His hand reached up to push the lock of hair from his eyes.

"It's too much. All of this. It's just too much. And it's my fault—at least some of it is. You should have your things—your clothes—your books. I wish . . . I wish I could . . ." He faltered. "I'm so sorry."

Words failed Beth too. She wanted to tell him that she wasn't angry about what had been stolen—Father had reminded her that such travel hazards were commonplace. And also that she realized now how very important his job as a Mountie would be. She wanted to thank him for traveling with her and seeing her safely to her destination—to know that his presence had been a comfort after all. She wanted to tell him that he was indeed her friend and that she hoped he could understand her decision to stay—even perhaps to gain his approval. But Edward was re-entering the car, and the driver had already started the engine.

"So soon?" she gasped out, taking a step forward before the door closed.

"Good-bye, Elizabeth. I shall do what I can on your behalf. I'm so sorry I couldn't do more." He pulled the door shut and the car pulled away, circling back awkwardly in the narrow street and moving again toward her. Beth caught one last glimpse of Edward's stern face. She turned her back against the dust that the automobile raised. He was gone.

CHAPTER

7

WHERE YER BAGS AT, MISS?" A man standing far too
near startled Beth with his question.

"I'm sorry, what did you say?"

"Yer luggage? I come to help carry. They forget to leave
yer things?"

She drew in a long breath. "I'm afraid I have nothing. My
trunks were stolen from the platform at the Lethbridge train
station."

His head tipped to one side. "Ya don't say!" There was a
pause as he digested the fact. "Then what'll ya do?"

"I don't know. . . ."

A group of women had followed Beth from the hall, and the
man waved them over. "She ain't got bags," he announced.
"They was stole."

Quickly the women once more surrounded Beth, their faces
showing the dismay they felt at this disclosure. "Poor dear,"
they clucked over her. "Oh my!" "Well, let's get you to Molly's
guest house and see what she says."

Beth followed obediently, asking no further explanation.

She had been promised room and board as a portion of her salary. Certainly this would have been known, and the women would direct her to her proper residence. She was led past the empty lot to the large weathered house facing the street. The ladies pushed back the wobbly gate, crossed the tidy yard, and mounted the porch, calling out, "Molly! Molly, she's here."

A plump woman in a dull dress of indeterminate color pushed open the screen door and smiled a warm, gap-toothed grin. "Bless us. She is at that." She wiped her hands on her apron and reached out to take Beth's hand. "Welcome, dearie. We're so glad ya come."

"She ain't got no bags" was bluntly repeated for Molly's benefit. "Somebody musta took off wit' 'em."

Molly looked from one to another, then shook her head. "No bags, eh? Well, that's a shame." And immediately she added sagely, "No sense cryin' over spilled milk. We'll jest have to make do."

Beth timidly stepped into the foyer and was passed on to Molly's care. The other women turned and walked away in singles and pairs. Molly, like a practiced sergeant commanding the troops, motioned toward two teenagers hovering in a doorway nearby.

"Teddy Boy, go see that the pink room is unlocked, and open a window so it airs." The boy rushed past and up the stairs. Molly cast a quick glance over Beth and then to the girl. "Marnie, go see Sarah and Miss Kate. Ask if they've some duds to borrow to the new schoolmarm. Tell 'em she ain't got nothin' 'cept the clothes on her back." Then she called after the girl as she whisked out, the screen door banging behind her, "And see Miss Charlotte too. Now she's in the family way she's laid aside most'a what she's got."

Without waiting further, Molly started down the hall

toward the back of her house. "Come with me, dearie. I'm fixin' pickles that need tendin', but we can jaw awhile till the kids get back."

Beth trailed behind and seated herself on a chair at a small table not far from where Molly was working. The room was scantily outfitted but neatly kept. A wood-burning stove stood against the back wall. Next was a small box half filled with wood, along with an oddly shaped bin of black coal beside an exterior door. There were two large pots and a kettle on the stove at which Molly stood. Along the far wall was a long, roughly built table with several crowded shelves fixed to the wall above and wooden bins tucked carefully beneath. A small doorway beside the table was half covered by a curtain, shielding an unlit pantry. On the third wall to Beth's right were a dry sink with a large metal basin and two pails of water waiting beside it, and finally the icebox. Though a remote location, Beth had not considered that homes here might not have plumbing or electricity. *How difficult life must be here in this place*, she marveled.

As Beth watched, the practiced hands scrubbed and measured, salted and stirred, her conversation never slacking. "We ain't got much here, dearie, but we know how to care for our own. And now yer among us, yer ours. I hear yer from the East, Miss Thatcher."

"Oh please, I'm Beth. I hope you will call me Beth." The room was warm and steamy, and she wiped at the sweat already rising on her brow. "Yes, my family lives in Toronto, but I do have family out here too. I have a relative who teaches in the North."

Molly set a glass of water on the table in front of Beth, and she reached for it eagerly. *How nice a cold drink will be.*

"My Bertram—God rest his soul—worked in Ottawa a short while," Molly explained as she returned to the stove.

"He drove a taxicab—not a fancy new one, though, a good ol' horse-drawn number. But he weren't cut out for all that city nonsense. He come from country folk, and so he left to find a more suitable place. Went west to the prairie and tried his hand at farming. But we ended here." She gestured to the house around them. "Bought it from ones who'd planned it for a fancy hotel. Got it real cheap 'cause the rails they thought would carry in rich folks came only for coal instead." She chuckled at her good fortune and then added matter-of-factly, "But Bertram died and left me here alone."

"I'm so sorry."

Using tongs, Molly pulled the last of the sterilized jars from the large pot, turning the steaming glass out onto a towel to let the water drain. "Don't help none bein' sorry. It's jes' the way life is sometimes." She hoisted the bubbling pot from the stove and kicked open the back door before Beth could rise to help, still chatting as she moved. "Bertram, he says to me, 'Molly dear, I ain't got much in life, but this old house will keep you when I'm gone.' I laughed and tol' him, 'No, sir, it's *me* who keeps this *house*.'" She tossed the contents of the pot into the yard. The door slammed shut again before the water hit the ground. "But he was right, my Bertram was. Somehow we do get by."

"Do you have family?"

"Ah, well, yes and no. We ain't got kids. But that's not to say I ain't got kin. Got good folk here, hardworkin' solid souls that suit me just as much as blood family." Then she sighed. "Leastwise, we still got some."

"What do you mean? What happened?"

"Oh, that ol' mine—it's stole 'em away from us. Weren't enough to only work 'em nigh to death—the whole thing fell in one day and buried most all our menfolk."

Beth's eyes widened at the horror of the story, and she held her breath as she grappled with the truth of their tragic loss.

Just then the young boy came down the steps and informed Molly shyly, "Room's ready, Miss Molly."

Beth smiled in his direction and watched him turn to leave. Molly sighed after him, "That's when Teddy Boy and Marnie lost their daddy—their momma'd already been gone awhile. They come to live with me instead. Were hardly a family in these parts didn't lose a man. And some of 'em lost sons as well."

"You mean, all these women—they're widows?" Beth felt a shudder go through her body. She could not conceive of such a dreadful situation. She saw again the faces gathered round her in the pool hall. Somehow knowing their plight transformed the image of them in her mind.

"Almost all—only a handful of their men still livin'. And then there's Helen's man—still claims he runs their place even though we don't see much of him. Keeps hisself to the woods mostly. Doin' what—who knows. Plus there's still the mayor an' his wife, and Toby Coulter runs the store with his wife, and all the big company men—though they're always comin' and goin' every few days—keepin' their own families in the city and well away from here. Was jes' the minin' folk bore the brunt of it all."

Beth watched as Molly stuffed small cucumbers into the scalded jars. "They brung in more men, soon enough—though it took 'em a while to dig out the mine from under. Single fellas this time—and foreigns. Didn't wanna bother with no more families. Got more'n enough of them to worry about already."

"How do these women, the widows, provide for themselves?"

"Pensions—small ones. And livin' in the company houses.

74

That'll keep 'em for a while. Most of 'em don't know what to do when that runs out."

"And the children?"

Molly paused, jar and spoon hovering over the pot, to contemplate her answer. "Don't none of us want 'em minin'— that's for certain. So I guess this is where you come in." She put down her utensils and lumbered over to lower herself onto a chair. She reached across the table to take Beth's hands. "Me an' Frances been talkin' about this. A lot. Them mines took her man, Lachlan, and her grown son, Peter, too. Nigh broke her heart in two. Had he been schooled, who knows what else might'a been. So we can't let the mines get the rest, Miss Beth. We gotta find a way to give 'em more. Can you help us do that, ya think?"

Beth squeezed the damp, calloused hands. "Education can open many doors. I do believe that, Miss Molly. I assure you that I shall do my very best in my year here."

"I know you will." The matter was decided, and Molly returned to her pickles, waving off Beth's offer to help. She saw the woman hastily wiping away a tear on the corner of her apron.

Once Marnie returned with a box of clothing items she had managed to gather, Molly sent Beth upstairs to find her room and to see if any of the clothes would fit. Cautiously opening the door, she peered around it. The room was simple—a bed with a pink quilt, a bedside table, a dresser, a washstand, and a row of hooks in place of a closet. Beth reached for the switch to turn on the light and found there was none. Her eyes rose to the empty ceiling and saw with new shock that there was no light other than three oil lamps placed in strategic positions around the room. She placed the box of clothing on the bed and began somewhat apprehensively to rummage through it.

She found simple homemade garments, but Beth quickly understood they represented both sacrifice and skill from women who had little. She slipped out of her traveling clothes and into a plain brown skirt and floral blouse. The fabric was rough and well worn, by far the simplest outfit she had ever donned. The skirt hem did not even cover her calves. Though comparable to the dress lengths that the latest fashion dictated, Beth felt terribly exposed. For the first time, she was grateful that she was shorter than most other women and tried not to think about how much of her legs were showing.

She hung the other garments from the hooks behind the door and tucked the borrowed underclothes away in an empty dresser drawer, happy that a simple shift would serve as nightwear. She steeled her resolve against the mortification she was feeling. As soon as Mother's shipment arrived, she would return the items to their owners. Until that time, she would care for them well, wear them with gratitude.

Her next thought was to look for the privy, and she winced as she realized it would likely be found in the backyard. Slipping down the stairs, out the front door, and around the side of the house so she wouldn't draw undue attention, Beth found the small structure. "One year," she whispered to herself, "just one year." Even as she spoke, she wondered if she would have consented to come had she realized the extent of the primitive living conditions.

Upon returning to her room, Beth poured water from the washstand pitcher into the waiting bowl and dipped her hands. The water was cold, the soap bar heavy and smelling of lye. She grimaced as she braced herself for a further adjustment. After drying her hands on the rough towel hanging on the nearby peg, she found paper and pencil in her handbag, seated herself on the bed, rested her back against the headboard, and dutifully began the first of her promised letters home.

It was impossible to claim that things had been going well. She did omit mentioning the incident while changing trains in which she had gotten rain-soaked and nearly missed her connection. It seemed unnecessary to burden Mother with those details—even though the omission made her feel uncomfortable. She tried to convince herself that her intention was to retain Mother's peace of mind. There were so many obvious difficulties which would have to be addressed. Beth struggled through an explanation of the lost trunks, though she knew her father would have provided a brief version of the whole sorry incident.

A soft knock roused her. At Beth's invitation, Marnie peeked around the door. "Miss Thatcher, Miss Molly says supper's on."

The meal at Molly's turned out to be a lively affair. Two company men were also boarding there, and two more joined them only for meals. Molly had explained that she never knew from one week to the next how many boarders she might have. Molly and young Marnie did not sit with the men at the table but kept busy filling and refilling serving dishes, pouring coffee, and gathering empty plates. Their hostess would not allow Beth to help. "No, dearie, yer a paying guest—same's the men," she insisted.

Beth had taken the seat to which one of the visiting gentlemen had gestured, and she pulled the too-short skirt over her legs and tucked her feet beneath the chair, hoping she was the only one in the room aware of her exposed calves.

Teddy spoke very little, which meant Beth became the focus of attention. Where was she from? asked the first man, the one with the glasses. How long would she stay? he wondered.

How much experience did she have teaching? came from one of those who joined the group only for meals. And what was happening back east? was voiced by several, almost at the same time.

"Oh, how I'd like to see a ballgame again. I miss everything about it!" declared the small man with glasses and a long nose.

"They have a league near Calgary, north of here, Walter. I've seen some games there."

"Yeah, but they don't have those grand stadiums out here in the West. I want the thrill of the crowds. The sound of thousands of people cheering so loud you can scarce hear the crack of the bat." Walter gestured broadly as if tracing the path of the ball as it sailed across the fence.

"I saw Babe Ruth play once," announced a third man, barrel-chested and loud.

"G'wan wit' ya, Henry!"

"I did! He hit a homer—first one ever as a pro ball player. Right here in Canada."

"You're a liar. His first homer was in New York," the last of the men interjected.

"No, sir! 'Twas on Toronto Island."

"Aw, not a chance!" The interchange was becoming heated.

The small man pushed his glasses farther up on his nose and turned to Beth. "You seen any ballgames, miss?"

Beth blushed and the room grew quiet. "My father felt it was not a suitable place for a young lady."

"What'd you do for pleasure, then?" he rejoined, looking startled.

"Well, we enjoyed the symphony, museums, and sometimes theater. We periodically attended lectures as well—but mostly I enjoy reading." As she spoke of the fine things she had left behind, the reminder brought a cloud of nostalgia.

"Reading? Well, that's not very friendly." Walter grinned toward the others. Beth smiled weakly and let the conversation proceed without her.

As soon as the meal had ended and she could move unnoticed, she slipped out the door and fled into the kitchen. "Please, Miss Molly, I'd really rather help in here."

"Then help you may," said the woman and tossed a dish towel toward Beth, pointing at the stack of dishes already washed and waiting to be dried and put away. Beth sighed in relief.

CHAPTER

8

BETH WOKE AT THE SOUND of a thump in the hallway, followed by footsteps moving away from her door. She crept from her bed and quietly drew the door open. There before her was a pail of fresh water, presumably so she could wash before dressing. She peered into the hallway in time to see Teddy setting another bucket outside one of the doors farther down the hall. She lifted the bucket inside and closed the door again softly.

There was a room for bathing off the kitchen, with an oversized galvanized tub, but Beth was doubtful she would often have the courage to request that it be filled for her benefit, considering how many buckets it would take. Instead, she washed up as thoroughly as she could, already hearing the sounds of machinery in the distance. She wondered how soon she would be able to tune out the incessant mine noise. Dressing again in the borrowed clothing, she sat on the bedside and silently recited a favorite Psalm and prayed. *Another item I'm going to miss is my Bible.* How many further items would come to mind during the next days . . . weeks? She shook her head and hurried down to the kitchen.

Molly was just beginning to fix breakfast, and Beth alternated between trying to help with preparations and avoiding getting in the heavyset woman's path. After hearing Molly huff more than once as they attempted to work around each other, Beth determined she would be less of an obstacle when setting the table in the dining room. It seemed a happy compromise until Molly entered with a heaping dish and placed it in the center.

She looked around the table. "How come you got so many forks?"

Beth blinked. "It's only two for each. I thought we needed one for the fruit and one for the eggs and bacon—"

"Only got one mouth," Molly tossed over her shoulder as she returned to the kitchen. "Take them extras off. Saves washin' up."

As Beth picked up the superfluous tableware and replaced it in its drawer in the sideboard, Molly brought in the plate of fruit. "And why's there jes' five plates?" she asked, hands on hips as she surveyed the settings. "Where's yours?"

"I thought I'd help in there." Beth gestured toward the kitchen.

"You gotta eat."

Beth lifted pleading eyes to Molly. "I'd rather not have to be the only . . . only female eating with the men."

The older woman paused, cast a thoughtful look toward Beth, and reached over to cup her face in work-hardened hands. The intensity held Beth fast as Molly said, "Those men are your kinda folk, dearie. Now, I'm not sayin' you rich folk're all the same—any more than all us poor. And maybe I'm selfish to ask—but if you could jes' make friends with them, jes' maybe you could help them understand our needs. Maybe you could speak to them sometimes on our behalf. Lord knows, they be too high-an'-mighty to hear what the likes of us has got to say."

Beth wanted to please her hostess. She wished it were not so difficult—*If only Julie could be here* . . . But Julie was not, and making conversation did not come naturally to her.

In the end she submitted to Molly's bidding and joined the company men in the dining room, doing her best to present a charming and clever façade. Molly smiled encouragingly toward Beth each time the woman crossed through the room.

Once breakfast had ended and dishes were done, Marnie walked with Beth over to the pool hall. She wanted to assess what preparations could be made for school. Her first task was to throw open the windows to let in fresh air. Marnie quickly caught on and helped open up the room. Beth feared the mustiness and stale smell from years of tobacco smoke would give her a headache.

With sunlight and a breeze filtering through the room, she turned and studied her surroundings. She quickly noted, however, that the open windows also increased the sound of the mine equipment grinding away in the distance, along with the periodic screech of engine brakes and sundry other sounds of the community. Beth hoped the students had grown so accustomed to it all that the noise would not be a distraction, for she was altogether unwilling to close it all up again. She found herself whispering once more, "It's only for one year." Yet Beth worried that it would prove to be a very long year.

True to her promise, Frances had made sure the blackboard was hung from hooks in front of the now-empty liquor cabinet. Beth wondered if she should laugh or despair at the thought of teaching before such a testimonial to intemperance.

What would Mother's ladies group have to say about this? Beth determined she would include this interesting tidbit in her next letter. After all, she had no way to change the situation and there must be *something* she was willing to share honestly.

Beth decided it was best to pretend the cabinet was simply an ordinary cupboard. There was nothing to be gained by making an issue of it. She only hoped the tavern did not store liquor elsewhere. She had heard that some of the company men frequented the establishment in the evenings. *Surely there will be no temperance laws broken in the very room in which we hold school!* But maybe that was naïve.

The round oak dining tables would make for awkward desks, but there appeared to be no alternative. And having no idea how many students would be enrolled or the span of ages, Beth tried to prepare herself for all possibilities. Then it occurred to her that the quiet young girl sitting on the bench near the door might be a source of some information.

"Marnie, how many students attended your last school?" she asked in her most pleasant teacher's voice.

"Don't know, Miss Thatcher."

"You don't remember?" Beth drew closer in order to better see the girl's face.

"No, miss. Don't know. Me and Teddy Boy, we didn't go to school."

"You didn't attend? Why not, Marnie?"

She shrugged self-consciously, turning her face away. "Our daddy, well, he didn't make us. Said it wasn't gonna help us none."

Beth sank down next to Marnie on the bench where the girl sat picking at her fingernails.

"Your father didn't believe in education?"

"Guess not. Not for us, anyhow." She hurried to explain,

"'Cause we're a minin' town. Don't need to spell to work the mines."

Beth held her breath. She would not say anything against the father that Marnie so recently lost, and yet she must elevate Marnie's view of herself and her right to schooling. Beth leaned a little closer. "Will you come to *my* school, Marnie?"

A slow smile broke out across the girl's face. "Can I? You mean I ain't too old? I'm thirteen, ya know."

"It would be awfully nice to already have a friend among my students. And since you're an older one, you can help me a lot, I know."

"Yes," she whispered guardedly. "Yes, I'll come. That is, if Miss Molly lets me, I will."

"Oh," Beth said with a grin, "I suspect she'll allow it."

Though Beth had spent much of the previous day preparing plans for how she would begin and what she would teach, the school day opened in some commotion. Several of the mothers had arrived on time with their children in tow, but it was immediately clear that the youngsters had been brought against their will. The building itself, even in so tiny a village, was unfamiliar—had been strictly off-limits before today. Some of the smaller children were crying and clinging, and their mothers lingered with them near the back of the room.

Beth stood at the front of the classroom, looking helplessly around, and then saw Molly appear in the doorway along with Frances. Beth had never been so relieved to see someone. If ever she'd felt the need for assistance and counsel, now was the time.

The two nodded greetings to the women gathered at the

back, then crossed the room to Beth. "Havin' a bit of trouble gettin' things settled down?" Molly whispered.

"Can I talk with you a minute?" Beth whispered back.

Molly merely nodded and placed a hand behind Beth's arm to lead her aside. "What's the matter, dearie?"

"Well, I'm not sure how to begin the school day. Back home, we—they always begin the morning lessons with a salute to the flag and the Lord's Prayer."

"Yes?"

"Well, for one thing—we don't have a flag."

Molly winked. "We can work on that. For now, just have 'em practice."

Beth cleared her throat. "And then—I was wondering, is the prayer—well, is it appropriate here?"

Beth couldn't read all the emotions that flashed through Molly's eyes. When the woman found words they were firm. "We ain't aimin' to raise us up any heathens, dearie."

"I didn't mean—"

"I know ya ain't familiar with our ways," Molly said gently. "You get out there an' get 'em started. Some of them kids will already know the Lord's Prayer, and they may as well learn yer pledge too. That's jest part of bein' civilized. Go on now." Beth felt a pat of encouragement on her shoulder as she returned to her place at the front of the improvised classroom.

Molly and Frances stood on one side, looking over the group, and their presence seemed to signal quiet and respect.

"I am Miss Thatcher," Beth began, turning to print her name on the blackboard. "Please stand beside a seat at the tables here," she said, gesturing along with her instruction. "We'll begin our day with the Lord's Prayer. If you don't already know it, you'll soon learn the words," she told them.

It looked like the children had grouped themselves rather naturally by age.

She noticed many voices joining hers as she recited the prayer. Next Beth asked her students to recite a pledge to the Union Jack. Here fewer children knew what to say, but with a little coaching, Beth helped them repeat with her, "I salute the flag—the emblem of my country—and to her I pledge my love and loyalty." It seemed incongruous with no flag displayed, but Beth seemed to be the only one troubled by the fact. "Please take your seats."

Beth noted the mothers slipping from the room, no doubt returning to a day full of the duties required simply to feed and clothe their families. Molly and Frances followed them out, smiling broadly toward Beth before departing.

She drew back her shoulders and set herself to presenting an appropriate disposition before her students—friendly yet strict, kind yet commanding, even though the room itself, the tables lit only by whatever light came in through the open windows, and all the outside noises, seemed to work against her. From time to time, usually just as Beth was calling for everyone's attention for another assignment, the hinges on the exterior door would announce the arrival of a new family, and all would turn to the doorway to see who would appear. Soon there were twenty-three students, from six to sixteen, randomly spread out before her. Beth struggled just to make eye contact with everyone scattered around. In order to keep each student's attention she had to wander the room in circles, weaving among the tables. *This will never do.*

Just as Beth was about to dismiss the students for lunch, a long whistle blast sounded from the direction of the mine. She had noticed the piercing noise the previous day at what seemed to be random times, but Beth now thought it must indicate the workers' breaks or changes of shifts. Apparently the sound would serve as a signal for school lunchtime as well. Clearly her students were attuned to it, rousing in attention as the whistle called to them through the window.

Because of the close proximity to the students' homes, the room emptied quickly, and Beth was left alone. Instantly her mind began to grapple for solutions to the immediate problems. It was simply imperative that she be able to address directly the students to whom she was aiming a lesson. During that time it was not as necessary for those particular students to sit at the tables, since some by turns would be working at the chalkboard.

It took all Beth's strength and determination to push and drag the most central of the heavy pedestal tables from the middle of the room and fill the open area with unused chairs. This provided a small cluster of seats near the front and a circle of tables surrounding them. In her busyness, she almost forgot to eat the sandwich and apple Molly had provided. She ate hurriedly now, hoping that the students wouldn't return before she had finished.

The thirty minutes she had expected them to take for lunch passed by without a sound in the hallway. Then forty—forty-five. As each minute ticked past, Beth was slowly resigning herself to her worst fears. *The students are not going to return for the afternoon.* Sinking into one of the empty chairs, she crossed her arms on the cool tabletop and dropped her head onto them in defeat, refusing to allow any tears.

At last, when a full hour had passed, a second whistle pierced the silence and, almost simultaneously, footsteps and voices filled the hallway as the children crowded in together. *An hour*, Beth chided herself. *They take an hour for lunch—just as the miners do. I wish one of them had thought to tell me.* A deep breath, and she was back to work.

Beth passed out paper and pencils, which she had been able to borrow from Molly, to each of the older students, and asked them to write a letter to her about themselves, conveying anything of interest to them. "Put your name at the top of the page," she instructed, "and then tell me what you like to do."

As they began—with some grumbling from the boys, she noticed—she moved the younger children to the central chairs and worked on simple phonetics on the chalkboard. Instantly, she could see they had become more attentive. She noticed too that pairs of eyes from the surrounding tables were intent on what she was teaching the younger ones. Perhaps she should not assume the older students had advanced beyond such a simple lesson. So, though Beth kept her eyes directed at the smaller ones before her, she raised her voice and wrote the alphabet in bolder print on the chalkboard for any on the periphery who needed a review of their letters.

It came as no surprise that she encountered a wide range of ability among the students. She had been trained that in a one-room school setting, the primary focus should be upon reading instruction. Once reading was mastered, the world would be unlocked to any student interested in pursuing more—it was the key to any occupation or endeavor. All that would be necessary to advance was one's personal desire and drive. The second objective would be mastery of writing and spelling. And, thirdly, teaching basic arithmetic.

Since there were no other teachers to share the load, Beth would use history and geography, science, literature, and music as tools to promote broader interests among her students—but always, the critical goal each day would be to reinforce the most basic, most essential skills known as the three R's. This was even more important as Beth recalled that her older students would be writing examinations at the end of the year to assess these primary skills. She expected already that her task would be enormous and that, in her duties of teaching, the year among them would prove rather short for what needed to be accomplished.

She was therefore not surprised when some of the papers remained blank—whether from unwillingness or inability, she did not know. Trying to catch a glimpse of the downturned eyes, she smiled and prompted simply, "Can you write your name on your paper, please?" The full group was able to accomplish this small task before she asked Marnie to collect them. It was a beginning, and the expression on the young girl's face when she brought the somewhat wrinkled pages up was another bright spot in the otherwise difficult first day.

Beth's steps felt heavy as she trudged the short distance back to Molly's house. It had taken Marnie and Beth longer than expected to put the room back in order for Helen Grant and Beth was quite exhausted even before they managed to heave the last table back into its original position. Beth was certain she could hear quick, impatient-sounding footsteps from the living quarters above them, where she assumed the Grants must reside. That thought had made her work even more quickly. Teddy, whose help would have been a great benefit, was needed at Molly's to chop extra wood for washday on the morrow.

Beth silently rehearsed what she would say to Molly—how she could put into adequate words a summary of such highs and lows. And, further, what she would include in her letter written later to those at home. Though perhaps there was little that would sound like an accomplishment, she felt at least a good foundation of trust had been laid.

As they mounted the steps of Molly's front porch, Beth and Marnie were met with the sound of clattering lids from the kitchen. *It's suppertime*, she thought with a quick glance at the watch pinned to her dress, and Marnie seemed to realize it at the same moment and rushed through the screen door toward the kitchen.

"I'm sorry, Miss Molly," the girl called, "I shoulda come back quicker."

Molly tossed more potato cubes into her pot. "I'm sure ya did yer best, child," she answered comfortably. "But now I need ya to ready the green beans." Marnie hastened to comply.

Beth set the table—with the minimum of utensils—and then pulled hot rolls from the oven, spreading butter across their crusty tops. Having watched two meals prepared, she imitated what she had seen previously. Next she chipped a large piece of ice from the block in the icebox and placed it in a basin. She set to work chipping off shards small enough to fit inside the glasses and poured each with fresh water. Just as Molly set the last of the serving dishes on the table, the company men, conversing in loud voices and stamping their boots, appeared on the doorstep.

Beth looked down at the wet splotches on her apron—even on her blouse. Her hair likely was disheveled, and there were deep wrinkles in her sleeves where she had rolled them up. She was not at all presentable—nor was she interested in sitting once again with the men. "Miss Molly," she began, "I really can't eat with them like this."

Molly frowned. "S'pose yer right, dearie. Fix yerself a plate, and you can eat in yer room. Though it would please me some if you'd come back for dessert."

"Thank you. I'll try."

While Beth helped herself from the pots on the stove, Molly

lingered next to her for a moment. "An' how was yer day? How many did ya have?"

Beth smiled. "Twenty-three."

"That's all of 'em, leastwise. They stay all day?"

"Yes," Beth answered, then sighed. "I worried for a time they wouldn't return after lunch, but when the mine whistle blew, every one of them came back."

"Then ya musta done somethin' right," Molly affirmed with a pat on Beth's shoulder and moved back to the sink.

This wasn't what Beth had pictured—no describing of all the day's details to Molly, who seemed to love conversation. But the simple encouraging statement carried more impact just because it came from such a busy, caring, and no-nonsense woman.

That evening Beth read through the writing assignments from the older students. Several were fairly long and described hunting, nature, or some other personal interest. Beth wiped away tears as most of them referenced the collapse of the mine and the loss of their daddies. The words underscored to Beth that theirs was a community far from the end of hurting and healing. *Lord, help me, please*, she prayed, *to know how to help them.*

The next day unfolded in much the same way. But from the opening recitation of the Lord's Prayer to working on the last assignment of the day, lessons were less frantic and more predictable, though still a struggle. Especially without all the materials and books she had planned to have with her.

Beth watched the clock carefully after school so she and Marnie arrived home sooner. Molly, as expected, made no comment but appeared appreciative. For a second time, Beth begged off eating with the men and was given reluctant permission to carry her supper up to the privacy of her room.

Setting her plate down on the dresser, she kicked off her shoes and decided to stretch out for a moment on the bed. She was utterly fatigued, but it was Friday, and she anticipated two days in which to recuperate and plan for the upcoming week. She was satisfied with what had been accomplished thus far. . . .

And before she could manage another conscious thought, Beth had drifted off to sleep, her supper turning cold across the room.

⚜

Despite Molly's declarations that it was unnecessary, that Beth was "a payin' guest," she chose to join Marnie on Saturday in the expansive garden, while Molly's skillful hands labored indoors to preserve the bounty for winter. The gardening proved far more difficult than Beth had expected, with all the bending to pull carrots, onions, and parsnips from the rich black soil. Soon she was sweating and stiff, her hands dirty and sore. *What would Mother say?* But the thought brought a small though victorious smile to her lips. *Truth is, I'm keeping up with Marnie fairly well,* she thought, glancing over at her partner. It had seemed rather ironic that morning as the two exchanged roles, the youngster explaining and showing Beth just how it should be done.

Molly's carefully tended plot stretched up the hillside in a broad sunlit clearing behind the boarding house, guarded by a picket fence, rows of thorny berry bushes, a sagging scarecrow, and several spinning whirligigs—all meant to ward off deer and other nuisances. The dreaded outhouse stood discreetly in its own corner. Teddy was busy nearby, cleaning out the

92

chicken coop for Molly's small flock and chopping firewood. Next he shoveled coal from the small shed into the hod, then hefted it into the kitchen.

By evening Beth had to admit she was physically exhausted. Certainly from the work of the day, as well as emotionally wrung out from her attempts to join in the wide-ranging conversations of the mine company's officials over supper. She was pleased to see them strike out together for the pool hall. Grateful for the quiet, she retreated to the parlor to grade a few papers and make further plans for Monday's lessons before turning in for the night.

She rose early on Sunday but found herself for the first time with little to do. There was no permanent pastor in Coal Valley, and this was a week when the itinerant minister was busy elsewhere. Beth felt strangely restless. The town was quieter than she had yet known it to be—each family observing some sort of Sunday rest. *If only . . . if only there were music somewhere. Singing, or a church organ, or a Victrola. . . .* Beth's heart ached to express itself in music—and the memory of the violin she would never play again dampened her spirits further.

She spent some time reading a borrowed Bible and sitting around Molly's house—though she found she was not truly enjoying her leisure. The inviting cool breeze on the front porch was not enough to lure her out with the four men already relaxing in Molly's rocking chairs. They seemed to view her as an odd but interesting diversion.

During the afternoon, Beth decided to take a stroll along the road that had brought her into the small town, and she was pleased when Marnie agreed to join her. Even with no one nearby, Beth could not successfully elicit conversation from the shy girl except for short answers to her questions. But it was pleasant to spend some quiet time together, picking fall berries growing not far from the road and walking through the speckled patches of shade.

There was little evidence of the woods attracting others until Beth noticed a faint trail heading away from the road and disappearing behind a tangle of bushes. "Marnie, should we go that way? Do you feel like a little exploring?" Beth tried to coax a smile.

"No, ma'am!" She shook her head with more spirit than Beth had yet seen from the girl. "That don't go nowhere." But Beth wondered at the look of fear her suggestion had seemed to stir and the quiet girl's emphatic protest.

"That's fine," she assured Marnie. "We can stay near the road if you'd like." Beth was unclear what had elicited such a response—whether wild animals or the idea of being lost, or something else. Beth simply put the incident behind her.

Rain fell in sheets on Monday morning, and several of the children were absent, but Beth forged ahead with the lessons. She was aware that it was difficult for her students to hear her over the sound of the heavy downpour through the open windows, but she chose the noise rather than the stuffiness of the closed room. All in all, Beth was pleased to note progress, mostly in the willingness of the children to take part and attempt what she was asking of them.

As each day passed into the next, she felt that small steps forward had been accomplished, and she thought her students agreed. But Beth subconsciously felt the weight of limited time with them—only one year. She had no way of knowing what or whom the following year would bring. The older children in particular were running out of time for the education their mothers wanted for them.

Also, Beth had begun to realize the significant sacrifice Molly was making in allowing Marnie to attend school. The bashful thirteen-year-old was grown enough to be nearly indispensable around the guest house, and Molly's responsibilities had been significantly impacted by the girl's absence. The woman rarely rested from the work of cooking for the men, washing linens, and keeping up the large house. Beth realized quickly that when this woman—who was not even Marnie's mother—had declared that the town's children should have an education, it meant she was also prepared to do what she could to ensure that it happened.

Further, even as tirelessly as the brother and sister worked in Molly's home, Beth heard no word of complaint from either of them. She couldn't imagine her own sisters back home—or herself—working so diligently without even a crossways look. She understood now that her older students would have little time for homework if they all helped out as much as Teddy and Marnie.

Beth pitched in around the house as best she could, and she was embarrassed to discover how few domestic skills she possessed. Molly had gradually given up reminding Beth that she was a "payin' guest," and she no longer discouraged her from assisting with domestic chores. Given the options of being alone, being with the four men, or being with the family, Beth found it an easy choice to make. She was pleased already with her own increasing ability to be useful in the kitchen. She found she enjoyed watching and imitating such a skillful cook. *Wouldn't Julie be surprised? Though, perhaps, not quite as impressed as she should be.*

At the end of another long but mostly satisfying week, Beth returned to the boarding house. Molly was waiting for her and motioned her upstairs with a grin and a wink. Beth discovered, crowded into the room in a row along one wall, three large trunks—the replacement supplies from Mother! Molly said she had to see to supper and went back downstairs.

Beth unlatched the straps and threw open the first to dig through the contents, which turned out to be mostly clothing. She drew out one frilly frock after another, held it against her, then laid it across her bed. The colors were lovely, in stark contrast to the faded browns and dull blues of her borrowed clothing. Some were in shades of soft pastels—even white. *In a coal-mining village? Mother, what were you thinking?*

Though Beth thought the dresses lovely, and exactly what her mother would have chosen for her, she couldn't help but wonder how they would fit in here. Absently fingering the beadwork on one of the new dresses, she could only imagine what effect such a display of finery would have upon her students. It wasn't until that moment that she thought of how readily the children had accepted her among them. *Can it be that since the borrowed dresses are from their own families and friends, this acceptance came more easily?* Still musing, Beth unbuckled the second trunk.

The topmost layer was an array of hats, and underneath were shoes. Beth was growing frustrated at the rather frivolous nature of Mother's selections. But beneath these were towels and soap, brushes and hairpins, candles and stationery, as well as sundry other sensible items. There was also a plentiful supply of the dreaded elixir. *Mother has not forgotten.*

However, packed carefully in the center to avoid damage in transit was a dainty tea set. At first it seemed an unusual addition, but almost immediately Beth began to formulate a plan. *Why not have two or three of the children at a time come for a visit and serve them tea?* This would perhaps promote a relationship with them outside of school as well as help them become familiar with some etiquette which Beth believed they would need if they were to travel beyond their small world. She was certain Molly would be in favor of such "lessons" given in her home. Beth arranged the tea set on her dresser.

As she unfastened the third trunk, she was greatly relieved to finally see books. Duplicates of all that Beth had gathered previously were there—as well as some additions made by Mother. And a precious Bible. Knowing how poorly the school was supplied, Beth appreciated the extra paper, pencils, and chalk. Also a flag, at last, a protractor for geometry, simple chemicals for science lessons, and paints for teaching art. There was even a set of percussion instruments—small triangles, bells, cymbals, and a tambourine.

The last items brought a heavy sigh as Beth remembered her stolen violin. How wonderful it would have been to be able to play for her students—to introduce them to music of the classical masters. Once more Beth fingered the locket and recited the verse silently. God was able to provide all that she needed. He had already done so—all these things in abundance for which she was unspeakably grateful. She asked once more for the faith to trust Him, and turned back toward the bountiful provisions spread out before her. All the extras Mother had included would be invaluable in providing new experiences to her students.

The last thing Beth opened was a long letter from Mother included in the third trunk. Beth smiled at the familiar looping handwriting, and welcomed the bits of family news. But as she had feared, there was much criticism about her "uncivilized" surroundings, including the school being "held in a *saloon*, of all places!" and staying in a residence "with gentlemen guests."

"Dearest Beth"—she could clearly imagine the reproof in

her mother's voice as she read the words—"I can't help but worry about your health, your safety, in such a place," she finished, along with promises to pray for her. Then she added a postscript: "There's no shame in coming home, dear, if you must. You know you will be welcomed with open arms."

Beth sighed and tucked the letter away. She had to admit that home sounded rather inviting. But she shook her head when Marnie's face filled her mind. No, she had followed the Lord's leading, and she would stay.

CHAPTER
9

$\mathcal{B}$ETH STOOD IN FRONT of the mirror early Monday morning, holding some of the dresses her mother had sent. *What am I to wear to school this morning?* After having begun a good relationship with her students, the last thing she wanted was to transform herself into someone else, someone visibly different from them. She chose the simplest of the dresses and held it up, scrutinizing herself carefully. It was still uncomfortably excessive. But perhaps something could be done. . . .

She reached for the pair of scissors her mother had included in the shipment. Fighting against long-standing principles decrying such a reckless and wasteful act, she began clipping away the lacy embellishments. She was well aware of the value she was destroying and that the dress had been purchased with Father's money. She told herself he would approve had he been standing next to her, but such a belief did not stop her hands from trembling. *And Mother?* Beth was quite certain she could predict Mother's shocked reaction.

At last Beth slipped into the garment and surveyed her

work. It was a vast improvement, much simpler and fairly unassuming. But the modern dropped-waist style still set it apart from the more serviceable skirts and blouses worn by most of the women around her. And the extra flounce on the bottom hem—lowering the length to near her ankles—would surely be viewed as a terrible excess by the mothers working to produce as many clothing items as possible from each length of fabric they could afford. However, if Beth had trimmed it from the dress, she could not possibly have hemmed it again before school. So what she had already accomplished would have to suffice.

Beth hurried to the classroom to set up some of the new items. Marnie helped carry over what they could. When the children arrived there would be a printed alphabet on cards tacked along the edge of the long bar counter. A world map was mounted next to the door, and the flag stood at the front beside a picture of the king. She now had individual slate boards upon which they could practice sums and spelling, saving precious paper. And there were three complete sets of readers ready for the children to share. Finally, with a little of the money that Father had sent with her, Beth purchased an oil lamp for each table from the company store, a great help when the sun was not shining brightly.

With effort Beth restrained her excitement and did not display all the school supplies immediately. These children had so little, and she did not want to seem like she was flaunting her affluence. She hoped she had chosen the correct balance. Just as she had expected, there was a hushed tone while each child, upon entering, surveyed the room with wide eyes.

"Now, children, please take your places quickly so we can begin." She waited until everyone was quiet. "You can see that we have received our classroom supplies. I'm sure you will appreciate these materials that will help each of you to succeed as we learn together. Remember to treat them with care so that *many* children will benefit from them."

She looked around at the eager faces and smiled warmly. "Now, as we begin our day together, let's say a special prayer of thanks to God for giving us everything we need. Who would like to come to the front and lead us in an opening prayer today?" Though Beth's words were matter-of-fact, her heart thrilled to see their glowing expressions.

However, as soon as the question had left her mouth, she suspected she had overstepped her bounds. She knew very little about the spiritual circumstances in the homes of the children who sat before her. Would any of them be willing to pray publicly—even if there were those among them who had been taught to pray? She held her breath and was about to suggest that perhaps she herself would lead the prayer. But she noticed a hand far to one side waving in the air.

It was the least likely one Beth would have expected to volunteer. She had already gathered that the neediest of her indigent families was the Blanes. The three children dressed more poorly than the others, with too-small, threadbare clothes. Their shoes were so worn they had strung grocery store string around them to hold them to their feet. Yet it was the youngest, six-year-old Anna Kate, who was eagerly offering to pray.

Beth stood in wonder, delighted yet worried about what might happen next. She nodded reassuringly, indicating with a gesture that the little girl should step to the front of the class-room. Anna Kate moved quickly, already folding her hands as she came forward.

"You need ta stand up and close yer eyes," the little girl informed her listeners in a soft voice. Then she waited while chairs scraped against rough floorboards. Each child stood and responded with bowed head and folded hands.

"Dear God," began Anna Kate in a hushed yet steady voice, and Beth, still working her way through the unexpected, was reminded that she too should close her eyes.

"Thank you, God, for bein' good. Thank you for the new teacher and the new books and . . . and all that other stuff. Help us to learn real good, and . . . and to obey like Momma says." She paused, as if contemplating what more should be covered. Then finished, "Okay—amen."

Beth heard some murmured amens. Children resumed their seats. But Anna Kate called out an afterthought. "Just a minute." All eyes turned back to her sober face as she looked up at Beth. "I forgot to say, 'Be-with-us-this-day-that-we-might-honor-You.'" The syllables rattled off so quickly it sounded as if they were all one word. She explained, "Momma always says that."

To Beth's surprise all heads bowed and hands folded once again so little Anna Kate could pronounce the benediction as she had been taught.

Beth blinked and swallowed a lump in her throat as she announced the pledge of allegiance, this time with the new flag in place.

With the new resources, lessons were suddenly a much more interesting endeavor—for Beth as much as for the students. After lunch, she selected a book of fairy tales by Hans Christian Andersen, first showing them on the map where the author had lived and telling them a few facts about his life. She began to read *The Little Match Girl*, holding up the book to show the colorful illustrations as they appeared. The children—all ages and both genders—listened to the story, their faces enthralled. Beth could hardly contain her own joy. This is *exactly* what she had envisioned teaching would be—*well, not exactly, but close enough*, she decided.

⁂

That evening, Beth wrestled again with what to do about her clothing. She had laundered the borrowed items, and it was time to return them. But she would be left with only beautiful things she was too embarrassed to wear. Lifting three of the new dresses over her arm, she slipped down to the kitchen, where Molly was preparing dried beans to soak for the next day.

It was such a difficult question to phrase. Beth hesitated. "Miss Molly, could you— May I ask for your advice?"

Not even raising her eyes, Molly answered, "Advice is free, dearie."

"I need to return the clothes I borrowed."

"Yes, 'pears it's time."

It seemed easiest just to let the new clothing speak for itself. When Beth didn't say anything further, Molly turned to look as she held up the dresses one at a time for Molly to assess. "My mother sent these to replace what was stolen."

Molly studied them and nodded. "I see." And Beth knew she truly understood.

Beth stumbled on, "I'm . . . I'm not sure what to do. I think my students will— That is, they'll see me . . ."

"As rich?"

Beth sighed. "Yes—and different."

"You are though, ain't ya?"

"I'm not different, not really."

Molly shook her head. "Then why ya teachin' 'em? If yer the same as the rest of us, how ya gonna change anything?"

"I don't want them to think I'm . . . I don't know . . . well, better."

"You ain't better—just richer an' better schooled." Molly chuckled, then sighed and dried her hands. "The world's not fair, dearie. It don't help 'em none to pretend otherwise. Yer comin' is gonna make it clear that others got more'n them. A child don't know what they're lackin' till they see somebody else got more. But I hope you can help 'em figure it out past that too—that with the learnin' comes better chances in life. Just help 'em see that books'll take 'em further than slaving away here."

"But I don't *want* to wear these clothes. There's no sense in rubbing it in. Couldn't I—I don't know—just ask to trade with the ladies who loaned clothes to me?" She knew it was a poor suggestion.

"An' keep them old things? Oh no, ya can't. That would make them gals feel small as a tick. Besides, they wouldn't wear the fancy ones either. For the same reasons you said."

"But I *can't* wear these." Beth sighed.

"Hmm." Molly pondered the dilemma. "Can ya make do till Saturday?"

"Yes, I have my traveling clothes and what I'm wearing now. I can manage till then."

"Fine. There's a car headin' to the city Saturday mornin'. I'm sending out for some things. You can ride along."

"How does that help?"

"Go on in and sell what ya don't wanna wear. Then buy some yard goods—ya know, plain stuff."

Beth frowned. "But I don't know how to sew."

"Now, let a body finish. Get them yard goods and ask one or two of the women here to sew up a few dresses for ya. That way, ya get yer common duds, and you can even pay 'em a little for their work." She winked. "I can even tell ya which mommas to ask. See?"

Beth smiled, understanding immediately. The idea had merit.

"Jest one thing though, dearie," Molly added. "Don't ya go and get cheap, ugly fabric thinkin' that's gonna help. You gotta split the diff'rence and still be dignified and fine. Yer their teacher, after all. And you be sure an' keep two or three of them fancy frocks for when you need 'em. Ya never know."

Beth was comforted to hear Molly's solution and awed by her wisdom. Then she paused. "But what if someone asks why I'm going?"

"'Least said, quickest forgotten,'" quoted Molly. "Ya just don't waste yer words explainin'. Ya got business in town, plain and simple. And you'll be back."

Beth stole up the stairs, pleased with the common-sense advice she had heard—and from someone with far less "book learnin'" than she had.

But her satisfaction was soon put to the test. Tuesday was dark and rainy, and she had to face some behavior problems from her students that she hadn't yet experienced. Little Emily Stanton cried for her momma and refused to take her seat when asked. Alice McDermott and Sadie Shaw whispered together despite multiple warnings, then were insolent when Beth forced them to sit apart.

"We can't share our book if we can't sit t'gether," Sadie shot back at Beth.

"Alice will have plenty of time to finish the reading while you're busy writing twenty times on the board, 'I shall speak politely to all.' You may complete the reading after you've finished." She motioned toward the blackboard as the girl slowly stood, muttering, "Speaking to all is what got me in trouble in the first place," and strutted to the front.

Beth had expected there would be bumps along the road,

but she had felt she was already beyond the worst of it. When David Noonan pinned Miles Stanton in the hall while they were supposed to be getting a drink of water, Beth had reached her limit.

"Children! Take your seats!" Pushing back those who had rushed out to watch the scuffle, she fumed at them, "I am very disappointed in your behavior today. I have no idea what is causing such disobedience, but I shall not tolerate it. We are striving for a fine school, and this conduct is appalling."

Emily had begun to sniffle again, and the boys were still glowering at each other. Without asking permission, Marnie slipped from her chair and approached Beth.

"Miss Thatcher," she whispered hesitantly, "can I talk to ya?" It was the pleading look in the child's eye that caused Beth to assent. They withdrew to the front of the room. "It's jest that David's momma is mad at Miles's momma on account'a Miles's daddy owed money—an' now he's dead, an' Miles's momma can't pay it. But David's momma needs it real bad. That's why them boys are fightin' an' Emmy's so sad."

Beth hung her head, embarrassed that she had lost her temper. "And the girls?"

Marnie shook her head solemnly. "No—the girls, they was just being ornery."

"Thank you, Marnie."

Beth seated the two boys on opposite sides of the room, called for order, and continued the lessons, giving a little more affectionate attention to little Emily Stanton. Beth understood that she would never know all the things happening in their lives, but she was ashamed she had lost her temper. It brought back to her mind the summary Frances had given her of the previous teacher—all yelling and cursing. She was the adult—and they were children. She should expect that they would behave childishly at times, but she was determined to remain composed despite it all.

On Thursday afternoon Beth brought in some of the chemicals Mother had sent so she could demonstrate the various reactions upon mixing them. As best she could, she explained the invisible aspects of what was occurring. Beth could see that even the older students among them were fascinated at the concept of atoms and molecules—the fact that all they could see around them, including themselves, was made up of tiny particles had captivated their imagination. Then Beth produced a science book and announced that anyone particularly interested in chemistry could take a turn reading during the remainder of class. Three of the boys were especially enthusiastic, pressing close together in order to share reading the book, even though most of the concepts were well beyond them.

Unfortunately, this resulted in Friday being another particularly difficult day. The three, Wilton Coolidge, Georgie Sanders, and Levi Blane, decided it would be a fine idea to play a practical joke on the class. The ingredients which they had tucked away in a trash can, hoping to create merely a loud bang, turned into billowing smoke and a small fire instead. The students were forced to flee the building, coughing and sputtering. Beth stood, hands on hips, over the three as they scrubbed at the floor, trying to remove the resulting residue. Somehow she managed not to lose her temper or say what she was thinking, but it was dreadful for Beth to try and explain the incident to Helen Grant, who was apparently not inclined to modify her own reaction.

The woman always seemed to be a bit out of sorts with the world, grumbling if the room was not back in order quite soon enough, or if the school items were not stored according to her instructions. Beth began to wonder if she groused just for something to say. She was cold and aloof, not even interacting with the other ladies in the community. But Beth dared not express her concerns to even Molly lest it aggravate the problem. She did not want to appear ungrateful for the use of Helen's building.

Beth had mixed emotions as she climbed into the car Saturday morning for the long ride back into Lethbridge with her bundle of dresses to sell. She sighed as she reviewed the week. She had felt the satisfaction of reaching for lofty ideals as well as the frustration of students whose behavior was disappointing and confusing. She was learning how to manage the classroom when things went well . . . and when they did not.

The trip was complicated by her discovery that the driver did not speak a word of English. Molly had explained that the replacement miners were mostly Italian immigrants, and this man was the only driver available. Beth decided she would just as soon sleep than attempt conversation and leaned her head against the door of the automobile.

A strange sense of being in another time, another world, descended over Beth as she stepped from the vehicle and looked around at the busy streets of the city. It was as if the previous weeks had not occurred—as if they had been pure fantasy and she had just awakened again. She had returned to what was familiar and modern. The driver motioned several times with three fingers raised in the air and then at the clock on the bank beside them. She understood that this was the time at which she should be ready to depart and nodded her agreement.

Her first stop was at a restaurant for a hot cup of tea and

a sweet roll lunch. She relaxed in the comfort of it all—the cushioned seats, the calm surroundings, the gentle voices. It felt like such a luxury to be waited on again—to not lift a finger and enjoy a pleasant meal. From there she proceeded to her main tasks of the day. The polite and helpful clerks made even the task of selling the beautiful dresses proceed smoothly, and purchasing lengths of yard goods had a familiarity about it that made Beth feel at home.

For a moment as she waited for her ride, she wondered—just a fleeting thought—what it would be like to remain in the city. She could easily turn her back on the difficulties she had faced in Coal Valley—the primitive housing, dingy classroom, laborious daily life. It would surely be nothing more than what most had expected. Determined as she was to fulfill her commitment to the full year, she did not truly consider such an option, yet the very contemplation had brought a gloomy cloud of discontent over her.

At precisely three o'clock the car drew up beside her, but this time a young man stepped from the passenger door and hurried to load her bags.

"Thank you." Beth could not hide her surprise. "I'm sorry, but I was expecting Mr. Giordano."

"My name is Paolo. I am Alberto's son." He spoke English clearly, though his accent was somewhat pronounced.

Beth motioned toward the car. "This man is your father, then?"

"Yes, miss."

She climbed into the back seat, still wondering at the unexpected traveling companion. Soon they were speeding across the prairie, and Beth managed to strike up a conversation with the young man in the front seat.

"My family—my mother, two brothers, and a sister—are

living with my aunt and uncle. My father, he heard that there was offered good pay for mining in the mountains. So he left us in the spring. I have not seen him since—until today. Now I will join him in the work. It is good. We will make money more faster, and I can be with my father."

"May I ask how old you are, Paolo?"

"Yes, of course, miss. I am fifteen. That is old enough to mine, no?" It was difficult to see the boy's expressions from where Beth was seated, but by his tone and the periodic looks he cast over his shoulder toward her, Beth supposed his stout emphasis was added for his father's benefit, even though Alberto apparently did not understand his words.

Beth smiled weakly. "I'm sure your family is very grateful for your willingness to assist them."

"No, not grateful," he countered. "It is just what is needed from me. I am the oldest son."

Beth's brow furrowed at the declaration. She pressed further. "Have you been attending school while living with your aunt and uncle?"

Paolo shook his head, a little forlornly despite his obvious attempts to appear resilient. "I left school and began to work when I was twelve, delivering groceries and chopping firewood—whatever I could find. But I was being poorly paid. Now that I am a man, I can hold a true job, help my family. It will be good." Then he forced a smile and asked, "And you, miss—do you work to help your family back at home?"

Beth suppressed her amusement. "No," she said with a warm smile, "my father is—he has no need of my help," she tried to explain. "I work because I wish to educate children and improve their opportunities in life."

He sighed. "If I didn't have to work—then I would go back

to school." The admission came wistfully, along with a quick glance across at his father.

"What would you study, Paolo?"

He considered the question for a moment. "I like to learn languages, miss. I would like to speak much better—in English and Italian also. And maybe then to teach others—men like my father. I think that maybe I could give better opportunities too."

Long after she had been delivered to Molly's home, Beth still contemplated the young man's words. *What if it were actually possible to find a way for Paolo to teach English to some of the other miners? Wouldn't that benefit all?*

CHAPTER

10

IT HAD BEEN THREE WEEKS since Beth had been to church. She missed everything about it—singing and prayers, the fellowship and the sermon. At last it was Coal Valley's turn for the arrival of the traveling preacher, and there would be a proper service to attend. She felt as if her soul had been starving for food and now was beginning to salivate at the chance to dine again. She helped Molly serve breakfast, hastened to dress in one of the finer outfits—for Father had always taught her to wear her best to church— and descended the stairs just as Molly and the children were gathering in the foyer.

"Ya look real nice," Molly remarked.

Beth gazed back at Molly in her soft blue print and clean white gloves, her hair swept up carefully and topped with a small hat. "You look lovely too."

They fell in line for the short walk down the street to the company hall. It was a large open room, built to serve many needs, now filled with rows of simple chairs. Centered in the front was a small table draped in purple fabric, holding an open

Bible and a large wooden cross. The minister, dressed in a black suit, sat on a chair to one side waiting for the service to begin. Molly led them into the third row of seats and Marnie slipped in next to Beth, who smiled and patted Marnie's arm affectionately. All around Beth were small families of mothers and children. She had noted only four men scattered among them—none of them the men who shared Molly's table.

There was no organ to accompany the singing, but Beth thrilled as she joined her voice with the others, blending in worship. What the community lacked in instruments was more than compensated for with sweet harmonies. Again she realized how deeply she had felt the lack of music here.

Beth studied the preacher as he delivered his sermon from the book of John. He was a young man, perhaps not far beyond college himself. But his passion was clear and his words were direct. This Jesus who had come was God dressed in human flesh. He came to love those He had created—to forgive and redeem and set free—to heal and restore. And there was no one else who held the power to do so. Jesus provided the only means of salvation from our world of sin and death. Beth's eyes sparkled with tears to hear him articulate the gospel so well.

"Brothers and sisters," he implored them, wiping a handkerchief across his glistening forehead, "I know that this world holds suffering—and hardship—and sometimes despair. But our God has a gift—a hope and a future for each of us. If only we accept the manner in which it comes: the surrender of our will to His—in faith and obedience."

"Amen," Beth whispered. "Amen." And in her heart she prayed for greater faith to heed God's voice more fully. They were then directed to open hymnals again and raise their voices to sing, "Trust and obey, for there's no other way to be happy in Jesus, but to trust and obey."

Beth's heart was full. She turned to follow the others retreating slowly down the aisle. When they reached the door,
they were met by the minister, who extended his hand warmly
toward Molly. "Mrs. McFarland, so nice to see you again.
Teddy and Marnie, I'm very glad you came today." Then he
turned to face Beth. "Good morning. Forgive me, but I don't
believe we've met. My name is Philip Davidson."

Suddenly Beth felt just a little shy.

"This is Beth Thatcher," Molly introduced her. "She come
to teach school."

His face lit up brightly. "Well, that's wonderful. I've heard
how anxious the mothers have been for your arrival. I trust
you've been made to feel welcome."

"Why, yes. Thank you."

"And have you already begun your classes?"

"Yes, we have." In that moment Beth could think of nothing
more to add. She struggled for intelligent words and hesitated
awkwardly.

The broad smile widened. "Well, perhaps we'll have another chance to chat. Mrs. McFarland has graciously invited
me to dinner—along with a friend of mine."

"How nice," Beth answered quickly.

"Then I shall see you soon."

Beth moved away, her face flushed over her failure to converse easily with the eloquent young minister. She chastised
herself as she followed Marnie through the sagging gate.

As soon as Molly's little family arrived home, each hurried
to help prepare the meal. Molly pulled roast chickens from
the oven, Teddy stirred up the fire and added more wood,
Beth mashed the boiled potatoes, while Marnie heated peas
in cream sauce. There was fresh-sliced bread, a bright Jell-O

salad, and apple pie for dessert. In no time Molly had finished the gravy and the meal was ready to set on the table.

The company men had already gathered in the dining room. For several moments more there was some fidgeting as they waited for the appearance of the minister and his friend. As soon as Molly's alert ears caught the sounds of their arrival on the front porch, she motioned that it was time to gather the serving dishes and carry them out to the sideboard.

Upon placing her bowls beside the others, Beth turned toward the men waiting to be seated and was shocked to spy a bright red jacket among them. Her face flushed. *Could it be Edward? Had he somehow become acquainted with this itinerant pastor?* The array of shoulders parted, and instead of Edward's unruly brown mop she saw the guest had coppery hair, cut short. He smiled around the room, a closely trimmed horse-shoe mustache framing his lips.

"Mrs. McFarland, this is my friend Jack Thornton," Philip said, introducing the man to his hostess, and Molly shook the extended hand. "Jack, I'd like you to meet Mrs. Molly McFarland. And this is Marnie, and Teddy, and Miss Thatcher—to whom I had the pleasure of being introduced just this morning."

Beth nodded to the brightly suited gentleman and willed her nerves to calm again. It stirred a strange mix of emotions to be reminded of Edward.

"Well," Molly broke in. "Let's all eat 'fore it gets cold."

They crowded tightly around the table with extra chairs from the kitchen. Teddy and Marnie were allowed to take their plates to the front porch. Beth found herself seated across from the minister and his friend. She was certain this was by Molly's design.

Philip's outgoing personality kept the conversation lively.

After leading discussions on several other topics with much laughter, he turned his attentions to Beth. "May I ask, Miss Thatcher, where do you call home?"

"My family lives in Toronto, Pastor Davidson."

He smiled. "Oh, please, I'm much more comfortable with Philip. You'll convince me that you think I'm old—and I suspect you're not *too* much younger than I."

"Well then, Philip," she repeated, "most of my family still lives in Ontario, but I have a relative who teaches school in the north and is married to an officer of the Royal Canadian Mounted Police." Beth had found her tongue at last. "And where do you live?"

"I roam around mostly." Pausing to pass a serving dish, he continued, "Jack and I shared a place in Calgary for several months. Now, *there's* a man who's truly old—almost thirty, by my last count. Though I doubt he'd admit to it." They exchanged lighthearted glances. "We got along well anyway, until I started to travel for my work. I'm afraid I fairly deserted him then."

"And I'm a worse man for it," the response came back with a chuckle.

Philip laughed. "That's all too true. You're a terrible cook and an awful housekeeper. And now you're out here alone. Whoever will take care of you now?"

Beth found herself laughing along. "And what of you, Philip? Did you do any better? How well do you cook?" she teased.

A loud voice piped up from the other end of the table, "Why, miss? You making him an offer?"

Beth felt her face flush scarlet. She wanted to flee from the room but instead dropped her gaze to her lap, knowing all eyes were watching her reaction.

Philip's even-tempered answer was spoken toward the man with not even a hint of rebuke or embarrassment, but was clearly for Beth's benefit. "Mercy, Walter! Miss Thatcher has just begun important work here in Coal Valley. It would be a tragedy for them to lose her now. Let's give her a chance to see what God has in store for her here." And then without pausing for even a breath he added, "Hey, I noticed that repairs to the mine are coming along well. When do you think you'll be shipping out coal again, Henry?"

Everyone's attention drawn away, Beth pulled herself together, so grateful to have been rescued from her mortification. But for the remainder of the dinner visit, she spoke very little.

Just as Philip and his friend were moving toward the door and Molly disappeared to wrap up some of the extra chicken for them, Philip made his way closer to Beth. "Miss Thatcher, it's been so nice to meet you. I'm sorry we weren't able to chat longer about your teaching. I truly do believe you've been given a great work to accomplish here." His eyes were intense. "These children—they need so much love right now, and it will require someone who can be with them often to reach out to them. That's one of the difficult aspects of preaching here as I do—there is never enough time to serve individuals well. I want you to know that I'll be praying for you."

"Thank you, Philip. I appreciate that so much."

Beth thought and prayed about what he'd said during the remainder of the afternoon. She wondered how much Bible instruction the children were really receiving when they sat with their mothers for one church service on every third Sunday. When she was a child, she was in church every week and also listened to Father read the Bible daily—Mother taking over the task a little begrudgingly whenever he was absent.

But what could Father do about that? It was his work that provided for the needs of the family. Beth guessed that some of the mothers in the little town could not read themselves. It was such a shame that her students received so little instruction. As she wrote her weekly letter to Mother, she poured out her concerns for the children, referencing some of them by name and describing their situation in more detail than she had done before.

In the evening, Beth sought out Molly for advice again. "I am thinking of starting a Bible club. Perhaps to meet a couple of times each week. Do you think there would be any interest in something like that?"

"That'd be real nice." Molly's answer was encouraging.

"So you think I could—that I should try it?"

Molly hesitated. "That ain't the same thing. I think the mommas would let 'em come. I think Bible teachin' is good. But I cannot say if it's somethin' God wants from *you*. Ya have to ask *Him* about that. But, dearie," she added, "pay Him mind. If He says yes, then don't let none deter ya. But if He says no, then He ain't in it. Don't do it just to please a man."

Beth blushed. "Oh no—it isn't—I wasn't—it has nothing to do with the pastor." But Molly's cautions sent Beth back to prayer, just to be certain.

⌘

By Monday morning she had come up with a plan and began steps toward achieving it. First she approached the mine superintendent, Henry Gowan, while he rocked on the porch with a final cup of coffee before heading off to his office. She asked for and received permission to use the company hall on Tuesday and Thursday evenings. So during her spare moments on Monday, she copied out a note to each of the mothers.

She described a Bible club where the children would act out the stories rather than just listening to them being told. She would help them put together the first skit about creation on the following evening.

After school she passed the announcement to each of the families. While she and Marnie were putting the room in order, some mothers appeared at the door, note in hand, with questions.

"What ages are you planning to let come?"

"What's this gonna cost?"

"Do you want that the mommas stay? Or do I jest leave 'em?"

Beth was greatly encouraged by their interest and hoped many of the children would participate. She had not expected, however, to discover the evening crowd almost as large as it had been on Sunday morning, with each mother seated prominently beside her children. Beth was a little uncertain how to proceed.

She tried a rather weak announcement. "Now, I believe I've explained that this club is for the children. It isn't necessary for parents to remain. Not unless you would like to." Not a mother moved. They merely smiled at one another and turned back to Beth.

What should be done? Beth began what she had planned. "Children, we are going to do some acting. Learning the Bible stories by participating in them. I hope you'll all be brave and willing enough to join in. I think it's going to be lots of fun. So let's begin. Tonight I have several parts to fill. I need a volunteer to be Adam." Gabe Stanton raised his hand, and Beth passed a short script to him. "I also need an Eve."

Giggling followed. Now that the children realized there would be a pairing up of a boy and girl, they were hesitant to volunteer. Beth chose a much younger Maggie Frazier and hoped the laughter would ebb. It did. She assigned the snake to Georgie Sanders, who received a round of hoots for playing the devil, and let Peter McDermott read the part of God to a chorus of even louder banter.

"Quiet, please. Now then," she instructed, "you other children will be the creation." It took several minutes to make assignments for trees and stars and moon and animals. "We shall read through the story once before we begin to act it out—so that we are well acquainted with the plot. Listen closely for your place in our drama. When we take the stage, you will need to know when you enter and what action you perform. For example, plants may lift their flowers and branches to heaven." Beth demonstrated each pose. "Stars and moon may shine, like this." She shot her arms outward around her head. "Animals may move a little—but please, no noises." More snickering. "For this evening only, I shall be narrator."

It was not smooth and well performed. Beth was nearly desperate at some points, trying to make any progress through the story at all. But in the end they managed to practice and present the story of creation and the first sin from start to finish. She walked to the front again, quite prepared to apologize to the mothers for such a disastrous performance of a Bible story. *What would Mother have thought about such a light-hearted form of presenting a Bible passage?* But to Beth's amazement, the women appeared to be delighted with what the children had done.

So instead, Beth addressed them all with an impromptu thought regarding the story they had just witnessed. She explained how sin had come into the world when that very first command was disobeyed, and that every person born afterward had inherited a sinful nature as well as the curse of death. She reminded them of what Pastor Davidson had explained on Sunday—about Jesus being the only solution. As she looked across the crowded room, she asked them to pause a moment, and she prayed aloud that the Spirit would stir hearts to understand and believe. Then she dismissed them, and the students went tumbling out in all directions at once, laughing and teasing each other about their various parts. Beth was very relieved that the children seemed to enjoy the evening.

The mothers crowded around her. "What story are you going to do Thursday, Miss Thatcher?" "I think my Thomas will want a part next time—now he understands how it's done. I'd like ta see 'im try." "Are you goin' to act out all the stories in the Good Book?" and on and on.

"Thank you so much for coming," Beth repeated to each one as she answered their queries as best she could.

Watching carefully for Esther Blane, Charlotte Noonan and Abigail Stanton, Beth drew each of the ladies aside when she arrived. She had divided up her fabric purchases to bring with her that evening, and she found opportunities to speak privately with these mothers about sewing for her. Each woman was visibly pleased to take on the projects.

Between teaching and grading and getting the room ready each day, Beth had very little time for preparation of the skits. She had thought just a little scenery and basic costumes could be included—but she was simply unable to prepare for such extras. Imagination would be essential—fortunately, the children were blessed with an abundance of that particular characteristic.

On Thursday the evening crowd was even a little larger. Molly had chosen to attend and brought along her friend Frances. This time Beth was going to present the much shorter story of Cain and Abel. Since there were only three parts to play, she had divided it into shorter readings and let several of the students have a chance to be the narrator. It seemed to work out quite well, with a bit of intervention needed when Daniel Murphy spent a little too much time "killing" his brother Abel. This was met with laughter all around, and Daniel basked in the pleasure of having stolen the show, even bowing low at the end, causing more giggles.

Beth quickly had learned it was best to undertake shorter passages—even though there would be fewer parts—and simply be certain to rotate the roles each week among all the children.

By Saturday she had already received two lovely dresses sewn with care. It blessed her heart to be able to pay Charlotte Noonan, David's mother, for her work. Perhaps this would help alleviate some of the conflict between the Noonan family and the Stantons. And Beth could imagine it would be a great help since Charlotte's baby was expected anytime.

Beth was also able to have the first of her tea parties, inviting the four oldest students. She had planned to purchase cookies at the company store, but Molly wouldn't hear of it. "Store bought! Might as well give 'em cardboard. I'll bake up a big batch. You can have some for your fancy doin', an' I'll have some ta put out for supper."

The lovely tea service Mother had sent was arranged on the dining room table. Right on time, Addison Coolidge and his sister Luela arrived dressed in their Sunday best. They joined Teddy and Marnie, standing stiff and awkward just inside her door.

"Please don't be shy. This is for you. You are the guests of honor today." She gestured toward the waiting table.

Still the boys hesitated. Beth felt it would help to instruct them. Keeping her voice matter of fact, she explained how the "men" were to assist the "ladies" by holding their chairs before taking their own seats. With a few awkward grins and some blushes, the task was accomplished.

Beth poured their tea and placed her napkin in her lap. She was pleased to see each follow suit, and they passed the plate of fresh oatmeal cookies from one to another. Once Beth finally managed to engage the boys in the conversation, she discovered that Teddy had plenty to say when bolstered by the presence of his friend. They described in great detail a nest of squirrels they had found, about how gentle and small the babies were, how soft to hold—at least until the mother returned. They had tossed her young back inside the shelter of the tree and skedaddled out of there, the poor mother chattering her anger, twitching and lunging after them. Beth found she immensely enjoyed the story and the chance to get to know her young charges better.

After their tea party was over, Beth was thrilled to be invited by the children to visit their favorite fishing hole along the river. The Coolidges ran home to change their clothes while Beth, Teddy, and Marnie did the same, and then they met at the river. Beth held a pole for a while, but soon passed it over to ones with more experience. Still she shared in their satisfaction on the way home with three lovely trout for Molly's supper preparations, while Addison and Luela would bring two of their own to their mother.

Leading the way, the boys holding high the poles strung with their catches, the two suddenly stopped still on the path. Beth hurried forward.

Addison was gesturing toward the river, and Teddy seemed to be drawing him in the opposite direction. Beth could see a man in the distance, hauling a small boat up onto the shore.

"Do you know him?" she questioned Teddy. He shook

his head firmly. "Ain't never seen him before." He looked at the figure again. "But we better not pester him. He's prob'ly fishin'. We'll keep goin'."

Addison started to speak, but Teddy cut him off tersely. "I said no, Addie."

Beth glanced from one to the other, wondering what was going on. But before she could find out, the boys were off again, and she and the girls were hurrying just to keep up.

Having already accomplished the story of Noah and the flood, Beth chose to present the Tower of Babel. She noticed during their rehearsal that an older gentleman, perhaps in his late sixties, had entered and taken a seat at the back of the hall. Since he was obviously dressed more like a miner than a company man, it seemed strange to Beth. She wondered if he was one of the newly recruited workers. Yet he was much older than she would have expected for such a strenuous job. She would introduce herself to him following the play.

Then the empty wooden crates being used to make the tower came clattering down during the performance. Beth was so busy afterward supervising their proper return to the company store that the man was gone by the time she might have greeted him. Later she inquired of Molly about him.

"Oh, yah, that's Ol' Man Stub. He's a miner—least he was. Lost a hand in an accident. 'Twas a shame. Had a good job leadin' a crew."

The meaning of his moniker slowly dawned on Beth. "You don't mean to say they call him Stub because of his missing hand?"

Molly chuckled and shrugged. "Guess so. I quit thinkin' 'bout that. But yah, that's what it means."

"Doesn't that . . . well, hurt his feelings?"

"Don't know. Never heard him say."

Beth grimaced. "What is his given name?"

It took Molly a moment to remember. "It's Russo. Frank Russo. From Italy—but he speaks English real good. Bin round these parts a lotta years. He's a good man. Knew my Bertram. They use ta play pool t'gether." She chuckled to herself. "Funny we call him Old Man—since he can't be more'n eight or ten years older than me. Guess Old Stub's had a long, tough road."

"What does he do—now that he doesn't work at the mine?"

"Helps out mostly." Molly sighed. "Sometimes at the mine—he bin blastin' fer so long they come to rely on him fer advice. Then, since the mine fell in, he's bin helpin' widows. Jest little things—extra wood in the stack, sometimes a bag of apples or a venison roast. Jest drops it off and scoots away 'fore they can thank him proper. Knew all their menfolk. Worked side-by-side with 'em—even led the crew fer some. Good man, Ol' Frank."

"I hope he comes again."

"I think he will."

Beth cast a sideways glance at Molly. "May I be honest?"

"Ain't ya been?" She winked at Beth.

"I don't even know why the adults are coming. I can see that the children are enjoying themselves, but the acting is poorly done, and we have a terrible time keeping to the script. There's so much chaos. I don't know why it's attracting a crowd."

"Ya don't?" Molly shook her head and chuckled. "They're learnin', dearie. They're learnin' right along with them kids."

Beth had not considered such a notion. "And why do *you* come?"

"I still got me some learnin' ta do." Then Molly's eyes twinkled playfully. "'Sides, it's powerful funny to watch all the nonsense—and you tryin' so hard to keep things goin'. Yer face when the tower fell—priceless!" Molly laughed heartily, and Beth couldn't help but join her.

CHAPTER
11

M ISS THATCHER, MISS THATCHER! There's a Mountie outside." Marnie had just placed the last of the chairs in order and was looking out the window. Beth, collecting her books and the papers, immediately thought of Edward. She had anticipated that he would make an appearance at some point. He would say he was following Father's request to keep an eye out for her.

Marnie was sounding rather frantic. "I think he's comin' in here! Should I let him in? Did we do somethin' wrong? Or one of the boys—?"

"It's fine, Marnie. Yes, please invite him in." Beth pushed at her hair and unrolled the sleeves on her dress. Edward no doubt would disapprove of the simple homemade dress.

The door in the hall banged open, but it was not Edward who entered the room. The coat was the same, but the face was that of Philip's friend with the copper-colored mustache. Beth took a step back, trying to recover from—her unexpected disappointment.

"Good afternoon, Miss Thatcher. I hope I haven't disturbed you."

"No, no—not at all. I . . . I thought . . ."

He seemed to read her confusion. "Would you have been expecting Constable Montclair?"

"Why, yes!" *How did he know?* She rushed once more to cover her surprise. "He is a . . . a friend. From home. I thought perhaps . . ." Then a new thought clouded her eyes. "He's not . . . not hurt, is he?"

"No, miss. Oh, no," the man quickly assured her. "I saw him just last week. He knew I was being stationed in this area, so he asked me to drop by and see how things are going for you here."

"Oh, yes, and thank you," answered Beth. "And where is he now?"

"He's just been transferred north."

"North?"

"Yes, Athabasca, I believe. He asked me to tell you he was sorry he couldn't come to see you before leaving."

"Thank you . . . for bringing the message, I mean." Then she added, "I'll admit you frightened me for a moment. I thought perhaps something had happened. His parents would be— Well, you see, they're family friends. And I—"

"No, no," he said, hastening to alleviate her concern. "Nothing of the sort. I'm sorry to have alarmed you. Maybe I should have sent word through the post instead. . . ."

She flushed and tried to begin again. "Of course not," she said, attempting to express heartfelt gratitude. "It was very kind of you to deliver his message. I'm sorry—it just caught me off guard somewhat. But I'm relieved he is fine. I'm sure he was excited about his new . . . posting?"

He nodded. "Posting—yes."

Finally she could recall her manners. "I apologize, but I don't remember your name—from when we met at Sunday dinner."

With an amiable smile and a playful bow, he said, "Corporal Jarrick Thornton at your service, ma'am. But my friends just call me Jack."

Prompted by the twinkle in his eye, she queried, "What does your mother call you?"

His eyebrows raised. "Well, that would be Jarrick, Miss Thornton. Always Jarrick." Now that she had turned the tables, she could see him wondering if she was poking fun at him or if it was good-natured teasing.

"I like your mother's choice." Beth extended her hand. "It's nice to know you, Jarrick." As they shook hands, she remembered Molly working on dinner. "I'm afraid I must excuse myself, though. It's been kind of you to come so far just to deliver Edward's message."

"Is there any way I can be of help?"

"Thank you, but no." Beth drew her hand away, then looked at his hand. "Oh mercy, I may have offered you some chalk dust with my handshake." She brushed her palm against her skirt. "It's something that goes with being a schoolteacher."

Jarrick turned his own hand over. "No chalk dust. I feel cheated."

Beth felt a bit unsettled by the conversation. "And you say you are to be in our area?" she asked, changing directions abruptly.

"Blairmore."

"Oh, is that close? I've heard it mentioned but didn't realize it was large enough for a— What do they have at a 'posting,' then, a jail?"

He smiled, and Beth noticed a small dimple nearly hidden

beneath his neatly clipped mustache. She wondered if he grew the mustache to cover it and appear more authoritative in his job. "Not much of a jail," Jarrick admitted. "It's a new location. More for security and aid than for enforcement, really. But we try to have postings scattered throughout the province in case we're needed."

Just then Marnie, waiting in the hall, dropped a book and startled Beth. "Oh my," she told him, "I really should be going. There's work to do at home."

"I apologize, Miss Thatcher. I've kept you too long." Jarrick stood just a moment more, though, shuffling the brim of his hat through his hands. "It was a pleasure to see you again."

"Yes, and thank you. That is, I do thank you for—for bringing greetings from Edward. I have often wondered how things were going for him. At times I've wondered if perhaps he had returned home."

"Oh no, I assure you. He has very much adapted to our work out here in the West. Very committed to the job. Doing well. He's developing into a fine officer and a particularly good investigator. It seems that part of the job appeals to him most. I expect he'll increasingly be found in that role."

Beth nodded and rubbed her hands on her skirt once more.

With a solemn nod, Jarrick returned his Stetson to his head and turned to leave. "Oh shucks, I almost forgot." He fished inside his coat pocket for something. "Edward would have been very annoyed with me. He told me to be sure you received this." He produced a small object. "I believe there is a bit of a note somewhere."

Beth's mind was whirling at the size and shape of the little box wrapped in brown paper. *A gift? Jewelry? What could it mean?* She tore open the package and gasped in disbelief. Instantly her eyes filled with tears and the room started spinning as she struggled to catch her breath. *Father's compass.* . . . She felt her knees go weak.

Jarrick quickly reached for her and held her up, then led her to a nearby chair and crouched down beside her. No longer aware of anything else, Beth dropped her head against his shoulder and sobbed. Several moments passed before Beth was cognizant enough to straighten and look away.

"I'm so sorry," she whispered, feeling humiliated at her emotional reaction. "I can explain . . ." she started, but more tears ran down her cheeks.

He quickly drew a chair over to sit beside her and looked at her with a mystified and concerned expression.

She wiped at the tears with one hand, the other clutching tightly to what had been returned. "It . . . it is the compass my father gave to me when I came west. It was stolen on the way—I never thought to see it again. However did Edward . . . ?"

He pointed to the floor. "Perhaps the note will explain. May I . . . ?" Jarrick reached down, picked up a piece of paper that had fallen to the floor, and placed it in her hands.

Her words tumbled out. "I'm so sorry I became emotional. It's just—it was my father's—and it's so special to us, to me especially, and he entrusted it to my care, and . . ."

"I see." But he appeared to be worrying more over her state of mind than her explanation. "I thought perhaps it was a gift . . . well, from Edward."

"Oh no. My father—he spent years at sea. This compass— he said I was to keep it so I would—I would always be able to . . ." Her voice trailed away, and she took a big breath. "To find my way home . . ." Her lip had begun to quiver and she quickly covered it with a hand.

"I understand. I do," he said quietly.

131

There were no words Beth could find to adequately explain her strong reaction to this man who was leaning toward her, assessing her condition. She could think of nothing else to say. Suddenly he was reaching for her hand and lifting it gently. "Miss Thatcher, I have a sister. I miss her terribly at times. And if she had lost something so precious to her, I know she would have responded exactly as you did. And I . . . I would have loved her for it." He held her gaze. Then the moment passed, and he patted her hand and released it, again assuming his role of caring bystander. "Are you certain you've recovered?"

"Oh yes. I'm sure." She pulled herself to her feet to prove it.

He stood with her, nodded, and turned to go. "I hope to see you again soon, Miss Thatcher." Beth watched him disappear around the doorway and heard his steps retreat.

Only then did Marnie's ashen face peer out from where she had been waiting in the hall. "Miss Thatcher, you okay?" she asked anxiously.

Beth glanced down at the unread note still clutched in her hand. She felt far too emotional to read it at the moment lest she burst into tears again. Molly would be waiting with supper. She nodded her okay to Marnie, rested her hand on the girl's slender shoulders, and turned them both toward home. She would read the note later in the solitude of her own room.

CHAPTER

12

$\mathcal{L}$AZY WHITE CLOUDS drifted across the sky, promising a lovely Saturday. Beth spent the morning with Marnie, gathering some last items of produce from the garden. She had offered to assist also with the process of preserving it, but Molly shooed her out of the kitchen, insisting that Beth find some way to relax. "You've gotten yerself some awful busy weeks, what all with teachin' and Bible club an' fancy teas to top it off. 'Sides, Frances and me been puttin' up the garden together for years. Kinda got our way of doin' things," Molly explained with eyebrows cocked and a meaningful grin.

Beth couldn't help but laugh. "So I'll just be in your way," she teased.

Frances nodded from where she sat at the table, her knife working quickly to peel and chop the last of the onions for canning. "Aye, and two in the kitchen is more than enough, Miss Beth. Even if the likes of you be no bigger'n a penny."

After hosting her second tea party in the dining room, this time for James, Bonnie, and Peter, Molly's suggestion about relaxing sounded awfully good. So almost by accident Beth turned toward the forest and began a walk.

She meandered downhill toward the creek. Using the same large rocks that Teddy and Marnie had, she crossed where it was shallow and wide, coming out on the far shore. It was easy then to find the deep, overhung spot from which she and the four youths had pulled out five large trout. She paused and smiled at the memory of the day, pleased about the opportunities to get closer to her students.

The day was warm, and Beth was pursued by a constant swarm of mosquitoes, but the peaceful sounds of water gurgling and birds chirping made up for the pesky critters around her head. The mountains provided a stately backdrop for the lush forest crowding down toward the broad rocky shore. The view reminded Beth of Mother's stereoscope, and of pressing her head together with Julie's to see the scenes in the viewfinder at the same time. She smiled at the memory and bent to pick a stalk of pale violet asters.

Gathering a wide variety of flowers for a bouquet, she stole along the edge of a clearing, her eyes cautiously searching around her for movement of any kind. She had never wandered so far alone. Caution and daring battled within her, yet she pressed on—always a little farther—exhilarating in the sense that she was the first to enter such a pristine wood.

A pair of chattering squirrels tumbled over each other, scampering this way and that in the woods as they gathered their winter fare. Beth followed them up the hill, having to laugh at their antics. When the two disappeared over the hill, she turned around to retrace her steps. But she could neither see nor hear the creek. For a moment she felt a small twinge of uncertainty—and then she told herself that as long as she went back downhill, it should be easy to locate the water, cross over, and be on her way home.

A patch of light indicated another clearing, and Beth made her way toward it. Pushing through the underbrush and dodging the low-hanging branches, she struggled out into the open. This meadow was long and narrow, stretching across the edge of the hillside. From her vantage point she could see the most beautiful view of the valley below and the range of mountains beyond. The trees on the far slopes were speckled with bright yellows and oranges. Cooler weather had coaxed out the fall colors, now brilliant against the dark green of the pines and spruce.

Looking closer she could see the town nestled against the opposite hillside, rooftops tucked here and there. The short stretch of the main street carved only a small gap between the trees. And far to the east was the road, long and narrow through the valley near the river. Up on the mountainside, the afternoon sun had exposed a dark area on the rock face. It appeared to be a cavern opening of some sort. *Is it nature's doing, or was it once another mining operation?* Then a curious occurrence as Beth watched it fade from view. It did not take her long to realize that only for a few moments did the sun's rays highlight the opening—and then it was gone, hidden in the deep shadows cast by nearby trees. *Almost as though it had never been,* she mused. She clapped her hands joyfully as she thought, *Wouldn't Julie and I have found that spot to be a wonderful place to explore and hide in?* The sound made a delightful echo around her.

Her eyes swept the valley again, and her gaze drifted just to the west of town. She puzzled for a moment over a wide, jagged opening in the trees and a jumble of structures. She quickly realized these were surely associated with the mine.

She then identified the spur of railway tracks which carried away the coal, extending along the valley. Beth marveled how close to the town all the mine work was taking place. *Small wonder that the noise of the mine operations is so easily heard in our classroom*, she mused.

Lifting her gaze again to the mountains around her took Beth's breath away—all this magnificent scenery surrounded her every day. And yet she had been so involved with her own responsibilities and cares she had not been able to appreciate the beauty of the setting . . . as if brushstrokes from the very hand of God were evident in the beauty surrounding her.

For the first time since she had arrived she tried to imagine the end of her time in Coal Valley. *What will it be like to leave this place and not return?* She determined to experience it more fully, taking longer walks whenever she was able.

Checking the sky, Beth concluded it was time to return. She had noticed that the sun dropped behind the tall peaks rather quickly here. Now that the sun had already begun its descent, she pushed her way through the sweet meadow grasses and came to the perimeter before the tree line. *I hope this is where I entered the meadow. . . .*

As she searched around her for anything familiar, Beth spotted a small, weathered gray cross just above the grass. Moving closer, she realized it stood upon a mound of rocks, marking what clearly was a grave. Curious, she stepped forward, almost stumbling over a crouched form. He slowly came to his feet. It was the miner called Old Man Stub.

Beth gasped her surprise and drew back, but he seemed unfazed by her presence. "Excuse me," she stammered. "I'm so sorry! I didn't mean to intrude."

"I knew you was'a there," he assured her. "No need'a to apologize."

She drew a deep breath. "I don't want to disturb you, sir. I'll just—"

"That'sa all right," he quickly said. "I been wanting to meet you anyway. Just as well it be here. I am Russo. Frank Russo." He extended his left hand.

"I'm Beth Thatcher," she answered, her right hand automatically reaching out, and then a quick correction, offering the left instead. "I teach at the school."

"Yes, miss. I know. I see you with the kids." Beth nodded. "The kids, they are'a lucky to have you." He smiled and motioned across the valley. "You admiring the Lord's beauty, yes?"

She nodded again in response. Then thought to ask, "Mr. Russo, I noticed a . . . a cave, or something, right up there. Is it—"

"That'sa ol' mine shaft," he cut in quickly. "Not for adventures, miss. Please don't go exploring. It'sa not a safe place for a young woman. You understand? Please do not—"

"I understand," Beth said to reassure him. She did wonder at his obvious agitation, though. But she shifted her gaze in another direction.

Beth felt a certain ease as they stood together in the stillness. At last she queried softly, "Mr. Russo, may I ask whose grave this is?"

He sighed and sank down again the way he was before, resting on a log. "My wife. My Colette."

"Oh, I'm so sorry." Beth knelt down in the grass and studied his face for a moment. He seemed neither despondent nor troubled by her question, only a tender reverence written there. Beth reached over and placed on the grave the flowers she was holding, next to a bouquet she knew must have been put there by Frank. His head bobbed in thanks.

Beth rose to seat herself on a large rock nearby and asked gently, "How long ago did you lose her?"

"So many years ago," he sighed, "and yet I miss her still—like it was'a yesterday."

"It's such a beautiful, peaceful resting place."

"She loved it'a here. Like she was a part'a the mountains—I couldn't bear to take her away somewhere else. And once she was'a here—I could not leave her alone. Never did I go back to Italy. Never did I want'a to."

"Can you tell me about her?"

He smiled, but not at Beth—it was an invitation to drink deeply from his precious memories once more. "I met'a her here in this valley—when I was'a just a young man and she was'a not much more than a child. I come from Italy to find work, and she was'a with her parents already here. After a while, we fell in'a love and married as soon as her papa, he give us his permission."

Frank sifted a handful of pebbly earth through his gnarled fingers. "She was'a so beautiful, my Colette. Her eyes big and'a brown, laughing always—so full of'a life. And we was'a so happy together. We moved away to live in the city awhile. But the mountains, they called us'a home again.

"Then she wanted a baby. I said, 'Colette, we don't need'a nobody else. We got'a each other.'" He sighed. "But a woman, she needs a baby. And so for a long time we hoped and'a prayed together. But still, no bambino. I said to her, 'Come with me back'a to Italy. We visit my family. They will love you like'a I love you.'" He smiled in recollection. "We made our plans. Saved up our'a money. And then, it happened." A tear sliding down his cheek went unheeded. "She was'a so happy. The baby, it was'a coming at last."

Several moments of silence hung around them. Beth kept

her eyes averted, not wanting to interrupt his emotion-filled memories. When his voice came again, it was controlled and resigned. "I lost my Colette in the spring when the baby, she was'a born. I lost'a them both. All the little spring flowers was a'blooming around her when we laid'a her here. And so I stay. How can I leave her alone?"

Suddenly he rose to his feet. "Miss Beth, it'sa already growing dark. You need'a to get home."

"Oh my, I didn't realize—"

"Please, miss, come with me. I will take'a you a much faster way."

"Thank you, Mr. Russo." She quickly rose and followed him along a narrow path leading almost straight down the hillside. They said very little to each other as he hurried her along. Ever so quickly the light had failed and it had become difficult to see. Beth stumbled after Frank as quickly as she was able, her arms raised in front of her to guard her face from tree branches. Then she noticed lights ahead. It was not the town—but there were voices.

"Where are we?" she called after Frank.

He motioned her to hurry. "We cross'a the footbridge here to the camp. And then only a short walk back'a to town." All around them forms began to take shape in the dusk. Beth hesitated at the first step onto the makeshift bridge. "It'sa okay. I'ma with you. Come along, miss. Please."

She turned her eyes to his and cautiously crossed the narrow structure. Several men began to move toward them.

"Eh, Francesco!" A deep voice drew attention from every direction. Beth understood none of the words that followed, filling the air around her with strange, animated voices.

"My friends," Frank called to them in English, "Meet'a the new schoolteacher, eh? Please, make a path for Miss Beth."

More words followed, but Beth understood nothing. She thought that perhaps he repeated her name along with a string of Italian. As he spoke, they worked their way into the center of the camp. Beth tried to shrink herself as much as she was able, feeling very uncomfortable and out of place. *What would Mother say if she could see . . . ?* But she put the thought out of her mind and, not a little afraid, followed behind her rescuer.

Frank called out to someone nearby, and two of the men moved closer. Beth could see that one was the driver who had taken her to Lethbridge. "Alberto, you meet'a Miss Beth before, eh? Come, say allo."

Stepping out from behind his father's form, Paolo greeted her with some astonishment. "Ah yes, so good to see you again, miss." And then added, "How is it you are here? And in the dark?"

"I went for a walk," she answered somewhat breathlessly. "I met Frank by the—in the forest, and he is showing me a quicker way home. I . . . I lost track of the time—"

"I did that once," Paulo said, smiling with boyish charm. "It will be the only time—I assure you."

Beth saw that Frank was moving away. "I wish we had time to chat, Paolo, but I must get home. If you ever have a chance, please drop by the schoolroom or the boarding house. It would be so nice to talk with you again," Beth said, turning toward Frank's figure in the darkness.

"I would like that, Miss Thatcher," Paulo called after her.

"Make'a way, *amici*," Frank directed the men standing around them. "We get the teacher back home pronto."

As they moved between the small structures of the little camp, Frank called out friendly introductions of Miss Thatcher. Although she could see no faces in the darkness, there was something reassuring in hearing Frank's confident greetings.

But as soon as they had left the camp behind, Frank turned to her and said in a low voice, "Paolo, he will not'a be able to come to town—you know that, yes?"

Beth stopped and stared at the elderly man. "He can't?"

"No, miss."

"Won't the mine boss allow him even a bit of time off?"

"It'sa not the mine boss. The foreign men, they're not welcome in'a town."

"But why?" Beth was startled at the revelation. "What—?"

"They think we can not'a be trusted," he explained simply.

"But *you* come sometimes—"

"Yes," he cut in. "I had a wife. A *Canadian* wife. You see, women, they don't live in'a the camp. So Colette and me, we make a cabin in'a the woods not far away. But it was'a long time before I was'a trusted. My Colette—she won'a their hearts for me."

Frank motioned them forward. "When I lost'a my hand," he said over his shoulder, "I could not work'a no more. But I couldn't leave—because she and the little one're up there on the mountain. Most people, they seem to understand. I had'a suffered enough, I suppose. I think Miss Molly, she made them change'a their minds. About me."

"I should think so!" Beth exclaimed.

His voice was soft with resignation. "No, miss, I understand. We are strangers. From a land far away. We come alone. No wives or families. We do not'a speak the same. They need'a protect their own. Especially now that their men, they are gone."

"But it doesn't seem right," Beth insisted.

"Right? It'sa how it is. Why should they let new men they don't even know near their little *bambinos*?"

With one more turn of the path in the darkness, Beth saw

they had come into the town just behind the company hall. She was almost home.

"Thank you so much, Mr. Russo. I would never have found my own way in the—"

"If we was not'a talking up there on the mountain, you would'a been home long before," he said quickly. "It'sa my fault. But, please, Miss Beth, no more walking up the mountain. Its'a better not'a to go on those paths. Please."

"You mean the men in the camp—?"

"No, no. Not the miners. They are good men. But, please— no questions. Just . . . just take'a the advice of an old man and do not go up'a the mountain. Walk to the nearby stream, perhaps—but not alone. And never up'a the mountain."

"I see," said Beth, though she puzzled over his intensity.

Beth extended her left hand once more. "I'm so grateful for your help—and so glad to have met you, Mr. Russo. I hope to see you often."

He smiled, his expression warm. "I thought I would'a like you, Miss Beth. An' I do. *Buonanotte*. Good night."

As Beth had expected, Molly held back nothing in rebuking her for being out so late. "We was fit to be tied, dearie! Almost ready to call in the cavalry lookin' for ya. Jest imagine havin' to seek out the new man—thet Jack Thornton, was it?—to come find ya. Or sendin' so many already tired-out men inta the woods in the dark to hunt ya down. . . ." And on and on it went. Beth was relieved when Molly arrived at "An' we couldn't *imagine* where ya might be . . ." but rushed right on with her lecture without questioning her.

Beth pictured how embarrassed she would have been to be lost in the woods and discovered by Jarrick. She determined she would never do something so foolish again.

In church the next morning, Beth did not know how much of her imprudent escapade already had been passed around. But she was able to put it aside as the richness of the hymns filled the simple room and Philip delivered another inspiring sermon. Beth found his message lifted her spirit as few had previously—so sincere and passionate and full of eternal truth. He was speaking the same biblical concepts she had always heard, but he spoke as if heaven and earth hung in the balance. And Beth was challenged to appropriate the same zeal into her own life.

So much had happened since Philip had last shared a meal with them, and Beth found herself wishing for a conversation with him. So she was pleased to learn that Molly expected him again for Sunday dinner. With the other guests there, she wondered how they might be able to converse in a setting where they would not be interrupted.

Philip offered to help with the dishes and refused to allow Molly to dissuade him. This meant Beth might have his attention rather privately while he washed and she dried. Molly would be bustling around them, putting away the leftovers, but only periodically commenting. *Ideal,* she thought. The two chatted congenially as they worked together before he turned the conversation.

"And I heard you've been quite busy too—with a new Bible club."

Beth's response came tumbling out as she described the joys and the frustrations of working on the short dramas with the schoolchildren—all happening right before the eyes of most of the community. He listened carefully, smiling and wincing appropriately by turn.

"I'm proud of you, Beth. I'm sure what you're doing will be used by God in ways you can't even imagine right now. God's Word never returns without fruit. That's a promise."

She smiled but admitted, "It isn't what I pictured it would be—it's been much more difficult and less inspiring than what I had envisioned. But I do think the children are learning. And that was always the point."

Molly inserted a comment once more. "An' I told her, them mommas is learnin' too."

"I'm sure that's the case," Philip agreed.

Molly retreated to the dining room, and Philip looked over at Beth with a gleam in his eyes. "I heard you had a little adventure last night," he teased. "Or maybe we should call it a misadventure." His expression assured her he was not scolding. But a chortle from Molly indicated she had returned as she now scooped leftover potatoes into a bowl. Philip glanced at Molly over his shoulder and handed the next plate to Beth.

She made slow circles over it with the dish towel as she tried to best phrase her answer. "Yes, I'm afraid I had a rather frightening experience. But I also met Mr. Russo—at his wife's grave in the forest."

Philip sent a surprised glance in her direction. "You did? Did you know about the grave?"

"No, I was just out walking and stumbled across him there. He told me a little about Colette and how she died. Such a sad story."

"Yes, it is. But he's a remarkable man."

"I agree. Miss Molly has already told me about the kind things he does to help the widows and their families."

Molly interjected, "He *is* a good man, no denyin' that."

Philip nodded. "Yes, Frank has a very good heart, and he knows how to love with his actions."

144

The conversation moved on, and Beth was wondering how to bring up the topic that had been on her mind most of last night. Then Molly dropped her apron onto its hook and excused herself, an opportunity for which Beth had been hoping.

"May I ask you," she began, her towel and the last cup held still before her, "I was wondering—is there anything being done for the men in the camp?"

Philip looked a bit startled. He paused, then asked, "Do you mean their personal needs or their spiritual needs?"

Beth found she couldn't answer his question as concisely as it was asked, so she tried another approach. "I met a young man who just joined his father in the mine. He speaks English well, but his father does not. The family is from Italy."

"You're referring to Alberto Giordano. I had heard his son would be joining him soon, but I didn't know he'd already arrived. You met the young man? Paolo, I believe?"

"Yes, Paolo. He's a very nice young man—but he's only fifteen. He has received some education, and he's clearly intelligent, with a gift for languages. It grieves me that the only life before him is likely one of toiling in the mine. It looks to me like there's little hope of achieving more."

Philip nodded.

Beth found it hard to explain all that was in her heart. "Isn't there something that can be done for him?"

There was another long pause. "It's a complicated issue, Beth," Philip said slowly. "I do understand your feelings, and I admire your tender heart. I also share your concern and, believe me, so does the district church board.

"When we first decided to begin this work, our district leaders approached the mining company. They own all the land where the camp sits, so we needed their permission to engage with them, invite them to a service. We were told that the men—the newcomers—had their own 'religion,' and we were not to confuse them by intruding with our 'Canadian brand of Christianity.' Simply put, their answer was a flat no. We could use their hall for others in the community, but not for the camp workers. Our hands have been tied." He paused a moment, staring at the plate he was working on.

"I'll admit we had hoped to reach out to them by discipling the other men of the community who worked alongside the Italians—encouraging them to share Christ's love with their peers at work. Now most of those men are gone." He stopped and shook his head. "I don't know. Maybe it isn't really that complicated. Maybe it's harder to ignore a problem that already existed, now that the majority of the miners are from across the ocean."

He handed the last plate to Beth, dried his hands on a nearby towel, and turned to lean against the work table. "I wish I knew what the answer was, Beth. I can't imagine what life is like for them. There isn't even enough space to adequately house them all anymore. When I was last there, I saw that some of them were still in tents. I think by this time they've finished building some additional housing, but it must be miserable—and now with the approach of winter . . ."

Beth had not even considered the very real concerns about housing and weather and the restrictions the mine company had put on them. "Paolo suggested to me once that he would like to teach English," she said. "If I worked with him, maybe that would help a little."

Philip's eyebrows drew together in concentration. "It might. At least it would begin to remove the language barrier that exists between them and the townspeople." He shook his head. "To be honest, though, I can't fathom a situation where it would be acceptable. The folks around here are duly concerned about safety and are not interested in inviting strange men into their midst—especially now that they've lost their husbands, their protectors. I think that would present your biggest obstacle—not the *if*, but *where?*" He looked into her eyes. "I can only tell you that if God is calling you to become involved in some way, then He'll provide the means for it to happen. And if there's any way I can help, I promise I'll do what I can."

"Has the mining company forbidden the men to come into town?"

"Frank Russo would know more about that than I do. I suspect that it's not so much a case of forbidding as a very strong suggestion. They no doubt are told it's better if they don't interfere with the life of the town—probably veiled behind some statement such as not 'making trouble.' Any miner who might do something offensive would be sent back to Italy. To be fired and sent back is a real threat. They came because they need the money for their families."

"So now the knife cuts both ways," observed Beth. "The company discourages the miners from mixing, and the town women are afraid of these men they don't know or understand."

Philip nodded. "It's really quite complicated and so sad. Here we have men on our doorstep whom we want to introduce to faith in Christ—and we can't converse with them, can't even invite them for coffee."

"But you've been to the camp?"

"I went in with Frank on a couple of occasions. Well—not really *in*. Frank had a few of the miners meet me on the opposite side of the road just across from their shacks. Not company land. Frank is gravely concerned about the men—and though he still draws a pension from the company and periodically is brought in as an experienced specialist, they don't seem to want him spending a great deal of time with the younger miners. Perhaps they feel his presence could make the men restless—more demanding of better treatment. There have been strikes at other mines. Still, Frank has a certain influence, I'm sure."

"So you don't think I will ever be able to help Paolo with an English class."

Philip hesitated and then answered, "Not as things stand currently. I've been as frustrated as you are. It seems we've come to an impasse."

"But what . . . what if something happens? Another collapse? Another accident—and they haven't heard the good news of the gospel? I'm . . . I'm afraid I'll have trouble sleeping just imagining such a disaster—both the physical one and the eternal one."

Philip shook his head, and Beth could see that he too was deeply troubled. Though she felt disheartened, she thanked Philip for being honest. There seemed to be no way for her to reach out. Even so, she determined that she would not yet give up. She would continue to pray for God to move someone—someway.

She wrote a long letter home describing the predicament of the miners, so isolated from the rest of society. But she once again found herself editing the truth. How would Mother respond to hearing about such a camp? How could she adequately describe Frank Russo? And what would Mother think about the possibility of her interaction with these men in the future? Beth wondered if her mother might not take the next train west to rescue her daughter.

She laid the letter down and pressed her hands against her face. It was a conundrum, one that was growing increasingly uncomfortable. Through her letters she wanted Mother to be reassured that Coal Valley was a safe place, one where her daughter's influence could be worthwhile and productive. Beth was convinced in her own heart that these things were true, but if the descriptions she presented were not the complete picture, was she actually being deceitful? Was she essentially conceding all independence and self-sufficiency through her feeble attempts to save Mother from worry? The guilty feelings clung stubbornly—even while she was trying so hard to work for good. . . .

CHAPTER

13

As Beth trudged along the dusty road to school on Monday, her mind was on Paolo and the rest of the miners in the rough camp outside of town. If one was not aware of their presence, it could seem they did not even exist. She wondered what it would be like to live so close to a town and yet be entirely excluded from it.

But even as she puzzled over it, she reminded herself that she was still a stranger herself despite her growing care for the people of Coal Valley. In truth, even Philip really was an outsider. Perhaps there was a reason—a good reason—why this unpleasant-sounding division was accepted by the entire town. Were the people here aware of issues of which Beth was not? Even Molly, in fact, had not brought it up. Beth knew that it would be prudent to use caution before meddling. And yet she could not help but worry about Paolo. He was a polite and articulate young man. Surely something could be done to help him. And maybe through him help the others.

Beth was entering the shadowed hallway leading into the schoolroom when she was reminded of those deep passageways into the mountain. She could not imagine what it would be like to spend one's days deep within the rugged walls of rock and timbers. No sun. No fresh air. The very thought made her feel claustrophobic.

And the dangers? Many men from Coal Valley had already lost their lives in the dreadful underground calamity. How could these replacement miners dare go back into the belly of that mine? How could their wives and families even consider letting them enter the tunnels? And young sons like Paolo . . . the very idea made Beth shiver.

As she pushed open the windows on the lovely autumn morning, she heard the sounds of her students arriving for another day of learning. It would be a perfect day to take the class on a nature hike. She wondered how the mothers would respond to such an idea and wished she'd had the foresight to ask Molly. Winter would soon be upon them, and such an opportunity might not present itself again.

With the feelings among the townspeople toward the miners' camp, though, would such an outing even be considered? Surely knowing that the miners spent their days deep within the mountain would provide the mothers confidence enough to allow such an excursion. Taking herself in hand, Beth hurried with last-minute lesson preparations before it would be time to ring the bell to call the students inside. They no doubt were enjoying every minute of the lovely fall weather and were in no hurry to leave the outdoors.

Beth glanced once more through the window and noticed Teddy and Addison engaged in an animated discussion on the other side of the street. Their hands were gesturing as part of the exchange, and their laughter was reaching Beth's ears—whatever it was must be highly amusing.

She stood gazing at them, deep in thought. *How much longer will the oldest students be allowed to be children? Already they have taken on responsible tasks as the eldest in their homes. Will they soon be called away from the schoolroom and required to take on some sort of occupation? How much longer will they have to prepare for life as adults?*

Sobered by her thoughts, she prayed, *Please, Lord—not the mines.*

It wasn't until that moment that Beth realized how much the mine disaster troubled her spirit. She had recently run across the account of another one, a slide that had occurred in 1903 at a town called Frank not too many miles away. Much of the town had been buried when the side of the mountain gave way and covered the town, and there was great loss of life. Beth tried to still her anguished heart with the truth she knew. *Yes—God is good. And God is in charge.* But in spite of her faith in Him, fear nibbled at the edges of her confidence. She wondered if her young students felt the uncertainty, the fear, as well.

And what of the miners themselves? The most frightening part was that she had no idea if they were ready to die. *What if they are not ready for eternity and no one is able or willing to share the truth with them?* Beth believed in Philip's sincere concern, but she wondered why someone who spoke Italian had not been sent here. Far better still, someone to teach them English, make friends with them, prepare them for the gospel's invitation. *Something needs to be done—and soon.*

A light rap on the outside door brought Beth up short. She lifted her hand and realized she was still holding the school bell . . . and that she had not yet rung it. She moved quickly into the hallway to the door. Her young students huddled together on the doorstep, wide-eyed and silent, staring at Beth until Sadie dared ask, "Are we havin' school today?"

Beth lifted the watch pinned to her dress and gasped. It was already fifteen minutes past class time.

"Oh my" was all she could manage. "Oh my. I am so sorry. I was lost in thought. I'm very sorry."

Sadie turned and waved a hand toward a group of boys kneeling on the ground by the bushes. "They're still playin' marbles," she informed Beth.

Beth looked again at the silent bell in her hand. "Come in," she invited the cluster of younger students before her, and gave the bell a firm shake. The boys scrambled to their feet, dusting off knees as they came. It was not long until she had all her students in their proper places, ready for the recital of the Lord's Prayer. But she did fervently hope none of the townsfolk had been watching the clock and noted the late school start.

Beth's day ended the same way it had begun—concerns for the town and for the camp so near—yet so far—were uppermost in her mind as she trudged back toward the boarding house. In whom could she confide? With all her heart Beth wished she could talk with her father, could seek his counsel. She was sure he would share her distress. Hadn't he advised her to find out what God had for her to do? Beth was becoming convinced that the task for her was much bigger than simply the classroom. Her students clearly were the main reason God had brought her to Coal Valley, but unless something more was done—something for the town and the miners—those growing up now would face the same troubles as those of their parents. In Beth's mind, the biggest need for the entire area and the one thing that would bring them together was a shared faith. But what could she do? She was just one person—and a woman. She felt helpless.

A sudden thought lifted her spirits. *Mr. Russo.* He knew both the town and the camp. He could speak both English and Italian. He was highly respected in both places. He was the common bond. If the miners could not come into the town, then she would go to them—with Frank. He would be her chaperone. Her interpreter. Her co-worker. She knew he had faith. He must be as concerned about his countrymen as she.

With a lighter step Beth hurried into the house. She would seek the very first opportunity to speak with Frank. But she would not share that fact with Molly until they'd had their discussion. If he vetoed her proposal, she would accept his decision and press the matter no further. In the meantime she would pray. In fact, she would spend time in prayer as soon as she entered her room. She would pray until Molly or Marnie called her for the evening meal. Surely God's concern was even greater than her own.

Now that she had the beginnings of a plan, Beth had felt both agitated and excited all evening. She knew she would not really be able to relax until she put the first piece of her plan in motion. Already she had spent time after the supper hour pouring over some school primers, sorting out what she might be able to use in the first English lessons for Paolo and his co-workers. She finally laid aside the books to prepare her lessons for the next day's classes.

It was almost midnight before Beth convinced herself to retire for the night. By the time she climbed into bed, she was frazzled and exhausted and wondered if she would be able to turn off all her swirling thoughts. Yet she must.

Outside her window she noted that the sky, previously bright from a full moon and a canopy of glittering stars, was now dark with a cloud cover. She could hear a wind whining among the branches of the large evergreens covering the hillside. *I hope it doesn't rain tomorrow, so Mr. Russo will be out and about,* she fretted. *We need to get started right away.* Eventually she must have relaxed enough to fall into a restless sleep, because the next thing she knew a bright light filled the window and a rolling, clamorous sound rattled the windows and seemed to shake the very foundation of the building. Beth leaped to her feet before her eyes were fully open. *It's happened! Another explosion*—and she was too late. Too late to teach them English. Too late to share the gospel. Too late . . .

Without waiting to slip on shoes she snatched up her robe and flung herself at her bedroom door.

"Wake up!" she cried into the darkness. "It's another explosion at the mine! Wake up. We need to help them."

Beth rushed down the hallway, knocking on each bedroom door, then back again, quickly lighting a candle on the hall table. "Wake up," she called once more. "It's happened again. Wake up!"

Doors began to open. Faces peered out, eyes heavy with sleep.

"What is it?" grumbled a husky voice from a dark doorway.

"An explosion," called Beth. "We've got to help them. We must get to the mine."

"An explosion? Well, even if it is, it won't do anybody much harm this time of night. Nobody's in the tunnels at this hour."

Beth had not thought of that. Was it true? "But what about the camp?" she asked. "It's not far from the entrance to the mine. We need to check," she insisted.

By now everyone in the house was astir. Teddy and Marnie appeared, rubbing their eyes and wondering what was going on. Beth took a deep breath and tried to explain as calmly as she could that she had heard a terrible explosion.

"I don't see nothin'," Walter insisted, sweeping back the hallway window curtain and squinting into the darkness without his glasses. "But I can't see much in all this rain."

And then it happened again. A flash in the sky that could only be lightning followed by a powerful, ear-splitting peal of thunder.

"That what you heard?" Henry demanded.

Beth couldn't answer. *Is that the same sound?* Was it merely thunder that had wakened her and caused her already troubled mind to jump to ridiculous conclusions?

"I . . . I don't know," she stammered. "I was asleep and I heard— I thought it was . . ."

Again a zigzag of lightning streaked across the sky followed by peals of thunder that seemed to shake the whole house.

"Well, I never!" Walter exclaimed. "Nobody's gonna sleep after all this fuss."

Beth was beside herself with embarrassment and regret. "I'm so sorry," she tried to apologize. "I—thought I— I'm so sorry. I didn't mean to . . ."

Molly pushed in and pulled Beth up against her round side as though to protect her from the irritated glares and muttering comments. "Look—it's too easy ta get spooked right now—what with the mine startin' up again after the trouble. Let's jest git on back ta bed and try fer some sleep. Nobody hurt here, so no harm done."

Grumbling to themselves, the other boarders turned back toward their rooms, and Marnie and Teddy slipped away quickly.

Beth stood dumbstruck. Molly had not removed the arm from around her waist. Beth turned to her helplessly. "I'm . . .

I'm so sorry," she said again, trying to keep from crying. "I didn't mean . . ."

"'Course not," said the older woman. "Coulda bin any one of us done the same thing. Wakin' from a sound sleep to a noise like that . . ." She was cut off by another booming round of thunder. Molly nodded her head toward the window. "Sure sounds like a blast ta me." Her arm tightened slightly. "Now ya better git on back to bed yerself. Ya got kids to teach, an' 'fore long it'll be mornin'."

Beth swallowed hard and nodded. She wondered if she would ever be able to live this down. She could imagine the dark looks that would come her way at the morning's breakfast table.

"I'm so sorry," she whispered again.

Molly said nothing in reply, simply gave Beth's shoulder a pat, then a slight push to send her on her way, blowing out the hallway candle before she departed.

As Beth moved toward her door, a flash of searing lightning lit up the world, followed by a booming roll of thunder that must have awakened the entire town. The wind lashed the downpour of rain against the windows in a new fit of fury. It was the most violent storm Beth had ever heard. Anxiously she crossed to the window for one more look at the angry night. No one—no one in his right mind would be out and about . . . and there was little chance she would find Frank in town on the morrow.

Wait! She swept the curtain back farther. *Surely I'm seeing things.* A figure was moving through the rain, leaning against the wind, head down and boots fighting for each step. *Who would be out at this hour?* The figure seemed to be moving toward the school. Fear struck her heart once again. But the unknown someone walked right on past the front door and turned the corner of the building. *Is he going up the staircase?*

Up to the Grants'? She had no idea why anyone would venture out in such weather. She shook her head and wondered if she was back to dreaming. Nothing was making sense. She had to get back to bed and try to get some sleep.

⟡

Beth dreaded facing her fellow boarders over breakfast the next morning. She wondered if they had slept as poorly as she after her ill-informed alert. She felt her cheeks burning as she slid into her usual chair, but no one even lifted his eyes. Teddy mumbled good morning as he slid in beside her, and it looked like the day was going to start as usual.

Molly came, followed by Marnie, with their breakfast. Beth took a moment to spread her napkin and bow her head for a table grace. By the time she said her silent amen, the men around the table were already filling their plates. Henry, on her left, passed on the dish without comment, and the simple meal proceeded in an almost comfortable silence.

Beth breathed a sigh of relief and settled in to try to enjoy the morning's porridge, eggs, and toast. She helped Molly and Marnie clear the dishes after the meal was over and the men had left. Even Molly had no comment about the previous night's happening. She did affirm, "'Twas a nasty storm last night. Saw some branches strewn round this mornin'. Ain't heard so much thunder for a long while. Glad it's stopped," she added, looking out the kitchen window.

Beth wondered if the comment was meant to salve her embarrassment. She was grateful as she gathered her books and supplies to begin the school day. But she had taken only a few steps off the porch when she spotted Frank Russo, his arms loaded with a bundle of freshly chopped wood. She waved a hand at him and hurried to catch up.

158

"I see you're busy, Frank, but would it be possible to stop by the school after classes are done for the day?"

For a moment he looked surprised, but then he nodded his agreement. "Yes, miss. Is there something you need'a from me right now?"

"Oh no," Beth was quick to reply. "It's not a need. Just your advice."

"Advice?" He smiled. "Nobody asks advice of this old man."

"I suspect that isn't true," Beth responded with conviction and a smile.

The elderly man's eyes twinkled. "Three thirty you let'a the kiddies go home, eh?"

Beth nodded. "Three thirty."

"I see you then," he promised and shifted the load in his arms.

She would figure out how to send Marnie home with the others so she and Frank could speak privately.

CHAPTER

14

FRANK WAS PUNCTUAL, arriving just after school was finished for the day. He stood in the classroom doorway. "I
am here, miss," he announced.

Beth greeted him warmly. "I'll admit, Mr. Russo, that I've
been distracted as I taught today—anticipating your visit and
what I'd like to discuss with you."

He helped her lift the chalkboard from its hooks and move it
into the closet. Beth talked while she pulled the alphabet letters
down from the edge of the bar counter. "I have an idea—but
I don't know if it will be possible, and I felt you were the one
who had the most familiarity with people in town as well as
the men in the camp."

He stopped pushing the large table and turned quizzically
toward her. "What'a you mean, Miss Beth?"

There seemed no better approach than to dive right in. "I'd
like to offer to teach the miners English. And Paolo, Alberto's
son, could help. That is, we would help one another. I've
already talked to Philip—Pastor Davidson. But I wanted to
speak with you before I mentioned it to anyone who actually

lives in town. I wanted to be sure that you felt it would be acceptable." She waited for him to process her words. "What do you think?"

He seemed speechless as he stared at her. "Why?" he finally managed.

Beth forced herself to slow down, to gather her thoughts before she explained anything further. "I don't want them to be left out of the community—like you were," she said. "And I know that speaking English won't change everything, but I'm convinced it will help. And—" she hoped Frank would understand—"I want them to be able to share in the church services with the rest of us. It's so important that they know about God and how much He loves us all." Beth's voice trailed away. It had all sounded so much more realistic and sensible before she had shared the plan aloud. "I know I'm new here, and that it's doubtful I'll be here for long. But I would so much like to accomplish this before my year is over."

Frank lowered himself into one of the chairs, deep in thought while his left hand, unheeded, rubbed at the stump where his right hand should have been.

Beth moved to take the seat across from him. "We would need your help, though, Mr. Russo. I don't think I could even ask Molly about it unless you were willing to be part of this—to be the chaperone whenever I would be teaching them."

He cleared his throat, and Beth could see that he was holding back tears. "I knew I would'a like you, Miss Beth. You have a good heart, like'a . . ." But his voice failed him.

Beth finished, "Maybe like your Colette?" Her own eyes were damp too.

He nodded. "She would like'a you too."

Beth reached a hand to touch his lightly. "But when I talked to Philip about it, he was concerned about where we would meet. And that might be a bigger problem than I had first thought. We can't invite the men into town—not yet, and Philip felt it would be considered inappropriate for me to spend time in the camp."

"That'sa true."

"What about meeting just across the road from the camp where, I understand, you sometimes gather with them?"

He shook his head. "No light—and the weather, it'sa no good now."

Discouragement bent her shoulders. He was right. With winter soon approaching, outside would not work.

Beth said sadly, "If we don't have a place to meet, it won't work."

"Don'ta give up yet. You have good idea."

"But where . . ." began Beth, and her words trailed off in sheer disappointment.

For a moment the man sat deep in thought, then flung his arms wide. "It'sa so simple," Frank exclaimed. "We meet at'a my place."

Frank had described his cabin as between the town and camp, making it an ideal location. "Do you think we could?" she whispered, her mind already working through the possibilities he had opened.

"It'sa not very big. But it'sa *my* cabin. I don't have to ask how I use'a my own cabin, eh?"

Beth returned his wide smile. "That would be perfect, Mr. Russo. I'll speak with Miss Molly tonight."

He stayed and chatted with her long enough to see that the room was returned to order and then excused himself with an encouraging nod. "You be doing a good job, Miss Beth."

"Thank you, Mr. Russo. Thank you so much!"

Beth followed him out the door. Just before departing,

Frank's eyes took on a mischievous shine. "Miss Beth," he said in a teasing tone, "please, can I say just'a one thing more?"

"Of course," Beth assured him.

"You said you doubted you would'a be here for long. When I came to this'a place, I planned on only short time too." He winked playfully. "An' that was'a fifty years ago."

Beth's eyes widened and she had to chuckle a bit as they said good-night.

But it was different for Frank, she told herself on the walk home. *He didn't sign a contract to serve for just one school term.* Still, the thought gave her something to ponder.

Beth knew she would have to broach the subject with Molly, perhaps the most difficult conversation yet. It seemed best to wait until supper dishes had been washed and Molly had a chance to rest with a final cup of coffee. Beth did not know the woman well enough yet to be able to predict how it would go.

To Beth's surprise, Molly was far less reluctant to discuss the endeavor than Beth had feared. Once the necessary constraints were set in place to provide for safety and propriety, Molly had more ideas to add to the plans. "You'll hafta keep them classes small since Frank's cabin ain't that large. Though small is sure to be better in the long run. But ya might get some a' the other English-speakin' men to help out. I bin thinkin' a long time that the company shoulda been teachin' 'em English all along—even before so many more come." Then she shook her head and announced, "I'll go along with ya. Now that the garden is all put up and it gets dark earlier, I can spare some time. 'Sides, gotta keep tongues from waggin'."

Beth breathed a long sigh. "That would be wonderful!"

"An' you say you talked to Pastor Philip too. Well, ain't you bin busy!"

Beth blushed and dropped her head. It felt so strange to be pressing ahead with something so far outside her normal sphere of influence. That was much more typical of Julie—to be drawing any number of others into her own plans. The thought was rather amusing. *Wouldn't Julie be surprised!*

Over the next couple of weeks, arrangements fell into place for the classes. Beth was convinced that the prayers concerning this idea were having a decided effect. Soon the first class was scheduled for a Saturday evening, and Beth was rushing to assemble something of a lesson.

In her enthusiasm and demanding activities in preparation for the new venture as well as her school and tea parties and Bible club, she refused to admit to Molly or anyone else that her throat was growing sore. By Friday morning she was coughing frequently. Rather than succumb, Beth managed to teach while sipping often on a cup of herbal tea. She was all too familiar with such respiratory symptoms—her body had frequently struggled to fight off what others seemed to take in stride. But on this occasion Beth was most frustrated with the timing. And she was determined that because of their prayers this affliction would be short-lived and incidental.

Undaunted, she and Molly met with Frank at his cabin on Friday night. Paolo and his father were also present. It was the exciting culmination of a great deal of effort, but at the same time it was all happening very quickly indeed, and Beth's foggy head made it difficult to concentrate on what each was saying. By speaking very little she hoped to deny her illness a little longer.

But she awoke Saturday morning with a swollen throat, stuffy head, and a slight fever. There was simply no alternative but to admit to Molly that she was sick. She knew from experience that once this illness had taken hold, it would only prolong her misery to ignore it. There was, in fact, little need to confess, for as soon as she began to speak Molly was alerted.

"How long yer throat bin hurtin' like that?" A practiced hand was already sweeping across Beth's forehead and cheeks.

"A couple of days," Beth mumbled, swallowing back the prickling pain.

"You shoulda said. Teddy Boy, git the afghan please. Marnie, pull the kettle forward. We'll clear out yer head over some steam, and then ya can gargle some salt water." When Teddy returned, Molly draped the blanket around Beth's shoulders. "Set down, dearie. We'll get ya feelin' better real soon. I think I got a few aspirins around here somewhere."

"No, please, Miss Molly. I don't want to waste your medication."

But Molly was already rummaging in the medicine cabinet despite Beth's protests. She slumped into a kitchen chair and pulled the blanket closer around with trembling fingers. Now that she had completely surrendered, she realized her whole body was aching and stiff.

"It's not fair," she whimpered pathetically. "We have the first class tonight."

Molly returned with a glass of water and two small pills. "Swallow," she commanded. "I'm sorry thet it come at such a bad time—but ya can't wish it away now." Once the water had begun to boil, Molly placed a steaming bowl of it on the table, added some type of liquid, and pulled a towel over Beth's head. "Now breathe it in till ya clear out yer head."

Beth, defeated, leaned forward and closed her eyes. *Why now? How can sickness strike now?*

She wasn't able to swallow down any breakfast. Molly made

some chamomile tea with honey and lemon juice for her to sip and then ordered her back up to bed. Marnie was sent to inform the guests that the day's tea party would be postponed. Alone again, Beth let tears slide unheeded down her face until she fell into a fitful sleep.

She woke shortly after lunch and was given chicken broth to sip slowly. Then Molly doled out two more precious aspirins. Following these, she crushed some dry ginger into some honey, had Beth swallow a little at a time off the spoon, and sent her right back to bed. Though she was deeply remorseful about being ill, Beth couldn't help feeling grateful for Molly's manner of treating her illness. Her mother would have been pushing nasty elixirs on her every few hours. Almost as soon as Beth laid her head down, she was sound asleep.

The remainder of the day was only a blur. Beth was vaguely aware of sounds when Molly left the house that evening. Mumbling a prayer that things would go well without her, Beth blew her nose and went back to sleep.

Sunday was equally uneventful, though she hung on every word of Molly's terse description of the previous evening. "Frances come with me—'stead'a you. There was four men— an' Frank, along with Paolo an' his dad. They did some talking—learned a few words—and seemed satisfied."

"Did Paolo teach?"

"Eh, he give some instruction in Italian, I guess. 'Cept I missed all that. Then we all said the words he told us t'gether."

Beth let the topic drop. Her head was beginning to clear. Now she could only hold out hope that she would be able to teach on Monday. Dutifully she began a letter to Mother. This time, however, Beth added more about the English classes that she had helped arrange and admitted her own disappointment that she had not been able to attend the first of them due to a cold. If Mother were to chastise her for becoming involved with foreign men and for working so hard that she had made herself ill, at least Beth knew she had been completely honest.

But it took another day for Beth to recover enough to return to her classroom. On Monday about a half hour before school was to begin, Molly asked Marnie and Teddy to deliver the message down the row of homes that class would be canceled for a day. They left the house at full gallop, like ponies set free in a spring pasture. Beth tried not to let their enthusiasm hurt her feelings.

CHAPTER

15

ℛESOLUTELY Beth hurried through her morning routine, feeling quite improved as she readied herself for another day in the classroom. Already the mornings were turning cold and gloomy in advance of winter. She hastened up the dirt street toward the schoolhouse, hunched down deep into her wool coat and pulling the collar tight around her neck. Her throat was still a little tender, but she knew she was beyond the worst.

She spent some time airing out the room, preparing her materials, and trying to light her first fire in the potbelly stove in the far corner. Having no success, she checked her watch pin. *Surely one of the older students will arrive soon and be able to help with the fire. Hopefully, no one is presuming another day off.* As she rang the hand bell with extra vigor, it echoed eerily through the misty morning air. Almost immediately her students appeared and filed in, but half-heartedly. She had the distinct feeling they were wishing she were still under the weather.

Only little Anna Noonan whispered as she shuffled past

with the others, "I'm glad God made ya better, Miss Thatcher. We been praying for ya." Beth returned her smile and felt her spirits lift a bit.

Addison soon had a nice fire in the stove. The school day began and their routine resumed. But when she moved the older students forward for their grammar lesson, Beth could sense there was something diverting their attention. Time and again she caught them casting telling glances at one another. Finally she stopped diagramming sentences on the blackboard, faced them fully, and surveyed the group.

"Would anyone care to share with me what you all find so distracting from our classwork today?"

Sets of eyes shifted around the room, watching one another to see who might have the courage to speak up. Teddy finally found his voice. "Some of 'em don't think it's right—them English lessons for the miners."

Beth answered evenly, "What do some find inappropriate about offering English lessons to people who want to learn it?"

Again, Teddy spoke for the group. "They think—leastways, their mommas think—that the new men are dangerous. An' that they'll jest start comin' into town and makin' trouble."

Beth drew up a chair for herself so she could meet their eyes from a more conversational position. "Is that what people are saying?"

"Yes'm," affirmed Bonnie. "My momma says they'll take over and be the ruin of our town."

Beth sighed, grateful at least that they trusted her enough to tell her what was going on. "What are you afraid they will do?"

Answers were tossed forward from every direction. "Steal!" "Get drunk." "Gamble." "Cuss." "Start fires." "Take our food." And then one little voice stuttered, "I d-d-d-don't want 'em to t-t-t-take me away to the w-w-w-woods."

"Oh, my dears!" Beth scooted her chair closer to them, motioning the younger ones to come forward and stand nearby so that she could talk to all the students. Jonah, the tiny stutterer, approached her side and Beth slid an arm around him. "These are men, fathers with wives and children. They're no different than all the people you've ever known. Their families cannot be with them right now, but they are working hard to send money back home to them. Most people are good and kind and helpful. I think you know that already." She searched their faces for acknowledgment of her words, reaching to tousle hair and brush a cheek. Her voice grew solemn. "But what do we know? How many people don't ever sin and do wrong things?"

For a moment the question seemed to puzzle them, and then Marnie whispered, "All people do wrong things sometimes."

"That's right, Marnie. We *all* have sinned sometimes. And so do those miners. But God loves them, and Jesus died to save them too—at the very same time He died to save all of us in this room. God knows them inside and out just like He knows you. He knew them when they were your age—at six—and ten—and thirteen—and sixteen. God even knows their mothers and fathers and brothers and sisters. You know what else God knows?" Beth let the question hang a moment. "He knows how much they miss their own families. Imagine having to move far away from everyone you know and go someplace where people don't even understand your language. Just imagine how scary that would be."

The room had become very quiet. Looking into their faces, so young and full of innocence, she felt compelled to add carefully, "Now, please listen to me. I want you to understand that these men are just like men you've known—the kind of people they are has nothing to do with what language they speak. But

I also want you to remember that they are still strangers to you. I am *not* saying that your mothers are wrong when they make rules regarding people with whom you're unfamiliar—rules such as 'Don't go to the camp.' Your mothers want to keep you safe. You must obey all the things they tell you, because those things are for your own good. Do you understand the difference?"

Beth remembered all her own mother's rules and understood a little more clearly the difficulty of protecting a child without causing the boy or girl to feel smothered. She wanted her students to view the men as ordinary people. At the same time she herself could not fully trust strangers without due caution, particularly where the children were concerned.

Beth was struggling to phrase these thoughts well, but she could see that the children were wrestling with what seemed to be conflicting information. She now understood that it was a lot simpler to teach prejudice. Children could grasp much more easily characterizations that were simply all good or all bad. The circle of children standing around her was growing restless.

Then she had a new idea. "Let's talk about Mr. Russo. You all know Mr. Russo, don't you?"

A few nodded in recognition. Finally Georgie Sanders explained, "Sure. The man that gots only one hand." Beth winced at his blunt words, but instantly every child acknowledged which man was being discussed.

"All right, Mr. Russo is also from Italy, just like the miners—but he came long ago. He speaks English now, but he didn't at first. You all know what a kind man he is—how he shares and helps out in our town."

Maggie Frazier chimed in, "He give us some berries. An' he brought meat fer the Blanes. Didn't he, Levi?"

"He did," Levi was quick to acknowledge. "It was some deer meat, and he shot it clean through the head so there wasn't no buckshot in the meat parts a'tall."

Some of the little girls turned squeamish, and Beth hurried to change the subject. "Well, suppose the other men who don't speak English are like Mr. Russo—kind and good, but when you don't know someone, you have to use discretion—that means good judgment, wisdom. You have to get to know people and learn which ones you can trust."

Thomas called out, "I trust Ol' Man Stub, that's fer sure."

"Yah, me too," others agreed.

"Children, listen, please," Beth said, her head spinning. "That's not a nice way to refer to Mr. Russo."

"Thet's what Momma calls him."

And from the back, "Thet's what *everybody* calls him!"

Beth shooed them back to their seats and stood before them, hoping to bring things back under control. She looked around at their faces. "We want to speak about others in the same way that we would want others to speak about us. Do you remember the Golden Rule, 'Do unto others as you would have them do unto you'? That means calling others by a name they would like. I would prefer you use my name rather than call me Old Miss School Teacher."

"But you ain't old!"

Beth determined to make one more attempt and then let the matter rest. "I would be unhappy if someone referred to my grandfather by the name 'Old Man Thatcher.' I would want them to show respect to him by using an appropriate title—saying 'Mr.'—or I would call him 'Grandpapa.' That's why we use titles that convey respect. Do you see?"

"Yes'm" came back the chorus.

And before anyone could pipe up with another comment,

Beth said, "Now, it's time we moved on with our lessons." She was relieved that the difficult discussion was over, but she was afraid she may not have explained it quite as well as it might have been. She whispered a prayer that God would open the little hearts to what He wanted them to hear.

After school, Beth felt depleted in body and soul. She hurried home to help with dinner and prepare what still needed to be done for the evening Bible club. The story they would dramatize was about Moses and the burning bush, and she still had narration to copy into parts. Had Molly not insisted she eat, she would not have taken the time. She had still not fully regained her appetite since her illness. Or her strength.

Beth felt the evening went fairly well. By reading the Bible stories aloud, the children were becoming familiar with Scripture, and despite the fact that they were clearly enjoying themselves, both their reading and oral skills had shown vast improvement. Additionally, most of them were much more comfortable in front of others. As Beth pushed the company hall's chairs back into straight rows after Bible club was finished, she knew that all the hubbub was worthwhile. If only she could manage to feel rested once more.

Then she noticed that Frank had joined Molly and Frances in setting things back in order. She had not even seen him among the audience of mothers.

"Hello," she called down the row. "Thanks so much for helping."

He smiled his acknowledgment. They worked together until the room could be left as it had been found—perhaps even a little tidier. Then they moved toward the door.

"I'm so sorry I missed the first of the English classes, Frank.

Molly told me a little about how it went, but she doesn't exactly—well, she doesn't exactly gush."

Frank chuckled. "Miss Molly, she dont'a waste no words." Then he quickly added, "How you feeling, Miss Beth?"

"I'm much better now, thank you."

"Good. That'sa good."

"So . . . how do *you* think class went on Saturday?"

"It was'a good beginning. Paolo, he did a fine job teaching the men. I think'a the men, they will all come back." Then he broke into a wider grin. "An' Paolo's papa, he was'a so proud."

Just then little Emily Stanton rushed back into the room, obviously in search of something she had left behind.

"Little one," called Frank. "Is that what'a you need?" He pointed toward a small jacket that he had laid on a table beside the door.

Emily nodded her relief. Then she smiled warmly and said, "Thank you, Grandpa Stub."

Beth felt a shiver run all through her. She dared not even move. *Is that what little Emily gleaned from the conversation today?* How had things gone so awry? Beth slowly lifted her face toward Frank's. His wrinkled countenance was still frozen in a smile, but there were tears forming in his eyes. Beth reached for his arm, not able to speak.

Emily snatched up the jacket and rushed out of the room. At last Beth found words. "I'm so sorry, Mr. Russo. I don't think—I'm *sure* she didn't mean to be cruel."

He waved away her apology and brushed at his eyes self-consciously. "No, no, Miss Beth. It'sa not what you think." She could tell he was also struggling for words, and she forced herself to wait while he gained his composure. "It'sa—" He smiled again and cleared his throat. "It'sa the first time I been called grandpa." Then he turned toward her. "I like'a the sound."

174

For one moment Beth stood silent—rethinking and sorting his statement. She realized how tenderly the simple, childish address to the elderly man had been received, and her breath caught in her throat. When she felt controlled enough again to speak she patted his arm. "It suits you well."

From that moment on, it seemed all of the children caught on to the new nickname, referring to Frank as Grandpa. Beth was pleased with any reference to Grandpa Frank or Grandpa Russo, but she insisted they choose one or the other rather than allowing any reference to Stub—no matter how graciously it had been accepted from the little girl by the dear man.

CHAPTER

16

ONE AFTERNOON the students returned from lunch pushing and shoving more than the usual rough-housing before yielding to the next lessons. Beth rose and called for order, and they calmed down. But as their faces turned toward her, Daniel Murphy called out, "Hey, Miss Thatcher, I seen a man goin' inta Miss Molly's. He was carryin' a big box. Bonnie and me asked him who it was for, an' the man said you."

"That's right, Miss Thatcher," his older sister, Bonnie, chimed in. "It was kinda long and a funny shape."

"Thank you, Daniel and Bonnie. But we have work to do. Let's all turn our attention back to our assignments."

However, as much as Beth wanted to pretend she wasn't excited about the idea of a package at Molly's house, she found she could think of little else. *Probably from Mother—or maybe Father*. But in their most recent letters, there had been no questions regarding what Beth might lack. On the other hand, Christmas was not far off. Perhaps it was an early present. And would she be able to wait till then? Probably not, she decided, unless it was so specified on the package.

176

The afternoon dragged, and she felt as impatient as the children to get their work completed for the day. When at last she was able to walk home and into the front hall, Molly met her with eyes dancing. "You got yerself a package."

Beth returned playfully, "Yes, I know. Daniel and Bonnie informed me." She looked around. "Where is it?"

Molly pointed to the dining room and trailed through the doorway behind Beth. The mysterious parcel lay on the table, still wrapped loosely in plain brown paper. Beth recognized the long, oddly shaped outline immediately and rushed forward in disbelief, stripping away the paper unceremoniously. "Where did it come from? Who brought it? What did they say?"

Molly had not expected such a robust reaction. "Well, dearie, he didn't say nothin'. Just dropped it off and was gone. What is it?"

But Beth could not speak right then. She was opening the snaps on the lid and carefully lifting an instrument from its case. She knew it immediately, but she turned it over regardless to trace the engraved initials. Her eyes were already dripping tears.

"Bless me! It's a violin," Molly exclaimed.

Beth choked out, "It's mine. The one that was stolen." Her knees went weak and she sank into a nearby chair, violin cradled on her lap, trying to recover from the surprise of it.

"There a note or somethin'?" Molly's hands searched the discarded paper, finally finding a small envelope. "Here." She thrust it toward Beth, but her hand was waved away.

Beth's eyes were still clouded with tears. "You read it. I can't even see right now, Molly."

Molly pulled the card from its envelope and read slowly, "Dearest Elizabeth . . ."

Beth knew immediately whom it was from and dropped her

face into her hands, a sob catching in her throat. *Edward—he's still trying to set right what happened.* After a moment she composed herself and Molly read on. "I hope this letter finds you well. I have searched for some time to recover your violin. Many of my fellow officers throughout the province have aided in my search, and with God's help, I know, I was able to locate it in a pawn shop. It is with a grateful and contrite heart that I return it to you at last. With fondest affection, Edward."

Molly pulled out a handkerchief from inside her sleeve and passed it to Beth. "It's clean—wipe up," she instructed, but then seemed to decide against prodding Beth for any further explanation. She passed her rough hand tenderly over Beth's hair and turned toward the kitchen, leaving the hankie in Beth's trembling hands.

At last Beth placed the violin back in its case, gathered up all the scraps of wrapping paper, and carried it all upstairs to her room. Her mind was spinning with questions no one would be able to answer. She would write to Edward. She would tell him how much it meant to have the violin returned. And she would try to express how grateful she was that he had worked so diligently to set things right again. *If only I could find an address for him*, she thought. With the compass safely tucked away in a drawer, and the violin recovered, he had accomplished the impossible. She could only imagine the effort it had cost him.

After dinner, Beth hurried back to her room and reverently opened the case again. A few trial tones and she soon had the strings tightened and tuned. Then she cradled the end in its familiar position beneath her chin, closed her eyes, and drew several long, sweet notes. Holding it again felt completely natural. Playing it was like a conversation with an old friend. Beth lost herself in the rise and fall of her favorite melody.

She did not even notice when Marnie slipped into the room, slid down to the floor, and curled against the wall beside the open door to listen. As the notes of a sonata by Mozart faded away Beth was startled to hear Marnie whisper, "That's real pretty."

"I . . . I didn't hear you come in," Beth said, voicing the obvious.

"You're real good at that, Miss Thatcher."

"Thank you, darling."

"Can ya bring it tomorrow? An' play for all the other kids?"

Beth nodded. "Yes, I can do that."

"Oh yeah," Marnie added, "an' Miss Molly said to ask you to come an' play downstairs."

Beth was happy to agree.

The next morning, the students were truly excited to see what their teacher produced from the strange-shaped carrier. Raising the instrument into position, she was soon playing one request after another of the hymns and songs that the children knew. She could tell that her fingers were clumsy and had lost some intonation accuracy—but she promised herself that she would devote herself again to practicing. *I know I can fit it in between the other things I'm doing.*

<hr />

By the time the students arrived at Bible club that night, it seemed that everyone had been discussing the arrival of her violin. Several of the mothers approached her as a group, clearly with some request they had come up with between them.

"Miss Thatcher, we're thinking you should do a Christmas concert—with the kids."

"Yah, they never bin in one before—an' now that they're so used ta bein' on stage an' all, I think they'd do real good."

"An' be sure to play your violin too," Emily's mother added enthusiastically.

The idea for a school program had not come to Beth, but she smiled around at the little group and agreed that it had merit. Not only would this be beneficial for her students, but it would also be a way to reach out to those in the community who had not been attending church, including the company men. On the other hand, she knew what Molly would say— what with teaching and grading, Bible club, tea parties, and English lessons, she was hardly giving her body a chance to fully recover from her recent illness. However, Beth thought of the locket containing Father's verse and renewed her determination not to allow physical weakness to come before an opportunity to do something good during the brief time she would be in their midst. She knew well enough by now how much her students would enjoy a chance to perform, this time in front of a broader audience. So Beth set to work immediately, gathering speaking parts and songs that could be joined together to make a simple program.

Upon introducing the idea during class the next day, she found the children wildly enthusiastic. Their own ideas flowed out unrestrained. This would be a chance to use the musical instruments she had brought. They could have costumes. They could have snacks. Who would be Mary? Who would be baby Jesus? David Noonan offered his baby brother, only one month old, for the job. Suddenly Beth was working hard just to keep things manageable. Preparations began immediately, using the last hour of each school day to practice and prepare. Only two weeks remained before their performance. It would be a whirlwind getting everything ready in time.

However, the children set to work with a will. This would be the first drama that would call for a simple set and basic costumes. With a little help from Grandpa Frank, they scoured the town for scrap wood, and the older boys framed up a primitive stable. Lacking proper boards to cover the whole frame, they attached rows of tree branches instead. The sides took on the look of a cabin, while the roof was formed from a lovely canopy of aromatic pine branches. Beth thrilled to see what they had accomplished with their own skill and imagination.

Teddy and Addison took the lead, organizing the ragtag crew and doing most of the heavy lifting. They seemed to relish the opportunity, and the work was nearing completion in no time. However, one evening just as the project was drawing to a close, Teddy was quieter than usual at dinner. With eyes diverted, he withdrew to his room immediately afterward. Beth cast a curious glance after him and then toward Molly. Little escaped the notice of the older woman.

"Do you think he had a fight with Addison?" Beth suggested later as she scraped the plates for washing.

Molly shook her head. "Thet pair don't fuss much. I wonder if it ain't that Teddy Boy's gettin' sick. I'll check on him after I'm done here."

"I can go check now," offered Beth.

"Yeh, you go—an' see where Marnie's gone too. Tell her the water's ready fer her to wash."

Beth had just mounted the stairs when she heard whispering around the corner. Instinctively she paused.

"Ya need to tell Miss Molly—or someone." It was Marnie's voice, pleading. Her tone brought instant alarm to Beth.

"Don't you say nothin'. It'll just git us in trouble."

"Yer in trouble now!"

"No I ain't. Long as we keep our mouths shut no one'll know we heard."

"I don't like it none."

"Trust me. Let it pass. Maybe he'll change his mind and . . ." His voice faded as the pair moved farther down the hall. Beth's pulse sped up in alarm. She heard a door close.

"Marnie," Beth called, and quickly she moved toward Teddy's door. Marnie's head poked out. "Molly's ready for you to wash dishes." The girl scooted past Beth and down the stairs.

Beth stood for a moment, considering whether or not to talk with Teddy about what she had overheard. After wrestling with it awhile, she felt it would be best to keep a watchful eye instead.

She did knock softly on his door, still open a bit. When he had pulled it wide, she asked gently, "Molly and I are wondering if you might be ill. Are you feeling well, Teddy?"

For a moment his eyes rose to meet hers. "I'm all right."

She pressed again, "Are you sure? We'd like to help if we can."

His face turned away. "Naw, I'm fine."

One last time she urged, reaching out to touch his shoulder. "Well, if you change your mind, I'm always ready to listen. Molly too."

Even as she included the troubled youth in her prayers before retiring, the single word that worried her most was *he*. If Beth had heard a name, perhaps she would better be able to keep vigilant.

                        ❧

All too quickly, the night of the performance arrived. It had been set for two weeks before Christmas, on the Saturday before their last week of school. Most of the mothers had helped with the preparations and were now buzzing around the stage, setting out props in their appropriate places and making last-minute fixes to angel costumes. The students themselves were a mass of nerves, chattering and shoving at one another. Beth managed to herd them to their places on the first two rows of chairs and then stepped forward to introduce the event.

As she glanced around the room, she was very pleased with the turnout. All of the school families were in attendance, as well as Helen Grant from the pool hall and the Coulters from the company store. In the middle of the room several of the mine company officers were seated together. Beth spotted Frank and Philip, and just as she finished speaking, she noticed Jarrick enter quietly from the back and take a seat beside Philip. There were even more people than she had dared to hope, though she forced away her disappointment that Edward had not made a surprise appearance.

Thinking of Edward, she remembered a recital in which she had performed at the age of twelve. He had been seated in the center of the second row. When Beth had taken her position on the stage with her violin, she had been annoyed to see him there, expecting that he would make faces or cause her to lose her concentration just for the sheer enjoyment of embarrassing her. Instead, more than anyone else in the audience, he had watched with admiration and amazement as she had played. Beth could still picture his young face, the green eyes fixed on her, not a hint of movement until she had finished. And then he had stood first, applauding with vigor.

"Elizabeth," he had said afterward with boyish enthusiasm, "I never heard anybody play like that. Bet you even made God smile." Strange that having forgotten them for so long, the words would come back to her now.

At first all went well. Luela recited a poem almost flawlessly, followed by a song from the five youngest in their school. Then little Jonah, standing with the other shepherds, managed to recite his lines with only a little stuttering and received an encouraging round of applause. All was progressing smoothly, and even a little cry from the manger brought only smiles as the baby's sister hurried to the stage to tend to her little brother.

But then Georgie Sanders faltered while trying to recite his piece, and it looked like he played up to the audience to cover his embarrassment. The laughter he received brought Anna Noonan to tears as she attempted to say her lines after him, and she promptly left the stage to seek shelter in her mother's arms. By far the biggest blunder, however, came just as Beth finished playing the last strains of "Silent Night." Marnie accidentally stumbled on her way across the stage, knocking the little Christmas tree to the floor. Colored balls rolled in all directions, and laughter again filled the room. Beth felt herself shrinking back in embarrassment . . . until she saw the look on Marnie's face and quickly rushed to her aid, assuring her that they would pick everything up later.

With one final hymn, the whole evening came to a close. Beth shut her eyes in resignation. She had so badly wanted it to be special for everyone. It was such a disappointment to have failed.

To her surprise, applause erupted, loud and long and sincere, as the audience stood to their feet. All through the room smiling faces affirmed that they had in fact enjoyed the performance. Beth was astonished, yet grateful. She began to recognize through their eyes what had been accomplished. They were appreciative—not critical. It was the children themselves, rather than the quality of their performance, that had won them over—missteps and all.

Pleasant relief swept through her as she made a little speech of dismissal, wishing the audience a most blessed Christmas. Then she saw Frank slowly raise his hand. Beth was quick to publicly recognize her dear friend. "Yes—Mr. Russo, do you have something you'd like to say?" Those around him hushed, and the crowd followed suit.

He stood slowly to his feet. "I . . . I was'a wondering, Miss Beth. Do you know the song 'O Holy Night'?"

Beth nodded.

"Could'a you—would'a you bless us with the playing, miss?"

There was a murmur of agreement, and those who had already stood to depart sank back down. Beth could feel each expectant gaze turning toward her. She felt a bit disconcerted as she again picked up the violin, checked the strings, and tucked the instrument into position.

As the first rich notes rose above the spellbound crowd, something happened deep within Beth's soul. It was no longer simply a beautiful song—it was a message. A message straight from her heart to these villagers. But it was even more personal than that. It was a message straight from her God to her own weary soul. She closed her eyes and pictured the night of long ago, the night of "stars brightly shining," the "night of our dear Savior's birth."

As Beth played, the words resounded through her mind. *"Truly He taught us to love one another: His law is love and His gospel is peace."* Never had she felt so at one with a piece of music as she did at this moment. By the time she reached the swelling chorus, she played with tears running down her cheeks. *"Christ is the Lord. O praise His name forever! His pow'r and glory evermore proclaim."* The music floated upward in rising, joyous thanksgiving. *"His pow'r and glory evermore proclaim."*

As the last strains of the instrument echoed through the hall, there was complete silence. Even the children did not stir. Beth lowered the violin rather quickly to bend her face and conceal the raw emotion written upon it.

It was Frank who broke the spell of silence. With un-ashamed tears rolling down his own cheeks, he stood to his feet. "Bravo! Bravo!" he cried, clapping his good hand against the other wrist. Others quickly joined in the applause. But as she watched him, Beth saw Frank lift his eyes upward and raise his hand toward the heavens. It was God to whom he was giving praise—not to Beth and her violin. She took a deep breath and a few steps backward, thanking God for the gift of music that was able to convey the wonder of His greatest Gift to these villagers of Coal Valley.

Beth was engulfed in compliments from those who crowded around her after the performance, thanking her for the evening. But what she realized they were actually grateful for was *hope*. She knew that things had not really changed. Their Christmases still would be skimpy if one imagined heavily laden tables or shimmering gifts with fancy bows. But they had just proclaimed with her something far more significant. "Christ is the Lord." What a wondrous difference that made in the lives of those who believed it. Beth silently prayed it would be so.

Gradually the families gathered into smaller groups and departed together, seeming reluctant to leave the warmth of community that hung about the room. The children in particular, who called a last good-bye to Grandpa Frank and received warm wishes or a pat on the head in return, left with smiles and reluctant steps.

As the last ones closed the door behind them, Beth took a deep breath and looked about. Everyone had pitched in to straighten the room and put things back in order, and the stage was cleared of everything but the Christmas tree and the manger. Philip had requested those items remain for the church service the next morning. There were only her own belongings to gather and carry home. Suddenly Beth felt extremely weary, and she sank into a chair.

She was startled by a movement out of the corner of her eye and quickly turned her head to see Jarrick standing in the shadows. He seemed almost shy as he approached. "That was a most enjoyable evening," he complimented quietly.

Beth let out a deep sigh and motioned him toward a nearby chair. "Thank you. I would say at times it teetered on the brink of disaster, but I suppose it did not actually fall apart."

He chuckled as he sat down, and Beth appreciated the warmth of his good humor. "I've seen worse kids' presentations. Shucks, I've been *the cause* of much, much worse. You've only to ask my mother." Beth joined in his laughter.

"But seriously," he continued, "if it were my child who participated in the program tonight, I would be convinced that they have a wonderful teacher deeply devoted to them."

"To him," Beth corrected. "Or to her."

"I . . . I'm not sure . . ."

"If your child were in the program, the teacher would be devoted to that parent's child—singular."

Understanding dawned on his face, and she added with a smile, "Sometimes it's difficult to stop teaching and correcting, I suppose."

Jarrick eyed her solemnly. "That . . . that final piece you played . . . Beth, it was—it was magnificent. It will resound through my mind over and over as I wait for Christmas, that holy night. I know it will. Thank you, Beth. I admit, I was rather dreading Christmas this year. Being so far from family and friends, I was already feeling . . . alone. I guess

I was forgetting that the most important Person is always present."

Beth nodded. "I've had some of the same feelings" was all she could manage in response. "I've been missing my family dreadfully."

"I understand. My own family is back in Manitoba—not really the East—but still pretty far from here. I haven't seen them for almost a year—well, last Christmas to be exact. My sister writes often, and I think the family counts on her to maintain contact."

Beth shifted in her chair, hoping to learn more about him but wanting to be discreet. "Does your family farm there?"

"Actually, no. My granddad worked for the Hudson's Bay Company, but my father became a preacher instead. I think my younger brothers will probably farm, though. They were hiring themselves out to neighbors when I left. I spent some time trying to convince them to come west and work for one of the big ranches out on the prairie—until I noticed the look in my mother's eye. Then I thought I'd better leave well enough alone. Besides, Laura's last letter said that my brother Will has quite a special 'friend' now—so I don't suppose one could coax him anywhere."

"Your mother must miss you terribly." Beth was imagining what a void his absence would create. "Couldn't you make the trip home this year?"

"No," he sighed. "There's just too much happening around this region right now."

"Oh?" Beth wanted more details, but chose to rein in her curiosity.

It was Jarrick's turn to shift in his seat. He changed the subject. "It must be a relief to get the play behind you." His brow furrowed and he added, "You do look quite fatigued, though, Beth. Is it all right if I mention that?" He studied her. "All the responsibility you have seems to be draining you somewhat. Will you get a chance to rest now?"

Beth was usually ready with an offhand answer to evade such questions, but she found it difficult to adopt a casual demeanor in the face of his sincere, attentive expression. She sighed. "The truth is, I do need a rest. In just one more week we'll begin Christmas break, and I'll be able to sleep as much as I like then."

His eyebrows lifted, but he scooped up most of her items on the chair between them and rose to his feet. "Come on," he said. "Let me walk you home. It might be the only way I can help lighten your load."

CHAPTER

17

MORNING CAME FAR TOO EARLY for Beth. The persistent tensions and activities of the night before and the weeks leading up to the program had managed to knot the muscles in her neck and shoulders. She found herself wishing for a hot bath, but not enough to go to the trouble of hauling water to the tiny bathing room and its galvanized tub. She managed only to lug a scant bucket of hot water up to her room. So instead of a good soak, she repeatedly dipped her washcloth in the basin, wrung it out, and draped it around her aching neck. It would have to do for now. She refused to request an aspirin of Molly, ashamed at how many tablets her ailments had already consumed. Perhaps soon the store would have some in stock, as she intended to replace them.

Philip would be conducting their service—the last before Christmas actually arrived in just under two weeks, when he was scheduled to preach at one of his other locations. Beth felt a twinge of disappointment at having to share his services on Christmas. But Molly, instead of complaining, suggested that the ladies from town meet over the holidays to pray for their sister churches.

So Beth was determined to make the best of the early celebration at their service today. She pushed aside her aches and prepared to worship with a surrendered heart, still so grateful for the way God had been with them during last night's performance.

She filed into their familiar row of seats, following Molly, Marnie, and Teddy. Someone had already redecorated the Christmas tree, so its ornaments hung neatly again. The manger, too, had been given a fresh armful of hay, a swaddled dolly tucked neatly into it—not nearly as precious a sight as Charlotte Noonan's baby. Beth looked around at all the familiar faces and, encouraged, realized how many more were in attendance now than were at her first service in Coal Valley.

Jarrick appeared at the end of the row, questioning with his eyes if he would be able to join her. Beth nodded and smiled an invitation, and he slid in beside her.

She soon lost herself in the words of the carols and the Scripture readings. She prayed with a heart overflowing in gratitude for the gift of a Savior and the hope He had purchased with His own life. She prayed also for the community, which had come to mean so much to her and with whom she could share in this Christmas celebration. She added a prayer for the young man seated next to her, for his family and the Christmas celebrations that would occur so far from him this year.

Philip's message was particularly moving and somewhat unexpected—more of a testimony than a sermon. He spoke of his childhood and the difficulties he had faced because of his broken home. Beth's heart immediately went out to the man. She had not heard any of his personal story before this.

As a youth, he told them, he had made some poor choices, involving himself with those who drew him further away from the church and his family. And then, finding himself at his darkest moment hiding from trouble and frightened that he might have sunk so low he could not recover, he had turned back to the faith of his childhood—a faith that his grandmother had modeled despite the failings of his own parents.

And God restored him, he said, looking around at the congregation. He admitted solemnly that it had not been an easy road—that he'd had debts to pay from items he had stolen and repairs on property he had damaged. But he testified that, looking back, he would not have changed even the most difficult aspects of the restitution process—through it all, Christ had been glorified in his life. The pain he had experienced had led to a surrender he doubted could have been so complete if he had not been through so much beforehand. Philip professed clearly that the most cherished gifts he had ever received were forgiveness and redemption because of Jesus.

After the service, Beth was pleased to find out once more they would share a meal with Philip and Jarrick. Molly had prepared a lovely pre-Christmas dinner—a ham roast steaming with a smoky maple glaze and scalloped potatoes. There was fresh-baked bread, her own dill pickles, and baked green beans in creamy mushroom sauce.

The company-men boarders had already ridden the coal train out of the mountains to join their families for Christmas. Philip and Jarrick chatted with two supervisors who remained, the ones responsible for shutting down the mine during the next week.

Jarrick asked them, "How close are you to heading out yourselves? I'm sure your families will be anxious to have you home again."

Pat reached for another thick slice of bread. "It'll take a few days for us to be sure things here are locked up proper," he said, spreading butter liberally. "But if it goes well, we'll be driving out on Thursday—'course, that's only if the road stays clear."

"That's a week before Christmas. I'm sure you're ready for a break."

The men exchanged nods. "You bet we are."

Beth interjected quietly, "What do the miners do for Christmas?"

"Huh?" Sid's face revealed his surprise; clearly he had given no thought to them.

Undaunted, Beth repeated, "What do the miners do—the men who stay here, whose families are far away?"

An awkward silence hung over the room. Molly eventually said in her direct way, "They stay here. Got no other choice."

"Hmm," Beth answered, and let the matter drop.

After dinner while the dishes were being removed to the kitchen, Philip stopped Beth, a quizzical expression on his face. "You seem pensive. I have a feeling you had more to say on the topic of the miners. What is it you might be cooking up now?" But his tone was friendly.

Beth sighed. "Nothing, really. I was just thinking that it's a shame not to share some kind of Christmas with them."

Philip had an eager look in his eye. "Then how about a service for the miners? Is that what you were thinking?" His own questions seemed to prompt a flood of ideas. "I wonder if the villagers are comfortable enough by now to allow such an event to take place. The company has already given permission for the church to meet in the hall on Sundays—even with the bosses away. Since there's nothing planned here during my absence, perhaps some of you could put together a special Christmas morning service for them."

Beth was torn—wanting badly to be able to accomplish such a feat, but not certain her strength would hold out through another busy week. In fact, the very idea made her want to sit down and cry. She was dreadfully tired.

Philip looked intently at her. "I'm sure there would be many who would help out," he suggested. "And it wouldn't be as complicated as the children's program—just music and reading the Christmas story. I'm sure Frank would lead the readings—he could share them in Italian." Philip was growing increasingly enthusiastic. "He can even help with the music. Frank plays violin too. Did he tell you that?"

"What?" Beth stared at him in shock. Not only was it hard to comprehend that a miner would be in possession of a violin, but to be able to play it with only one hand . . . "Now you're just teasing me," she said.

Philip shook his head. "I'm very serious, Beth. He played for years—long before he lost his hand. And the fact that his right hand was the one to be crushed was a particularly difficult blow. But he's able to strap the bow to his wrist and his left still works the strings. Frank rigged the contraption himself. As I mentioned before, he's a most remarkable man."

"Why didn't he say something to me?" she asked, feeling just a bit hurt.

"Well, I think he would have felt he was stepping on your toes—to mention he played just as you were taking on the role of accompanist for the children."

Could this be something Frank and I share? Is there a chance to play together? The possibility was delightful.

"I'll speak with him tomorrow," she whispered.

Jarrick crossed the room to join them. "What secrets are you two guarding?" he asked with a twinkle in his eye. Noticing Beth's expression, he sobered and said, "You look rather shaken, Beth. I hope there's nothing wrong." He reached out to grasp her arm. "Would you like to sit down?" But she shook her head.

Philip chuckled. "Well, Jack, I've just been telling Beth that Frank Russo still plays violin, and she's having a very difficult time believing me."

"Well, that *is* a surprising bit of news."

"I suggested she might do a special Christmas service for the miners. As you recall, Beth is concerned about their being on their own for the holiday."

Jarrick's gaze swept over her face. "Actually, I think that's too much to ask of someone who's expended much of her energy in preparing for the last event." He turned back to Philip. "I don't mean to overstep my bounds, but I'm afraid adding another Christmas will tax her beyond what is prudent. Don't you think that would be too much, Beth?"

Philip was quick to agree, "Of course, if it's too overwhelming for you, Beth, it was only an idea. Perhaps another time— when you're feeling more rested."

Beth glanced back and forth between them, dismayed that these two men were making their own pronouncements on her ability to recover from ordinary fatigue and forge ahead. *Having a simple church service would not be much additional work,* she told herself in some indignation. *If something can be accomplished for these miners who have no one else with whom to share Christmas, it is more than worthy of pursuing.*

"I think it's a very good idea," she answered evenly, drawing her arm away from Jarrick. "I'll speak with Molly about it later tonight." Both pairs of eyes watched her closely as Beth excused herself and retreated to the kitchen.

Later in the afternoon Beth drafted another letter to Mother. With steely conviction, she admitted to her lingering illness and the hardships of preparing for the Christmas program. She also enthused about how much God had blessed it for so many in attendance. And then she asked for prayer that she would be strong enough to accomplish one more event before Christmas.

"There," she whispered as she sealed the envelope. "It's honest. She knows I'm not quite back to full health, and she knows I'm working too hard. That's the worst one yet. I can only imagine how she'll respond to that."

It took surprisingly little convincing to obtain permission for the miners to have a Christmas service in the company hall. The English lessons had begun to have their effect, bridging the gap between town and the camp. It gave the residents a reason to be concerned about the welfare of the miners who lived so near to them. Soon Frances had enlisted the aid of some of the women to bake and decorate. Beth was more than surprised when they agreed to allow the children to help serve refreshments. This was far more than she had hoped.

Deciding on an approach to Frank, however, had seemed more difficult than Beth had expected. Suddenly she felt reticent asking about his musical abilities, still wondering why he had chosen not to disclose the talent to her. But he agreed immediately to participate, very pleased along with Beth about the positive response from the families in town. She learned it would be no surprise to any of the miners that he played the violin. They had listened to him often as he lifted their spirits with his gift of music.

Beth awoke to another busy week of teaching. Besides the usual classroom work with her students, her Monday evening was spent in English lessons, Tuesday and Thursday were club nights—the last before their Christmas break—and Wednesday evening had been the only time for rest, such as it was. Beth had spent it with Molly, organizing tableware for Sunday morning's refreshments. Friday involved another English lesson in the evening, and it was also the last day of teaching before Christmas break.

Saturday morning Beth insisted on hosting the last group of students—the youngest of them all—for tea. Although tempted, she could not possibly see her way to postpone the event. They all looked forward to their turn at tea. She smiled when she overheard the children reminding one another about simple things—like boys needing to hold chairs for girls to be seated, or asking for the cookies to please be passed instead of reaching across the table. They were learning. And the best part, it seemed to elevate their opinion of others and give them confidence.

Saturday night was devoted to setting up the hall and practicing the songs Beth and Frank would accompany. He was in charge of all of the readings and had chosen hymns familiar to both cultures.

As they stood at the front of the room for their initial rehearsal, Beth watched in awe at how well Frank had adapted to the violin's makeshift apparatus. "How beautiful!" she gasped.

"It was'a my great-grandpapa's," he informed her proudly, assuming she had been speaking of the instrument. "He played with the symphony in Milan. When I was'a just a small boy in Italy, he saw my love for the music. He let'a me hold it—such a precious thing. He showed'a me how to search for the notes, trying this and that till I found what I wanted them to say. He gave'a to me this violin before he passed on'a to glory. I was'a five years old."

The story touched Beth, and she wondered what tragedy

or circumstance had brought such a talented young man from possibilities in the music halls of Milan to the coal mines of Alberta. The thought made her even more pleased that Frank would have this opportunity to share his music with the people of the community—townspeople and miners alike.

⁂

Beth groaned and crawled out of her bed on Sunday morning. *Just one more event*, she told herself. She straightened the covers and tucked them in neatly, all the while repeating to herself that after lunch she would be able to snuggle right back into them, sleep until she had no more need of rest. It was the one thought that helped her as she dressed, ate a quick breakfast, and went to the hall.

When she arrived, chairs had already been set neatly in rows and the front was decorated with red candles and evergreen branches, filling the room with a sweet pine aroma. Several women were arranging the dessert table, and coffee was brewing in large pots on the hall's wood stove. With a quick cup herself for added energy, Beth tuned her violin and awaited Frank's arrival.

It was almost heartbreaking to see how timidly the miners arrived in the hall, gathering just inside the doorway with hats in hand. Here were robust men, diffidently standing back to await an invitation before venturing forward. Molly took charge immediately, directing them toward the coat racks, where they could hang their all-too-thin jackets, and then beckoning them to come and help themselves to the food items.

As soon as Beth noticed Paolo arrive, she hurried forward to greet him.

"Miss Beth," he called to her, "Merry Christmas—perhaps a little early, but merry just the same, eh?"

"Merry Christmas to you, Paolo. Isn't this exciting?" She squeezed his arm and gestured around her.

In all directions were miners enjoying the warmth and welcome of the resources that the town had to offer. And scattered throughout the hall were ordinary, everyday exchanges, their significance magnified by the fact that this had not ever happened in Coal Valley before. Children carrying simple cups of coffee to men whom they had feared as thugs and thieves just a few weeks before. Mothers sharing their best baking with strangers who had been brought from afar to take the jobs of the husbands cruelly lost to the same hazardous profession.

"It could never have happened if God had not intervened," Beth whispered. Paolo merely smiled at her and took another large bite out of a muffin on his plate. "This is a big room," he commented, his eyes wide as he looked around inside the building he had not previously been welcome to enter.

Promptly at ten o'clock, Frank called for their attention in both Italian and English, then instructed everyone to take a seat. Beth was increasingly amazed at his confidence and poise in front of the villagers and the miners. She had never seen this side of him before, the natural but effective leader. He read from the gospel of Luke, first in English and then in Italian.

During the singing of carols, Beth's violin led with the melody line, strong and sweet. Over the sound of her instrument she could hear voices all around, the tune shared but the words a blending of English and Italian. Truly uplifting and unique.

Standing beside her, Frank played a harmony that gradually swelled, filling the pauses with beautiful counterpoint phrasing. Beth was in awe. This was not the way it had sounded in rehearsal. Frank was feeling the music in the moment and instilling it with pure, worshipful emotion. It did not take long for Beth to understand their varied styles. She had been skill-fully tutored to play by note and by memory. Frank, on the other hand, had a naturally developed talent. She wondered if he had ever received private lessons, except perhaps what his great-grandfather had taught him at such an early age. Frank played by ear—and by heart. Just listening to him was a blessing that overwhelmed Beth to the core of her being.

Though she also was exhausted—entirely spent—the music flowed, filling the room with sincere expressions of worship. She could see faces change from weary and lonely to relaxed and joyous. But Beth could sense in every muscle in her body the sacrifice of praise she was offering up at this moment.

Her mind filled with the struggle required to achieve the gathering. The ladies too had given of their own meager re-sources to contribute to this worship service. And Frank, with his bow tied to his disfigured limb, had perhaps offered the greatest sacrifice of all, presenting his gift of worship through music in spite of his devastating injury. The thoughts washed over Beth in a flood of emotion, too tired and worn to hold herself in check. Not the glorious rush of ecstasy she had felt in the Christmas concert, this was altogether different—a painful, aching praise in which she was entirely aware of how emptied she had become, and still grateful that the truths of God's love were real, even in this moment.

Beth struggled to finish the song. Instead of returning to her seat, she slipped out a side door into the frigid air without stopping to grab up her coat, while the Bible readings con-tinued without her. She dropped her face into her hands and wept alone, overcome by the churn of emotions filling her soul.

It was with Herculean effort that she was able to force herself back into the building to finish the last of the Christ-mas songs. She knew her puffy red eyes betrayed her state, but she refused to let herself fail her responsibilities. Once the service was completed, she even managed to speak with several members of the miners from the English classes before Molly noticed her condition and sent her home immediately, no questions asked.

Beth crumpled onto her bed, pulled the quilt up around her, and fell into a deep, fitful sleep. When she finally awoke, it was morning. There was a plate of food sitting nearby on the side table, but she was completely unaware of who'd brought it or when.

A sudden cough reminded her of how much her throat hurt. Then the physical inventory began. She could tell she had a fever, her nose was congested, and her stomach felt queasy. Her next thought was a rush of relief that there was no school all week. If sickness was going to take her down once again, she was grateful that at least it had waited until now.

A soft knock sounded on the door. In answer to Beth's call, Marnie entered. "I heard ya stirrin'. Can ya eat?"

"I'll come down." Beth slid her feet from under the covers.

"Oh no," Marnie said with a firm shake of her head. "Miss Molly said you was to stay right there in bed. We're bringin' what you need up here."

It was rather easy to acquiesce. Beth doubted she would have been able to stand up anyway.

CHAPTER

18

MOLLY SUITABLY FUSSED OVER BETH in the days that followed, mumbling about taking more seriously the illness that had stolen away so many in the flu epidemic of 1918—still vivid in Molly's memory—and chastising Beth for having gone out into the wintry air without even having the sense to put on a coat. Apparently David Noonan had noticed his teacher rushing outside during the service and had reported such to Molly.

Once she was finally allowed to leave her bedroom, Beth spent much of the remaining week bundled up in the kitchen, and reading where she could be close to the best light and the warmth of the stove. Molly and Marnie quietly mended and knitted and put final touches on small gifts for friends. With all the company men away—all, that is, except the one most recently arrived—the house was calm and rather quiet.

This new gentleman would be residing at Molly's for only a short time, he said. His name was Nick Costa and he spoke Italian, though not as his native tongue. Beth learned during pleasant conversations with him over the dinner table that his

British mother insisted he learn the language of his father's family along with the English spoken in their Canadian home. He was well educated, well read, and professional. Beth liked him immediately and wondered how he would fit in with the other company men. He seemed the obvious odd man out. She wanted to ask what he was doing there while the mine was closed, but she held her tongue.

Nick was married, and his wife had borne him a son of whom he was very proud. The baby was just a little older than JW, Beth discovered. It was a delightful diversion in the evenings to hear him tell of his son's amazing feats. Beth hung on every word, picturing little JW during the discourse. Unfortunately, Nick was rarely present except at suppertime. So the rest of her recovery was rather quiet.

Frank dropped in to see Beth several times, bringing some little token he had whittled or a puzzle he had crafted using only wire. He joined them in the kitchen, drawing a chair up to the small table to play chess with Beth or Teddy, lingering over each move contentedly because there were no other demands upon their time. On December the twenty-third, Jarrick surprised them with a visit, chatting amiably during the short break he was able to spare from his responsibilities. Beth brushed aside his concerned glances, assuring him that her health would soon be fully restored.

"Surprised to see you out in this weather," Molly said to him as she came over with coffee and a plate of gingerbread cookies Marnie had made. "How are the roads?" she asked.

"I've got chains on the tires. If it doesn't snow any more I may even make it home again," joked Jarrick.

"You're brave to give it a try. It ain't often folks come out here over the winter roads."

"Police work doesn't pay much mind to seasons, I'm afraid."

"Yer policin' during Christmas? Investigatin' something—"

"Saw a big moose just down the road a bit," Jarrick broke in without letting her finish the question. "Biggest fella I've ever seen. It's a wonder he's managed to outdo the hunters for as many years as he has. Makes one rather admire him."

"Might admire him more as an oven roast," Molly said with a laugh.

The conversation turned easily to other things, and it seemed no time until Jarrick was gathering his hat and gloves and bidding farewell to them all.

Beth said a little prayer that he would make it back safely over the snowy roads.

Even with such visits and the family's companionship, a heavier melancholy settled over Beth as they moved another day closer to Christmas. She couldn't help but imagine her own home and the whirlwind of activities, the bountiful table, the cheerful décor, and heaps of presents—even Mother's parties. Christmas was always festive and eventful back home, nothing like the quiet days she faced now.

What Beth perhaps missed the most was Christmas Eve, when they gathered before the blazing hearth and Father read the story of that first Christmas. Just closing her eyes and thinking of it brought back the sound of his voice, the scent of his aftershave . . . Beth missed him dreadfully.

Even recalling Julie's unrestrained merriment and Margret's composed conversation brought a lump to her throat. Baby JW would no doubt be taking tentative steps, getting into the wrapped presents if someone didn't turn him in another direction . . . *and enjoying his first Christmas without me.*

For some reason she didn't explain, Molly just at that moment decided to teach Beth to knit. She carried a basket of yarn scraps to the kitchen and set Beth to work on a scarf. Even in her current physical condition, Beth had to admit it helped to fill the time. But the variety of colors which Beth drew from the basket created quite a medley as the scarf began to take shape, and Beth wondered when she might ever wear such a thing. Then she thought with a little smile that perhaps the children would enjoy seeing her in it. *And I made it myself*, she would announce, no doubt to some giggles.

⬥

Carefully making her way down the stairs with the quilt bunched around her on the afternoon of Christmas Eve, Beth looked through the windows at the snow falling. *A white Christmas*, she exulted. Then she heard muffled steps over the snow on the porch. She'd already heard Frank arrive, and he would be waiting in the kitchen with Molly and the children. Through the glass in the door she could see a bright red tunic. Whisking open the door, she expected to greet Jarrick and tease him for crashing the party. But Beth drew back in surprise when dark green eyes peered down at her from beneath a Stetson. She stood motionless.

"May I come in?" He grinned.

Beth blinked away her bewilderment. "Yes, of course—but, Edward, how did you get here?"

He stepped through the doorway, stamping new snow from his boots, removing his hat, and putting down a bag. The lock of hair over his forehead was conspicuously absent—a short, professional cut now gave him a more mature and rather handsome appearance.

"I was given Christmas Day off and decided that what I'd like most would be to finally pay you a visit."

"You came for Christmas—all the way from up north?" Beth sounded as incredulous as she felt.

"Well, no." He hesitated and shifted his gaze away. "I was not so far away as that. I've been working farther south for a period of time." He lifted his gaze again to her quilt-wrapped figure and pale face. "Are you ill, Elizabeth?"

"No—that is, I have been. But I'm much better now."

Molly and Frank appeared, moving toward the stranger at the front door. "Welcome," Molly said, her hand stretched toward him. "Thought ya'd never git here. Glad the weather ain't too bad for ya."

"You *knew* he was coming?"

"Sure." Molly was shaking hands with Edward. "Jack told us last Sunday. Jest seemed more fun ta let it be a Christmas su'prise. Put yer bag in the third door on the right upstairs," she instructed him, "an' join us in the kitchen."

Beth watched in amazement as Edward disappeared up the stairs. She cast a glance down at her clothing—nightgown and house robe with a quilt over all. She wondered what her hair must look like . . . but she pushed the thought aside. There was no way of fixing anything now. She wilted onto a chair.

"Jack told me this Edward was practically kin." Molly was looking carefully at Beth, clearly trying to make her own determination about this new man and what his presence meant.

"Well, I suppose that's one way to describe it." Then Beth lowered her voice and said, "Miss Molly, please, in the future if someone's coming to visit me—particularly a man, would you—could you *please* let me know?"

Molly reached to push a strand of Beth's hair into place. "You look jest fine, dearie."

Beth frowned. *Is Molly, like Mother, doing her own match-making?*

Edward on a chair in Molly's kitchen was like a swan try-ing to seem at home in a peat bog. His polite manners were a little too stiff, particularly across from Beth's pale face and quilt-wrapped form. He managed, however, to convey deep sympathy for her.

"There is nothing trifling about the flu," he was saying. "I've seen it put vigorous men on their backs for weeks. But I'm glad to hear you've been well cared for. Have you heard from your mother? No doubt she'd be quite worried about you."

"I've already written to her about it, but, please—I'd rather you didn't mention it to anyone who might tell her. That just makes it seem all the more serious. It's just the flu. I'm nearly back to normal."

Edward's eyes crinkled in the teasing way Beth knew so well. "So you're emancipated from your mother's watchful eye. You certainly had to travel far from home to achieve that."

Frank mercifully changed the subject. "Where is'a your posting, Mr. Montclair?"

"North in Athabasca. Though I'll be in Lethbridge for the foreseeable future. Some of us were brought back for an additional assignment."

It wasn't so much the vagueness of his answer but the subtle change in his expression that drew Beth's attention. *Is there something Edward is omitting?* But Beth chided herself, *Of course, there is much he would not be able to tell us.*

"And you enjoy the work?"

"Very much. It's been taxing, to be sure, but there are frequent-enough moments when order has been brought to a community—it makes the rest of it worthwhile. But if I've learned anything in my job, it's that the threats are closer than one would expect."

207

"I'm sure that'sa true. I have seen crime and disorder drop as'a the law it moves closer."

Just then Beth remembered the recovered compass and violin. She broke in, "Oh, Edward, I have wanted to thank you so much for finding my things—for sending them along. You can't imagine what a relief—what a thrill—it was to see them again!" she rushed on.

He leaned closer, speaking in a quiet tone. "I wanted so much to set things right again, Elizabeth. It was vitally important for me to do so. I wanted to repair the damage I had caused. For things to be the same between us."

Beth frowned. "It wasn't your fault—not really. I already explained that." She drew back a little. "But I know it took a great deal of effort to recover them, and I *am* very grateful."

"It was my pleasure, I assure you." There was an awkward silence.

Molly filled it with, "Frank, why don't ya ask Beth's friend here if he plays chess? I'll bet the farm he does."

Christmas Eve passed quietly, Beth observing Edward and wondering what might be behind his earnest words. She suspected now that there was more to his attempt to set things right than simply concern for an old friendship. *What do I feel where Edward is concerned?* Beth couldn't sort out her emotions—at least not right then.

That evening Molly suggested that Edward read the Christmas story, and then they shared some fruit punch and special pastries. Molly eventually shooed Beth off to bed, leaving Edward in the kitchen with Frank and her.

Beth had no way of knowing their perceptions of Edward, but they would be viewing him without prior prejudices of station or reputation. And as she contemplated this, another thought rose. *There is something different about Edward now—*

he has matured. Perhaps she should reconsider her long-held opinions.

Christmas morning dawned with Beth feeling better than she had for some time. She washed up and brushed her hair, hoping to present a much better appearance than she'd had the energy for over the past week. It was difficult to choose which dress to wear. The ones Mother had sent seemed over-reaching for a day spent at home, while the working dresses seemed too plain. She chose the one she had restyled, hoping that it was somewhere in the middle of the spectrum.

"Merry Christmas, dearie," Molly called as soon as Beth's footsteps sounded in the kitchen, throwing a quick hug around her shoulders. "So glad yer here ta share the day with us this year." Then she added, "You look real nice."

"I'm glad to be here with you," Beth answered sincerely. "How can I help?"

"No, no. I got it almost ready. You set yerself down and put yer feet up."

Marnie and Teddy had dug in to their Christmas stockings, and Teddy was already sucking on a hard candy he'd found. But Marnie carefully tucked hers away for later. Her face glowed as she showed Beth the new wool socks Molly had made, along with ribbons for her hair.

Edward soon joined them in the kitchen for a delicious breakfast. They chatted amiably about his work, answering his questions about the town. Beth was astonished at how frequently he traveled, how he'd become acquainted with much of the province. In fact, he seemed to know their own region quite well—as if he had spent time in the area. *If that is correct, why is this his first visit?* she wondered idly.

Molly gave an unusually animated review of the Christmas programs. Beth and Frank looked at each other with some surprise and not a little discomfort at her enthusiastic compliments, but Edward seemed fittingly impressed.

They were seated together in the parlor for their gift exchange before Beth realized she had nothing for Edward. *If I'd only known, I would have found something*, she thought with dismay.

Teddy was in charge of distributing the packages that were around Molly's little Christmas tree perched valiantly on its table, a few ornaments and tinsel hanging from it. He reached for a little box and handed it to Marnie, and she was thrilled at the small bottle of perfume she found inside. One by one, the gifts were unwrapped.

Beth had tucked her own contributions among the presents around the tree. A new pocketknife for Teddy and a book of poems she was sure Marnie would enjoy. For Molly, a set of ivory combs with little pearl beads across the top, and for Frank she had managed a pair of store-bought red wool mittens. Then she watched as Marnie opened the new dress which she and Molly had worked on together from the leftover material Beth had purchased in the fall. Teddy, who was somewhat less enthusiastic, opened a new shirt.

When Beth was presented with a small box, she smiled around the room, curious, since it had no name on it other than her own. She pulled off the wrapping and drew off the lid. Inside was a bright gold chain and a lovely dove-shaped pendant made from mother-of-pearl. Beth drew in a breath, shocked at such a lavish gift.

"I was thinking it was kind of a peace offering," Edward said with some chagrin. "I hope you like it."

Beth could feel her cheeks flush. What could she say? The gift was far more extravagant than any of the others—out of proportion, she felt, and unwarranted. She was sure it was not purchased on a Mountie's salary. She thanked him politely, embarrassed to say anything further.

A small fuss rose across the room as Molly pressed Teddy toward the next package, one she was insisting be given next. "An' this says, 'To Edward from Beth,'" he announced.

Beth could not hide her shock and cast a confounded glance toward Molly, who shushed her with a finger to her lips.

Edward accepted the package and played up the suspense, turning it over and over, even shaking it—though it clearly was soft and some type of clothing. Finally tearing the paper away, the multicolored scarf—uneven rows and all—that Beth had labored over tumbled out. He held it up with a surprised grin as Beth covered her face with her hands.

Undaunted, Molly announced proudly, "Beth knitted it."

Edward chuckled. "Yes, I see—I'm sure it's her first, and I hope not her last. I'm honored to have it. I'll set a new fashion trend in Athabasca."

He wound the scarf around his neck and smiled around the room, his gaze at last resting on Beth. His words came slowly and carefully, as if there were no one else listening. "You have so many wonderful talents, Elizabeth. I'm convinced there is nothing you could not accomplish if you try. I will cherish this gift as a tribute to what an amazing woman you are, and on frosty winter evenings I'll find some way to tuck it under my tunic."

For a moment Beth was spellbound. The green eyes gleamed with sincerity in a face distinctly more weathered and masculine than she remembered. His expression bore no resemblance to the mocking, irritating boy she had once known.

For the rest of the day, Beth avoided Edward's gaze, confused by the stir of her sometimes-contradictory thoughts and feelings. She spoke cordially to him as dictated by her upbringing, but her muddled emotions couldn't manage more interaction than was unavoidable. After supper he gathered his bag, expressed his gratitude, and turned to head back out into the frozen landscape.

"Thank you for coming, Edward," she said politely before he exited Molly's foyer. "Please try to take care of yourself—I shall pray for your safety."

His eyes held a warm expression. "I'm grateful that you might remember me charitably in prayer." And then he was gone.

Beth had already tucked the expensive necklace away in a drawer and tried not to dwell on her conflicted feelings regarding Edward's visit. She stole sheepishly into the kitchen, taking up a dish towel to work her way through the stack of clean plates.

"A nice fella," Molly commented in her forthright way. "Ya like him?"

A deep flush rose into Beth's cheeks. "I am not enamored with him, if that's what you mean." Her answer sounded clipped and terse.

"Ya sure?" A chuckle sounded from Molly, and Beth felt it was just too much. She dropped the dish towel onto the counter and hurried from the room, up the stairs, and retreated to her bed.

She buried her face in her pillow, opposing thoughts churning her stomach into knots. She had in no way intended to offend Molly, had wished she'd given some kind of response. But her emotions were all tied up with memories regarding Edward, and it was all too complex for her to sort out right now.

A soft knock sounded at the door.

"Who is it?" Beth called, though she was certain who was there.

"Can I come in?"

Beth sat up on the edge of the bed and tried to recover her composure. "Yes."

Molly peeked around the door and entered cautiously, closing it quietly behind her. She crossed the room and sat down heavily next to Beth on the bed. "Appears I owe ya an apology."

Beth shook her head. "No, no, Molly. It's not you—I don't know why I'm feeling so touchy."

"Well, I didn't mean ta upset ya none. An' I'm truly sorry I did. Can ya talk about it?"

Beth drew in a long breath. "The truth is—" She covered her face with her hands. "Oh, I don't know what the truth is. I suppose that the truth is I don't know what I feel or why."

"Well then, why don't ya start with what made my question so upsettin'."

Beth studied a speck on the carpet. "I've always rather disliked Edward," she began slowly. "And I've always known some people expected us to marry, mainly our . . . our mothers." Beth could hear Molly sigh quietly.

"And I'm beginning to believe Edward's expecting as much," she continued. "But he . . . he has never been the type of man I want to share my life with. That is—well, at least, he wasn't the type of *boy* I could respect. It's different now. He's not the same. I don't know, but maybe he's truly changing."

Beth lifted her eyes to Molly's caring face. "But the whole idea makes me feel trapped somehow—as if there's some unseen force *pushing* me toward him. I thought for sure I was leaving all of that behind when I came out west, and suddenly he appeared on the train. At first it upset me, and then I found myself expecting to find him at every turn—and finally *hoping*, in fact, that I would. But then when he didn't show up here for all these months . . . Oh, Molly, how can I *want* to see him, yet draw away from it at the same time? It just doesn't make sense. . . ."

"Feelin's often don't" came Molly's frank response. She put her hand on Beth's arm. "So we can't live by 'em. An' we can't be a slave to 'em either. We have ta live accordin' to what's right—not what we feel. Feelin's ain't bad, ya know, we just have to remember they can change themselves into somethin' else for no reason we can tell."

Beth nodded.

"Was it my teasin' that set ya off?"

A small hesitation and Beth replied, her voice low, "It was more than that. All the things wrapped together. . . . You didn't tell me he was coming, and you didn't tell me about the gift. I guess I felt like you were doing what others have done—pairing us up against my will."

Molly put her arm around Beth and pulled her close. "I don't want nothin' for ya, dearie, but what you an' God want. I guess when yer older, ya find some fun in watching the young get matched up. But I would *never* press ya one way or another. Ya gotta make up yer own mind."

With all her heart Beth wished that Mother had been able to bring herself to articulate such words. She whispered, "I feel as if my family wouldn't say the same—that my mother in particular feels she knows what's best and would be most happy to dictate my future to me—if I were to allow it."

Molly chuckled again. "Oh, it's different in a family. It's harder ta take a step back when the future of a loved one's at stake. I'm sure it's yer momma's love for ya that makes it hard to let ya go. Even make a little mistake or two." Then she squeezed a little harder. "But yer here, ain't ya? An' that's a long, long way from home and Momma—sayin' a lot, eh?"

Beth was able to produce a little smile, but she also shrugged. Molly was undeniably right, but somehow it felt like a temporary freedom, measured out cautiously—one that would all too soon be withdrawn.

"How can I pray for you and yer momma, dearie?" Her question was unexpected, but conveyed gentle love and support.

Beth looked away, then into Molly's face. "For peace between us. For submission, the right kind, I guess. That I wouldn't feel so stubborn and resistant to whatever she says or wants."

"If I may," Molly said carefully, "I'll pray that ya submit to God first. An' once that's done, you an' yer momma'll work through th'other parts. Yer a woman now, true, an' ya gotta make the decisions for yer own life. But first ya gotta obey God's call—the little things and the big things. You'll understand better some day, though, that you'll always be her girl. An' ya gotta honor her no matter how old ya get. That part'll be somethin' ya do in yer mind, not yer feelings—just you an' God workin' it out together. We all got mommas— and at some point we gotta figure out what it means to be a grown-up daughter."

Pressing a kiss against Beth's hair, Molly rose and left, softly closing the door behind her. Beth sighed, but one of release, not sorrow. It was so easy to talk with Molly. After spending only a few months in her home, they had already grown to love and understand each other. *Maybe it's Molly I'll miss most when my year is over. . . .*

At last Mother's reply to Beth's pre-Christmas letter arrived. Not surprisingly, Beth found many remonstrations about not caring for her own health adequately. Mother, in fact, came very close to threatening a visit to see to it that she had sufficiently recovered before continuing with her teaching responsibilities. Reading between the lines, Beth deciphered that Father had been the one to repudiate such an idea. Hot tears stole down Beth's cheeks as she realized there wasn't a single reference to her Christmas program. She wiped her eyes, blew her nose, and prayed that Mother would someday come to see her as more than merely an invalid who needed coddling and someone's watchful eye.

Snow had continued to fall after Christmas, and the world outside was blanketed with a lovely cotton batting of white. As alluring as a walk seemed, she knew it would be unwise until she was back to full strength. Instead, from the safety of Molly's parlor window she could occasionally watch some of the children playing in the street, chasing and throwing snowballs or making tunnels through the drifts.

She soon learned that this was pleasant so long as it was only for a short while. Any longer, and she quickly felt the need to reprimand them for some childish infraction. *Hmm,* she thought for a moment, *does that sound a bit like Mother?* And if she did call out to them through the open door, Molly immediately hollered from the kitchen to close it again "afore ya catch yer death." Beth shook her head at the irony of being reproved as if she were a child at the very moment she was thinking of reproving her own students. But it was not a battle she could win—nor did she actually want to go against this loving woman who was such a guardian of her well-being. *Like Mother wants to be . . . so why does it feel so different coming from Molly?*

Beth had lots to mull over during this week of quiet before school resumed. *Lord, help me to sort out all these thoughts and feelings, to become more like You,* she prayed, *more understanding and forgiving.*

She was grateful Frank continued to call every day. He was a pleasant diversion from the quiet that had settled over the house since Christmas. Whenever he arrived, there was laughter, games, and impromptu singing, and sometimes two violins in lovely harmony—everyone's spirits rising to meet Frank's.

CHAPTER

19

ATHERING TOGETHER PAPERS SHE HAD GRADED
many days before, Beth had mixed feelings as she set
out for school again. The two weeks of rest and fellowship
had come just at the right time, and she would miss it. But she
also was looking forward to being back with the children—to
feel she was accomplishing something significant.

Her students, though, seemed restless and preoccupied as
she faced them from the front of the room. Apparently they
did not share her desire to be productive once more after the
Christmas break. Beth simply stood before them, waiting till
they noticed her silence and gave her their attention. She knew
she had to be particularly vigilant and creative to keep them
on task, pressing forward with the lessons despite their lack
of concentration. By the end of the day she felt drained and
trudged home disappointed—in herself and in them.

Molly noticed immediately, and without Beth saying a word,
she patted her shoulder and told her it would be better tomorrow. And it was. As the winter days moved along, their
routine was established once again.

Beth was somewhat nervous as she opened another letter from Mother, then pleasantly surprised when she read of Mother's regret over having lectured Beth about her activities in her last correspondence. Next followed much more detail about the family's Christmas celebrations, along with a wish that Beth had been present. Mother also wrote of upcoming plans and news about some friends Beth knew. In the very last paragraph she added, "I'm so glad Edward was able to spend Christmas with you. I do trust you were congenial."

There it was—Mother's thinly veiled suggestion that Beth cultivate a relationship with him. *Did he find some way of communicating his visit to her? Or perhaps his own mother had passed along the news. . . .*

The winter days were short and often drab, and Beth found herself walking to school before the sun was up and coming home in twilight. The meager lamps on the school tables worked hard to provide sufficient light for the students on the cloudy, snowy days. Beth worried about the stuffy room, now that it was far too cold to open the windows. But she was managing to get more sleep, even though she continued Bible club and English lessons each week.

Three additional miners had joined the class at Frank's cabin. It was now a lively mix of interesting personalities, which Beth enjoyed greatly. The men were learning far more quickly than Beth had ever imagined. She was certain this was due to Paolo's efforts to coach and challenge them throughout the week. By far, Alberto was the most proficient. Beth suspected that he had already known more English than he'd been willing to admit.

But partway through January a blizzard hit, the first Beth

had experienced since arriving in Coal Valley. Molly told her there was no need to send Teddy to put out the word that school was canceled—the mothers would not allow their children to leave home in this kind of weather even if Beth had managed to get to school herself. For two days icy snow blasted against the windows and whipped over the roof. The howling wind through the trees drowned out all other sounds, including the ever-present mining equipment. At Beth's question, Molly assured her that the work underground would continue.

Frank also surrendered to the storm, giving up his frequent visits for the duration. Beth had no doubt he'd likely taken in guests too. It would not be the first time he'd invited some of the miners to sleep on his floor when the weather was particularly nasty. His cabin was not large or extravagant, but it stalwartly held on to the heat of its potbelly stove much better than the thin boards of the camp buildings. Some of the miners, Beth was told, would shovel snow up against the sides of their dwellings, hoping for some insulation against the driving winds and bitter cold.

When the storm was finally spent, Beth peered out into a crystal world, polished fresh and clean and bright. Several of her students were already bundled up and playing in the new snow, and she hurried into her own coat and hat and mittens. She'd been ill when she'd last watched them from inside the window. She determined that today she would enjoy some of the pleasures of the snow for herself.

They seemed genuinely surprised at Beth's appearance but quickly accepted her into their fun. She helped in their efforts to build a snowman—though the powdery snow proved poor for such construction. So they worked instead on digging a tunnel. Her cheeks were rosy and her fingers almost numb before Molly called them all to sit on the porch for some hot chocolate and cookies. Beth stayed with them, enjoying their chatter and answering their questions.

"Didn't ya have snow where you grew up?"

"Of course," she explained, "we often had a great deal of it. But my mother rarely let me play outside in the cold. I was quite sickly as a child."

"So is Levi. His momma keeps him in too," Georgie informed her. "Says he gots to stay warm."

"Did ya have any brothers an' sisters?"

Beth answered solemnly, "I have two sisters. But I also had a baby brother who died. I still miss him," she said quietly. The children stared at her with new interest. She smiled around at them and added, "One of my sisters is older, and she's married. The other sister is younger. And I also have a sweet little nephew named JW."

"JW? What sorta name is that?"

"It stands for John William. It's kind of a nickname."

"Bonnie has a nickname," Daniel said with a grin. "Want to know what it is?"

Bonnie rose to her feet in a menacing manner. "Stop it, Daniel. I'll tell Momma!" He laughed, but chose the better part of wisdom, hunching down inside his parka as if the coat would protect him.

"Miss Thatcher, bet yer glad you didn't grow up with a brother," muttered Bonnie.

Beth changed the subject. "In the city where I come from it's quite flat—and there are people and buildings everywhere."

"I bin to the city," Maggie piped up. "When I was real small, Momma said. I don't even 'member. And then we come out here with my daddy." Speaking the word aloud brought silence all around. "I miss my daddy," she added softly.

Beth reached to brush her rosy cheek and answered tenderly, "I'm so sorry, darling. I'm sure you miss him very much."

Jonah muttered, "Momma says not to t-t-t-talk about him. But I l-l-like to 'member."

Beth scooted forward in her seat. "She's probably still feeling very lonely, because she misses him too. And sometimes when we're still feeling bad, it's easiest to try not to think about it. But you can talk about your daddies with me."

"Don't it m-m-make you feel bad too?"

Beth could feel her tears welling up and blinked them away quickly. "It makes my heart hurt for *you*. But that's a different kind of pain. So if you'd like to, you can come and talk to me whenever you want."

Molly brought one more plate of cookies and offered them around the small circle. "Can I have one fer Levi?" Anna Kate asked. "He don't get much sweets."

"He don't get much sweets 'cause he don't get much food," Maggie blurted out.

Anna Kate was too young to be put off by the comment. "Anyways, he'd wanna cookie." She stuck out a tongue at Maggie.

Beth turned to the pair of little girls. She asked solemnly, "Is that true, Anna Kate? Do you not have enough to eat?"

With childish candor, she answered, "Momma says it's jest till the s'ply train can get through again."

Beth tried not to meddle, but the idea that any of her children did not have enough to eat brought serious concern. She thanked them for allowing her to play in the snow with them, stealthily tucked a few more cookies into Anna Kate's pocket, and waved at them all as they left.

Later Beth approached Molly to see if she were aware of the problem.

222

"I knew they was hard up, but I didn't know they was quite so low."

"Is there anything that can be done?"

Molly dropped down onto a kitchen chair. "Esther Blane's a real tough nut. She don't take help none. Even turned down Frank flat out when he tried ta give 'em some fish."

"How many other families do you think are having a difficult time?"

Molly shook her head. "Three or four. Maybe more. Them pensions is startin' to run out, dependin' on how long their man worked in the mine. The gals is jest scared to death what happens next. Problem is, nobody knows."

Beth would not be deterred. "Then whatever we do can't be targeted at one family—or even a few. It must be offered to all the children."

Molly looked at her for a long moment. "What're ya suggestin'?"

"How about if we see they get a good breakfast? Many schools have done that much. And it's one of the cheapest meals to provide." She watched for Molly's reaction.

"Careful what ya start, dearie. Might be bitin' off more'n you can chew. And sometimes failin' is worse 'an not tryin'— when it comes ta stirrin' things up."

Beth sighed. Unconsciously she touched the locket again. She could not drive from her mind her recent illness, no doubt brought on by overextending herself. She would need much prayer before she moved ahead.

"How much does it cost to buy a cow?" Beth asked. She had pulled Philip aside to a secluded corner of the hallway after Sunday dinner.

He stared back as if she'd lost her mind. "A cow?"

"The children need milk," she explained. "I thought we could call it a school project, maybe teach them each to milk it. That way we don't have to make any of the mothers feel we're giving charity. The children are the ones providing for it. It would kind of belong to them all. . . ." She could tell she hadn't been very convincing.

"Have you spoken with anyone else about this idea?"

She looked away self-consciously. "No, I thought I'd try it out on you first—sort of a test run."

Philip shook his head. "It's an awful lot of work to keep a cow—you'd be amazed at how much they eat. And have you given any thought to where it would be kept? You had best discuss it with someone who knows cattle a lot better than I do before you move much further with your plans."

Beth clasped her hands tightly in front of her, her knuckles white. "The Grants have a big shed behind the pool hall. I'm wondering if it might be kept there. I know we'd have to bring in hay too. I just hoped it wouldn't be *too* complicated."

"I know you want to help, Beth." The pastor reached out to squeeze her arm gently. "But what would happen to the cow when you leave at the end of the school year? I admire your good intentions, but perhaps you would be biting off more than you could chew."

Beth blew out a long breath. "You just repeated Molly's very words." She had hoped Philip might be more positive. Now she would have to go back to Molly and see if she might have further ideas.

Molly immediately vetoed the cow as impractical. She was unwilling to even discuss it. "If yer set on gettin' 'em breakfast, then porridge is yer best bet," she maintained.

Beth had a difficult time imagining the children would be

very enthusiastic at the idea of porridge every morning, but perhaps if they were hungry enough it would suffice. However, it did not satisfy the wide nutritional range her mother had asserted was required.

"A while ago," Molly said thoughtfully, "some o' the mothers were talkin' 'bout settin' up somethin' like this. You should ask Katie Frazier—or Frances. They'd know who else."

After a quick lunch, Beth walked to Frances Tunnecliffe's home for a visit. Molly's friend was able to offer additional information about which families were suffering most through the difficult winter. It was a painful conversation, underscoring to Beth how very poor some of the families were.

As Beth rose to leave, Frances cautioned, "Don't be lettin' the gals hear about this. They won't like to know their private affairs are being discussed. And they wouldn't take kindly to charity—especially from an outsider." Beth tried not to let the label hurt. She so wished she could be considered a neighbor among them—but she knew all too well that it took time to earn their trust. And her year was passing quickly.

Still, she had expected much more support than she'd found. Surely the welfare of the children should be paramount, but others seemed to perceive only obstacles. Late in the afternoon she lay down on her bed for a rest, pouring her heart out to her heavenly Father.

"I don't know what to try next, Lord. I need somebody to help me determine what can be done. The children need food, proper nutrition. Maybe I could get word back home to my parents. I'm sure they would be willing to help, though maybe it's not fair to ask it of them. But then, what can I do? We can't get a cow—even though they need milk. Porridge alone is not enough—and I can't even offer them that without finding others who are willing to help. And my health,

Father—now that I'm feeling stronger again, I don't want to start all over. . . ." Soon tears accompanied the words.

She whispered Father's verse once again. "'I can do all things through Christ which strengtheneth me.'" Yet somehow this time it failed to fill her with courage. She tried to convince herself that all she needed to do was rally the others in support of her ideas, but she had become much more aware of her own weakness and limitations. She sighed, wiped her eyes, and rose from the bed.

If anything were to happen, it would begin with Molly.

Beth entered the kitchen quietly and took a seat at the table, waiting to be acknowledged. Molly was setting out bread dough to rise at the back of the stove. When she had greased the top and covered it neatly with a towel, she turned toward Beth.

"Ya been cryin'?"

Beth nodded. "I've been praying about the breakfast idea."

"Hmm" came the calm response. "An' did God speak on it?"

"That's the problem. I don't know if He did." Beth wiped her eyes again on a handkerchief already wet with her tears. "I just don't know yet what I'm supposed to do."

Molly set the teapot on the table, spooned in the loose tea, pulled the kettle from the back of the stove, and carefully poured hot water to fill the pot. She worked slowly, as if there were no crisis. Beth found her methodical motions aggravating. The herbal aroma drifted through the room while Beth watched Molly make her way around, gathering the honey and spoons—even setting out a plate of sweets. At last she settled into her chair.

"Ya seem troubled 'bout it all."

Beth nodded again and blew her nose quietly.

"I ain't no preacher." Molly stirred her tea slowly, deliberately. "Can't tell ya all the ins an' outs of prayer. But I done my share of it, I guess." She clinked the spoon on the edge of her cup before placing it on her saucer. Finally she looked over at Beth. "Wish I could give ya yer answer, dearie. But it ain't my call ta say. I seen ya work real hard for all them kids since ya got here. An' I know ya done plenty ta help 'em out—them kids and the rest of us too. I also seen ya laid pretty low by it all."

"But I can't just overlook the fact that they're hungry—"

"I know all that, dearie. I know." Molly was shaking her head, her hand held up to quiet Beth's arguments. "Some folks say God don't give us more'n we can handle. Some say God helps them who helps themself. An' I suppose there's plenty enough who wanna just wait fer some kinda sign to show 'em what to do next. I guess I figure it's best to listen *first* to what God already said, 'stead'a all them folks. So I'm reluctant ta add my own thoughts till we look in here." She drew a well-worn Bible from a shelf beside the table.

"Good Book says ta cast yer cares on Him for He cares for you. Also says, 'My yoke is easy, and my burden is light.' Now, like I said, I'm no scholar, but maybe if yer gettin' crushed by it all, then, dearie, jest maybe yer tryin' to do something that isn't yers to do . . . or doin' something wrong."

Tears threatened again. "I don't know," Beth whispered. "I'm trying so hard to find out what God wants me to do about this."

Molly reached across the table and took Beth's hand. "An' I'm not aimin' ta criticize. Please hear me out. I jest wanna say that it don't appear that cares are the same as burdens. Yer to cast your *cares and worries* at His feet, and in trade He gives ya a *burden* you can lift. Amazing how hard it is to carry all them worries—and then it turns out that the burden of the real work ain't near as vexin' as yer worries been. So we gotta let go of all that frettin'. Thet's the key ta knowin' how to rest in the Lord. An' it seems ya gotta be able to do 'em both—not jest the workin', but the restin' too." She leaned back and took a slow sip of tea, shaking her head. "I seen folks who don't know how ta rest—an' I seen other folks who don't know how ta work. Wish we'd all jest learn ta do the right amount on each."

Beth gave Molly a shaky smile and went back to her room and back to prayer, unloading before her Father all of her worries about the children, including the fears that she would create hurt feelings or cause damage to relationships in her genuine attempts to help. Trying to align her heart as best she understood to the correct attitude God wanted her to take, she laid down all her concerns, presented her willingness to be used, and asked God to direct, claiming in faith that He already had an answer waiting.

It was so different than her previous prayer. Instead of feeling wound up afterward, she truly did feel a kind of release—an increased trust that something would work out—with or without her. Each time in the coming days when she felt worry return, she did her best to place it back into God's hands through prayer. It was more of a struggle than she had imagined—not to be anxious for her desired outcome to happen on cue.

On Tuesday morning before school, Molly presented Beth with a wrapped platter. "It's muffins," she explained. "Guess I made too many. Jest set 'em out an' see if any kids're interested."

Beth wasn't sure what to expect as she explained to the children that Miss Molly had sent the muffins and they were free to help themselves. *Would there be a rush? Would the children share?* She was very pleased to observe Luela Coolidge, who had five siblings, take charge and divide things up in such a way that there were three leftover.

Luela wrapped them up again in the cloth and said, "Levi, why don't ya take them extras home. It can be your turn today," as if this were a common occurrence. As Beth walked past Luela during their opening exercises, she laid a hand on her shoulder and smiled her gratitude.

Wednesday morning while Beth was still preparing the schoolroom for the day, she was surprised by the arrival of Frances. The older woman looked rather sheepish as she passed a large burlap sack to Beth. "It's apples," she explained. "And why I bothered to keep 'em so long I can't say, as they were just gettin' wrinkled in my cellar. You can give 'em to the wee ones if you want."

Beth knew Frances was trying to diminish her act of kindness but couldn't resist reaching out for a quick hug. She was surprised to feel Frances's arms tighten firmly around her. No words were spoken, but when Beth closed the door behind the shawl-wrapped figure, she knew God had begun to answer her prayers in the best possible way.

There was no offering of food on Thursday or Friday—but there were still apples in the bowl that Beth had placed at the back of the room. Even the children seemed to understand the unspoken arrangement—these were to be shared by all with an extra portion going to the ones among them who had less at home.

Thank you, thank you, Father, Beth's heart sang.

On Saturday, Jarrick stopped in at the boarding house and shared lunch with them. As he chatted amiably with Molly, the children, and Beth, he told them about some of the other communities where he worked and things happening elsewhere. Having rare interactions with the outside world, Beth was delighted to get some news through Jarrick.

Just as he was leaving, he drew Beth aside. "I have something to show you." He helped her into her coat and ushered her to where his car was parked in front. Raising the lid to the trunk, he grinned. "Word's gotten out, and some folks started sending things. Before long we couldn't stop it."

Beth's eyes took in six large crates of food, and her hands went to her cheeks as she stared at the bounty.

"There's cheese," he began. "Big blocks of cheese—so I guess you don't need a cow after all."

Beth shot him a glance. "Who told you that?"

"We Mounties are trained to know things—you haven't heard that?" He grinned at his quip and then sobered. "I talked with Philip." He paused to search her face. "You're not angry, are you?"

"No, of course not. I have a feeling it wasn't mere gossip but concern."

His brow furrowed. "You can be sure of that, Beth," he said. "Anyway, there are also potatoes, powdered milk and eggs, flour, oatmeal, and some jars of canned foods—fruit and whatnot. I think it's more than enough to hold you for a while. And every bit of it was donated by folks who are simply concerned about your town—your kids."

Beth wanted to throw her arms around his neck but held herself in check, grasping his arm instead. "I can't tell you what a blessing this is. It will last most of the winter, I'm sure."

"There's just one more thing," he cautioned. "Philip wanted

230

to be sure this was handled properly. He has a suggestion—he explained it in a note that he put in one of the boxes. I think it would be wise to consider carefully what he has counseled about this program."

"Of course," she answered, eyes shining, "I'll make sure I read it. Oh, I can hardly believe this, Jarrick—I would never have been able to do this on my own."

"Then let's get it all inside. You go get Teddy to come help. And let Molly know what it's all for. I didn't say anything to her yet, but she's going to have to find room to store it." Jarrick hoisted one of the large crates, and Beth held the gate for him and then opened the front door. They made quite a ruckus hauling it into the kitchen.

"Molly," Beth called. "We've got our answer."

CHAPTER

20

After all the bustle of putting away food and saying good-bye to Jarrick, thanking him again and again, Beth retreated to her room to read the note from Philip. It was not long, but very specific.

My dear Beth,

I would advise you against simply beginning to distribute food or offering it before school starts each day. This shall surely lead to offense. What I would suggest instead is that you take on a service project, and invite interested students to participate each day before school. This maybe could be done at Molly's home—which would make the food preparation easiest. I would caution you against making a request of the Grants at this time, though I would rather not go into reasons just now.

That comment gave Beth a moment's pause. *I've rarely seen Helen Grant out and about in the town.* And, even more unusual for Coal Valley, she did not recall ever having seen her husband, Davie.

Philip continued,

As far as the actual project goes, I have a strong prospect for it. My mission board has acquired dozens of boxes of donated yarn to be used overseas. It all needs to be sorted and rolled neatly. I am willing to provide this yarn if you can find children who are willing to do the work of rolling it. This would benefit many, as well as instill in your children the idea that they can, in turn, help others. I would encourage you to feed only those who are willing to work. I know they're children, but you are planting the seed of a concept that will grow into life-long attitudes as they move into adulthood. Please do so carefully and thoughtfully.

I suspect that you will be excited to start on this project, so I will plan to deliver the yarn to you this Saturday.

Yours very sincerely,

Philip Davidson

P.S. It is difficult for me to adequately express how your love for this community encourages me personally. I am grateful for you, Beth.

Beth folded the note slowly and tucked it away inside the cover of her Bible. God's answer had been so much more efficient and effective than what she could have even imagined. She prayed her gratitude.

Molly offered her yarn scrap basket to begin teaching the children the proper technique for rolling yarn into tidy balls. So on Sunday, Beth wrote out notes to each of the mothers, explaining the new school project and inviting their children to participate on Monday. She slid into her boots, pulled her coat tightly around her shoulders, and braved the wintery wind to deliver what she prayed would be seen as the giving and receiving of a blessing.

On Monday morning, Molly's front entrance filled with children. She had cooked a large pot of oatmeal over which she planned to spoon some of the canned fruit. Beth could not help but notice the hungry eyes of Levi and Anna Kate as they waited politely for their turn to be served, but there were others who seemed just as interested. Beth dragged the basket of yarn to the parlor, where they would work together. As the children finished their breakfast, Beth set each one to work rolling the yarn scraps, demonstrating how to start each ball and how to tie a new piece on when the end was reached. It took some of them several attempts before they had a nice tight ball of yarn.

All too soon it was time to bundle them off to school. Beth no longer had the preparation time in the early quiet of the makeshift schoolroom, but she felt what they were accomplishing more than compensated. With just a small effort on her part, and much help from Molly and Marnie, who had taken on all of the cooking, they were able to offer breakfast.

As he had indicated, Philip arrived on Saturday with several boxes of yarn for the children to roll. He assured Beth that there was plenty more once she and the children had managed to detangle and tidy it, and that he would periodically bring replenishments of food along with the yarn as he made his Sunday circuits.

Frances, sipping a cup of coffee, shook her head as the boxes were carried past her into Molly's kitchen. "An' just where are ya plannin' ta put it all, Moll?"

In answer, Molly drew back the curtain to reveal the small

pantry already crowded with the children's food. "Blamed if I know," she said with a shrug.

In the end, half of the boxes of yarn were stacked in Beth's bedroom and half in another room that was rarely needed. Then Beth began the work of managing it all, carrying it down one box at a time as the children worked their way through, satisfied little smiles on their faces.

Weeks settled into a contented routine. The one thing that was difficult for Beth to adapt to—even more so than the bitter cold of a mountain winter—were the short, dark days in the classroom. She checked her watch pin in the mornings, noting just when she could see the sun brightening the windows on the east and then noting again during the afternoon when it faded on the other side of the building. Each day it rose a little earlier and set a little later, but the tedious progress toward a full day of light was exasperating.

One day when a coal train had gotten through the snow with mail, Beth received a letter from Julie. Her sister had written only twice since Beth's departure, with the exception of a few lines tagged on to the end of most of Mother's letters. Beth would have recognized her sister's showy handwriting on the envelope without even reading the return address.

Waiting until she had gone to her room, Beth fell across the bed and tore open the letter. Anticipating a long, newsy report of the goings-on of Julie's peers along with her own plans for the near future, Beth was stunned to read Julie's enthusiastic announcement—with many exclamation points— that she would be traveling west for a visit. *Surely Mother and Father are aware that Coal Valley is still in the grip of winter,* Beth thought, but scanning down the page further she learned that

Julie's trip was still weeks away. Beth had long ago dismissed the idea of a possible visit from Julie. She was thrilled to write back and begin planning for it.

Beth could not immediately think of special outings with which to entertain her gregarious sister. And just the thought of Julie in the midst of so many trees and so few people was daunting. But she put all that aside in light of sharing her new life with someone from her family. Julie would certainly be stretched and challenged by the experience.

Beth and Molly discussed the implications of the visit and made a plan for how Julie would be brought from the city and where she would sleep. As Beth walked through her days, she began envisioning each situation through Julie's eyes. How would she explain the pool-hall classroom? Beth had never had the courage to fully describe the building to Mother. *How will Julie respond to the townsfolk? What will she think of Molly's rather primitive boarding house—no indoor plumbing or electricity?* Beth hoped winter would have spent most of its fury before the visit in May. It would theoretically be spring—if only the Rocky Mountains would acknowledge the fact.

Beth also received a letter from Edward, describing in detail his return to his post in Athabasca. He seemed to be very pleased with the work and confident in his expanding abilities. Beth was happy for him. Of all their peers, it amused her that she and Edward were the ones to wander farthest from home. They no doubt would have been considered two of the least likely candidates.

Since Julie's letter, her thoughts more often drifted back to home and family. She imagined JW taking his first steps. She wondered too if there was news of another baby on the way. Mother had not mentioned it in her letters, but Beth would not be surprised. Margret had spoken often of her hopes for a large family.

Beth considered how opposite Margret seemed to be from their mother—and yet how well the two of them got along. Her older sister was gentle and compliant, reserved yet warm. In many ways the kind of woman that Beth hoped one day to become. She wondered why, despite this, she felt a strong aversion to being perceived as having the same personality, the same characteristics, as Margret.

Beth wrapped herself up and took a walk down to the river's edge. She found the water still hidden beneath ice and banks of snow. She leaned against a pine tree to think, and she came to the conclusion that this issue had very little to do with Margret. Instead, Beth was feeling pressure to follow in her sister's footsteps. Though they were similar in disposition, the two sisters shared few of the same goals. Margret was utterly fulfilled as a wife and mother. She had found her calling. Beth was convinced that she herself had been called to something different. *Perhaps this is the source of the angst where Mother and I are concerned.* Margret was satisfied to follow, where Beth preferred to cut through the thickets and make a trail of her own.

Walking back again toward the small town, Beth contemplated the implications of it all. Idly, she noted the wet patches of shrinking snow giving way to spaces of muddy ground. But she had been cautioned not to perceive these warmer chinook days as the end of winter—only a windy respite. She would enjoy being outdoors for as long as it lasted, though.

Saturday afternoon was particularly springlike, and Beth felt an inclination for music. Lifting her violin in its case, she went down to the parlor, but Henry already had stretched himself out on the long sofa with a book. Beth turned to the dining room, only to find Teddy and Marnie, along with Addison and Luela, engrossed in a game of pick-up-sticks. She smiled at the youths and wandered into the foyer, turning slowly to take stock of her options. She could play the instrument in her bedroom, but even upstairs her music might intrude on the rest of the household. On impulse, Beth reached for a wrap and wandered out into the warm sunshine, case in hand.

Beth turned toward the road leading out of the town, strolling some distance before finding a small clearing close to where she and Marnie had picked berries in the fall. Her skirt brushed at small mounds of snow clinging stubbornly to branches and dry grasses. Her shoes, not as pristine as they had once been, showed signs of her frequent walks, along with a bit of today's mud.

Already Beth was anticipating the poetry of the experience—standing alone in a patch of warm sunshine amid the quiet sounds of nature, playing before only the Creator of such beauty and of music. Beth raised the violin to her shoulder and brought it into tune. Then she let the bow play across its strings, moving from note to note in exploration of their sounds rather than in practiced form. Could she—would she?—ever be able to play with the natural fluidity and artistry of Frank? She would not have dared to try—except that she was now out of sight and sound of others.

She began with three simple chords, exploring a movement from one to another until she was pleased with the sound. She closed her eyes, feeling the notes more than listening—working with and then against the desired effect. Finding it even more difficult than she had hoped, she continued to attempt it, oblivious to all else.

"Ain't you awful far from home?"

Beth gasped and snapped her head around at the sound of the raspy voice. She stumbled back a step and her pulse quickened as she realized she did not recognize the man.

"I'm sorry if I've disturbed you," she finally said, her voice sounding high and tight. "I'll just pack up my . . . my things and be on my way." Beth made a move toward the violin case resting on top of a nearby stump. But the man stepped between, blocking her way.

"Don't know me, do ya?" He spat on the ground defiantly.

"I'm sorry. But no."

"Go ahead. Make a guess." He was toying with her in an ugly tone.

"I'm . . . I'm not good at guessing games," she dared reply.

"Then ask me." His sneer as he spoke made Beth's skin crawl. Was he serious or just baiting her? She dared not test him further.

"Well then, sir, what is your name, please?" she responded in as firm a voice as she could manage.

"'Sir,'" he repeated. "I like that," he said with a snort. "And ya better be showin' me respect."

He tipped his weathered hat, then hooked his thumbs through his overall straps as if still considering her request. Looking down at his worn boots, he kicked at a clump of dead grass, then slowly let his eyes sweep back up to Beth's face. "Funny I'm still a no-name to ya since I bin supportin' ya so long."

Beth was certain she had never met the man before. "Please, I'm at a loss—"

"Yup. I s'pose ya are. But ya spent plenty a' time in my building." He snapped a twig he had been holding. "I'm Davie Grant. Use'ta have a profitable tavern—now all I got is a school squatting in my place, usin' up my wood an' drinkin' up my water. Strange—as I ain't got no son no more, so that there school don't do me a lick a' good. An' now I find ya here in *my* woods. Ain't ya got no respect a'tall fer what ain't yers?"

Beth tried again to step around the man. In a flash, Davie had snatched the violin and held it away, high in the air, a slow grin spreading across his face as he loomed over her. "Thet's real fancy, missie. An' you was playin' it jest so well."

She could hear Father's voice commanding that she run—that she escape before danger could befall her. But she hesitated, casting a pleading look at her precious instrument. "Mr. Grant, please," she whispered, "I just want to go in peace."

He took a menacing step forward. "An' thet's what I want too—ta be left in peace. But you had to come in here—all high an' mighty, changin' our town with all yer learnin' and all yer religion and all yer fancy ways. An' then bringing in all them vagrant foreigners—right here among us. Who the blazes ya think you are, anyhow?" He lowered the violin from the air and clutched his other hand around its neck. The strings made a sickening sound.

"Leastwise, the school year being most over, it's 'bout time fer ya to leave. An' I say ya best git to it, then. I say let them widders take their kids an' git too. What this here town needs is *men*—real men—not none of them there Eetalyuns either. Real red-blooded men. And the sooner them houses is rid of non-payin' folks, the sooner new folk'll come. Pro'bition won't last—an' it'll all go right back to how it was. Ya hear me? All ya gotta do is git. Outta town. Outta the country, far as I'm concerned—jest git."

For a moment he raised the violin as if offering it back to Beth, then snatched it away before her hands could receive it. "See this perty thing? Bet it'd be easy jes' to snap its skinny neck. Now, I ain't a bad fella, so I'll let it go—fer now. But ya best be careful, missie. 'Cause I don't think it'd take much ta break a thin little neck like this. Best ya keep it in mind."

Slowly he passed the beloved instrument back to Beth, glowering into her eyes. With one last sneer, he turned on his heel to head toward the woods. Only then did Beth notice the gun he had left at the edge of the clearing. He hoisted it conspicuously to his shoulder and walked away, whistling.

Beth's heart was pounding as she stood alone once again. She frantically thrust the violin back into its case, snapped it shut, and struck out quickly toward town. It wasn't until then that she recalled Frank's warning about not venturing into the woods. Was Davie Grant a dangerous man? He had referred to the woods as his. She had not realized they were privately owned—if that indeed was Davie's meaning.

Beth almost ran past the pool hall and on toward Molly's home, closing the door behind her and leaning against it. She struggled to catch her breath.

It appeared that her absence had not been noticed—nor her agitated return. Beth hurried quietly up the stairs and stowed the case safely back under her bed. Then she dropped onto the covers and wept silently, realizing the danger in which she had found herself. And now she was terrified to return to school. *Will Mr. Grant make good on his threat? Who can help?*

Surely Molly would react too strongly—maybe even confronting the Grants and risking their classroom—to be considered a confidante. Beth shook her head. Frank too. And Jarrick—Jarrick, who could best protect her—might also react with the most negative results. She still needed the Grants' pool hall to finish out the school year. If she were to disclose the conversation now, all her hard work and that of the students would be in jeopardy. Beth wiped her eyes, determining that she would tell no one for the time being. It was clear that she had been threatened if she did not leave—but he had not stipulated that she do so before the end of the school year.

Setting the table for supper and assisting Molly in the kitchen, Beth kept her eyes averted as much as possible. She was certain if Molly paused to look deeply into them, her maternal affection would read the fear Beth was struggling to conceal. Her mind churned with wild and garbled thoughts. Memories that had once seemed disjointed and unimportant flashed before her. Was there more than she knew about Philip's suggesting she not serve breakfast in the Grants' tavern?

What exactly is this man capable of doing? How worried should I be?

⁂

On Sunday morning, Beth had not shaken the nagging sense of fear from yesterday's frightening encounter. She picked her way across the rutted road, placing each step into Teddy's footprint as she followed him toward the company hall for church.

Upon entering the building and feeling engulfed in its sense of safety, she smiled toward the circle of children and adults gathered inside the door and joined them in exchanging boots for indoor shoes. The floors would have been impossible to keep clean if it weren't for this practice. Beth tucked her boots under the bench. Soon there was a large jumble of boots spilling over near the door. Something about the sight warmed Beth's heart. It spoke of community and closeness—of sharing and consideration. With a little smile she wondered if it would make the same impression on Mother.

She moved forward to chat with a group of ladies. Philip was speaking with three of the mining men. With increasing frequency the miners had been attending services since the Christmas concert—first Paolo, Alberto, and his cousin Lucio. And then young brothers named Saverio and Roberto, each in their early twenties. Now there were others whose names Beth did not yet know. Thrilled to see them making an appearance, she was growing hopeful they would be fully accepted into the community in time. Then Davie Grant's comments filled her mind and her heart clenched in fear. *If he has his way, they will be banished from Coal Valley—from the mine too.* Did anyone else resent their inclusion? Were there others who felt the same way as Mr. Grant?

Philip spoke from the book of Psalms, introducing it as a whole collection of praise and prayers, and mentioning some of his favorite passages. He challenged the townsfolk to read through one psalm a day and to share the reading with a neighboring family if Bibles were not available.

At the end of the service, Beth watched Philip from across the room and edged over in case she might be able to converse with him. She wondered if perhaps she should confide in him about Davie Grant. But she hesitated, uncertain.

Philip had motioned toward Alberto and another man, drawing them aside, directing them toward a small box at the front of the room. They seemed to be surprised and pleased by its contents. Curiosity got the better of Beth, and she inched closer.

She overheard, "Bardo and Giacobbe, they can'a surely read. Others also. I take and give out. *Grazie, Pastore!* Thank you." They scooped up the box and carried it away, leaving Philip to finish packing away the other church items.

Beth felt like a schoolgirl, shy and sheepish that she had listened in but too intrigued to draw away. "I'm sorry, Philip, I couldn't help but notice. Were they Bibles? In Italian?"

He placed the last hymnals in the box and turned to smile knowingly at Beth. "I thought you might like that. It wasn't even my idea. Two older ladies from a church in Lethbridge heard me talking about what was happening with the men up here and immediately began asking if they had the Word in their own language. Imagine my delight when they tracked down several copies in Italian and brought them to me."

"That's wonderful! Such a gift."

She lifted the cross from where it had been set aside, wrapped it back in its cover, and placed it on top of the crate of hymnals. "I knew Frank had a Bible, and I suspected Alberto might too. But it never occurred to me to find more. How lovely."

Philip pulled the purple cloth from the table and began folding it. "Sometimes God answers before we even know what to ask." His comment stirred Beth's heart. She had not prayed more than a few desperate words about her current difficulties. Ashamed of herself, she determined to spend some time in prayer that afternoon.

She began by confessing her foolish decision to go into the woods alone. She prayed for Davie Grant. She asked the Lord for safety, for peace. But peace did not come. For the first time, Beth talked to God about her fears that perhaps He did not want her to return to Coal Valley—and that if true, it might have nothing to do with whether she had failed to stand in His strength. She wondered if there might no longer *be* a school in which she could teach—or enough children remaining in town. *Will Davie Grant be able to accomplish his wish to send all us "outsiders" back to where we came from—get rid of the widows too?*

Feeling dejected, Beth could not bring herself to do the one thing she had promised herself she would not neglect—the letter home to Mother on Sunday afternoons. She knew she would never be able to present an honest assessment of the week without mentioning Davie Grant. And that was something Mother should never know.

Fewer children came for breakfast and yarn rolling on Monday, which Molly insisted was good news—at least some of the mothers were feeling it was no longer necessary. But Beth could not shake the dismal thought, more frequent with each passing day, that they might have just a couple more months together.

As she prepared to teach each morning, Beth grappled with her concerns about Davie Grant. She paid close attention now to any sound she heard from the residence above their classroom. Any thump might cause Beth to freeze in place, any squeak of the floorboards put her on alert.

She found reasons—any reason—to never be alone in the pool hall, asking the bigger boys to help rearrange the furniture after school each day, inviting Marnie to help her with study materials in the morning. She of course did not expect the children to protect her should there be another altercation, but she was certain if anyone else was present there would be none.

M ISS THATCHER, Miss Thatcher! You gotta come
quick. An accident!"

The loud rapping on her bedroom door startled her, but
the frightened look on Teddy's pale face when she answered
brought fear to Beth's heart. She couldn't even voice her
questions—*Who? What?*

"It's Grandpa Frank," Teddy said, reaching for her arm and
pulling her into the hallway. "He cut hisself. Bad."

Frank is hurt! Clutching Teddy's arm tightly, she headed
down the stairs—now pulling him along with her. "Where
is he?"

"Out back—at the woodshed." The boy's voice was un-
naturally shrill.

"What happened?"

"He was—he was cuttin' wood. Guess the ax musta slipped."

Oh, dear God, please— Beth's silent prayer was cut short
with her question, "How badly . . . ?"

"His leg—it's bleedin' buckets."

The back porch door banged shut behind them, and they

were running across the yard toward the woodshed. *I should have brought supplies,* she thought frantically. But what did she have at hand to deal with an open wound?

"Get Molly—"

"Already there."

Beth felt the air return to her gasping lungs. Molly would know what to do. But she tried to imagine their strong, dependable Frank in jeopardy. *What will we ever do if . . . ?* But Beth would not allow her mind to finish the thought.

At the open door of the small shed, Beth saw Molly on her knees beside Frank, who was sitting on a stump and leaning against the wall for support. Quiet and pale, he looked woozy and uncomfortable with Molly's ministrations, and blood was still flowing down his leg. Molly looked flushed yet determined.

"How'd ya ever manage . . . ?" Molly was gently scolding as she worked. "Ya gotta slow down, Frank. Teddy here can chop wood now. Ya need . . ." She shook her head and ripped another strip from a bed sheet nearby.

Beth moved forward. "How bad—?"

"Yer here." Molly did not even turn her head. "Good. I need ya to help me get this bleedin' stopped. Teddy, run git the kettle from the stove—and mind ya, don't slosh hot water on yerself. An' bring the basin too. We gotta clean this wound." He rushed to obey, and Molly called after him, "An' git the disinfectant from the shelf by the basin." She glanced at Beth. "Tear off some more strips while I try to stem the bleedin'."

Beth sank to her knees, following Molly's instructions with shaking hands. The sight of so much of Frank's blood made her feel sick, and she took little panting breaths to keep nausea at bay. Molly had already torn away his pant leg, and blood washed over his bare lower leg and covered Molly's hands. Beth had to look away as she handed over the next strip.

"Not too deep—an' that's a blessin'," Molly was saying. "Once we git the bleedin' stopped." She took the new strip and wound it tightly above the wound.

Frank seemed to rouse himself, forcing some strength back to his voice as he stared at his leg. "It'sa gonna need stitches."

Molly's head came up. "Stitches? I ain't no doctor, Frank."

He managed a weak smile. "Doctor, no. But stitcher, yes."

"Humph," puffed Molly. Teddy returned from the house with the additional supplies, then was sent back for the sewing kit.

Beth was tearing more strips of cloth but had to keep her face turned away. She shuddered, finding it impossible to imagine such a task, but Molly set to work. She steadily stitched the wound, with only an occasional groan from her patient. She got the blood flow stopped and bandaged the leg with more of her sheet strips after pouring on generous amounts of her precious antiseptic. Finally she rinsed her own hands clean with a deep sigh. Then the two women and Teddy half carried, half led Frank inside to a chair at the kitchen table.

"Make a list an' we'll send Teddy to yer place fer what ya need," Molly instructed.

Frank stared at her.

"Well, ya can't go back there, even if you was able to git there. Which ya ain't. This is gonna take some tendin' to, and I ain't got the time to be hikin' out to yer cabin two or three times a day. You can have the long sofa in the parlor fer a bed, since you can't climb them stairs. We'll jest watch over ya here for a while." Her tone invited no discussion, and Molly placed a cup of strong coffee near Frank's elbow, placed a piece of paper and a pencil on the table, and went to wash the blood from her apron. Beth guessed she probably washed additional tears from her eyes at the same time.

⁂

Frank's wound healed well over the days that followed. Molly took her nursing seriously and fussed or scolded by turn. They shared coffee in the kitchen, where Frank was allowed to do small tasks to help with meal preparation. Beth observed a few games of dominoes or shared work on a jigsaw puzzle. Once he could put weight back on the injured leg, Molly even escorted him to the dining room table at mealtime. In all of Frank's previous visits, he had never taken a meal with the company men in the dining room.

"Truth be told," Molly muttered to Beth, "he got far more right to be settin' there than those stuffed shirts I feed every meal." Beth only smiled. Molly was doing far more than inviting a man to the dinner table—and well she knew it. Molly was making a statement to the entire town—company men included—that they were all on level ground. Well—almost. Beth was certain that in Molly's eyes, Frank was one step above them.

Almost as soon as Frank joined them at the dinner table, Nick Costa returned unexpectedly. It caused some consternation for Molly—who was faced with the task of finding room for him when all her guest rooms were in use. With Frank sleeping in the parlor and four other men already settled in the rooms upstairs, Beth quickly volunteered to have Marnie move in and share her room so Nick might board in Marnie's for the time being. Marnie's eyes shone at the prospect.

Even at this arrangement, Nick was such a gentleman that he did not complain—not even a flicker of annoyance. Beth was certain none of the other company men would have stood for such a small room—with a view of the shed to boot.

Frank was getting restless and antsy, impatient to get back to his usual activities even while he obviously appreciated the care Molly was lavishing upon him. In his typical manner, he had taken upon himself some useful tasks. Virtually behind Molly's back, he would slip away to fix the hinge on the front gate, drive the fence posts deeper so the pickets stood straight again, and pound more nails into some loose boards on the front porch. Molly clucked at him disapprovingly whenever she caught him, but no one doubted how pleased she was to have Frank getting well and near at hand.

At last Molly was convinced Frank could manage well enough for himself at home. She wrapped an extra loaf of nut bread, his favorite, and ladled a jar of some leftover stew for him to take home. Beth watched in amazement as he expressed his thanks, smiling warmly into Molly's eyes just a little longer than necessary, and Molly blushing ever so slightly when he praised her. "You make'a the best I've ever had!"

TEDDY WAS BUSY coaxing the pool hall's large iron stove into a controlled warming blaze as Beth worked at the chalkboard, posting the day's arithmetic assignment for the older class. An unexpected visitor slipped into the schoolroom while they worked, and they both spun toward the sound of a loud, questioning meow.

"A cat!" Beth exclaimed.

Teddy stood and shut the iron door. "Mrs. Grant's tabby," he volunteered. "Don't know how it managed to git out. She keeps it tucked in close upstairs."

"Maybe you had best take it back up to her," Beth suggested.

"That cat? She'd scratch the freckles right off yer face if ya even tried to pick her up."

"She's mean?"

"*Mean*? She's wicked. Won't let no one but Mrs. Grant touch her. Not even Davie."

At the mention of Davie, Beth felt a chill. Dared she ask questions of Teddy? He knew the cat—did he also know the man?

As quickly as the idea came, Beth dismissed it. She would not involve Teddy in something that might mean danger.

"If we can't get the cat back, what will we do with it?" she wondered. "If it's mean, I don't want anybody getting hurt. . . ." Silently she was praying that Davie would not be the one sent to reclaim the wayward animal.

"Mrs. Grant'll come," asserted Teddy matter-of-factly. "Surprised she ain't—*isn't* here already."

Just as Teddy spoke, Beth heard steps stomping through the hallway. She turned, fearing she would be facing an angry Davie Grant, but instead it was Helen who trudged into the room.

"Penelope," she said, staring at the cat with a frown. "How come ya down here?"

In answer the cat dashed from under one table to another.

Helen turned accusing eyes at Beth. "It's the food ya been bringin' in here to feed those kids. She never come down here before."

Beth stood dumbly—chalk in hand. Weeks had passed since she had last brought any food to school.

Teddy spoke into the silence. "Miss Thatcher said I should bring her on up, but I told her the cat don't like no one touching her but you."

"You mind you never lay a hand on her, boy" was Helen's terse response.

"No, ma'am," responded Teddy evenly.

Helen blew out a breath and let her gaze travel the room. "Humph," she puffed, "almost looks like a true schoolroom in here."

It is a true schoolroom, Beth wished to retort, but she bit her tongue.

"Yes, ma'am," said Teddy. "It sure does."

Helen shuffled. "Well—the year's most over. Then we'll be back to some peace and quiet again."

Beth felt she should say something—anything to break the tension. But her mind refused to produce anything that sounded reasonable.

Teddy saved her again. "We sure do appreciate Mr. Grant lettin' us use his building for the year, ma'am."

Helen's eyes sparked. "*His* building?" she snapped. "That man ain't done nothin' in his life to earn 'im no ownership of nothin'. Was my money bought this here building—then he goes and makes a saloon outta it, 'stead of the supply store we'd agreed upon. Then Prohibition come along and takes even that away. No store. No nothing but a two-bit pool hall thet don't even pay me to open the doors. I watch my money tricklin' away for no good reason. And now my husband is—" She stopped abruptly and tugged her worn sweater across her front as though to hide behind its tattered wool.

Beth finally found her voice. She carefully laid aside the chalk and stepped toward their visitor.

"Mrs. Grant," she said with all the kindness she could convey, "you will never know how meaningful and wonderful the use of your building has been to this town. Without it there would have been no chance for these children to receive an education. I sincerely—*most* sincerely—thank you on their behalf for your generosity. We owe you more than we can ever repay."

As Beth's words washed over the woman, the changes in her demeanor were reflected in her eyes. She said nothing more, simply scooped up her delinquent cat and took her leave just as the students began to clatter through the doors. However, as Beth watched her go she was certain the woman's back did not look quite as stiff as it had when she had entered.

As Julie's visit drew close, Beth was bubbling over with excitement. She referred to it often, repeating, "Molly, when Julie comes . . ." numerous times a day. Her sister would follow Beth's western journey, arriving in Lethbridge by train and catching a ride to Coal Valley in the company vehicle. Beth put the finishing touches on Julie's room, including a little bouquet of the first spring wild flowers, grateful there were fewer boarders at the time so a room was available. She stood back, assessing it in hopes that her sister would be comfortable and feel welcome.

The big day finally arrived, and Julie stepped out onto the streets of Coal Valley as if the road itself were contaminated. Beth rushed forward to hug her close, overlooking her sister's aversive behavior. "I can't believe you're really here," she exclaimed again and again, pulling Julie into Molly's yard. They climbed the porch together, Julie looking around stiffly and oddly silent.

Introductions came first. "This is Molly McFarland. She's like a second mother to me."

"Delighted, I'm sure." Julie nodded and offered her hand.

"And these two are Teddy and Marnie, Molly's—uh—family."

Julie smiled politely. "Good afternoon."

"H'lo," the teens answered in unison, their faces devoid of expression.

"Come upstairs, Julie. We've got a room for you just across the hallway from mine. I was going to suggest that we share, but this way you'll have space for your clothes and your other things."

The man carrying Julie's trunk dropped it at the front door

and turned away, looking somewhat put out. "Teddy Boy," Molly said, nodding at the trunk. He silently hoisted it to follow Beth and Julie up the stairs.

Beth motioned toward her own door and then opened the door to Julie's room. "See, I'm just across the hall." The two girls entered. "I think you'll be very comfortable here," Beth hurried on. "The men boarders are farther up the hall."

Julie was surveying the room slowly. "What I'd really like, Bethie," she said, "is to freshen up. It was a horrific trip—the roads were positively dreadful. I thought that old beat-up car would surely fall to pieces before we arrived. Will you show me the washroom, please?"

Beth smiled. "Well, there really isn't one. But you do have a washstand here, and I made sure the water is fresh for you. Here are your towels and soap."

Julie was bewildered. "But where . . . where is the privy?"

"Oh, well, you have two rather old-fashioned choices, sister dear. There is a chamber pot—" she gestured toward it—"and the outhouse in back." Her eyes were coaxing Julie to see the humor and adventure in their surroundings. But then Beth remembered her own feelings upon arriving in Coal Valley—the dismal main street, the simple accommodations, the strangeness of it all. Her bearing relaxed in empathy.

Julie was clearly overwhelmed. "I had no idea that your town was so . . . so primitive."

"You'll get used to it," Beth reassured her.

Julie snorted and walked around the bedroom, testing for dust on the dresser and pressing down on the mattress.

Beth was taken aback by her reaction. "I don't remember you being quite so prissy," she blurted before she could stop herself.

Julie flashed a frown, then quickly softened. "Is that what

I'm being? I'm sorry, darling. I really was determined to be ever so bold and daring—and here I am, already fit to be tied."

"You're here, Julie!" Beth raised her arms in delight. "You're really here. You can't imagine how I've looked forward to this!"

Together they unpacked Julie's trunk and began to chatter again as they had when they were young. There was so much news from home that Beth could hardly drink it all in. Friends had become engaged, hearts had been broken, babies had been born, and extravagant purchases had been made. Julie gushed over all of it, just as she used to.

After everything had been put in order, Beth suggested they take a walk around town. "It won't take us long," she said with a chuckle. "There is really only one street."

They walked over to the company hall while Beth pointed down the little hill to the mining families' houses. She had already shared with Julie about the plight of the women and children. Julie was even more dismayed to see their homes. "They're so small," she whispered. "Are some of them where those foreign miners live?"

"Oh no, they live in the camp. It's a little ways from town, and much humbler than these."

"I can hardly imagine!"

The hall was locked, so Beth continued next door to the company store.

"We can go inside the shop, but I doubt they have anything you need."

"Can I see your classroom?"

"I suppose—yes, we can go there," Beth answered guardedly, her mind wrestling with the chance of encountering Davie Grant. She had not seen him since being accosted in the woods, and so she was nearly certain he would not appear now. But still her heart raced at the very thought—heightened by her desire to protect her sister from any possible harm. She rather warily led Julie across the street toward the pool hall. Inside, the dim lighting showed the main room where the tables were now set up to serve company men in their leisure. There was no evidence of her classroom at all.

"But, Bethie, it really *is* a saloon, just as Mother said."

Beth led their retreat out onto the road before anyone had noticed them. "No, it is indeed a pool hall and a coffee house. But on weekdays, it's also our classroom."

"Unfathomable." Julie shook her head. "How can your tiny hamlet even support a pool hall? Are there enough patrons with so few men? Does the school pay rent?"

It had never occurred to Beth to wonder. "Possibly the mothers do" was her best response.

Already Julie had seen almost everything that made up the small town. They stood together in the road for a moment, turning in one direction and then another. Beth shrugged. "Other than the mine and the camp—and I suppose the river and woods—there's really nothing else. If it were warmer we might go for a walk—" But she stopped abruptly. A walk through the beautiful woods was no longer an option.

"Let's go back to the guest house," Julie said. "I feel as if we're being watched."

"Well, I suppose we are." Beth laughed at the thought. "You're new—and that creates a stir. Mostly among the children—who seem to notice everything."

Beth and Julie spent a little more time sitting in chairs on the sunlit porch before they were summoned for supper. They shared the dining room with three of the company men and Teddy. Beth felt a little like she was a newcomer too tonight, not assisting with the meal service as she usually did. She watched with some apprehension as Julie conversed with the men who shared their table. Her sister's manners were impeccable, but Beth was concerned her demeanor conveyed a lack of respect. It made Beth wonder if she herself had seemed as aloof when she first arrived in Coal Valley.

In the evening, Beth invited Julie to join their English class at Frank's cabin, but she declined, saying she was weary and wanted to retire early. As Beth trudged the short wooded path behind Molly, she was pleased to remember that Sunday morning would bring the arrival of Philip and a church service to share with her beloved sister.

Molly and the others were waiting in the foyer ready to leave when Beth rapped on her sister's door for the third time. Julie had skipped breakfast and now insisted, again through the locked door, "Just a few more minutes." Beth descended halfway down the stairs and suggested that the others go on ahead—she would follow when Julie was ready.

Molly obviously was holding her tongue. She managed to smile up at Beth and motioned the others out the door. Beth returned upstairs.

At last Julie emerged. "How do you like it, Bethie? It's new." From head to toe she looked the fashion plate. Cloche hat tipped smartly over swirls of extravagantly coifed hair, liberal use of rouge and lipstick, a shift-style dress of expensive silk fabric—the shorter fashion their mother disdained—modern hose with patent leather shoes, three long strands of beads clicking against one another as she moved.

Beth stepped back in alarm. "Julie, no one dresses like that here."

"I know," she answered calmly, gesturing with one hand

as if she were modeling the ensemble. "I thought I would show them how it's done. Maybe they can learn a few tips. I'm considered somewhat of a master at accessorizing back home, as you know."

Beth quickly pushed her sister back inside the room and shut the door, leaning her back against it. "We don't have much time, Julie—but the makeup and jewelry have got to go. I suppose we'll have to put up with the rest."

"But there is nothing wrong with the way I look!"

"For pity's sake, Julie, it's *church*!"

Despite her sister's shrill protestations, Beth persisted until the makeup had been removed, the long strands of beads and gaudy earrings returned to the box on Julie's dresser. Then as quickly as possible, Beth tossed a coat to Julie and propelled her out the door. She could already hear singing from the hall before they entered and moved into the row to take the seats Molly had saved for them. Beth noticed Philip's eyes following them curiously. In fact, in every direction she could feel people observing them intently.

For the first time since arriving in town, Beth had difficulty concentrating on Philip's sermon. She found herself dwelling instead on what she would like to include in the conversation she planned to have with Julie after Sunday dinner. She tried not to be too embarrassed that Philip would meet Julie dressed as she was. It was a shame, since Beth had been so looking forward to presenting her sister to her new community.

But Sunday dinner turned out to be a special event planned by Molly to introduce Julie to as many of the townsfolk as possible. The generous woman had gone to unusual lengths to organize a potluck meal to be held at the company hall. With great effort, Beth controlled her emotions through all of the repeated introductions.

"Philip, I'd like you to meet my younger sister, Miss Julie Thatcher. And Julie, this is Pastor Philip Davidson."

Philip took her hand congenially. "So nice to meet you, Miss Thatcher. I know that Beth has been very enthusiastic about your visit. I'm sure you have a great deal of catching up to do."

"I enjoyed your sermon so much," Julie enthused. "Not nearly as stuffy and academic as those we have at home. It was a breath of fresh air. Really."

Philip smiled and asked, "And how long will your visit last? I hope you'll be able to make good use of the time together."

"Yes, we have two full weeks together," Beth answered for her sister. "It will be so nice to have an extended visit."

"To be sure."

Beth felt her knees turn weak when she noticed Jarrick approach. *What on earth might Julie say to him?*

"Julie, may I present Constable Jack Thornton," she said, hoping the formal wording might keep Julie in check. Jarrick's eyebrows lifted slightly. For some reason she had not been willing to share his given name, the one she had chosen to use.

"Welcome, Miss Thatcher," he offered cheerfully. "I trust you've been made to feel at home."

Beth held her breath while a coy smile from Julie answered his inquiry. "It's not much like home, but I'm glad to be with Bethie again. And it's awfully nice to meet an officer of the law so far from civilization. I'm sure you have stories to tell, do you not?"

Jarrick cleared his throat. "I suppose I do, Miss Thatcher. But I'm afraid it's our policy to keep most of those stories classified."

Julie refused to be put off. "Come now, Officer Jack. I'm sure there must be some interesting goings-on nearby. A few horse thieves, perhaps? A band of outlaws? It simply can't be all miners and farmers, now, can it?" There was a twinkle in Julie's eyes that Beth found alarming. She turned to Jarrick, watching for his reaction.

"I'm afraid I couldn't say." He smiled and nodded just a little to soften his remark. "It was so nice to meet you, Miss Thatcher." Something in the way he avoided her questions caused Beth to wonder what it was that *did* consume his hours of work.

Julie, however, seemed puzzled by the man's rather un-affected reaction to her—nothing at all like the attention she was used to receiving from the young men back home.

Having made the rounds and managing a few quick bites of food between conversations, Beth and Julie had finally re-treated to their seats when Addison and Luela Coolidge took to the stage and signaled for everyone's attention. To Beth's surprise, there was to be a short performance by the children.

She was delighted, watching Julie's expressions from the corner of her eye as her beloved students sang an amusing rendition of "Billy Boy" and presented a short skit. Surely, she thought, Julie would quickly understand what delightful, precious children she had been given to teach. However, she was shocked to hear Julie whisper, "Oh dear, Bethie, have they no better clothes to wear? Most of them are worn through and don't fit properly at all." And then she added, "Poor little waifs," as if the afterthought removed the sting from her comments. Beth cringed. *How can Julie so entirely miss their endearing faces?*

In preparation for the next song, Frank took the stage and quickly tuned his violin. Five of the girls stood before them in a row, fidgeting until he was ready. Beth recognized the tune in just the first few notes of the introduction, one of her favorites. "What a Friend We Have in Jesus," the girls sang in lovely harmony, blending beautifully with the strings. Beth felt she had never heard anything sweeter and once again found herself clapping heartily. This time Julie seemed pleased, but her gaze was on Frank and his violin rather than the children.

At the end Beth stood and expressed their thanks to the full room, and the sisters retired to Molly's home again, changing out of their church clothes into simpler garments. Beth had every intention of confronting Julie immediately about her attitude and conduct, but she did not want to dispel the goodwill created by the welcome they had received at church. They spent the afternoon enjoying each other's company.

As supper approached they heard Molly's voice call up the stairs, "Frank's here, girls."

Beth rose quickly and motioned to Julie. "Good. You can talk to him now. I want you to get to know him."

"Who's Frank again?"

"The violinist—the one who played today."

"Oh." Julie rose to follow. "He was really good—better than some musicians I've heard in concert back home. Who would have thought I'd hear such lovely music from an old coot like that?"

Beth froze, her hand on the door handle. She drew a deep breath and turned back toward Julie. "Please don't ever talk like that about Frank Russo again. If you knew him at all—if you could get off your high horse long enough to see who he is—you'd truly be ashamed of yourself."

It was Julie's turn to recoil. "Don't be such a stuffed shirt. It's not as if he can hear me."

"*I* can hear you, and that's enough." Beth took another step forward. She whispered tersely, "I won't hear you speak against anyone in this town, Julie. You are *not* better than they.

In fact, I've been more embarrassed to be seen with you than I ever was of them. You have acted like an unabashed snob."

Julie's lip began to quiver. "How can you say that? I've been . . . I've been congenial, even friendly."

Beth shook her head, trying to find the words to explain the difference to her sister, who clearly could not comprehend how her actions were perceived. "Don't treat them any differently than any of Mother and Father's friends. They're just as dear to me as any guests ever brought to our home. In fact, more—many of them are practically family."

"*I'm* your family," Julie said with a sniff. "And you've never talked to me like this before."

"Maybe I've never seen you as clearly before." Beth took a breath, trying to stifle her own anger. "I've learned that these people are more than what they appear on the outside—and much more difficult to assess than their surroundings would imply. Please, please try to view them with an open mind. I think you'll be surprised if you do—most of them are as agreeable, as interesting and cordial, as any of our friends and family back home."

The two sisters stared at each other. Then Beth went over to Julie and embraced her. "I'm sorry to have sounded cross, darling, but I had to get your attention . . . get you in another frame of mind as quickly as possible. These two weeks can be a truly wonderful and memorable experience for both of us if you can open your mind to another world from that in which we grew up."

Julie sniffed again and shakily whispered, "I'll try, Bethie."

Beth and Julie spent a lovely evening with Molly and Frank. Beth smiled in pleasure as she watched these two she had come to appreciate and love looking so comfortable together. Molly was still checking on how well his leg was healing and managed to find a reason to send home more food. Beth remembered what she'd said to Julie about family and knew how much it rang true when observing the older couple. In all the world, she felt they were in her circle of very favorite people.

Julie retired early again, leaving Beth to share the cleanup with Molly. Beth dutifully scraped the plates and stacked them beside the sink. Molly poured a second kettle of hot water into the basin, and Beth began the process of washing.

"I feel I should apologize about Julie," she began.

Molly smiled but queried, "What ya mean?"

"Well, she's rather . . . childish, spoiled I think. I hope she hasn't hurt anyone's feelings with her silly talk and vanity."

"Words can only get at a body if ya believe 'em."

Beth paused, hands still in the water. "Certainly, but even if you don't take someone seriously, the words still sting."

"Oh? How's that?" Molly reached for another bowl to dry.

"If I called you a name, it wouldn't hurt?"

"Depends. Were ya intent on being mean? Or jest by accident?"

"Hmm," Beth contemplated, thinking back to the times she had been teased. "Let's say I found it amusing."

"Then it ought'a roll right off. I might jes' laugh right along with ya. 'Course, ya also have ta ask, is it true? If it is, maybe a body should take it to account." Molly put an arm around Beth's shoulders affectionately. "I know she's a bit rough 'round the edges, dearie, but we ain't none of us fit fer glory yet. Gotta let God do His job. An' it ain't the rest'a us she's gotta please—only Him."

Beth couldn't help but chuckle at "rough around the edges" applied to her finishing-school sister and imagine Julie's response to such a description. Then she sobered and tried to process the full meaning of Molly's counsel. "Well, at least she should try a little harder."

"Now, dearie, ya gotta take care. That word *should*, it's a slip'ry one. Who gets ta measure *should*s? Only God gets ta say. If He says ya should, then ya mind Him. If folks say ya should—ya jest go back an' ask God. Don't need more'n that to measure up to." She smiled to herself and reached for the next plate. "Good thing 'bout gitting old—ya don't think near so much 'bout what *folks* think of ya—what they say ya should do. Ya spend more time wond'rin' what you still *can* do. Wish I could go back over my own life and not bother with all the silly things folks said I *should*. Sure woulda made life more simple—less confusin'."

CHAPTER

23

JULIE WAS BETH'S SHADOW for the remainder of the week. She took a seat in the center of the parlor sofa while children rolled yarn all around her, sat next to the window in the pool hall while Beth taught school, helped as best she could in the kitchen, and observed both English classes and Bible club in quiet amazement. It seemed to come as a sobering realization that Beth was working much harder, with more creativity and energy, than Julie had ever envisioned.

On Saturday a happy respite occurred when Jarrick returned for a visit and took the sisters riding in his car. Beth had seen little of the local countryside from such a vantage point and was pleased to explore it with Julie and Jarrick. However, the fact that Beth had introduced him to her sister as Jack provided an added complication. She now had no idea how to refer to him when they were together. Out of sheer stubbornness she called him nothing at all during the entire day.

Beth was surprised at the little off-road trails Jarrick had found, winding in and out among the hills, and even more flabbergasted at the kinds of terrain over which he was willing to drive his automobile. "Are you sure we aren't lost?" she teased.

"I've been in and out of here before. There's a beautiful small stream just ahead with a beaver dam that makes its own little waterfall. Thought you would enjoy it. If we're lucky, we might even get to see one of the beavers at work."

Though they did not have the pleasure of watching the beavers, the two young women did enjoy the falls. Julie even produced a camera and took delight in snapping a couple of photographs. Beth found herself blushing as Julie insisted upon a picture of Jarrick and Beth sitting on a large rock beside the stream. She had wished to object, but making a fuss about it seemed worse than just going ahead with Julie's instructions.

Jarrick seemed especially keen on studying the surrounding hills with his heavy-duty binoculars. "Looking for bears?" Julie had asked, sounding like she might really be worried.

Jarrick laughed. "Well, you can never tell what you might find in this expanse of wood." He let the ladies also have a look, and Beth could not believe how close it brought everything, vistas she knew to be a good distance away.

Jarrick produced a picnic lunch which he had arranged for with Molly. It was delightful to sit under the sweeping trees waking from their long winter nap and listen to the birds busy among the branches, making plans for nest building. The water from the beaver dam filled in the harmony for the birds' songs. Beth wanted to lean back, close her eyes, and be lost in the day. At the same time, listening to the lively conversation between Jarrick and Julie made Beth determined not to miss a thing.

When Jarrick dropped them off at the boarding house, Julie hurried in to brush away some of the day's soil from her new shoes. For a moment before Jarrick departed, Beth lingered at the gate.

"Your sister is . . . nice," Jarrick offered, standing beside the driver's door.

Beth smiled and turned her head self-consciously. "She really is, you know. She's got a very sweet heart, even though I'm afraid we've all spoiled her terribly. I didn't realize how much until this visit."

"Regardless, I enjoyed our drive. It was a perfect day with two fine young Thatcher ladies."

Beth dipped her head. "I enjoyed myself too. Thank you so much for taking us, Jarrick."

He laughed. "Oh, so I'm Jarrick again?"

She had hoped he hadn't noticed. "I only— Well, I just didn't have your permission to . . ." She sighed. "All the others call you Jack," she finished weakly.

"Yes, they do. You—and my mother—are the only ones who seem to prefer my given name. But I'll admit that I do like to hear you use it. At any rate, I'm pleased to have shared the day with you." And then he called over his shoulder as he disappeared into his car, "Have a nice evening, Bethie."

Beth felt her face flush, and she couldn't help a little smile at his use of the nickname. She turned back toward the house. Only then did she notice Julie watching through the window and was grateful her sister could not have overheard.

❧

Sunday afternoon a picnic had been planned for the children of their church. Philip was providing candy as prizes for the games, and the townsfolk were to organize and manage it all. Beth and Julie offered to assist with the three-legged races. For most of the afternoon they watched the other games, cheering along the youngest children and laughing at the antics of all. Beth was pleased to see that Paolo and his father were among the crowd as well as several of the other miners. They were interacting well with the townsfolk, chatting—not easily, but congenially—smiles flashing affably.

Beth filled her plate from the selections of potluck dishes at the crowded serving table and took a seat on one of the makeshift benches, enjoying the peaceful moment to observe interactions around her. She heard a disturbance coming from between the buildings just behind her. Beth turned to see Addison with his small brother, Wilton, who was doubled over and appeared to be retching into the bushes.

Mothers converged from all directions. Beth reached the boys first, placing a hand on Wilton's back and bending down to look into his ashen face. She turned back toward the older brother. "What happened, Addison? Is it something he ate?" As more and more gathered around them, the confusion made it difficult for Beth to hear his answer.

"No . . . I . . . I don't really—" Just then Wilton's knees buckled and he slumped to the ground. Hands reached out for him from every direction. Addison begged, "Oh, Willie—you okay? I'm awful sorry! Don't cry."

Wilton shook his head, even in his pitiful state insisting defiantly, "I ain't cryin'!"

"Good boy." But Addison's expression was full of uncertainty and fear.

Despite the crowd, Jarrick was able to lift Wilton up and carry him toward one of the nearby tables. All the dishes were whisked out of the way to clear it for the limp boy. "You're going to be just fine, buster," Jarrick encouraged him, tucking a towel beneath his head and peering closely into his eyes. He chatted on as he assessed the boy. "You're a brave fella. Now,

Willie, did you eat anything unusual—anything strange? Berries from the woods? Or some kind of mushroom you found?"

Without an answer, the eyes became unfocused, then closed. Jarrick leaned over him. In panic Beth watched him sniff into Wilton's gaping mouth. He turned away to quickly search the bushes where Wilton had been discovered. The mothers crowded around Beth, waiting beside the table, all murmuring conjectures about the little boy's condition.

Addison hovered over his brother and stroked his forehead. Almost at once Jarrick returned. He drew the boys' mother, Heidi, away and motioned for Beth to follow. "I'm not a doctor, but I'm quite certain this is serious. He needs to be taken to the hospital in Lethbridge right away."

Heidi's eyes grew wide with fear. "How'm I s'posed to git him there?" Before Jarrick could answer she cried out, "What's wrong with 'im? Do ya think ya know?"

Jarrick drew in a long breath. "It looks like some kind of poisoning to me. I have a car. We'll give him as much milk as he can hold and take him into the city right now."

"Ain't no milk!" she nearly screamed.

"Then water," Jarrick insisted.

"But my babies," she wailed. "I can't leave my babies." Heidi's eyes jumped from the sick boy on the table to the two smaller children clutching at her skirt and the infant bawling in her arms, then locked on Jarrick's face.

"I've got to have someone ride with me, in case . . ." He let the words hang unfinished.

Beth was quick to volunteer. "I'll go."

"Thank you, Beth. I'll bring the car." Grabbing up a bowl as he passed by a table, Jarrick unceremoniously tossed its luncheon contents underneath. "Take this, Beth. If we're lucky, he'll vomit some more."

In stunned silence Beth followed, frightened yet obedient, uncertain she was up to the task ahead—providing nursing duties for a deathly ill child while they drove for hours across rough roads.

Only then did she notice her sister at her side, frightened eyes betraying obvious distress. "I'm sorry, Julie dear," Beth said. "I must leave."

"I understand. I'll be fine. He needs you. Just go."

Jarrick and Alberto managed to wrap the boy in a blanket and move him into the back seat. Someone else ran up with a jug of water. Beth slid in beside Wilton, cradling his head in her lap and keeping the bowl at hand.

They started down the dusty road, Jarrick driving as carefully as possible to miss the largest of the potholes, but keeping up his speed. Beth could see his hands gripping the wheel, knuckles white. Beth pushed the hair from Wilton's eyes and laid her other hand on his chest to keep his body from bouncing so much. From time to time he needed to use the bowl. Afterward Beth raised his head, attempting to keep him drinking sips from the jug of water.

"Let's sing, Wilton," Beth coaxed him, hoping her voice expressed much more calm than she felt. She began with the song the children had sung at the welcome event for Julie. "Oh, where have you been, Billy Boy, Billy Boy? Oh, where have you been, charming Billy?" To the best of his ability Wilton sang along, his face pale and his voice thin. Beth rubbed his stomach and his arms, hoping to somehow distract him from his obvious pain.

It was a dreadfully long, difficult ride until the mountain roads were behind them and only the wide expanse of prairie lay ahead.

Beth noted the boy's eyes had closed. "Wake up, Wilton." She shook him, and his eyes fluttered open again.

"I'm tired, Miss Thatcher," he murmured.

Beth shook him again. "You must stay awake, darling." She tried another song, but his eyes continued to flutter.

"Hurry, Jarrick. I think he's passing out. Or falling asleep—I can't tell which. Is it bad if he sleeps?"

"Try to wake him again. Pinch him if you have to."

"Oh, Father, help this child," she choked out. "Wilton, wake up!"

"I'm awake." He stirred. "I'm jes' so tired."

At last the city came into view, and—finally—the hospital.

Jarrick scooped up the boy and ran into the waiting room to summon help, Beth hurrying along behind. Almost immediately two orderlies and a doctor appeared. Soon Wilton was wheeled away on a gurney.

Beth grasped at Jarrick's jacket. "Will he—do you think he will be all right?"

He placed a comforting arm around her shoulders. "I think so." Leaning against Jarrick, Beth let him lead her to the waiting area. He found seats for them, and then they began the long watch. Beth sat stiffly in her chair and Jarrick paced anxiously. "It seems like he would have gotten rid of much of the poison during the trip," Jarrick said, trying to comfort her. "And the water would also help—"

Just then a white-coated doctor appeared. "I want to assure you both that the boy is doing much better now. He's resting peacefully and appears to be out of danger. Are you his parents?"

"Oh no." Beth felt her cheeks growing warm.

Jarrick took a quick step away from Beth. "No, his mother was unable to come. I am a local officer, and this is the boy's teacher."

"I see. Well, it's a blessing that you were able to bring him to us in time. Eventually his body will clear itself of the toxins, but he has certainly ingested a dangerous amount of a very noxious substance."

"I was afraid that might be the cause of his illness. What happens next?" Jarrick sounded calm, contrary to the flurry of emotions Beth was feeling. She was relieved beyond measure that whatever Wilton had ingested was not going to take his life, but she also was horrified to hear how close he may have come. She breathed out another prayer for his full recovery.

"Well, he will certainly need to rest overnight. In the morning, he may be well enough to travel home again. We'll have to assess that later."

"May we see him?" Beth asked.

"For now, he's sleeping soundly." The doctor turned his attention back to Jarrick. "I'm sorry, Officer. I didn't get your name."

"Constable Jack Thornton." Jarrick extended his hand.

The doctor shook it. "I will provide a written report of the diagnosis when the boy is discharged. There's also the matter of the bill, Constable Thornton. How soon will you be speaking with the boy's parents?"

"That presents some difficulty," Jarrick answered evenly. "Would it be possible to give us a written copy of the bill? I'm afraid arrangements will have to be made. His mother is a widow, and from a mining community—"

"Now, Constable," the doctor said quickly, "you understand that the hospital is required—"

"I do understand, sir. And I assure you that arrangements will be made," Jarrick answered firmly.

The two stood face-to-face for a moment. The doctor finally conceded, "I'll see that a bill is prepared for you. I'm sure someone will need to contact our director if payments are to be arranged. An appointment will be required for that. The person doing that can stop at the desk or just telephone the office." He paused. "Are there telephones in the boy's community?"

"No, sir."

"Well, then, I trust that you personally, Constable Thornton, will see to it that arrangements are made." He turned and disappeared down the hall.

Beth had not considered what would happen after the boy had been examined and diagnosed, or how the bill would be paid. They walked from the building in silence to the car, waiting where Jarrick had abandoned it at the front curb.

"Heidi Coolidge doesn't have much left of her pension," Beth whispered.

"I know."

"Then how will she ever . . ." But she didn't complete her thought.

Jarrick opened the car door for Beth, and she slid into the front seat. He retraced a path around the back of the vehicle and into the driver's seat.

Jarrick sat quietly thinking for a moment. At last he answered her unfinished question. "We'll have to pray for a miracle."

<hr>

Beth found it difficult to enjoy the unexpected treat of a restaurant meal, picking at the fresh greens which she would normally have found delightful after so many months without. Her mind was on Heidi Coolidge and how she would pay for an expensive hospital stay, and on the question of where and how Wilton had ingested such a dreadful poison.

"I'd offer you a penny for your thoughts, but I'm pretty sure

I know what worries you." Jarrick seemed to be having just as much trouble with his own meal. "The important thing, of course, is that little Willie is going to be well again soon."

Beth fiddled with the tassels on the tablecloth, avoiding Jarrick's eye. "I just can't help but worry about all of the children. What if—"

"Yes," he agreed quickly. "I assure you that I will be tracking down the source of that toxin."

"But if Wilton found it, there's always a chance that any of the others could be in danger. If not now, sometime in the future . . ." Her voice trailed off.

He eyed her thoughtfully. "Please trust me, Beth."

For a moment she considered confiding in him her own concerns, and then decided against it. She sighed. "I hope you can find out something soon. I don't think I'll rest at all until I know."

Beth glanced through the window at the people walking past. It was a perfect spring evening in the fading light, and she was back in the city. She wished she could shake off her melancholy demeanor enough to enjoy it.

"I did hear some good news," Jarrick told her. "Paolo has found a job here in Lethbridge. He'll be leaving soon to live with his mother again. But I'm sorry for Alberto. He'll miss his son, though I'm sure he's pleased that the boy won't have to work in the mine. In the long run, it will likely open more opportunities for him—to be in town."

"That *is* good news." Beth smiled. "I had hoped he wouldn't stay long even though I'll certainly miss him. Our English classes won't be the same with his absence."

She took a big breath, let it out slowly, and set her mind to involve herself in the conversation Jarrick was continuing. Beth could feel the tension leaving her shoulders, the headache that had been threatening slip away. She eventually was able to relax and enjoy cuisine she hadn't tasted for many months. *Actually,* she told herself, *the setting seems almost romantic,* and she felt herself blush as she watched the light from outdoors fade. A candle on the table flickered against the white linen cloth, and the polished silverware beside her plate glittered with each dance of the candle's flame. Beth felt at ease, expressed in a soft sigh of contentment. Jarrick was good company. Attentive. Communicative. And sincere. *Not like those silly boys who vied for my attention in the past,* she thought, then dropped her eyes to her plate in case her expression gave her away.

They lingered over dessert and coffee, Beth reluctant to let the moment go. Just as she wondered if Jarrick might be getting ready to call for their bill, he summoned the waiter to refill their coffee cups, apparently enjoying the time as much as she was. Beth stirred actual cream into the rich coffee and, cup in hand, settled back to enjoy the pleasant, meaningful conversation. For the moment, thoughts of little Wilton, now in good hands, ceased to trouble her.

But Jarrick's demeanor seemed to alter. In the light from the candle, Beth thought his eyes now held a seriousness, an intensity, that hadn't been there before. He studied her with a pensive expression. "And what about you?"

"Me?" She looked at him.

"How long do you think you'll stay in Coal Valley?"

The unexpected question caught Beth off guard, her mind a jumble of reactions. She shrugged, feeling a bit shy. "My teaching contract is for just one year. I have started to wonder—to consider—what I would do if I were offered an extension to that time, but there's no way for me to know if it will even be a possibility."

"Well, before long summer will be upon us again. And the

school year will have ended. I just thought you might already know what comes next for you this summer."

Beth frowned and sighed again. "I suppose I'm going home. Mother would never forgive me if I didn't, and I've no reason to stay here. . . ." She let the words trail away.

It was silent for a few minutes, until Jarrick asked, "What do you think of the West? How do you like living out here? I'm sure it's very different from what you're used to—far fewer amenities, even here in Lethbridge. Would you ever consider making your home here—permanently?"

She could feel a prickle of fear at his inquiry. Or maybe it was hopefulness? At this moment the palpitations of her heart were indistinguishable. *How can I answer such a question?*

"As I said, my parents expect me home," she said slowly, "at least for the summer. But should I be asked to teach again, I would certainly consider the option." She blushed and hurried on, "I would be *very happy* to consider the option."

He leaned forward, moving his hand closer to the center of the table. "I know the town would be grateful to have you return." He hesitated for a moment, looking intently into her eyes. "I would be . . . well, pleased to hear that you planned to return."

The moment was filled with an intensity Beth had never experienced before. It both disturbed and energized her. She did not know how best to manage such emotion. Julie would have navigated it well, but Beth . . .

She allowed herself a little laugh. "It's funny that I hadn't thought of it before. But the truth is, if I chose not to return to Toronto, my mother would probably send Edward along to escort me home—forcefully, if necessary."

"Edward?"

She could feel herself fiddling with her napkin. "Oh, he's

somewhat of my mother's pet. She dotes on him." Beth gave a little laugh again. "Did I ever tell you that he's the one who found my violin? Just like the compass—the one he sent with you. The violin had been stolen, and Edward searched high and low until he recovered it. I can't even begin to express how grateful I am to have it again."

Jarrick was slowly leaning back in his chair, withdrawing his hand. The change in his disposition confused Beth. His gaze turned toward the window and he said, "That's . . . that's wonderful for you. I'm glad he was persistent. You must have truly missed the violin—you play it so beautifully." He paused for a moment and then continued in an almost off-hand manner, "Well, I certainly hope you'll consider teaching out here again. The town would be blessed to have you."

CHAPTER

24

ARRICK ARRANGED FOR BETH to spend the night in the home of friends, a young couple working with the same church organization as Philip. A warm reception and a comfortable room meant a good night's sleep. Jarrick bunked out at the RCMP post on the edge of town. The following morning, Beth was relieved to learn that Wilton would be able to return to the mountain town with them. *"Thank You, Lord, thank You."*

On the way to the hospital, Jarrick cleared his throat. "I'd like to ask you for a favor—even though you might not understand the reason just now."

Beth nodded and waited.

"I know you heard Wilton's doctor refer to the toxin that the boy drank. In reality, Beth, the drink was alcohol based. It was bootleg liquor."

"But I thought you said it was *poison*," she contended.

"And it was." His tone was sad. "Beth, I'm sure you have no idea what is in the kind of stuff that is bought and sold as 'hooch.' It has an alcohol base—but it's made with anything

279

that can be found—including antifreeze and dead animals. The doctor was correct when he called it toxic. Indeed, it was almost fatal."

Oh no, Lord, our worst fears . . . Horrified, Beth turned to him, her thoughts churning. *Liquor—to the children—a kind that could easily kill someone! Are we all in danger? Who would give that to a child?*

Seeing her reaction, he hurried on, "I am most definitely determined to discover more about it—that has been and will continue to be my own top priority during the coming days. But I'd like to ask you, Beth, to keep that information just between us for now."

"Why?" she demanded, appalled. "Shouldn't the families be warned?"

"I'm afraid that if others know, it will make my job much more difficult—and there are aspects to my investigation I can't reveal at this time, even to you. So it's essential for the time being not to mention this to anyone. If you do it may well jeopardize the whole operation, which we've been working toward for months." He turned his eyes to meet hers. "Can you do that, Beth?"

At first she sat as if numb—then finally nodded, more questions rising now than before. *Investigation? This has been his work, what he has been doing? And where?*

⸎

"They gave me ice cream," Wilton announced once he was settled in the vehicle. "An' I got ta sleep in a bed that folded up. Like this." He gestured with his hands. "An' the doctor said I'm a brave little buckaroo. Miss Thatcher, what's a buckaroo anyways?"

Beth smiled as best she could from the front seat as he

jabbered on without waiting for an answer. The car pulled out onto the highway. Even though she was listening to Wilton's tumbling stream of narration about his experiences, her eyes were studying Jarrick. He was strangely withdrawn, though Beth was uncertain as to why. Perhaps he was more worried than he had let on concerning the source of the deadly liquor.

Her gaze drifted along the grassy roadside rushing past her window. She wondered what Julie had done during her absence. She thought about the interrupted church picnic and felt sorry the event had not gone as intended. Then her thoughts went to the hospital bill they must deliver to poor Heidi Coolidge and the anxiety it was certain to create. Her thoughts shifted again to the man beside her. *Is he lost in concern about the Coolidge family?*

And so the hours went by, Wilton once more asleep in the back seat, and the other two silent in the front.

As if their arrival had been predicted, a crowd quickly gathered on the street. Heidi hurried forward, clutching her youngest baby on one hip. "Willie, Willie, you all right? Goodness, I'm so glad to see ya up and around! I've been so worried." She pulled him close against her, lips trembling with emotion. "Thanks be to God, you're home again safe."

Julie made an appearance. "Oh, he looks so much better now. How was the trip? I hope it went well." Beth fell into her arms, relishing the comfort of being held by her sister, though Beth knew there was nothing much she could explain about Wilton's illness.

They were not given the opportunity to be alone again until after the noon meal. Though it was Monday, school had been canceled in Beth's absence, and the afternoon remained empty before them. Despite the troubling events, Beth would need to use at least some of the day to prepare her lessons for the remainder of the week.

Molly had gone to pay a visit to Frances, and Marnie and Teddy were fishing. This meant that the kitchen table was unused and quiet—a perfect place for Beth to spread out her work. Julie fumbled around for a short while, fixing some tea for both of them. Beth knew the conversation ahead would be difficult because of the secrets she was required to keep, but she must not let on that there was anything distracting her.

"Well, Julie, what did you do while I was gone?"

A teasing smile crossed Julie's face. "Why, Bethie? Does it make you worried? That I was here, and you were not around to make sure I was behaving?"

"Even more so now that I see you find it amusing." Beth set down her pencil and gave her full attention to her sister, willing herself to focus on Julie instead of her own troubled thoughts.

Julie giggled. "I didn't do a single thing. Or rather, I did many lovely things—helpful, friendly things. You would have been quite proud."

"Hmm." Beth was doubtful. "Tell me about it."

"Well . . . first I helped carry on with the picnic. Philip wanted to soothe the fears of the other children, so he asked me to help rally everyone to enjoy the remaining games. He's such a dear, Bethie. So thoughtful and kind." Julie set the teacups on the table in front of them, offering Beth a sugary-sweet smile.

"What did you say to him, Julie?" Beth's tone was as firm as she could make it.

"Nothing! Nothing, I promise. Just whatever was necessary for the task at hand."

"And then?"

"Then we gave out the prizes, and the picnic was over. Everyone went home and I returned here. Nothing dreadful—nothing out of order. To be frank, it's been rather boring. Philip wasn't even around today. He'd already returned to wherever it is he goes when he's not here."

Julie frowned, then continued. "But may I say, sister dear, that you are missing a golden opportunity where he is concerned."

"What do you mean? Or should I ask?"

Julie rolled her eyes. "Don't be obtuse. You know exactly what I mean, and there's no reason I should keep from expressing my opinion. Philip is a handsome, educated, gracious man. What more could you possibly be looking for in a husband?"

"Julie!" Beth reached again for her pencil and turned her focus back on her work, hoping the issue was closed.

"No, I won't be put off. If Mother were here, she would say exactly the same thing. He's a perfect match for you. You're both . . . kind of . . . well, solemn."

"I shall not discuss it."

"If not Philip, then who? Perhaps that Jack Thornton is more to your liking."

"Julie, please! I'm trying to prepare my lessons."

Julie absentmindedly stirred her tea. "I was wondering, Bethie, did you—were you able to spend time with Jack? Without the little patient?"

Beth could not lie to Julie, but determined not to mention their dinner together. "Most of the afternoon was driving, and I was tending a very sick child. Then there was a long wait at the hospital. And I spent the night with some friends of his." She hurried to change the subject before additional questions could be posed. "What makes you waste your time worrying about my personal affairs, anyway? What benefit is that to you?"

"None—at least not directly. Except that I'm genuinely worried about you. Your happiness and fulfillment. And I had hoped you had moved on from . . . well, from Edward."

"Edward? What on earth do you mean? I've never—"

"Oh, Bethie, he's always been your best prospect. Mother and Mrs. Montclair have long seen the two of you together—dreamed of it, I'm sure. But if you're too foolish to see what is right before your eyes, surely you wouldn't begrudge me the opportunity, would you?"

"Edward? You're interested in Edward?"

"Whyever not?" Julie feigned surprise. "I had honestly hoped to see him while I was here. I didn't realize his posting is so far away that you don't even cross paths. It's disappointing, really. I had hoped to catch a glimpse of him in his uniform. I'm sure he's very debonair."

"Julie—please. Don't even think of leading Edward on as you've done with so many others."

"I thought you didn't care."

"Of course I care. I mean, he's . . . he is a friend of our family. He doesn't deserve someone toying with his affections."

"You surprise me, Bethie. I think you care far more than you admit."

"I . . . I care—of course, just not in that way. . . ."

Julie turned her large, expressive eyes on Beth, half smiling, half smirking. "Now, big sister, you don't need to be mothering Edward. He's a man—and quite able to care for himself. He's a Mountie, for goodness' sake!"

"I just don't want to see him . . . ill used, hurt." But Beth was confused by the turmoil she was feeling. *Edward? Julie?* She was surprised how much she resented the invasion, and yet quickly reminded herself that she had claimed no ground where Edward was concerned.

"You're right, of course," at last Beth admitted calmly. "I truly have no designs on Edward. If he should be interested in you, then I would wish you both well." Secretly, though, Beth wondered how difficult it would be for her to achieve such an attitude if it were required. "But I shall also say, Julie dear, that I will not allow you to meddle in my personal life."

"I'm not meddling," she shot back. "I'm giving advice. You must admit I know bushels more about men than you."

Beth could see immediately it would be best not to expend too many words on that subject. She merely responded, "We have very different objectives where men are concerned," and turned back to her papers.

"In what sense?" Julie demanded.

"You seem to be looking for . . . well, for different things than I am."

"What do you want that I don't?"

Beth sighed. "I don't care about money, Julie. I don't care about status or appearance. I want a man who will love me for who I am—one whom I can love and support in some worthy endeavor which he is pursuing. I want a man of whom I can be proud."

"Pish-posh, I'd be ever so proud of Edward. He's more than just rich and handsome—he's a Mountie too. Just like your darling Jack."

Beth was quickly losing all patience. She feared her fragile hold on her reactions to her silly sister was slipping away. "I shall say this and then I shall have to return to my work." She swallowed hard, collecting herself so she could answer calmly. "What I'm doing here is important to me. It's what I've studied hard to accomplish—and I believe God is using me. So I'm not looking for a life partner until I feel God is leading me in that direction."

Julie drew a deep breath to interrupt, but Beth waved her off. "I haven't even planned beyond this school year. There are far too many unanswered questions in my life right now to confuse the issue with pursuing marriage. My intention is to be patient and prayerful instead." She looked directly into Julie's eyes, willing her to understand. "I'm asking you to do the same—to be patient and prayerful on my behalf. Can you do that for me, darling sister?"

Julie softened immediately. "Oh, Bethie, you know I can. I only want what's best. I don't really understand your reluctance, but I will honor your wishes and not talk about it anymore." With a hug around Beth's shoulders, she asked, "Friends again?"

"As always, dearest." Beth managed a weak smile.

Julie retreated to the wood stove, pouring herself a second cup of tea and smiling broadly—as if she had accomplished what she'd determined to do.

Beth ran a hand across her forehead. "You're still going to think about it, aren't you?"

"Pardon me?"

"You promised not to *talk* about my finding a husband—but that doesn't mean you're not going to *think* about it, use your influence where you can—does it?"

Julie smiled in response. "I'm sure I don't know what you mean, Bethie dear."

Beth had mixed emotions over the fact that Jarrick had been able to keep the exact nature of Wilton's illness concealed. However, it did not take long for word to filter through the community that Wilton's mother, Heidi, had received a bill from the doctor which she had no means to pay. When Julie heard Molly and Frances discussing it, she pulled Beth aside immediately.

"Why don't we telephone Father? He'll help. I know he will."

Beth grimaced and shook her head. She had often had such thoughts—a plea to Father could swiftly solve some of the problems her neighbors were facing. "We can't," she sighed. "This is our town—our responsibility. Not his."

"I don't see why not."

Beth tried to articulate what she had not fully settled in her own mind. "Philip says that would be charity without love. Like Paul describes in 1 Corinthians 13. That it's not just the meeting of needs which God wants from us—it's also the importance of seeing the faces of the ones through whom it came that matters. To connect the personal sacrifice to the gift. That's important too. Or else it has a different effect on the receiver somehow."

"Hmm." Julie's face wrinkled up in puzzlement.

But the sisters watched in amazement as the drama surrounding Heidi's bill unfolded over the course of the next few days. A collection was begun immediately. Small amounts trickled in at first—only what could be spared by the widows themselves. The few dollars and coins were merely seeds of a gift—a hope and a prayer that somehow God would make them grow. And then Frank delivered what had been collected among the miners. To everyone's amazement, it covered almost half the bill. Such generosity was overwhelming to all. There was no doubt that the miners' cash too was needed elsewhere.

And at last the mining company, moved perhaps by the example set for them, paid the remaining balance. Tears streamed down Heidi's face, trying to find words to express her gratitude as Molly and Frances placed the precious bills in her hands. She, in turn, would deliver the money to Jarrick, who was to carry it back to Lethbridge.

"I can't ever repay it," Heidi lamented.

Frances patted her hand. "We've all been where you are, dear. It's not easy to take help sometimes—but, sure, and you're not alone. We all share in the good and the bad together."

Watching the woman's pinched face, Beth's heart hurt to see Heidi bearing the weight of her responsibility, caring for the needs of her family of seven without a husband to provide for them. She wondered how different things would have been for Wilton's mother if her husband were still alive.

Then suddenly Beth's mind retraced again the recollections of her childhood. She imagined what it had been like for Mother to manage her own small family when all three of her young children had fallen sick with whooping cough, and Father had been away. True, there had been ample resources for doctors—but that would be small comfort to a devastated woman whose baby boy had died in her arms and there was no one in turn to hold her as she wept. For the first time in Beth's life, it broke her heart to realize the weight that Mother had carried alone. Then Beth began to wonder how often Mother had been forced to bear such solitary burdens. Looking back on her childhood now as a woman, a strong sense of empathy began to weave itself into Beth's memories.

⚜

Beth was brushing out her hair in preparation for bed, still brooding over her contemplations, when she heard a light tap on the door and Julie's voice, "Bethie, are you still awake?" She hurried to open it for her sister.

Julie, in nightgown and robe, darted past Beth into the room. Before closing the door behind Julie, Beth poked her head out and gave a quick glance down the hall to confirm it was empty. Mother would be scandalized if she knew a daughter of hers might have been seen by one of the male boarders *in her night clothes!*

"I was just remembering when I used to come sleep with you—and we'd be whispering together until all hours of the night," Julie explained. "I find myself missing those times— those talks—more than anything else since you've been gone." She turned toward Beth with persuasive eyes—the look she knew Beth could not easily dismiss. "May I join you?"

"Oh, I'd like that, darling. I've missed it too. We've had so many wonderful memories together, haven't we?" At Julie's nod, Beth continued brushing out her hair and Julie turned her attention to the dresser top and the open jewelry box—fingering the objects within—the watch pin, the locket, the dove pendant. Beth hurried on before difficult questions could be asked. "It's fascinating to realize how much more I appreciate *family* when I've been away than when we were together all the time. I suppose it's true what Mother used to quote, 'Absence—'" and Julie chimed in along with her—"'makes the heart grow fonder.'" The two laughed merrily at the shared memory. "I think she would quote that to us," Beth added, "whenever we complained about how much we missed Father."

Julie tossed her robe across the end of the bed and climbed in, pulling the pink blanket up to her chin to shield herself from the chill in the air. Beth set down her brush and moved toward the other side of the bed, sitting on its edge to remove her slippers.

"Bethie, I really am astonished at how you've adjusted to—" Her eyes swept around the room. "—to this kind of life. I'm thinking about your lovely bedroom at home—twice as large as this room. . . . with electric lights instead of oil lamps and a privy just next door—*indoors*," she emphasized. "I would think you'd wake up every morning, look around and wonder why you ever left home."

Beth sighed and slid under the covers beside her sister. "I admit I appreciate pretty things and enjoy the comfort of modern conveniences. But for me those are rather inconsequential, not nearly as important as. . . ." She searched deep inside to find expression for what she was felling. "What's important to me," she started over again, "is that I believe right now I'm supposed to be here in Coal Valley, teaching children ro read and write—ones who likely wouldn't be learning these things if I hadn't come. At least, I hope I'm effective in that task—I want to make a difference in their futures—and in this town."

Julie sighed, "But you're all alone here."

"Oh no," Beth countered. "I've made better friends here than I ever had at home. There are the children, and Frank, and Jarr- uh, Jack, and Philip. And then there's Molly . . ." Beth's voice trailed off and she blew out the lamp beside the bed, easing herself onto the pillow thoughtfully. "Well, the truth is, Molly is without a doubt the wisest, most loving and caring woman I know,"

As soon as she had said the words, Beth cast a guilty glance toward Julie, who was staring back in shock.

"And Mother?" Julie questioned, eyebrows raised. "Where does that leave Mother? I believe that's what she wants to be for us, don't you think, Bethie?"

Beth nodded slowly, frowning toward her sister. "Yes, I suppose she does—in her own manner."

"You and I don't view Mother the same way. You see her as someone trying to make all your decisions for you—but I think she's just being a—a mother." She finished with a chuckle to herself. Beth allowed herself to snicker a little along with Julie, who continued as she rearranged the pillow under her head, "You see, you take it all to heart. I think, sister dear, that it's more upsetting to you when you do something other than what she wishes than it is to Mother herself!" Julie laughed again at her own insightfulness.

This time Beth did not share in her humor, "What do you mean?"

"To hear her brag about you teaching here—so far from home—you'd think it was her idea in the first place."

"She does—she brags about me?"

Julie's laughter was fuller now. "Haven't you figured out Mother yet, Bethie? She wants to be appreciated—and she wants to be right. If you want her approval, all you have to do is succeed, and then she'll always talk as if she were supportive from the first."

"But that's not honest—it's manipulative. I want her to approve because my decisions are right—not because I'm successful."

"You mean to say that you honestly expect her to *belive* that it's right to send her daughter into the wilds *before* she knows if it will be safe. She can't do that, Bethie. She needs to know first. So if you ask her opinion she'll always opt for keeping you close. Just stop asking. You're an adult. Just tell her your plans—and ask her to pray for you. She does that, you know."

"I know," Beth whispered, tears forming in her eyes. "I know."

Silence stretched between them. Then Beth whispered, "Thank you, Julie."

The second week of Julie's trip passed quickly. It seemed that before they had even stolen several precious moments together, she was packing again and preparing for the long trip back home. Alberto had been given another errand in Lethbridge, and the sisters were to travel with him. He strapped Julie's trunk carefully to the back of the company car while she gathered the last of her belongings. Beth was already feeling as if she would cry. They'd had far too little time together.

They sat together in the back seat and used the long miles talking over many things there had not yet been time to say. This time Beth felt the road was not nearly long enough.

Alberto unloaded the trunk at the station and set it on its assigned cart. "I pick'a you up again—two hours, yes?" he said to Beth.

"Yes, thank you, Mr. Giordano. I'll be waiting right here."

Beth slipped an arm through Julie's, and they walked together into the station. Upon checking at the window and being assured that the train would depart on schedule, they found a quiet nook where they could spend their last moments together. Arriving passengers from Julie's train had already alighted, and from where the sisters sat they could see the hasty attention the linked cars were being given—food for the dining car, water and coal for the engine. For some time they continued their forced chatter, watching the train being loaded with all that was to be shipped back east. Then they could avoid it no longer. Sadness descended between them and tears threatened.

Beth sighed, then took a long breath. She had not intended to ask her sister—had even hoped to be able to avoid the question altogether. But her curiosity could no longer be restrained. "What are you going to tell Mother?"

Julie glanced sideways, wiped her eyes, then grinned, as

if she had been expecting the question. "Whatever do you mean?"

Beth offered only a stern look in response.

"Oh, I see. Well, dear Bethie, you know how Mother has worried about your safety. I intend to speak only the truth." She paused for dramatic flourish. "Actually, I have no idea why you would ever *want* to endure life in such a primitive place. It's simply unbearable, if you ask me. But I assure you that despite the lack of privacy, the lack of comforts, and the lack of good company—or rather, relatively rare examples of good company—I shall tell Mother not to worry. That you are well cared for and in no real danger. Satisfied, sister dear?"

Beth managed a crooked smile and shook her head. *If Julie indeed shares all those details with Mother, if all the difficulties of living in Coal Valley are laid out in candid array—without Julie understanding and articulating the reasons for such to be endured— Mother will not simply overlook it. Julie's list will be enough for Mother's level of concern to rise.* Beth was grateful, at least, that her sister knew nothing of Beth's greatest worries.

"Julie," she began carefully. "You needn't share *all* about it—don't you think?"

A sparkling laugh, with Julie fully enjoying the power she possessed.

Beth felt her temper rising. "I'm not teasing about this! This is extremely important to me."

Just then the train whistled to alert its passengers. Julie stood and began to gather her bags as if their conversation had not been interrupted by her impending departure. Beth scooped up the items remaining and hurried after her sister. "Julie," she called anxiously, "please wait."

Already the porter was taking Julie's bags. Beth passed along what she had been carrying and the bundles disappeared up the stairs into the train's vestibule. "Julie," she commanded, drawing in a deep breath. "Julie, please don't tease just now. I would very much appreciate some assurance that—"

"Bethie," Julie said, reaching out a hand to grasp Beth's, clearly savoring the tension. "I'm your sister. Whyever would I do you harm?"

Beth tried hard to believe the coaxing eyes. But there was an alarming mix of emotions concealed within them—such playfulness, such pity, such pleasure. "It's my life, Julie, my calling at stake. Much of it resting on what you say to Mother—don't you understand?"

Julie raised herself up onto the first step, the porter motioning her along impatiently. She paused. "Dear sister," she called out over the clatter of the engine, "surely you'll find it in your heart to trust me."

Beth hoped with all her heart that Julie's words proved true. If Mother ever knew about the need for police intervention in their little town, of a child being poisoned, and worst of all, that she had been accosted in the woods, she would have no hope of returning. *And if anything had happened to Julie during her visit, then Mother* . . . With a sigh, Beth was grateful that Julie was safely on her way home again.

CHAPTER

25

NOW THAT JULIE WAS HEADING HOME, much of
Beth's attention was centered on her own return
east, and all too soon. She needed the last weeks of school for
review and preparation for the exams the older students would
write, and simple testing that would evaluate the progress of
each of the younger ones. Copies of the results would be submitted to the provincial school board, given to the mothers,
and also entrusted to Frances, who had offered to hold them
and make them available should another teacher arrive in the
fall. If there would be "another teacher," Beth hoped whoever
it was would benefit from having a written assessment of each
child's development.

For the most part Beth was pleased with the students' progress, but two of the older students gave her grave concerns
about the upcoming exams. She was grateful, though, that all
of them were reading on a far more proficient level than had
been the case upon her arrival. She had remained committed
to that primary purpose, and she was pleased to see the results
of their hard work together. Beth spent an inordinate amount

of time each evening preparing the materials needed for the final school days.

Philip shared their table on Sunday, as well as five of the company men. Through the conversation going on around her, Beth gathered that there were plans in the works to open a new spur in the mine. With the increased activity, several more miners were being sought.

Philip frowned and questioned the officials, "Where will they be housed?" Beth knew what concerned him. The miners were already crowded.

"Some of the houses in town will be vacated soon. The company already sent notices to three of the widows."

Beth gasped, then tried to cover it. But Philip probed further. "And what will happen to the families who live there?"

"That is not the company's affair. I believe in those cases there was already a debt owed at the company store, so their pensions were used up sooner. They will have to make other arrangements."

Beth felt herself wince. She was certain if there had been other possibilities available to them, the mothers gladly would have used them long ago, leaving Coal Valley before their pensions were depleted. She glanced toward Philip but remained silent rather than voice her concerns.

As she gathered the plates after dinner, Beth approached Molly uneasily. "Did you know?" she whispered.

"Yep."

"Do you know who?"

"Yep."

"How long?"

"Diff'rent fer each."

Beth sighed. "I suppose it was bound to happen. But I wish there was something we could do about it."

"Gotta be faced, one way or t'other, dearie. Everyone knowed it was jest a matter of time."

Beth curled up in the parlor that evening, intending to read a new book Philip had loaned to her. Her mind, however, refused to concentrate. A walk, even considering the muck outdoors after strong spring rains, would be most beneficial at the moment.

Pulling on her boots and wrapping herself in her coat, Beth plunged out into the fading sunshine and struck out in the direction of Frank's cabin. *Only a short ways, and surely this direction offers safety,* she assured herself. Frank would be home, and perhaps would enjoy a visit. At any rate, it would still be a walk.

A loud group of men was gathered on Frank's porch. Beth stopped midstep, wondering whether she should approach. Something about the demeanor of the men made her freeze in place. They sounded angry.

The words were foreign, but the faces left no doubt there was serious trouble afoot. Beth took a step back and hesitated. Just then she recognized Alberto's voice shouting something she could not understand. It was enough to send Beth hurrying back along the path toward Molly's house. She prayed with every step that no one would be hurt and no lasting damage done. But she couldn't help but wonder what had caused such turbulence.

Beth immediately reported what she had seen to Molly. Much to her surprise, Molly seemed untroubled.

"They bin all worked up before. Doubt it's nothing Frank can't handle."

"Are you sure? Even Alberto was angry and shouting."

"Ain't got no police 'round today. Can't do nothing myself. Guess we'll jest wait an' see. But as fer me, I trust old Frank."

Beth did a fair share of pacing the floor while waiting for Frank to appear for their customary evening of games and music. It seemed an excruciatingly long time before he arrived, whistling and cheerful.

Beth met him at the door. "I . . . I was at your cabin this afternoon. I heard the men yelling. Is everything all right?"

He paused a moment, then looked past her into the house. "Do not'a worry. Just a little disagreement, eh? But now—it'sa okay."

Beth eyed him with some apprehension. There were beginning to be far too many mysteries around. Beth could feel her stomach tighten. "Please, Frank. I've been so anxious. Can't you tell me what happened? At least enough to set my mind at ease."

He motioned her to follow him outside and rubbed at his stubbly face. "Okay, the men they had'a some trouble. But it'sa good now. One'a the boys, he was accused of'a drinking. Berto, he found out, and we had'a meeting." Frank paused. "Maybe that's all you need'a to know, eh?"

"Drinking?" Beth felt a chill pass through her. "Who? Where?" She couldn't get past the image of a very ill Wilton.

Frank sighed his resignation. "The boy—he was'a not drinking. It was a mistake—you see?"

Beth did not understand at all. Tears were blurring her vision. She was too desperate about her children to keep quiet any longer. "Frank, I need to confide in you. I don't know where else to turn. The day that Wilton got sick—"

"I know, Miss Beth. I know." Frank reached a hand to grasp her arm. "It was on account'a the liquor."

"You know?" Beth gasped. "Did you see Wilton with it? How did you ever figure it out?"

"No, it was'a Jack Thornton—he tol' me."

"But . . . but do you know why? He made me promise not to tell anyone—not even Molly."

Frank's voice grew increasingly strained as he answered, "You must'a trust me, Miss Beth. There are reasons for'a to keep it quiet just now. Please. I would never hurt'a you. You know that, eh?"

Beth's heart pounded in her chest. She leaned closer to Frank, tipping her face as close to his ear as she could, and lowered her voice. "Frank, I have to tell you something I haven't told anyone else. I think it might be Davie Grant." She watched him stiffen. "He . . . he found me in the woods one day. He threatened that if I didn't stay away from there . . . well, he told me he wanted me to leave town. He said all the miners should leave too, and the widows."

"Miss Beth," Frank said, his brow furrowed as he looked into her face, "did'a he hurt you?"

"No, no," Beth was quick to assure him. "But I've been frightened ever since. I have no idea if he has anything to do with the alcohol that seems to be around—I can't help but suspect him, though. Oh, Frank, what can we do?"

Frank put a hand on her shoulder. "Miss Beth, I'ma gonna tell you something—something you can'a not tell nobody else. Jack, he knows about Davie—has known a long, long time. But he has to catch him with it so he can'a make the arrest. You see?" He paused as if determining what all he could say. "The boy at my house today—he was'a not drinking, but he was'a trying to buy. Jack, he asked the boy to do it, just so we can'a catch that evil man, an' bring'a him to justice far away from here."

Beth was astounded. She had never guessed that so much criminal activity was happening around her. She doubted that any of the townswomen would suspect—even Molly seemed completely unaware.

"Miss Beth, you can'a not tell nobody—and you must not get involved. You must'a wait—even if that'sa the hardest thing to do."

Startled awake, Beth sat up in her bed. The bedroom was completely dark, not a sound that she could detect. There seemed to be no reason for such an abrupt awakening, except for the worries that were consuming her. *The children—the town—the dreadful drink—the dangerous men.* These thoughts seemed to have invaded even her sleeping mind.

Now alert, she lay back and turned several thoughts over again to explore their implications. Davie seemed to be the center of it all, yet there was nothing specific to connect him to it. She wondered what was missing from the picture. Then slowly bits of memories began to return—small moments that had meant nothing at the time. As each flashed into her mind, she became more agitated.

The man in the rain I saw through the window—he had moved around the corner of Davie's home. What if he was not an intruder—but Davie himself? And when I first came here, the wooded path where Marnie showed such fear—it was close to where Davie later found me alone. . . .

A shock pulsed through Beth's body. *What does Marnie know? Why would she have refused to set foot in that direction?* Once Beth's mind had begun to wrestle with Marnie's possible connections, her thoughts spun to Teddy. *What of the mysterious "he" to whom Teddy had referred in the hallway? And what was it Marnie had said—that the boy was in trouble? With*

Davie? Were Teddy and Marnie somehow involved? An audible groan escaped Beth's lips, and she sat bolt upright in bed.

Her mind was whirling more quickly now. *There was that moment in the path with Addison when Teddy had seemed to know— or at least to know of—the man by the boat, yet he had not wanted Addison to go near him. Was the man a smuggler? Had Teddy ever been involved with such men?*

By the time it occurred to Beth to wonder where exactly Wilton had come into possession of the lethal liquor, she was very worried—and then convinced—that Addison too somehow had become embroiled. *What else could possibly be revealed?*

In another flash of memory she saw Jarrick peering across the mountainside with binoculars. *For what was he searching—even while picnicking and sightseeing? And Frank—on the day by Colette's grave where I saw a cave in the distance, he gave a warning about certain places in the woods that were unsafe for walking. And for what reason had Jarrick been so frequently in the vicinity, but for his need to investigate further?* It seemed that all her memories were converging—things she had not for a moment considered related. By this time, Beth was pacing anxiously back and forth across her room.

Beth lay back against her pillow, but sleep had fled for the rest of the night.

CHAPTER

26

AWN ARRIVED AT LAST. Beth had spent those wakeful hours scribbling her thoughts on a piece of paper, turning and retracing each memory until it took clearer shape. And slowly, ever so slowly, she began to determine what to do next—despite Frank's warning merely to wait.

Teddy was easy to locate in the woodshed behind the house. He seemed surprised to see Beth appear out of the cool morning mist, but he greeted her warmly as usual, then asked, "Miss Thatcher, why ya up so early?"

"I need to speak with you, Teddy. Please sit down."

His eyes grew wide, but he sank onto the chopping block and laid the ax on the ground beside him.

"Teddy, I need you to tell me the truth. And I want you to believe that you can trust me with exactly that—with the absolute truth. Do you understand? I am not here because you're in trouble. I'm here because I think you need help to get *out* of it."

"Ma'am?"

"I know about Mr. Grant's business," Beth said, looking him straight in the eye. "I need you to tell me the rest."

Instantly, his head dropped to his chest, and he refused to meet her gaze.

"Teddy Boy, please believe me, I want nothing—absolutely nothing—but to help you find a way out of the mess." Beth crouched down before him and placed a hand on his knee, shaking it gently. Tears were already streaming down his face as he lifted his eyes to hers. "Please, Teddy, for Marnie's sake—and for Wilton—please, please tell me what you know."

"I didn't want to do it. I jest couldn't find a way to make 'em stop," he said through sobs.

"Do what?"

He wiped the back of his hand across his dripping nose. "The men. The ones my daddy use ta work for. They made me do it—when he couldn't no more 'cause he was dead."

"Oh, my dear boy!"

Now that he had begun, the tale seemed to rush out all at once. "My daddy, he use ta pass the stuff along—so's nobody would know where it come from. And when he died they said they'd give me money if I'd do it, 'stead of him. But I said no, Miss Thatcher—I really did." He briefly raised his pleading eyes.

"I believe you, Teddy. I do." Beth pressed her handkerchief into his hand.

"But when I wouldn't, they started in sayin' what they'd do to Marnie. I couldn't let 'em—I had to do whatever they said." He gulped back another sob. "All I did—all I did was pick it up at a place in the woods, and then I'd leave it by the boat downstream. I don't know what else happened to it. I don't know who took it from there or nothin' else."

"Do you have any idea how it came to be in Wilton's hands? Think, Teddy. It's so important we know."

He covered his face with his hands, muffling his words.

"Addison found one of the bottles I left hid in the woods. He thought it was a joke—took it to his fort, laughed about drinkin' it someday. I couldn't tell him 'bout what I knew. . . . Then Willie found it. It wasn't s'posed to happen like that." He sobbed into his hands.

Beth pressed further, "Do you know who made it?"

"Yeah," he whispered. "Mr. Grant did. But he'll kill me if he ever finds out I told—an' Marnie too. Maybe Molly—"

"No, he will not," Beth assured him. "We will go to Jarrick—Mr. Thornton. He's going to keep you safe."

A flash of fear. "No, ma'am. I can't. I can't. What about Marnie?"

Anger and purpose crowded out Beth's own fear. "This is what you will do," she said firmly. "Finish chopping the wood, then go to your room. When Jarrick arrives—and I think he will be here very soon—I want you to let him take you with him. If he is worried about Marnie too, he'll take her along. He'll keep you safe. He already knows most of what you told me."

"He does?"

"As I understand it, Teddy, there are many who are striving to put a stop to all this. And I assure you they will all work tirelessly to keep you safe. Nobody—and I mean *nobody*—is going to bring you harm. They'll have to go through me first . . . and Mr. Thornton, and . . . well, I can't tell you exactly who else. But it's a whole team of people who love you very much and will stand between you and any danger that might come."

His gaze said he was anxious to believe the things Beth was saying.

"And, Teddy darling," she whispered, a smile flickering on her face, "Miss Molly doesn't even know yet. Can you just imagine what she'll do when she finds out somebody has been mistreating you and Marnie? I just don't even want to imagine!"

"Yeah," he said, returning a feeble grin. "I wouldn't wanna cross her."

Beth loaded her arms with the piles of wood as Teddy chopped them and together they quickly filled the bin in the kitchen, even before Molly made a first appearance for the day. Then Beth shooed the boy up to his room and warned him to stay put.

As quickly as she could, Beth wrote a short note to Jarrick, explaining what she had been told. She folded it and tucked it deep inside her sleeve. Then she descended the stairs and stood in the center of the foyer, uncertain of how she would get the note to him.

Peering through the curtain on the front door, she noted a car parked before the house. For a moment she was puzzled, and then she heard Nick Costa at the dining room table. *He must have come late in the evening—or very early this morning.* Her mind began to whirl once again. *He came in a car. Why does Nick always come by car? The others, the company men, they come and go by train. Almost always by train.*

Beth pushed her way into the dining room, past the men who were standing waiting for breakfast to be served. She moved with determination straight toward Nick Costa.

"Beth," Nick smiled in greeting. "So good to see—"

"We must speak," she said evenly. "Please, follow me."

Retreating into the entryway, Beth turned without explanation. "I must ask you to deliver a note to Jack Thornton."

He stared at her.

"I need you to pass on a note to Jack," she reiterated. "It's important. It's an emergency, in fact."

"But why me? Why do you—"

Beth leaned closer. "Can you, or can you not, deliver my note? Or do I have to find a way to get it to him myself?"

His eyes squinted slightly, but he admitted, "I can."

"It must go right now."

He merely nodded.

Beth reached inside her sleeve and pulled out the paper. She hesitated before releasing it to him. "No one—no one else can read it. No one but Jack."

"I give you my word," he answered soberly. And in a moment Nick was gone, his car sputtering away up the road.

Beth patrolled the main floor of the house as inconspicuously as she could, watching that Marnie stayed in the kitchen with Molly and that Teddy remained upstairs. She was not surprised that she did not wait long. Jarrick's car slid to a stop beside the front gate, followed closely by Nick's vehicle.

Jarrick entered with resolute steps. "Get the children." Beth hurried to comply, leading first Teddy and then a dazed Marnie to where he waited.

"You are both going with Mr. Thornton," Beth told them, keeping her voice as calm as she could. "We can't talk about why right now. Please just go as quickly and quietly as you are able. I'll explain to Molly."

Teddy reached for his sister, putting an arm around her protectively, and they disappeared together into the waiting car. Beth breathed a sigh of relief. Then she reached for her coat and felt a hand grasping her arm. Molly stood in astonishment, staring out at the departing cars.

"I'm sorry, I can't explain now, Molly. But I'm bringing all the children in to roll yarn today. I think that's what we'll do for school."

Molly was still gaping as Beth rushed out. It took very little time to knock on all the doors in the little row of houses, informing each of the mothers that all students would begin the day at Molly's home for a special project. Then Beth hurried back again, her breathing labored under the weight of the events she had set in motion.

Soon they appeared, two or three at a time, all her treasured children. Beth ushered them in to the parlor and seated as many as possible, then led the rest into the dining room. "I don't know what I was thinking," she said, waving her arms. "We still have a great deal of yarn to roll, and time has gotten away from us. Pastor Davidson gave us one last box when he was here last week. So we need to finish up this morning. But we can do it." She made a good attempt at a smile. "You've all done such a wonderful job so far—let's see how quickly we can finish." She was grateful that they were compliant and didn't ask any questions.

However, upon closer inspection of the circle of students, Beth noticed that Addison was absent from among them. "Luela, why didn't Addison come?"

"Oh, Miss Thatcher, Mr. Thornton—he come and got Addie in his car. I thought ya knew that."

A shiver ran through Beth's body. Then she quickly reminded herself that Jarrick had them all together. They would be safe with him. "Oh, yes, Luela, that's right. . . ." Fortunately the exchange had not prompted any questions.

The clock made awfully slow circles measuring off the morning hours. They were running out of yarn, and Beth was trying to think of how she would keep the children occupied once that was depleted.

Suddenly a frantic knock on the door, and Frances rushed inside without waiting for someone to open it.

"Molly," she called out, "Molly!"

Beth followed her to the kitchen. "They caught that

wretched man," cried Frances over her panting breaths. "They caught him, I tell you. With all his spite and wickedness—right there with his own hand in the cookie jar, so to speak. Those Mounties are goin' through his place, both up and down—this very minute."

Molly shushed her with a finger to her lips, gesturing toward the children with her eyes. "Lookin' fer what?"

"Hooch!" Frances almost shouted, despite the warning.

Molly's face instantly went white, and then she turned slowly toward Beth. "Where's my kids?" Beth was taken aback by her severe expression.

"With Jack."

"Now, I let you be all mornin' long—I asked ya nothin' at all. I didn't like it, but I let ya be. Now yer gonna tell me right this very moment why my own kids ain't here."

If Davie is truly in custody, what harm will it cause now for Molly to know? Frances has found out already. Beth answered quickly, "Teddy, he didn't want to, but they were making him deliver the liquor for them. Marnie and Addison knew. I believe the children went to show Jack where the still was kept and to testify that it belongs to Davie Grant."

"No need for testifying now," Frances asserted. "I heard they got him stone-cold guilty."

⁂

By noon Jarrick's car had returned, along with several other official-looking vehicles all crowding the short street of Coal Valley. The children, no longer able to be restrained indoors, were gathered in the yard, watching the amazing sight in excitement and disbelief. When, at last, Davie himself was led from the company hall toward a waiting car, shouts erupted, followed by a cheer. Beth tried to hush the children but was ignored.

Suddenly, from the corner of Beth's eye, she spotted Molly pushing past the crowd of children and out through the gate, crossing between the cars and the men in blazing red uniforms who were supervising the scene.

"Davie Grant," she shouted, marching defiantly toward him, "ya despicable coward! Usin' *children* ta do your dirty business—*my children*. You answer me now! You answer me now!"

"Molly, no." Frank came from nowhere to reach for her arm and hold her in check.

"No, Frank, ya best let me go. I'm gonna tell him just what he is."

Frank held tight his grasp. "Just let'a him go, Mollina. He can'a hurt them no more."

Molly struggled. "I'm jest gonna tell 'im what kinda man he is."

"No, Mollina. No. You're'a better than this."

Her anger broken, she turned and wept on Frank's shoulder, his stub of an arm patting her back comfortingly. A moment later, Teddy and Marnie fell into her embrace, and all Molly's attention was lavished upon them.

Beth noticed that one of the officers who had turned toward the commotion was Edward Montclair. She had never guessed he might also be part of the inquiry, even though Jarrick had as much as told her when he remarked that Edward's specialty was investigation. In fact, Edward himself had admitted he was in the area for a special assignment. Beth was certain nothing could surprise her now.

⚜

Beth sat on the front porch, her head resting against the cool wood of Molly's rocker, and watched the sunset tint the

309

clouds in beautiful shades of scarlet and orange. Once more she was mulling over the string of preceding events.

The evening after Davie's arrest, Jarrick and Nick Costa, who was now in full RCMP uniform, had called a town meeting in the company hall. They had presented much of the information that had been gleaned and about which many rumors had quickly spread. Davie was not the only person to be detained. They had also taken into custody two of his partners, along with poor Helen Grant. Beth's heart ached to think that the beleaguered woman had been implicated due entirely to her husband's actions. But she soon was relieved to hear that Helen was expected to be released quickly.

It was explained to all that the miners had nothing to do with the trafficking in prohibited liquor, except of course for the one man who had aided in their sting operation. It came as news to Beth that the company men had been instrumental— and entirely cooperative—in the process of the investigation, assisting in many unspecified ways.

Lastly, the townsfolk were assured that a thorough search had been completed in the Grants' home and business, as well as around the two stills in the woods, now destroyed—one near the meadow and one in the cave, just as Beth had eventually suspected. They were assured that there was no longer reason to be concerned for the safety of their children.

Beth smiled even now as she recalled the look on Frank's face when Molly had first mentioned her concern for Helen Grant's cat, all alone in the upstairs quarters. "But she'll die if no one helps her," Molly had prompted. So Frank, head shaking, carried little plates of food from Molly's kitchen to the Grants' second-story home and pushed them gingerly through a very small opening of the door, the beastie hissing and clawing its vehement protest all the while.

310

As Beth sat basking in the lingering glow of the sunset, it seemed as if all the world was at peace at last. School would be over in only a handful of days, and then Beth would be packing up for the trip back home. The thought wrenched out a deep and sorrowful sigh. One year had seemed so awfully short.

Did I get done what You wanted me to do, Lord? she asked. And then words from deep within seemed to be telling her, *I don't measure in time but in what happens inside a person. These children have learned life lessons that will be with them long after their school days are over. . . .*

<hr/>

"Miss Thatcher," Marnie said, stepping forward shyly, "we got somethin' for ya." It was the end of the last day of classes and all the mothers were standing at the back of the room, ready to share in their children's accomplishments.

Beth's breath caught in her throat.

"Can ya come see?" Marnie urged her toward a table hidden behind several figures crowding in front of it.

Beth followed Marnie and soon was in the center of the group of children. She reached her arms around as many shoulders as she could, already fighting back tears.

"We wanna thank you fer—for teaching us this year. We learned a lot. And you were our best teacher ever." This from Addison, his voice strong and steady.

James passed to Marnie a small bouquet of flowers. "We got you these," the young girl said quietly, putting them into Beth's hands.

Beth blinked away emotions as she viewed the small bouquet of spring flowers. *How and where this early in the season did they manage to find enough to tie up with a pretty pink ribbon?* Beth accepted the bouquet and smiled around at the group.

"An' that's not all." Miles gestured toward a small box in the center of the table. "We all wrote ya letters—like we did at first. Miss Molly said you'd like that well as anything."

Beth nodded wordlessly. *A perfect gift.*

"So here, Miss Thatcher." Marnie passed the box to Beth and stepped aside.

For a moment Beth struggled to find her voice, surveying the room around her—the smoky tavern which had served as a schoolroom, filled now with mothers and children. "It's been my great pleasure teaching in Coal Valley this year. I know I've learned much as well—from you and from everyone here. I have to say, I've come to feel such fondness for this community—and so much hope for its future." She again scanned the room. "Your friendship is such a priceless gift to me. When I leave here in just a few days, I will not be the same woman as before I came."

Applause followed. Beth stepped out of the center of attention, preferring instead to speak individually with the mothers, to somehow express all the emotions pent up inside her.

One of the last to approach was Esther Blane, with whom Beth had managed little interaction previously. She came quietly, awkwardly. "I know I ain't good at sayin' what I mean. But I just want to try—so you can understand." She lowered her head and took a deep breath. "When my husband was . . . was killed I . . . I died too—kinda. I mean he . . . he was gone but I . . . I was still here, in body. My spirit was kinda gone too, I think. I didn't care, I didn't *feel*—'cept all that hurt. I was jest goin' through my daily work and not doin' it well either. My little ones—they needed me, but I jest wasn't able to help them. Not really. I . . . guess I gave up tryin'." She shifted nervously before continuing.

"We all been talkin' 'bout what ya done for our town. An' I

'preciate it all—along with the rest a' the town. Ya brought a lot to us—to our children. But to me ya brought more than what ya done. Ya brought back hope—an' faith—things I didn't know I lost. I'd stopped goin' to church. I'd stopped prayin'—right when I needed it most. An' then when my kids got excited 'bout those little Bible plays, I decided to go along with 'em.

"That one about David and Goliath. That was me. I was fightin' somethin' way bigger than me—me bein' a widow now. But I . . . I wasn't goin' in the name of the Lord. That was my problem. I come back home that night and went to bed cryin'—but I ended up prayin' too. If David could fight that big ol' giant Goliath—and God could make him win—then I could start fightin' again too. The same God who helped him could help me. My life ain't easy—but it got better. God's been helpin' me—every day. I know that. I'm so thankful that ya told us that story. I needed to hear it again."

Beth reached to hug her close and they cried a little together. There were no words left to say. Esther pulled away and breathed in deeply, then turned to gather little Anna Kate and Levi, directing them toward the door. Beth wiped away the fresh tears. "God, keep them," she whispered. "God, keep them all."

Molly came next and hurried Beth away from the last few, pulling her out the door before she could try to pitch in with tidying the room. Now that Helen had returned home, her evening pool-hall business was in operation again.

"Ya done enough," Molly declared as they stepped out together into the cool afternoon. Beth lifted her face to the tree-covered slopes surrounding them, and to the white peaks reaching to the skies. She stopped for a moment to take it all in.

Suddenly, there beside the path stood a man dressed in civilian clothes. Should she be afraid? He stepped forward with a smile. *It's Edward!*

"I DIDN'T WANT TO INTERRUPT," Edward said. "I was in the back of the room, but I didn't want to be a distraction from what the ladies and the children were saying to you."

"But what are you *doing* here, Edward?" Beth stared back at him. It had been so long since she had seen him dressed in anything other than his uniform. He still looked every bit as distinguished as Beth remembered. Those dark green eyes showed his new maturity.

Molly was excusing herself. "I'll meet ya back at home," she called as she hurried off.

"They said you went back to Athabasca. What brings you so far, Edward? Surely not just the last day of school."

"I wanted to speak with you. I hoped this would provide a good opportunity and a measure of privacy."

Casting a glance toward the pool hall, Beth suggested, "Perhaps Miss Molly's front porch would serve us."

He motioned her forward with a sweep of his hand, and they silently walked to the boarding house. Once Beth was comfortably seated on one of Molly's chairs, Edward pulled the other closer and dropped into it.

Beth could sense he was unsure of himself, an unusual frame of mind for Edward. There was a hesitancy, yet determination, in his voice. "Elizabeth," he began, "you know I have always regarded you highly. Indeed, I'm certain I have held you in an esteem which you often neither recognized nor could return. And seeing you today—in your moment of triumph—I cannot begin to express how proud I felt to know you. And more than that, to admit I was emphatically wrong about you. I'm so pleased to discover I misjudged you when I criticized your motives—" he paused before completing the thought—"when I called you stubborn and headstrong."

Beth assured him, "I haven't been angry at you, Edward. I forgave you long ago. Even before you had asked me—do you remember?"

He nodded. "That's very kind." He repositioned himself in his chair. "You know that our mothers—at least my mother— have always assumed that you and I would one day marry. I have thought so too. I know—I realize that you have never given me cause to . . . to expect your agreement, but Mother consistently advised that I must let you grow up first—not press you with a proposal until it was the proper time. Even after your coming-out party, I waited in hopes that your feelings toward me would begin to change." He floundered to a halt. "Oh dear, I'm afraid I'm making a terrible mess of this, aren't I?"

With everything in her being Beth wanted to nod in agreement with his statement but held herself in check. Surely Edward did not consider this an appropriate time to present his case.

"The fact is, Elizabeth, I had always intended to ask for

your hand. Had never thought of anyone else. My . . . my admiration has only grown. Seeing you here, watching the respect you have earned in this community. You have indeed revealed yourself to be an astonishing young woman, and I . . ." He hesitated again.

Beth's heart cried silently, *Please, Edward, you don't even know me—not really. Please don't assume . . .*

He was speaking again. "And since—well, since it's been widely presumed both by members of my family and yours—I felt it was important that I should speak with you. You see . . ." He put a hand on her arm to bring her eyes to his. She raised her gaze while he struggled for words, his eyes entreating her to hear him out. "You see, Elizabeth, I have met a young woman. Her name is Kate. I feel she is . . . is . . . Well, simply put, I have fallen in love. Quite madly in love. I feel she is exactly what I want—what I need in a wife. And she seems to return that feeling." He stopped and took a deep breath.

Beth breathed in deeply too—a refreshing breath of relief.

Edward continued, "Before . . . before pursuing any further relationship with Kate, I felt I needed to speak with you. To be sure there is no misunderstanding . . ."

Beth stood from her chair and stepped away toward the railing, only then looking back at the young man. Her brain wrestled to make sense of what had just transpired. *Has Edward come to ask for permission to court another young woman?* She had not thought she had any claim on him, though certainly she had been aware of their family's hopes and plans for them. She also remembered Julie's attempts to bait her about Edward during her visit. Beth's mind quickly took another turn. Here he was, sincere, almost apologetic, seeking her understanding, and obviously desiring that a friendship could continue. She could not help but admire his honorable conduct. He

316

was acting as his mother had taught him. A gentleman, in a difficult circumstance.

"You've changed, Edward," she heard herself say.

He stood with a wry smile. "For the better, I hope," he said as he joined her at the railing.

"You've matured into a man of whom your mother has good reason to be proud."

"And you?"

"I admire you for the gentleman you have become—and wish you every happiness with your Kate."

"You do understand that—"

"There is nothing I need to understand, Edward," she said quickly. "God leads—it is up to us to follow."

He reached out to take hold of her hand. "You are a remarkable woman, Elizabeth. I shall always think of you with fondness."

Beth turned back to the railing, her eyes sweeping across the town around her.

He cleared his throat. "Elizabeth, there is one other issue," he admitted, moving a step closer. "I . . . I have noticed that my colleague Jack Thornton seems to think highly of you as well." She looked at him and saw a flush on his cheeks. He swallowed before hurrying on. "I'm afraid I may have misled him . . . to some extent."

A frown creased Beth's brow. She cast another sideways glance at the man beside her. He had stopped to once more clear his throat.

"I'm afraid I gave the impression . . . I mean . . . well, I rather staked my claim to you when I had no right to do so," he finished in a rush.

"I see" was her only verbal response. *So that is why Jarrick has not sought to further a relationship.* And this was the true reason Edward felt the need to speak to her—to disclose the extent of this strange one-sided connection. Her indignation began to rise until she considered that he could have allowed her to leave for the East without confessing what he had done. She would have never known. . . .

"I'm sorry, Elizabeth. Very sorry."

Beth barely heard the softly spoken words. She turned to face him and looked at Edward's pleading eyes. When she spoke again her voice was low but confident. "Edward, if there is one thing I have learned over the past year, it is that God is in charge of my life—every area of my life. I trust Him. In each relationship."

She stopped. There was no need to go further. Jarrick, or someone else—or no one at all—as a life's partner . . . It was in God's hands. As much as her heart beat faster at the thought of the one man from whom her heart had hoped to receive attention, she would not need to do anything about it.

Again she gazed up at the familiar face before her. She extended her hand. "Thank you, Edward, once again, for your persistent work in retrieving my compass and my violin. You'll never fully understand what it has meant to me. I have heard that you also helped to apprehend Davie Grant, something for which I shall also be eternally grateful. And thank you for the years of friendship. I expected nothing more—and with our family relationship—nothing less. May God be with you—and Kate—if she accepts you." Beth stopped, then smiled. "And, Edward, I think she would be a very silly young woman if she does not."

Even as she said the words she was surprised at how much she truly meant them. In the distant recesses of her mind was a niggling question. Given the way Edward had changed, given the difference in her attitude toward him, and had he not come with hat in hand, asking her blessing on a new relationship with another woman, could she—would she—have eventually learned to care for him? She shook her head. She would never know.

CHAPTER

28

THE NEXT AFTERNOON, Beth returned to the pool hall to collect the school items she kept in a closet there. Should she return in the fall, Beth was determined that school would never again be held in this building. It was easy to surrender it since the pool hall had always been an inappropriate location. She wondered if perhaps the company would allow the school to meet in their hall—even if they were not paying the teacher's salary. They had been very generous in the recent months with all they had allowed to occur there.

Molly mentioned with a sly smile that it had proven beneficial after all for Beth to cultivate a relationship with some of the men over their shared meals. And then quickly added more seriously, "More'n that, dearie—if ya hadn't offered yer good will, they might never have begun to come to church, neither."

Frank recovered Beth's trunks from where they had been stored in Molly's attic and set them again under the window in Beth's room. The decisions involved in repacking them brought much consternation and emotion.

Beth brooded over the handmade dresses she had commissioned as she folded them neatly. "Molly, I think I should just leave these behind. I don't suppose I'll have opportunity to wear them once I'm home again—and I know there are women for whom they could be useful here."

Molly shook her head. "Ya don't know the future yet. Might jest as well hang on to 'em fer a bit."

Beth wondered too if she should leave the books and school supplies behind, but Molly insisted she pack them up. "Should ya come back, you'll still have yer things. But if ya don't—we ain't got no use for 'em if there's nobody ta teach. Won't do fer the likes of me to try an' fill yer shoes." Molly's voice was heavy with feeling, even though she was trying hard to suppress it.

The trunks were to be shipped on the company train into Lethbridge, and Beth would follow the next day. It was a strange feeling to see them loaded on a truck and borne away, leaving Beth as she had arrived—with almost nothing. She shook her head as she thought back to that first day in Coal Valley . . . how much had changed. *How much I have changed,* she thought.

Jarrick had offered to drive Beth into Lethbridge, telling her he would be traveling out of the mountains anyway on an assignment. Early Wednesday morning, Beth whisked back the curtain as his car pulled into the space in front of Molly's picket fence and straightened her hat. She was wearing a traveling suit, her hair tucked neatly beneath one of the new hats Mother had sent. The fancy blue suit felt awkward and unfamiliar to her now—seemed inappropriate for every day. She felt it rather false to don these clothes—as if she were not that person anymore. Then she paused to wonder if such attire had always misrepresented her somewhat. Perhaps she had long been intended for a humbler station in life. One thing she knew, she would miss terribly her community and the dear friends she had made.

A light knock at the door, and Jarrick stepped inside. "Good morning." He nodded around to all those gathered in the foyer to bid farewell to Beth.

Beth turned toward them, reminded of similar feelings when saying good-bye to her family before boarding the train not quite one year ago. And then the tears came. . . .

Frank reached for a quick hug. "Now, you come'a back to us, Miss Beth. We don't want'a to wait too long."

"I'll do my best." She patted his whiskered cheek. "Take care of yourself—and my family here, won't you?" She leaned close to his ear. "And Molly," she whispered.

He nodded back, clearing his throat brusquely.

Beth turned to Molly next with a lump in her throat, making it difficult to speak. She threw her arms around the ample woman, receiving a strong hug in return. "I love you, Miss Molly. I'll miss you so much. Who will I be able to talk things over with?"

"I think you'll be back," Molly murmured softly. "At least, thet's what I'm gonna tell myself."

Marnie fell into Beth's arms, burying her face against her shoulder. "You'll come back. I'm gonna believe that too," she whispered through a sob.

Beth stroked the girl's hair and placed a kiss on the top of her head. "I'll miss you, darling. You're so special to me. We've shared some very precious memories together, haven't we?"

Marnie smiled up at her. "I think so too."

Teddy reached out an awkward hand and Beth gave a shaky laugh. She pulled him into a small hug, then stepped back and searched his face for a moment. "I'm proud of you, Teddy.

You've grown so much while I've been here. Taller and so much older too. You're becoming a fine young man."

He blushed and turned his face away. Molly came forward and put an arm around him, then pulled Marnie up next to her as well.

With a schedule to keep, Jarrick was reaching for the door, and Beth picked up her handbag. She looked back over her shoulder at the small cluster of faces that had grown so important to her and wiped away her tears while Jarrick ushered her into the car.

As the engine started up, Beth noticed first one and then several of the children hurrying toward the road to wave one last time. She waved back to them through the window glass, sadness spilling more tears onto her cheeks. The children followed the car, running behind and calling words of farewell until the automobile disappeared around the bend. Jarrick passed a fresh handkerchief to Beth, and she wiped more tears from her face.

"You mean a great deal to them, Beth."

Her voice cracked as she replied, "It's mutual, to be sure."

The long road stretched out ahead. Beth planted a foot on the floor of the car and reached for a good handhold on the door. She now knew better how to keep herself from being bounced around mercilessly by the rutted road.

"You've had a good year," he commented.

"Oh, it's been wonderful—well, perhaps not wonderful all the time—but I'm so grateful for it all."

Jarrick nodded. "Are you looking forward to getting back to the city—to civilization?"

Beth's brow furrowed as she contemplated the question honestly. "Well, I'm ready to see my family again. I've missed them very much." She thought wistfully about her little nephew, already walking—and about Father and Mother. "I wish I could have them all together—my new family here and also my original family at home." She smiled at how divergent the people were that she was including now as family—hardly able to envision them gathered in one place.

He nodded, and another mile slipped away. At last, she heard him draw a deep breath, and she knew he was working toward a topic he was having a difficult time raising. "Edward Montclair told me he paid you a visit this week."

"He did. He came to the school."

"Hmm." After a pause, he spoke again. "Do you know . . . do you realize I was uncertain for some time about the nature of your relationship with Edward?"

"Oh?" Beth answered evasively.

"Yes, when I first met the man, he made it rather clear that he had intentions toward you—that the two of you had somewhat of an arrangement."

Beth held her breath for a moment before answering carefully, "He explained as much to me when he visited. I was quite surprised by his assumption." She turned her face toward Jarrick just a little, watching his reaction from the corner of her eye.

"We also had a second conversation recently," he went on. "Edward at that time made a point of admitting that the understanding was one-sided. That it was his presumption and not an agreement you had made."

Beth nodded quietly.

"It's funny," he said, pressing further, "that day we spent together—taking Willie Coolidge to the hospital—I was going to ask you if you might be open to having a gentleman caller."

Beth looked back in surprise. "What stopped you?" Then she blushed as she realized how straightforward her question had been.

He shook his head. "Your references to Edward at dinner. I had come to believe he had overstated his relationship with you until you were rather candid in your appreciation and esteem of him that night. It made me wonder if you didn't feel for him as he felt for you."

"I see." Beth replayed the moment in her mind. As she recalled, in a bumbling way she had described her gratitude that Edward had found her stolen items.

Jarrick continued, "I knew without your telling me how hard he'd worked to recover your violin and compass. I felt he must have cared for you a great deal to be so vigilant on your behalf."

"Jarrick," Beth answered gently, "do you know the story of how the trunks came to be missing in the first place?"

"Well, no—except I heard they were stolen."

"But you don't know under what circumstances."

"No, I have never heard that part."

Beth laughed softly and shook her head. "Edward chose a porter at the station who did not work for the railway company. He handed my trunks over to . . . well, to a thief." She let the words take their effect, then quickly added, "It was an easy mistake to make—but it was Edward's error, not mine."

Jarrick chuckled. "No, somehow he missed sharing those details. All I heard was how much effort he was expending recovering the items. I assumed he was working to please you—to rescue you from your distress—not to assuage his own guilty feelings."

Beth waited a moment longer, trying to find an adequate way to express what she wished to say. "I had never considered Edward a suitable life partner. In fact, in our childhood—and even youth—I quite . . ." She fished for the right word. "Perhaps *despised* is too strong a term—but nevertheless . . . I'd never seen in him the characteristics of a man with whom I would wish to share marriage. I will admit that he seems quite different now—that choosing his occupation and coming west seems to have matured him greatly. I know his father will be delighted to see how much he's changed. But at no time did I have a serious interest in Edward's companionship, other than merely as family friends—and for the most part, before this trip I was not even interested in that."

"I see." Another mile passed. Jarrick seemed to be deep in thought. Beth felt somewhat uneasy, wondering about his silence.

"There's something I would like to say, Beth, but I can't decide if it's a suitable time to do so—with you preparing to leave. And yet I find it difficult not to speak up at all."

"What is it?" she asked, her voice low.

Jarrick cleared his throat. "You said you did not find Edward to be a suitable life partner. I suppose I would . . . would like to admit that I've seen in you the very qualities I've hoped my future wife *would* possess. I've seen you giving of yourself and striving to serve in ways that few others would. I've seen you pouring out your love on the children you taught and making a great difference in their lives. I've seen you being honest in difficult moments, and patient and wise. And I've seen you rise to the occasion to defend those you love. I have to tell you, Beth, I've come to admire you greatly. You are what I would see as the best of women, and any man would be blessed to share his life with you."

Beth was so overcome she found it hard to catch her breath. "That's . . . that is v-very kind," she stammered. "I—"

He hurried on. "Now, I know I have no right to ask for your permission in a formal way—there being no assurance you'll return again. But I hoped at least to express my admiration and my wish that if God brings you back to us, that you would allow—that you might consider—my request at that time."

Beth breathed in deeply and managed a nervous smile as her hands fumbled with the gloves she held in her lap. She scarcely dared lift her eyes to the young man at the wheel. "If . . . if I return to the West, I would be very pleased to hear from you again. Unless you've changed your mind by then." She dared catch a peek at him out of the corner of her eye, and he was smiling and shaking his head.

He sobered and posed another question. "Would you consider me too forward if I asked for a way to contact you over the summer?" He seemed painfully uneasy even as he made the request.

"That . . . that would be fine—a pleasure." Even as she spoke, thoughts of her mother whirled through her mind. What would she think? Would she allow such interaction with a young Mountie, unknown to her? Beth determined in her heart to be forthright in explaining this relationship to Mother—at least to the extent that she herself could summarize it.

Jarrick was explaining, "I never know when I might be transferred, and it sure would be a shame to lose touch . . . to lose you."

Beth could not speak for a moment. "Of course," she said, "I will write my address on a slip of paper." She began immediately to fumble in her handbag, looking for a suitable scrap.

"Would you mind noting a telephone number as well?" he pressed.

Beth could not hide the little smile that quirked at the corner of her mouth. *He is persistent.*

"Of course," she said again with another smile.

Seeming relieved and satisfied, Jarrick turned the conversation to other things.

⌘

Though her heart was full, there was little Beth could put into words in their last moment together at the train station. Jarrick seemed to feel the same. Beth was surprised when he asked if he could say a short prayer. They bowed their heads for an intimate moment together. Beth closed her eyes and heard him bless her travels, leaving in God's hands her direction for the future. Just then the conductor called for final boarding, so he led her toward the familiar steps.

"Thank you, Jarrick," she repeated one last time, conscious of nearby eyes and not wanting to draw attention.

He answered gently, placing a hand over hers. "Safe journey, and enjoy your time with your family, Beth. I can only imagine how thrilled they'll be to have you home again." He glanced down at the slip of paper he still held, then tucked it carefully into the breast pocket of his red tunic. "I will give you an address when I first write." And with a nod and a tip of his hat, he released her hand. Beth mounted the stairs and followed the porter waiting to usher her toward the sleeping compartment that would carry her home.

Upon entering the room, to her astonishment, she saw before her a long, open box containing red roses. *Who could have . . . ?* And then a smile played across her lips. The card read, "Affectionately, Jarrick." *What a lovely surprise. It must have been difficult for him to have made the arrangements. And he must have done it before he knew for sure my response. . . .*

She hurried over to the window to look out on the platform. Among the many unknown faces milling about to wave their good-byes, she spied the bright red coat. Jarrick stood, his eyes sweeping over the windows of the train. He spotted her just as Beth felt the train begin to move. She lifted the flowers, mouthing her thank-you.

In reply he smiled, then patted his breast pocket that held her Toronto address. As the train drew away, Beth fixed her eyes on the man in the prominent jacket among those crowding the platform. Surrendering at last to the plush seat, she cradled the beautiful box of flowers on her lap.

"Father," she prayed, "I know You are in charge of my future. I can see Your hand in everything that has happened over the past several months. Truly You have been my strength—just as my father said that You would." Unconsciously her fingers clasped the locket that contained the small, cherished paper where her father had written the promise.

She continued her conversation with her God. "You know I feel . . . torn. I long to see my family again. To reconnect—or perhaps to *finally* connect—with Mother, to be held close again by Father, to put the compass safely back into his hands. To see how big JW has grown. And to be with Margret and Julie. Family." She paused for a moment.

"But . . . but I love the people of Coal Valley too," she continued. "They've become so, so precious to me—each of them." Beth stopped again as a number of faces paraded through her memory. Dear Molly. Frank. Marnie and Teddy. Each child in her classroom. Their needy but courageous mothers. Paolo and the miners. Philip. Jarrick.

Jarrick? She felt her cheeks flush as her pulse quickened, her gaze returning to the gift of roses. She pressed cool hands against the warmth rising in her cheeks, then took another deep breath and continued her prayer. "So, dear Lord—if—*if* it fits Your plans, please—*please*, I would so love to come back here." *Home.*

About the Authors

Bestselling author **Janette Oke** is celebrated for her significant contribution to the Christian book industry. Her novels have sold more than 30 million copies, and she is the recipient of the ECPA President's Award, the CBA Life Impact Award, the Gold Medallion, and the Christy Award. Her novel *When Calls the Heart*, which introduces Elizabeth Thatcher and Wynn Delaney, was the basis for a Hallmark Channel film and television series of the same name, and *Where Courage Calls* tells even more of the Thatcher family's story. Janette and her husband, Edward, live in Alberta, Canada.

Laurel Oke Logan, daughter of Edward and Janette Oke, is the author of *Janette Oke: A Heart for the Prairie*, as well as the novel *Dana's Valley*, which she co-wrote with her mom. Laurel and her husband have six children and two sons-in-law and live near Indianapolis, Indiana.